The

MEMORY
TREE

BOOKS BY JOSEPH PITTMAN

Linden Corners Series

The Memory Tree

A Christmas Hope

A Christmas Wish

Tilting at Windmills

Todd Gleason Crime Novels

California Scheming

London Frog

Novels

Beyond the Storm

When the World Was Small

Legend's End

The Original Crime, Part One: Remembrance

The Original Crime, Part Two: Retribution

The Original Crime, Part Three: Redemption

KENSINGTON BOOKS are published by

Kensington Publishing Corp.
119 West 40th Street
New York, NY 10018

All Kensington titles, imprints, and distributed lines are available at special quantity discounts for bulk purchases for sales promotion, premiums, fundraising, and educational or institutional use.

Special book excerpts or customized printings can also be created to fit specific needs. For details, write or phone the office of the Kensington Special Sales Manager: Kensington Publishing Corp., 119 West 40th Street, New York, NY 10018. Attn. Special Sales Department. Phone: 1-800-221-2647.

Kensington and the K logo Reg. U.S. Pat. & TM Off.

ISBN-13: 978-0-7582-8943-8
ISBN-10: 0-7582-8943-X
First Kensington Trade Paperback Printing: October 2013

eISBN-13: 978-0-7582-8945-2
eISBN-10: 0-7582-8945-6
First Kensington Electronic Edition: October 2013

10 9 8 7 6 5 4 3 2 1

Printed in the United States of America

The

MEMORY
TREE

A Linden Corners Novel

JOSEPH PITTMAN

Kensington Books
www.kensingtonbooks.com

This one's for . . .

the Menter family

AUTHOR'S NOTE

It's always nice to come home, especially for the holidays. Seeing friends and family, you can't help but remember good times, special moments that define what Christmas means to you. After three previous novels—two of them with a holiday theme—it's time for another return to our friends in Linden Corners. Here, in the land of the windmill, a new story awaits faithful readers and new alike. Though many of these characters have appeared in previous novels, I intend each story to stand alone.

Brian Duncan remains, of course, the focal point of the series, as it is his story that has fueled so much of the action. Other favorite characters return, including Gerta, Nora, and Thomas, all in supporting roles, as well as the regular denizens of Linden Corners. Sharing the lead this time is Brian's best friend, Cynthia Knight, who finally gets her moment to shine—and just in time. A new character to Linden Corners is Trina Winter, who shares a surprising connection to someone we've met before. Lastly, the surprise appearance of Brian's parents, Kevin and Didi Duncan, adds drama to the coming holidays.

But the heart of the book remains Janey Sullivan, now ten years old, and her devotion to the endlessly spinning sails of the windmill. In *The Memory Tree*, the residents of the sleepy hamlet of Linden Corners are once again faced with how to make this year's Christmas celebration the best ever. What follows are all the hallmarks readers have come to appreciate in the Linden Corners series—gentle warmth, subtle humor, and an endearing, enduring sense of family, no matter its origin.

Not with whom you are born, but with whom you are bred.

—Miguel de Cervantes, *Don Quixote*

$\mathcal{P}$ROLOGUE

Clocks turn even when you're not looking, the sun rises and falls as the passing days move gently into the quiet of night, and so time effortlessly glides by, unseen but ever present. For those with little to look forward to in life, time can drag on till it seems the earth has stood still, while for others the endless rotations of its axis move far too quickly, leaving them with a sense of time running out, always planning, seldom living. Time is universal, yet it represents so many things to so many, and while it can be enigmatic, even mysterious, it also represents one of the few constants in the universe. What no one has in common with time is how much of it they have.

In reality, the world marches on, and before anyone realizes it, time has flown by on the currents of the wind, with another day, month, and year having elapsed, leaving us all a little older, perhaps a bit wiser. And always wondering, Where has the time flown?

Sometimes people anticipate the arrival of a certain day, a birthday or anniversary, a trip that will take them to the far reaches of the earth, feeling it will never come. And then suddenly it's gone, whisked away by time's inevitable advancement, leaving in its wake those things called memories. Sometimes people wish

*time would grind to a standstill, allowing them to forever trea-
sure a moment so hard to catch, like witnessing a falling star, the
first bloom of love, a long-planned wedding, only to realize that
time is a part of life no one can lay claim to—its hold on us strong,
our grip, at best, tenuous.*

*Time is always present, but it's remembered in the past,
thought about for the future.*

"Remember that time . . ."

"Time will tell."

*Time means everything and yet it ultimately means nothing,
leaving a place like the small village known as Linden Corners
somewhere between yesterday and tomorrow. For eager kids down
at Linden Corners Middle School, a year of studies can feel like
forever; for anxious adults in the simple act of waiting for a cup of
coffee down at Martha's Five O'Clock Diner, time can come to
mean impatience; and for the elderly folks down at Edgestone Retirement Center, who have seen their lives fall behind them, time
taunts like an enemy. Even the iconic, majestic windmill that
looms over this countryside knows of time's unstoppable dance, its
spinning sails silently recording every step.*

*But then come those special times of year when folks dream of
better lives. Holidays are like time-outs from the rigors of daily
life, filling out days with Memorial Day picnics and Fourth of
July fireworks, these events like time caught in a bottle. At
Thanksgiving, we take time for our families and ourselves, giving thanks for all we have, all we share. And then of course there's
Christmas, which stretches the notion of time to extremes, for it is
not just a single day amidst a cold month, but something joyfully
referred to as Christmastime, a time built on a giving spirit, on
tradition. And what is tradition but time told in reverse.*

Only one thing in this world can halt the passage of time.

*Only one thing in this world can transport you to another time
and another world.*

That thing is called a dream.

For one wide-eyed girl in Linden Corners, she with freckles on her usually scrunched-up nose, dreams were sometimes all she could cling to.

Shutters clattered against the old farmhouse as the wind took shape on dark currents. A willowy shadow emerged, sweeping in through the open window, washing over the sleeping figure in the bed. Instead of blocking the moonlight that flowed through lace curtains, the figure was cast in a golden glow. From the small bed, the little girl stirred, although if truth be told—and why not? didn't nights call for honesty?—she couldn't be called little anymore. She had reached double digits, a whole ten years old for just over a month now. Independence, always a trait that ran rampant inside her, had recently begun to assert itself on the outside. So much so that she didn't need to be tucked in anymore, to be babied, and she didn't need to sleep with a night-light anymore. Janey Sullivan was growing up.

But the elapsed time couldn't change everything.

She had memories, even at her tender age.

The moonlight glinted in her eyes and she opened them, green twinkles in the darkness.

For a curious moment, her tired mind was unsure where she was and she reached for her constant companion, a purple frog that remained with her despite another birthday, despite this supposed streak of independence. At night she still sought comfort from a friend made from stuffing, a friend that had never uttered a single word but had seen her through days—and nights—way darker than this one. Nights when not even the moon visited. Then, popping up, elbow on her pillow, she looked at the shadow on the wall and saw it smile.

How did it know to do that? How did such a gesture manage to soothe her?

"Mama?" she suddenly asked.

"Yes, Janey, it's me."

The shadow morphed into something more concrete, light hitting it. Yes, there she was, Annie Sullivan, her body floating like something crafted from the heavens, vibrant in the starlit night. The young girl felt warmth spread over her. She tossed back the blankets, and even as the wind howled against the side of the old farmhouse, calming heat continued to surge around her. She couldn't remember ever feeling so warm, not even on those cold nights when Brian had to light a fire in the fireplace and they sat beside its flame sipping hot chocolate—with tiny marshmallows—while orange embers burned and he invented silly stories of a girl who could ride the wind. She would giggle at times, scrunch her nose with doubt at others. Those were special times, the best. At least, the best she could remember since her mother had gone to sleep at a secret place only she knew. Beads of sweat formed on her brow now, and as a drop found its way to a blinking eye, she wiped it away.

The vision—if that's what it was—remained.

"Come with me, Janey. Let me show you."

"Show me what?"

"What it was."

Why was she speaking in riddles? Janey almost giggled.

"What what was?"

"Our life, from before you could remember."

A hand suddenly stretched out toward her, and Janey felt its pull even without touch.

This woman before her, whether real or conjured from her imagination, or perhaps locked somewhere in between, spun her dreams. And while the girl named Janey would follow her anywhere, there was only one possible destination for them both. They were headed where their lives remained connected, forever bonded.

The windmill.

Across the open field they journeyed, down the hill, which tonight was a swirling carpet of fallen leaves and dying grass. Yes, it was windy on this warm autumn night, and the sails of the giant windmill spun like they were producing gleaming straw. But once they had gained entry inside the tower, magically not needing to turn a key or to open the door, the windows remained closed and no one would be letting down their spun golden locks.

Annie had loved coming to the windmill to paint her dreams on canvases, only to close them in a drawer. Never thinking to show them, never thinking her talent commanded attention. Yet several hung now inside the homes of Linden Corners—in the farmhouse and on Gerta Connors' living room wall, just above the mantel. But Annie had mostly come here to contemplate life and all she had been given, all she had lost. Now it was Janey's turn to rely on the windmill's power, some days more so than the reassuring presence of Brian Duncan. He was real, always dependable, but sometimes Janey enjoyed living out the dream inside her mind.

"Mama, why have you brought me here?"

"What do you see?"

"Why are you answering my question with a question?"

"Because, Janey, sometimes when you listen you hear your own answers."

Janey didn't know what to think of her wisdom; it sounded far too grown-up for her to understand. But then she gazed about the inside of the windmill, her feet taking her one step closer to the iron staircase that curled upward to the second floor. Janey made a dash for it suddenly, almost as though a gust of wind had taken her. When she arrived there, Annie was already waiting.

"How did you do that?"

"The world in which I live, we think of a place, we're there."

"Is that how you keep an eye on me?"

"Both of them," the glowing Annie said, her smile giving light to the compact room.

Janey gazed up at her mother, recognizing her features, the way her eyes sparkled. The worry she had often seen inside them was gone, replaced by something that sent a wave of relief Janey's way. Her mother was forever at peace. Janey instinctively reached out her hand and felt it pass through the translucent figure before her. Again, warmth spread through her, even as on the nearby window frost suddenly appeared like spiderwebs along its edges. The pattern of snowflakes was left frozen against the glass, leaving Janey wondering how that could have happened.

"Mama, did you do that?"

"Peer through the window, Janey, and tell me what you see."

"I'll see outside, the big hill, and the farmhouse where we live."

"Look again, but this time close your eyes first."

"When you close your eyes, you can't see anything."

Annie cupped the young girl's chin, her touch electric. "Of all the people I've met, you, my sweet Janey, know that when you close your eyes you can see the world as you wish it."

Janey would trust her mother to tell the truth. Didn't she know all truths now, traveling to places beyond the world? Which is maybe just where they'd gone now, because as Janey leaned in close to the window, she could no longer see familiar sights, least among them the farmhouse she called home. But she wasn't afraid, not in the presence of her mother. So she did as asked; she closed her eyes and immediately she saw sparkles of light dance inside her mind. Those sparkles soon took shape, stars of varied colors. She saw red and green and blue and gold, and they shone like ornaments, and when she opened her eyes she saw that all those lights dotted a tree that seemed to tower toward the sky.

"Mama, it's a Christmas tree," Janey said, wide-eyed. "But how . . ."

"Just watch, Janey."

More images appeared, brightly wrapped presents underneath the tree, strands of fallen tinsel atop them, aglow from the lights of the tree. It was beautiful, just like those she and Brian had decorated the last two Christmases. Janey had a sense this tree was not one of them, but one from another time. When she spun around to ask Annie, Janey Sullivan found that she was alone inside the windmill.

"Mama?" she asked, a bit nervously.

There came no answer, and Janey, wondering if she was soon to wake from this all-too-real dream, considered closing her eyes again, wishing to be home, safely tucked in her bed with her purple frog clasped tightly in her arms. Her feet, though, wouldn't move, so Janey peered again through the window, seeing the sails of the windmill pass by, as though aiding in turning back the clock. As one of the latticed sails disappeared and allowed a clear view, Janey saw an image melt into the frame, the figure not quite solid. Janey blinked, and then there she was, her mother, part of that Christmas scene she had watched develop before her very eyes.

"Mama," she said, the word breathless.

Annie was moving inside the farmhouse living room, a cup of coffee warming her hands. Wrapped in a snug robe, she settled on the floor near a crackling fireplace, sneaking peeks at the gifts placed under the tree. A smile lit her face as much as did the warm glow of the fire, but neither was a match for the glow when she gazed up and saw another figure before her. It was a man Janey knew but didn't remember, handsome in his matching robe, and in his strong arms he cradled a little girl. It was this little person who elicited such a glow from her mother.

"Oh my," Janey stated with wonder. "That baby . . . that's me."

The man, whose name was Dan Sullivan and who was the father she'd known only from photographs, placed the sleeping baby in his wife's arms. She held her tight against her body, kissing her exposed forehead. Janey had recent experience being around babies, their neighbors Cynthia and Bradley allowing her to help out with baby Jake, so she knew that this infant version of herself was a newborn, or just beyond. Two months, she thought, her birthday being October and this scene before her obviously Christmas.

She realized that unfolding before her was her first-ever Christmas.

This was Christmas of the past.

How had time managed to take her there? Was it because of the power of the windmill, of its sails and the strong wind coming off the land? She placed a hand upon the window, felt the cold of a winter long since passed. Inside the windmill she was still warm, almost feverish, yet just beyond the glass lived a wonderland of snow and ice and the joy of a holiday Janey had come to embrace despite recent tragedies. She had no mother and she had no father, but she had Brian, whom she called Dad, and together with the residents of her home of Linden Corners, she'd seen the joy Christmas could bring to all.

But this story that was breathing before her, it was about one family.

A family that back then lived for a tomorrow filled with dreams.

Dreams, the girl named Janey Sullivan knew, didn't always come true.

But on this magical day they did, as Dan and Annie exchanged gifts, their laughter filling their home, their love for each other apparent. Janey watched as her father opened a box and grimaced at the sight of shirts and ties, even though she had seen many pictures of him wearing such clothes. He'd been a businessman, like Bradley, the two of them friends. She watched as Annie opened a cardboard box and withdrew, with a wow of exclamation, a ceramic Christmas tree. Janey pointed her finger, the window stopping her. She knew that piece; they still had it stored upstairs in the attic, taking it out for Christmastime. What she didn't know was when her mother had received it, nor did she realize it had been a gift from her husband. Janey smiled as the two of them kissed, a loving sight that Janey couldn't ever remember seeing.

"I love you, Dan Sullivan," Annie said.

"I love you, Annie Sullivan," he said in response.

And then they looked down at their bundle of joy, kissed her cheek.

"And we love you, precious Janey Sullivan."

Janey felt her heart lurch inside her chest, felt it thunder with emotion.

She didn't cry; she just continued to watch. Curious to see what was to come next.

There had to be a reason her mama had taken her here to share their Christmas.

Dan reached under the tree and pulled out a small, square package.

"What is this?" Annie asked.

"It's not for you . . . well, not really."

"Dan Sullivan, what have you done?"

"I'd have Janey open it . . ."

"Should we wait until she can, perhaps next Christmas? Will it spoil?"

He laughed, the sound deep and masculine. "Are you sure you can wait?"

Dan Sullivan must have known his wife well, since, with little Janey still cradled in her arm and beginning to fuss, she slid a fingernail beneath the wrapping. When she struggled with the tape, Dan took hold of Janey and together father and daughter watched as Annie opened the box and removed from it . . .

"Oh, Dan, you remembered . . ."

Janey didn't hear the rest of her mother's statement, her excitement filling the windmill.

"My frog!" Janey exclaimed. "That's my purple frog!"

Her voice reverberated inside the empty windmill and then inside her mind. That was when she closed her eyes and awoke in the utter darkness of her room, the wind still howling at the old farmhouse, the images of yesteryear gone.

"Mama?" she asked the night.

But it was as if Annie hadn't been there, even though Janey was convinced she had been.

She got up out of bed, gazed out the window to see if the magic from inside the windmill would transfer here, to her home and to the room in which she felt most secure. But all she saw was the early rise of tomorrow over the horizon, just beyond where the windmill loomed, its sails turning forward.

Not backward.

She slept, and then hours later, Janey felt a chill seep into her bones, her little body grabbing at the pillow, hands fruitlessly grabbing at blankets. She stirred, woke, popped up. She was in bed, the blankets pushed all the way to the edge of the bed. Grabbing for the comforter, she snuggled beneath it and sought out warmth she no longer felt.

"Mama?" she asked the empty room.

There was no answer other than the light of morning sneaking in through the window. It should have warmed her, but a chill had swept over the land sometime during the night. She felt tired, as though her sleep had been interrupted, even if she couldn't remember why. She looked out the window and saw the first flakes of snow she'd seen since last winter.

Then she reached under the pillow and sought out her steady companion, a stuffed purple frog that had seen better days. She might be ten years old, but that meant so too was he. He'd been a gift on her first Christmas, when she'd been barely two months old. Wait a minute, *she thought, looking down at the frog's silent, sewed grin,* how do I know that? And why a stuffed frog? After all these years, she still didn't know its significance. Either she'd never thought to ask, or her mother had told her and she'd forgotten.

Unlikely, that second scenario.

All she knew was that the frog had always been there, constant but unnamed. Back when she was old enough to understand the idea of naming things, she'd refused to give the frog one. People with names only disappeared, like her father had, a man with the name Dan.

Many things were uncertain for Janey Sullivan, most of all her future.

For now, though, on this morning when she felt the first chill of the season, she knew one thing was certain: Christmas was coming.

PART 1

THE SULLIVAN FAMILY

CHAPTER 1

BRIAN

In the blink-and-you-miss-it downtown area of tiny Linden Corners there stands a local bar once called Connors' Corner, now named George's Tavern after the kind, wise old man who had first welcomed a just-passing-through Brian Duncan to town and who later left the bar in Brian's care when his own time on earth came to an end. Since then, Brian had honored the traditions George had instilled all those years by running a friendly bar as best he could, and that included knowing when it was time to close up after a long night. He was tired, and tomorrow, a holiday, promised to be exhausting, mostly because he'd volunteered to do the cooking. He flicked a switch on the wall, dimming the lights until just soft yellow bulbs over the long stretch of oak remained. The open room developed a ghostly glow, with only shadows sitting at the empty tables. Except for one last straggler, the midnight hour chasing him away before Brian could.

"Any bigger hint and you'd be hitting me over the head with a hammer you bought down at Ackroyd's. I'll be heading out now. I'll see you tomorrow night, Brian," said Chet Hardesty, an out-of-work welder who'd been coming to the tavern more and more of late. He rose from his bar stool with a crack of his knees.

"Closed tomorrow, Chet. It's Thanksgiving."

"Oh, right, the holidays. They kind of sneak up on you, don't they?"

That would normally be the case if not for the defrosting twenty-five-pound turkey hogging precious space inside the refrigerator back at the farmhouse he shared with his young ward, ten-year-old Janey Sullivan. Still, he supposed weathered old Chet raised a good point. It was hard to believe that special time of year had arrived again, when not just turkey, but trimmings, tinsel, and trees would dominate the local conversation. Whether here or across the county road at the Five O'Clock Diner over a cup of coffee or down the street at Marla and Darla's Trading Post, at the counter inside A Doll's Attic, really anywhere in Linden Corners that the locals liked to gather, Christmas had a way of consuming their lives.

"Take care of yourself, Chet. Get home safely, you hear?"

"I made it to sixty-four with few problems, knees notwithstanding," he said. "Don't see why tonight would be any different."

Chet responded to his time-honored wisdom with a hearty laugh, but to Brian it sounded hollow. He briefly wondered if Chet had any family to go home to tonight, a place in which to spend the holiday, and he nearly extended one more invitation to the festivities scheduled to take place within the gentle warmth of the farmhouse. Perhaps his wife was out of town visiting relatives and he had stayed behind. But then Chet was gone into the night, the zoom of the truck's engine disrupting the night's silence. Brian might be a bartender, but that didn't mean he was cut out to solve everyone's problems. Didn't he have his share of them? As much joy as he'd experienced here in town, certain things in his life remained unsettled.

Linden Corners was usually discovered only by unsuspecting visitors who had made an inadvertent turn off the Taconic Parkway. Existing on a stretch of highway that sliced through the rolling green hills of the Hudson River Valley of New York State, it was a place that liked to roll up its sidewalks as dusk arrived, George's Tavern one of the few exceptions. By midnight, it was only his lights that allowed unsuspecting travelers to know they were passing through civilization. Brian had made decent money with such a business mode, as some folks just didn't like staying home alone, and so the bar offered up a regular place to kick back and relax, watch a ballgame on the wide-screen television on the wall while knocking back a few beers, a chance to make new friends. Otherwise, on weeknights like this, the downtown area was as dark as night preferred, lights doused, a sleepy village living up to its reputation.

Brian made his way across the creaky wood floor, wondering if maybe the converted old home needed some repairs before winter, turned the lock on the front door to avoid any possible last-minute customer. Back behind the bar, he set about cleaning the remaining glasses quickly so he could get back home to Janey, even though he expected she'd already be fast asleep. Sara Ravens was watching her tonight, no doubt catching a few needed winks on the sofa. Sara, one of the waitresses over at the Five-O and Brian's tenant who lived upstairs from the tavern with her husband, Mark, had recently volunteered to look after Janey a couple of nights a week, practice, she said, for when she and Mark had a kid of their own.

Which would come soon enough. Sara Ravens was eight months pregnant.

Brian flipped on the faucet, letting warm water wash

over his hands. It wasn't cold out, the usual winter chill not having swooped down on them, surprising given the amount of snow the region had suffered the last two Christmases. Last year, in fact, he remembered a snowstorm hitting them on Halloween and little relief after that until April. At this hour, though, despite the unseasonal temperatures, there was something about the big sky and its shroud of darkness that produced a natural chill, and it reminded Brian of his solitude. Or was that loneliness? Sure, he had Janey to light his life, she who filled his days with boundless joy. But then there were those nights, especially when he was off from tending bar and Janey was helping over at the Knights' with baby Jake, when he found himself pacing the farmhouse with no purpose. He stopped, setting the clean glass down on the washcloth, and let out a sigh. Taking a look around the place where he spent most nights, the quiet jukebox and the empty chairs, the smell of beer wafting through the air, he wondered, not for the first time, what more he could be doing with his life.

Just last Christmas he'd asked the same question of himself, and rather than seeking out answers, he'd wrapped himself up in the complex lives of others, like Nora Connors Rainer, like Thomas Van Diver, strangers then, now friends and expected tomorrow for Thanksgiving dinner. He'd solved their issues and ignored his own, and then a new year had begun and life just chugged along, Brian's life the lone whistle at the end of the journey. And suddenly it was Thanksgiving again, and along with Nora and Thomas, several other guests were expected, and so Brian supposed he ought to stop wallowing in his brand of self-pity and get on home. His life wouldn't be changed tonight, and that turkey wouldn't cook itself tomorrow.

A rap of knuckles against the glass pane of the front door caught his attention.

He waved, said, "Sorry, I'm closed."

He could see a deflated expression cross the face of the person on the wrong side of the door. Brian noticed through the panes of glass that it was a woman. He didn't recognize her.

She knocked again, persistence winning out. Maybe she was in trouble.

Tossing down the towel, Brian crossed the floor again but didn't immediately turn the lock.

"Sorry, I just closed up," he said. "Taps are turned off."

"I'll be quick," the woman said.

"Quick about what?"

"This is a bar, yes?"

"Yes. A closed bar."

"Your sign here says you're open till two." She pointed toward the HOURS OF OPERATION placard that dangled from one of the panes.

"True, but I hardly ever do. Maybe weekends. Look . . . miss, I'm sorry . . ."

He again saw defeat crumple her weary features. He sighed again, turned the lock, and let her in before turning the deadbolt behind her. *No other strays allowed tonight,* he thought, *just this one. And she better be not just quick but a good tipper.* As he made his way back to the bar, the woman, whom he guessed was around thirty, trailed after him and hopped up on one of the stools found midway down the bar. He turned to her just as she was removing her fur-trimmed overcoat, a bit bulky considering the mild temperatures outside.

"So what'll it be?" he asked.

"Scotch, neat," she said. "You got Johnny Blue?"

Brian's top shelf didn't reach that high. "I think I have Dewar's."

"It'll have to do in a pinch."

Brian poured the requested drink, sliding it over with a gentle push. She peered through the glass, judging its contents' clear brown character before taking a sip. Satisfaction apparently met, she knocked back the rest of it with one gulp, setting the glass down with a loud thunk. Her gesture indicated that Brian should hit her with a refill, not that she ever voiced such words. He did so, her hand helping him tip the bottle until it had produced a double.

"Better?" Brian asked with a hint of sarcasm.

She took a sip, then settled down like she was getting ready to nurse it. Which meant she wasn't leaving anytime soon. "I needed that first one. Thanks."

"Mind telling me what's got you so eager for a few shots at this late hour?"

"You a bartender or a shrink?"

"Aren't we supposed to be both?"

"Ah, Linden Corners. Home to stereotypes."

"Is that comment directed at me, or you?"

"Touché, Dr. Barkeep."

She sipped at her drink again and Brian wondered how long this second drink would take.

"Trina," she said. "My name's Trina. And who might you be?"

"Late for home, apparently."

She laughed, the sound producing a smile for the first time since she'd appeared, virtually out of nowhere. Brian observed her appearance, from her mousy brown hair matted against her head, like she'd worked up a sweat, to her simple jeans and a blue chambray shirt. A speck of makeup but otherwise no noticeable signs of jewelry, no necklace and no rings, and her ears he couldn't see, what with the flat head of hair. As hard-edged as she seemed, her smile softened up her face, her lips widening.

"Sorry to mess up your plans. The little woman waiting for you?"

In a way, Brian thought, thinking of Janey. But this Trina woman, she meant otherwise.

"Just my daughter; she's with a sitter."

"Sorry," she said with a raise of her glass. "Guess I was a little presumptuous, George. I'm really good at jumping to conclusions."

"How are your landings?"

"Generally sucky. I'm here, after all—don't take that as an insult. I don't mean your bar. Just . . . Linden Corners," she said, the name of the town falling off her tongue with more than a hint of derision. "Let me guess—your name's not George."

"Brian," he said, extending his hand.

"But the sign outside says . . . Never mind. It's nice to meet you, Brian," she said, taking the proffered hand. "So, Brian, what's a guy named Brian doing running a place named George's?"

"Long story."

"I'm happy to listen. I'll even spring for a round."

Brian shook his head. "Kind offer, but I'll pass."

She looked around the empty bar before returning her focus to him. Her eyes were wide, a soft blue in the dim lighting. "Afraid of setting a bad example in front of your customers?"

"No, I just don't drink."

She had her glass up to her lips, where it lingered. Like she was deciding whether to take a gulp and suddenly felt bad about Brian's late-hour confession. She set the glass back down, gave him a curious look. "Can I ask why not?"

"No, you may not. Drink up, Ms. Trina."

She did, quickly. "Okay, I'll get out of your hair. I just needed to get away for a bit."

"Where you staying?"

"At the Solemn Nights," she said, sounding like it was the last place she wanted to be.

Not surprising, really. It was hardly the ideal place to rest your body. The Solemn Nights was the only motel in town, located about half a mile down Route 23, and was owned by Mark's uncle, the eccentric recluse Richie Ravens. Brian had once stayed in the motel's less-than-deluxe accommodations when he'd arrived in Linden Corners, and for a second he questioned what this woman's story was and why she had chosen the roadside location. Now, though, wasn't the time to get into it, not when he'd put the bottle away and he was anxious to get home.

"Well, maybe you should wait a bit before driving back. Those shots are strong."

"It's okay, Dr. Barkeep. I walked over. Like I said, I needed air. My father was driving me nuts."

"Your father? He's staying with you?"

"More like the other way around," she said, offering up no more explanation.

Brian let it go, deciding her business wasn't his. He let Trina finish the last drops of her drink while he finished cleaning up, hoping his actions were as subtle as when he'd chased Chet out. She set down a twenty-dollar bill and told him to keep the change. Brian just pocketed the money for now, his register closed. Trina busied herself with putting on her heavy coat.

"I was expecting snow by now," she said when she saw Brian watching her.

"Weather's been weird this autumn," Brian answered. "Supposed to be sixty tomorrow."

They walked together toward the front door, where Brian turned the lock again.

Trina stepped through the doorway onto the front

porch. "Thanks. Maybe I'll see you again," she said. "Like tomorrow."

"Closed tomorrow," he said, parroting himself. "It's Thanksgiving."

She nodded once but didn't say anything. A fresh darkening of those blue eyes told him all he needed to know. Some people found holidays less than happy occasions. Trina looked to be among them. She made her way out to the parking lot, gone as quickly as she had come and leaving Brian once again to his familiar solitude.

Back at the bar, he took hold of her glass, noticed a faint stain of lipstick on the rim.

He stared back at the door, almost wishing she would return. He'd actually enjoyed her company. She had made him forget that he'd been lonely.

But then the glass hit the warm water and the red gloss melted away.

It was getting on toward one o'clock in the morning before Brian had fully washed down the bar and turned up the chairs and stools. He'd sent a text Sara's way, saying he was running a bit late, and her reply had buzzed back quickly, telling him not to rush. All was fine, she'd typed, Janey was fast asleep, even if baby Ravens was kicking up a storm inside her belly. No longer in such a hurry, Brian gazed about the darkened bar, amazed at how much his life had changed in nearly three years and how much it still amazed him. His New York friend John Oliver liked to joke that Brian had traded the noisy subways of Manhattan for the endless cornfields of Linden Corners, from corporate maven to early-rising farmer, and while the lifestyle was admittedly a 180-degree turn, Brian was still a night owl. He could often be found rattling around the farmhouse at two in the morning, unable to sleep, his mind unable to shut down.

Tonight was no different.

He'd probably be making chestnut stuffing at five A.M.

Still, best to let someone get rest, and that someone was Sara. If Brian's life represented time standing still, Sara's was the picture of progress. A year ago she'd been pushing Mark for a wedding date, and now eleven months later they were married and the birth of their first child was fast approaching. Brian, on the other hand, still worked at the bar. Period.

"Okay, Duncan, enough wasting time. Get on home."

He heard the echo of his voice before it too dissipated. Silence again ruled the night.

Flipping off the last of the lights, he grabbed his keys and exited the bar, turning the lock for the final time that night. Tomorrow was a much-needed day off from pulling the taps and refilling the pretzel bowls, and he allowed himself another sigh. He refused to give those sighs a name, fearing they would reveal a level of dissatisfaction he didn't want to believe. Once out on the porch, he went toward the stairs, and suddenly he stumbled, feeling something connecting with his foot. Only a quick grab of the railing saved him from stumbling down to the walkway.

"What was that . . . ?" he asked.

His eyes adjusted to the darkness, and he noticed a parcel on the top step of the tavern's entrance. Curious as to why someone would leave it there, he bent down and was surprised to see his first name written across the brown paper covering. There was no mailing address on it, no return address either, and no postage anywhere. Which meant someone had dropped it off in person. But who, and why? And for that matter, how long had it been there? Also, what should he do with it?

All those questions came with no apparent answers.

He considered leaving the package just where he'd found it, somewhat suspicious of the intent behind it.

But then the former New Yorker remembered this was Linden Corners.

So he tucked the box under his arm and headed out to the parking lot, where his old truck waited to take him back to the farmhouse. How the battered vehicle had managed to survive another year, he couldn't say. Like an old lady going from home to church, Brian supposed he didn't get out much beyond the world that was Linden Corners. But he couldn't trade it in; it had been Annie's and it represented one piece of history for her daughter, Janey, now in his care. So he fired up the engine, listened as it coughed up spumes of smoke from the exhaust, then set off with a rattle down Route 23. A couple of miles west, he turned up Crestview Road and along the driveway to the house he called home, once upon a time belonging to the Van Diver family, the Sullivans next, until Brian arrived, the current tenant.

He hopped out of the cab, closed the door quietly so as not to wake anyone.

Sara tended to favor the sofa in the living room, which faced the front.

Janey's room looked out over the back field, with an unimpeded view of the windmill that defined their landscape.

The thought of the windmill had Brian considering a quick jaunt down the hill. This late hour was often when he would venture to its endlessly spinning sails and talk with Annie, whose spirit seemed to inhabit it as much now as it had when she was alive. He liked to fill her in on the details of Janey's days and of their holidays together, the gentle wind that turned its sails her way of answering him. But tonight there was no discernible wind, and with the warm air it hardly felt like Thanksgiving, much less the official start to the Christmas season.

That was when Brian turned back to the front seat of the truck, where the parcel waited.

Brian withdrew the box and walked to the porch of the farmhouse. There he grabbed at the cardboard corners, releasing the tape that held the brown paper secure. As it came away, he noticed another box wrapped in gold paper, its shiny surface reflecting off the light of the moon high above. A silver-colored ribbon was tied around it, and attached to that was a card with a grinning Santa Claus staring back at him, like he was in on the mystery. Flipping over the card, he easily made out the message, written in block letters:

DO NOT OPEN UNTIL CHRISTMAS

Surely this was a joke, was his first thought.

And then he remembered the last two Christmases he'd spent in Linden Corners and the wonderful residents who inhabited this endearing little town, and the joyous times they had shared trying to out-gift each other. He thought first of Gerta Connors and her daughter, Nora, and Nora's young son, Travis; and of the elderly Thomas Van Diver and the coarsely funny Martha Martinson; of the newlyweds Mark and Sara too, and lastly his best friends and neighbors, Cynthia and Bradley Knight, all of these people he'd helped in some way and who had helped him. One of them must be behind this gift, an opening gambit in a game of Secret Santa.

Which was odd, considering it felt nothing like Christmas outside.

At last, he thought of Janey Sullivan, who had been his greatest gift.

Had she somehow pulled this off?

Nah, she was too impatient to let a gift go unwrapped or to keep a secret like this for long, much less a month. Just then Brian realized he had to hide the gift, if not for himself then for Janey. If she found the package she would want to open it right away, her curiosity the opposite of his. She would insist they open it now and not wait until Christmas. So Brian indeed paid a visit to the windmill on this unseasonably warm night, carrying the shiny gold box down the hill and inside the wooden tower of the old windmill, hiding it in the closet on the second level. It was just as he'd done the past two years with their Christmas gifts, knowing this was one of Annie's traditions.

"Okay, the holidays have officially begun," he said to Annie's lovely self-portrait, which hung on the wall of what had once been her art studio. "Christmas is once again on its way. Not that you can tell outside. Not a flake of snow yet and barely a chill."

As he began his journey back toward the farmhouse, Brian instinctively turned back and noticed that the sails of the windmill were now turning like gentle giants. A sudden gust of wind blew past him and swept up the hill and into the dark sky, carrying with it a blast of warmth. At this late hour of the night—or was it early morning?—with a holiday celebration looming just hours away, it still felt like late summer.

Brian Duncan had a sneaking suspicion that this Christmas in Linden Corners was going to be unlike the last two, with its own share of unforeseen surprises, and it all began with a gift he'd not seen coming. But didn't such a thing define his life here?

CHAPTER 2

CYNTHIA

Jake Knight might be only eighteen months old at this point, but he sure had the right idea—sleep the day away. For his mother, the perpetually tired and always-on-the-go Cynthia Knight, getting ready for Thanksgiving meant overseeing the preparation of the vegetables, and she supposed it was only natural, since during the summer months she ran a fresh fruit and vegetable stand just on the edge of their property, itself on the northern edge of the village of Linden Corners. The produce she'd sold for years had come courtesy of their farm and backbreaking hard work, but in recent years the tilling of their fertile land had been taken over by workers for hire, who all got a portion of the sales. She was busy being a mother, and Bradley's job as a lawyer had continually stolen more hours from their lives. Other local farmers had begun to contribute to the stand as well, to the point where it was the best place in the county to get in-season corn, blueberries, and anything else you could ask for. A communal effort for a close-knit town.

She supposed it was good that Knight's Vegetable Stand had other people caring for it. It meant she could let it go that much easier, helping to ease the separation she was bound to feel. At least, that's how she pictured the scene unfolding in her head, practical woman that she was, even allowing a new owner to change its name if not its traditions. To everyone and everything there is a season; isn't that how the song went? And then you moved on. Her heart, though, told another story, and as if needing a fresh reason to infuse her heart with an energetic jolt, she gazed lovingly over at the corner of her kitchen.

"Lucky you," Cynthia said to her son, who slept quietly in his portable crib.

She knew she could collapse at any second, as she'd barely had any rest. For once, her sleepless night hadn't been Jake's fault; the little tyke had taken to sleeping through the nights the last few months. No, the other man in her life was responsible for her wide-awake nights and yawn-inducing days. Her husband, Bradley, and all the news he'd brought with him the past couple of weeks; news that would bring about big changes. Just then she checked the kitchen clock, noticed it was just after noon. They needed to get going. Where was that fool husband of hers?

"Bradley, are you about ready? We've got to get over to Brian's."

It was Thanksgiving Day and the three of them were expected at the Duncan farmhouse, just down the hill from them, for a jam-packed afternoon of food, friends, and family. And, she supposed, one major announcement that was forever going to change the landscape of their town and their own lives. She thought of Janey Sullivan and felt a regretful stab at her heart. Could she really go through with this?

She didn't have time to contemplate an answer as a refreshed-looking Bradley Knight made his entrance into the kitchen, dressed in khaki pants and a casual sweater. His thick blond hair was neatly combed, but then again, it always was. He planted a warm kiss on his wife's lips before settling his gaze on his resting son.

"Should we wait till he wakes?"

"If we're late, Brian will kill us. He's so nervous about hosting his first big dinner."

"I think you're the one who's nervous."

"Bradley, don't. I don't need any reminders . . ."

He pulled her into his embrace, held her slim frame tight against his. "I love you."

"Bradley Knight, you are not going to distract me now."

"I think I'm the only husband who says those three little words and gets admonished."

"That's because you're using them to manipulate the situation."

But she wasn't mad at him, the smile on her pretty face too broad. He patted her behind teasingly, kissed her again. Bradley was certainly frisky this morning, she thought. But of course all the pressure had been lifted from him, at least for the present. The stress of the business world would invade his life soon enough and he'd be ever the distracted lawyer again.

"Okay, I'll get Jake's stuff into the car."

"I'll grab the dishes," she said.

"See what a team we make. Us against the world."

"Indeed," Cynthia said with a hint of derision.

So the Knights packed up, Cynthia feeling like they were taking half the house with them for just a short trek to Brian's. She couldn't imagine how she would feel seeing filled boxes and empty rooms. With Jake in her arms, she grabbed hold of the front door, but not before she stole a wistful look at the quiet living room and its fireplace that stood cold and the television with no sound or image. Like a frozen silence had already fallen on their old home.

Jake settled in his car seat, Cynthia in hers, Bradley pulled out of the driveway and turned right onto Crestview Road, journeying only a half mile to their destination. Cynthia watched as barren fields passed her by; winter was coming, not that you'd know it on such an unseasonably warm holiday, but the ground knew better and was already well into its natural hibernation. The land was littered with a cornucopia of fallen leaves, leaving the countryside aglow in orange and yellow, all set against the skeletal remains of branches. She couldn't get the idea of change out of her mind. The slowly turning, latticed sails of the windmill rearing up over the cresting hill added to the effect. Everything was changing; time couldn't be slowed.

Before long Jake would be talking, he'd be walking so fast she'd barely catch up to him, to time also, one day out the door and to his own life. How she wished she could remove the battery from the kitchen clock and keep them locked in the here and now.

"Uh, Cyn, we're here."

"Oh, uh, I guess I was thinking."

"Care to share?"

"I was wondering where Jake would go to college."

"Hey, Cyn?"

"Yes?"

"Jake's not even two. I think we can leave that discussion to another day."

Cynthia was about to ask her husband of twelve years if he ever gave the future a thought when she realized that was all he'd been doing for the past few months. If she voiced her concerns, he'd think she was losing it. Thankfully their non-discussion was interrupted by the opening of the front door of the farmhouse, ten-year-old Janey Sullivan bounding toward them, her effusive smile leading the way. Cynthia was about to forewarn Janey that Jake was sleeping, when the little guy stirred as though he knew his favorite person in the world was closing in on him.

"Hi, Jake!" Janey said, opening the back door.

"Hello to you too, Janey," Cynthia said.

"Oh, sorry, hi, it's just . . ."

"Yes, I know. Have at him. I'll take the dishes into the kitchen."

Bradley, unfolding his long legs from the driver's side, said, "Where's Brian?"

"In the backyard. It's so warm out, he decided to use the grill for the turkey."

Bradley laughed, brushing his hair back from his forehead even though it wasn't needed. "I've tasted his burgers, so I think I'll go help."

Cynthia grabbed two of the three dishes she'd prepared—beets in one, sliced zucchini in the other—and was prepared to make a return trip for the green beans topped with fried onions when Travis Rainer stepped out onto the porch, offering his assistance. His mother, Nora, standing behind him, appeared to have made the decision for him, for the thirteen-year-old boy slumped his way over to the car like it was the last place in the world he wanted to be. Perhaps that was true of the entire day. Janey was closest to him in age, and they were friends but hardly had much in common. Cynthia took in his sullen teenage look and wondered if Jake would grow into such a mood too.

"Thanks, Travis. I appreciate it."

He took hold of the first two dishes from her, Nora coming up to take the third.

Janey had Jake in her arms, cooing over him. His bright blue eyes were wide-awake.

So that left Cynthia empty-handed and feeling a bit useless as she made her way toward the house, feeling as though once she stepped over its threshold there was no going back to the cocoon inside her own home. Because not only was today Thanksgiving; it represented the countdown to her new life—or perhaps to the end of the life she had known.

She paused, causing Nora to take a look back. "Cynthia, you okay?"

"Oh, sure. Why?"

"You look like you're a thousand miles away."

Cynthia couldn't help it as a sharp laugh escaped her lips. "I'm right here," she said.

Nora's expression no doubt mirrored her own. Not believing a word of it.

Fortunately the arrival of another car interrupted their moment.

"Oh good," Nora said, "now everyone's here."

An SUV pulled up beside the other cars in the driveway, where Cynthia noticed Nicholas Casey, the handsome, bespectacled art curator whom Nora had been dating for the better part of the year, emerge, dash around to the passenger door to assist his elderly companions. From the front seat came Gerta Connors, Nora's mother, and from the backseat, Thomas Van Diver, clad as always in his trademark bow tie; today's was a burnt orange with pumpkins on it. Nicholas took hold of Gerta's arm, leading her up the couple of steps of the porch and into the house.

"Oh, we mustn't forget the pies," she said.

"I'll come back for them," Nicholas said.

"Oh, you, such nice manners," Gerta said with obvious delight.

It was little secret she approved of her daughter's choice of boyfriend.

Cynthia found herself accepting Thomas' arm, helping the eighty-five-year-old man along the uneven path. It didn't go unnoticed by her that in the span of twenty minutes she'd gone from holding her young son in her tight grasp to assisting the elderly Mr. Van Diver, reminding her again of the tenuous nature of time. One day you're young; the next, big decisions aged you before the mirror.

Once they settled inside the comfortable living room, where extra chairs had been set, the sliding door that led from the kitchen to the back patio opened up, bringing in not just the wind but Brian Duncan, adorned in an apron that said DON'T BLAME THE COOK. Cynthia saw her still amused husband follow behind him.

"Well, it looks like everyone's here," Brian said to the assembled group. "Welcome to all our guests, to friends we think of as family."

"Wait, where's Mark and Sara? I thought they were coming."

"They had to cancel at the last minute, a family situation," Brian explained. "So, yes, this is everyone."

Indeed, in the shadow of the turning windmill it was a full house for Thanksgiving this year, a celebration not just of the community that was Linden Corners but of the bond that existed between the generations represented here as well. Thomas and Gerta, Nora and Nicholas, Travis and Janey, and even little Jake, who might just be the start of a new era. Bradley sidled up beside his wife, wrapping a comforting arm around her waist. She felt herself letting out a heavy sigh. Yet she realized she wasn't the only one here clinging to an unsettled feeling, as she saw a sudden sense of loss cross Brian Duncan's face.

They exchanged a quick look, one understood by best friends.

He was missing Annie Sullivan. So too was Cynthia, and in more ways than one.

"She's here," Cynthia silently mouthed, gazing about the farmhouse.

He offered her a smile before saying, "So shall we get this celebration started?"

"I have just one question," Janey asked.

"What's that, sweetie?" Brian asked.

"Well, I mean the holidays are here, but we haven't had any snow yet and so it doesn't feel right. It's not even that cold outside. During the parade on television this morning, even Santa Claus looked warm in his red suit. How can his sleigh even land when there's no snow?"

There came a couple of genial chuckles from the elder folks. Janey wasn't arguing the logistics, just indulging the fantasy that all children embraced at this time of year. Christmas had to be just perfect, from the tree to the gifts to the setting. And if one knew anything about Janey Sullivan, one knew she was expecting an answer.

"That's why they call it the Miracle on Thirty-fourth Street," Brian told her.

That got an even bigger laugh, until Janey, unaffected by the amusement around her, said, "I sure hope your cooking is better than your humor."

That got the biggest laugh of all from the group. Suddenly the festive celebration began in earnest, even with no snow falling and no cold wind, no fireplace blazing to warm their hearts. Cynthia realized that the warmth filling the farmhouse had nothing to do with the weather.

How she was going to miss Linden Corners.

"I'm stuffed."

"Couldn't eat another thing."

"The turkey turned out great, Brian, very moist."

"I could take a nap."

"That's from the tryptophan," Janey stated, staring across the table at Thomas.

"No, I need a nap because I'm old," he replied. "If you'll excuse me for a bit, it's been a lovely meal."

Thomas wasn't kidding, as he shuffled his way from the dinner table to retire to his chair in the living room. Jake was resting near there too, thankfully, which had allowed Cynthia to enjoy her meal. Which she had, as evidenced by her near-spotless plate. She'd even splurged on seconds, thirds for her beets. Most had skipped them, but it was a favorite recipe of hers, the vegetables straight from her garden. She wouldn't have that next year, she doubted she'd have the chance to even plant seeds. Life would take a while to regrow. As young and old alike refreshed themselves, she rose from the table, started to take plates in her hands.

"Cyn, you don't have to do that . . ."

"Relax, Brian. You cooked; I'll clean."

"You cooked too," he reminded her.

"Shush yourself, Brian Duncan," Gerta told him. "Me, Nora, and Cynthia will clear the table and get dessert ready. You menfolk can watch football or whatever it is you do."

"How'd I get dragged into cleaning?" Nora protested.

"And what should I do?" Janey asked.

"You go have fun until dessert is ready. We'll call you."

"And then before we cut the pie, we play my Thanksgiving game, right?"

"Ugh," Travis said with a roll of the eyes.

"What's that?" Nicholas asked.

"Oh, it's a tradition I learned two years ago at Brian's parents' house, where we go around the table and everyone gets to say what they're most thankful for."

"Sounds perfect. I know I'm thankful for much," Nicholas said.

Cynthia noticed he was staring at Nora when he said those words. A wineglass, tipped to her lips, hid Nora's nervous smile, making Cynthia wonder if there was trouble between them. Nora was a cautious, reserved woman by nature, and it had been surprising for them all to watch the effortless charms of Nicholas Casey steadily win her over this year.

But Janey's game of thanks would have to wait for Gerta's famous pies to be set out. For now, Janey and Travis went outside into the falling light of the day if for nothing else than to escape all those adults, while the men—Bradley, Brian, and Nicholas—dodged KP duty. So the kitchen was full with Gerta, fussing with the six freshly baked pies she'd brought over, and Nora, pouring herself a fresh glass of wine, keeping Cynthia company as she attacked the dishes like a woman on a mission. A plate went crashing into the sink, the sound unmistakable. She'd broken it.

"Whoa, Cyn, you all right?" Nora asked.

"It slipped from my hands," she said, again her voice betraying her. It seemed everything that came out of her mouth sounded unconvincing, not least during dinner, when Janey, sitting beside her, had told her how happy she was that the Knights were with them today, her especially. Cynthia knew that Janey missed her mother, Annie, every day and every starlit night, and while Cynthia had tried to be there for her best friend's impressionable daughter, she feared that since Jake's birth she'd been less attentive to Janey's needs. The rest of the meal had lingered, which had Cynthia feeling like she had a hole in her stomach; perhaps that was why she'd eaten so much, a poor attempt at filling it. She allowed herself a rueful smile at her own joke, knowing the emptiness she felt stemmed from what was still to come, not just today but in the coming weeks.

"Here, I think you need this more than I do," Nora said, handing over a glass of red wine while taking over before the sink.

Cynthia accepted the glass, took a sip before setting it down.

What was wrong with her? Why was she feeling so guilty about her choices?

And besides, it wasn't just about her, but about Bradley and Jake as well. Their family.

Change was unavoidable; it was coming as sure as tomorrow was.

The scent of baked goodness stirred her from her inner turmoil. Just then she saw Gerta peeling the tinfoil off her signature strawberry pie, its fragrant smell filling the kitchen. She realized that as much as life changed with each rising sun, there were moments in time, slices of life, that were just like Gerta's pies—unforgettable. Cynthia made her way over to Gerta and gave her a sweet hug.

"My goodness, dear, not that I'm complaining, but—"

"That's it," Nora said, tossing down a wet dishcloth onto the counter. "Cynthia Knight, tell us right now what's going on."

"I . . . I . . . can you wait a few minutes? Bradley has an announcement."

"That sounds . . . ominous."

Cynthia grabbed for the glass of wine, not really drinking it, just using it to hide behind. Two could play at that game, she thought as she watched Nora's brow furrow. But all answers would have to wait, as Janey came in from outside, her cheeks reddened from running down the hill toward the windmill and up again, announcing that she was starving and so was Travis. Kids, full of energy, growing fast, needing a refuel of sugar. Gerta smiled with anticipation, telling them to round up the rest of the troops, and moments later the friends were gathered back around the table, where pies were laid out in formation, coffee cups and plates at the ready.

And so began their game of Thanksgiving testimonials.

"Well, I suppose I'm thankful for another year," Thomas Van Diver began, "and to have another holiday spent inside the place I once called home. I suppose there's not enough thanks in the world." Gerta, sitting next to him, agreed with him, thankful for the gift of another year and for the year she had spent with her daughter and grandson, ending by thanking everyone for being there, especially Brian for hosting.

"I do have three other daughters and six more adorable grandchildren," Gerta added, "but today of all days I know that family means more than blood relatives."

Travis was thankful for the food and six kinds of pies, his shadowed eyes unwilling to meet others. Thirteen years old, a child of divorce, he was perhaps the most unsettled of them all here, and Cynthia could hardly blame the boy for his reserve. The exchange progressed to Nora, who was thankful that her life had settled down and that her business, the consignment shop A Doll's Attic, was seeing some decent traction in an otherwise depressed marketplace, and watching her son blossom in his new school. Then she paused, looking like she'd left something out, and then gazed over at Nicholas.

"And for Nick, who somehow puts up with me."

Nicholas Casey appeared to take her comment in stride. "I'm very thankful for being part of this celebration, something the fractured Casey family doesn't seem to value much. So thanks to all," he said, "and to Nora, and Gerta, I'm thankful like Travis for your fabulous pies despite the protests coming from my waistline."

His attempt at levity energized the room, and Cynthia

found herself smiling, even as she realized the round-robin game was fast making its way to her and Bradley. Even Jake was part of this moment, sitting on his father's lap, his blue eyes seemingly transfixed by the flicker of the orange candle in the center of the table. But before it came to them, it was Janey's turn. If this ragtag group of friends and family represented a living, breathing entity, then surely Janey Sullivan was its beating heart, and as she began to talk, a silence settled over the room.

"First of all, I'm thankful for all of you being part of my life. I'm a lucky girl."

She paused, and Cynthia could see Bradley, thinking it was his turn, about to open his mouth. She grabbed his arm, caught his eye, and silently told him to wait. Janey wasn't done.

"But I guess I wouldn't know any of you if not for two people, and it's them I most want to give my thanks to," she said. "My mother and my father, who you know as Dan Sullivan and Annie Sullivan. They gave me life and they gave me things like wishes, and they gave me the gift of hope, and they instilled in me that dreams are possible, so long as you open yourself to them. I know that when we go to sleep at night we're supposed to allow our minds and bodies to rest, but sometimes I think . . . I think . . ." She hesitated, her lips quivering, as though she were unable to get the words out, a rare instance for the garrulous Janey. Cynthia wanted to reach out to her but knew to baby her in this moment would only make it worse. "Sometimes I think dreams are real, and that the people we see in them still exist. I dream of those I've lost, and so I'm thankful that they remain with me."

No one said a word for a moment, not until Jake opened up his mouth and emitted a cry.

Laughter ensued, especially as Janey added one last comment: "Oh, and I'm thankful for Jake, who is like a little brother to me."

Cynthia's heart melted right there, and she nearly let a tear escape from her eye.

Bradley's comforting hand on hers stopped it.

"Uh, I guess it's our turn," Bradley said, using his best lawyer voice. "Thanks can mean many things in this world today, and not enough people express them. So I applaud Janey's game, and her bravery for speaking so eloquently. So, on behalf of Cynthia and Jake, we are thankful for our friends, and for all that we share. But we are also thankful for memories made, memories shared. Knowing that they keep friendships alive even when we're apart, when life takes us . . . elsewhere."

"Elsewhere?" Janey asked. "What do you mean?"

"Well, I guess there's only one way to say this," he said. "Cynthia and I—and of course Jake—have been given a new opportunity. A new job and all that comes with it, including a new home and . . . gosh, this is harder than I thought it would be."

It was Cynthia who finally finished his thought. "We're leaving Linden Corners."

Again, silence hung over the surprised group, interrupted only by the abrupt ringing of the telephone. The scrape of Brian's chair against the hardwood floor snapped Cynthia back to reality, and she watched as her friend—silent, confused—retreated to the kitchen to answer it. She heard him wish the person on the other end a happy Thanksgiving, and then heard several "uh-huhs" and "okay, sure," and lastly, "fine, we'll settle later on which day. Yup, great, we'll talk later. Thanks. Bye." During the entire exchange, no one said anything, and the group all turned eyes toward Brian, who looked a bit pale in the cheeks.

"Brian, is everything okay?" Nora asked.

"Yeah," he said, sitting down at the head of the table. Cynthia, at the other end, held his gaze, and she could see a mix of emotions coursing through him. Had their announcement done that, was it because of the phone call, or maybe it was a combination of both? Only after he made his own announcement did Cynthia realize how upside down Brian and Janey's life was about to become. She and Bradley and Jake might be leaving town, but company was coming.

A door closing, a window opening. Time advancing.

"I can't believe it," Brian said, his voice toneless, as though he were speaking to himself, despite speaking aloud to the group before him. "My parents are coming for Christmas."

CHAPTER 3

TRINA

On a scale of one to ten, today's Thanksgiving celebration, if you even dared use that word, had to rank a four. She'd experienced worse and she supposed she'd had better, even though she was hard-pressed right now to recall one. The Ravens family wasn't exactly known for its ability to bond, and this was never made truer than by the fact that the man she sat across from, her father, was a virtual stranger to her. Fortunately, there had been two other guests at the dinner table to help ease any tense conversation. Trina Winter and Richie Ravens had little to say to each other; such was the history between estranged biological father and diffident, difficult daughter.

The scene was the back office and makeshift apartment at the Solemn Nights Motel, just off Route 23 on the eastern outskirts of Linden Corners, and in addition to Trina and her father, assembled for their makeshift reunion were her cousin, Mark, whose late father, Harry, had been Richie's brother, and his pregnant wife, Sara. Sara had brought dinner, courtesy of the Five-O Diner, where she worked, and Mark had brought the pie, saying it had come from some woman named Gerta Connors. All Trina had had to provide was the beverage, sparkling cider for her father and Sara, beer for Mark and herself, though Trina throughout the day found herself thinking about a healthy shot of whatever the local tavern down the street had on offer. Had she not known the bar was closed for the holiday, she'd already be making plans to escape.

Instead, it was dessert time.

"It's pumpkin," Sara said, "a special request of mine."

"Let me guess, a craving?" Trina asked.

Sara rubbed her considerable belly. "I've had stranger."

"Sara, you're eight months pregnant. I think the cravings have lapsed," Mark said with a genial smile, dimples lighting his face. Then, as an aside to Trina, he added, "Right about now she'll eat anything. Just look at how she cleared her dinner plate."

"Is that remark directed at my appetite or at Martha's cooking?"

"I'm not sure I'm safe with either answer," he remarked.

Sara nodded appreciatively. Pregnant wives always got their way, and Mark seemed to have developed an understanding of said fact to the point that he leaned in to his wife, giving her a quick kiss. Trina couldn't tell if the two of them had just had an argument and the fastest makeup in history, or if their interaction was just how they were: cute banter, sickening display of affection. It was enough to make Trina wish she were anywhere but here.

But that had been true since her arrival a week ago and each night as she went to sleep in her motel room right next door to the office. What was she doing here, and why had she agreed to come care for a father she barely knew? Their relationship subsisted on the occasional phone call, even letters back when they were more fashionable. No e-mails, since her father was one of those old-world men who preferred old-world ways. His only acknowledgment of the modern world seemed to be his forty-five-inch flat-screen television, which had been on all day—football games—and it was this that continued to command his attention now. He'd missed the entire exchange between Mark and Sara. Trina wished she'd inherited her father's sense of obliviousness.

"Richie, you about ready for pie?" Trina asked.

Her father, whom she never called father because she also had a stepfather, who had been more of a role model growing up than he, gazed up absently from his frayed couch. He was sixty-seven, sallow of face, with sunken cheeks and thinning hair that had lost its battle with the bald a while ago. He also at the moment had a cast on his left leg, reaching from his ankle to his calf. He'd broken his leg in three places. "What's that you ask?"

"Pie, Uncle Richie," Mark said.

"Wouldn't be Thanksgiving without," he said with a nod. "Do you mind if I take it here? It's too much effort to get up again and hobble over to the table."

Mark tossed Trina a quick look, as though seeking approval from her.

Both his doctor and the physical therapist had said it was important to keep Richie active and not let him get too complacent. But Trina was too drained to argue with him at this late hour, so she gave in, her expression showing obvious displeasure. She suggested that Sara make herself comfortable in the other chair; it would be dessert in front of the Cowboys game. So while Mark helped his wife get settled, Trina made her way to the small kitchen, which required her to pass through the front office of the motel. All was quiet, the only sign of life coming from the neon red VACANCY sign in the window.

In the kitchen, she took hold of pie plates and small forks, surprised that her father even had such specific items. His kitchen wasn't exactly one fit for a gourmet. Figuring it was easier to serve here and carry the plates back into the living room, she set about cutting the pie when Mark came up behind her.

"You doing okay, Trina?"

"Sure, why wouldn't I be?"

"I sense sarcasm."

"Gee, and I was going for a direct hit."

Her bite didn't seem to have any lasting effect on him, but then again, that matched all she had heard about her cousin on her father's side. Mark was patient, good-natured, understanding, a smart guy with lots to look forward to, and add to that his ambition. He was working two jobs to achieve his goals. He was handsome, with an easy, winning smile, and, as far as she could tell from the few times she had seen him since her arrival, a perpetual dark scruff laced his cheeks. And now with his pretty, perky wife and a baby on the way, Mark Ravens was one of the family overachievers. Neither Trina nor Richie fit that mold.

"You know, you're doing a good thing here," he said.

"What, caring for someone who doesn't want to be looked after?"

"It's hard for Uncle Richie; he's been on his own for so long."

"His fault, not mine."

"Trina, it's not about fault."

"Well, who told him to climb up on the roof and try and clear the gutters? At his age?"

"Like I said, he's independent. Like father, like . . ."

She held the knife in front of him. "Don't go there."

"Still, it's nice you're here."

"It's just what a thirty-year-old single woman wants, to suddenly be the de facto manager of a roadside motel in a town that doesn't seem to need one. I mean, Mark, we've got two guests right now and no reservations for the next two weeks. Even the days here are solemn."

"He makes a killing in the summer season, lots of weekend antiquers. It will also pick up right before Christmas."

"Oh God, can I endure Christmas here too?"

"Uncle Richie's going to be out of commission for a couple of months, so yeah, I guess you're going to settle in. I mean, first the cast has to come off, then weeks of physical therapy appointments. But don't worry, Trina, Christmas in Linden Corners can be real special. Sara and I were married last year on Christmas Eve in the village gazebo, with practically the entire town as our witnesses. You just have to get involved; otherwise, Linden Corners can seem like a lonely place."

"Sure, I'll keep that in mind, from behind the front desk."

"Sara and I will relieve you sometimes, help you get out and about," he said. "You know I'm pretty busy between my two jobs, but Sara is around. She's cut back on her hours at the Five-O, since the baby's due date is a month away."

"A Christmas wedding and a year later, a Christmas baby. You sure didn't waste time."

"If you want to keep life interesting, Trina, you have to have things to look forward to."

"Okay, Mr. Optimism, let's get this pie served so you and your bride can escape."

"It's hardly an escape . . ."

In a rare display of affection, she touched his arm and let her hand linger. "Look, Mark, I know you and Sara had other plans with your friends. I appreciate your being here."

"Family first," he said. "Uncle Richie's not a bad guy, just quirky."

"More like stubborn."

"See, you two are finding more common ground with each passing day."

"You want a pie in your face?"

With his easy laugh filling the kitchen, Mark grabbed hold of two plates and returned to the living room. Trina hesitated a moment, steeling herself for the final leg of what had been an awkward holiday. When she arrived with the last two plates, she saw that her father had already plowed down half of his slice, not bothering to wait for everyone else. Silence had also fallen over them, the three of them seemingly engaged in the game. She went and sat by herself at the collapsible card table that had served as their Thanksgiving dinner table. A candle had burned down to a nub before being doused. Trina Winter, surrounded by blood relations, by family—more concept to her than reality—realized she was the only one here whose last name was not Ravens. Even Sara had that over her.

Again, she wondered just what had possessed her to accept this assignment.

What had Mark said? Life was about having something to look forward to.

She couldn't recall the last time that had happened to her, and she knew prior to her arrival here that she'd been going through the motions. Work, home, sleep, rinse, and repeat, and be careful along the way that you don't yawn yourself to death.

Richie's phone call to her had happened at just the right time.

Funny, she'd needed an escape from her life, and now that she was here, she was still on the topic of running.

She took a bite of the pie, felt an involuntary smile cross her face. The smooth, savory pumpkin filling was the best thing she'd tasted all day, and for once, Trina's sour expression wavered. Mark's comment continued to taunt her. For one's life to be fulfilling, one needed something to look forward to. In this foreign place called Linden Corners, where not even the local tavern was open on the holiday, perhaps she'd start with thinking about a second slice of this amazing pie.

It was progress.

But once the pie was gone, what then?

"Thank you. I hope you enjoyed your stay with us."

"Everything was clean," the man said gruffly as he handed back the key to his room.

Trina, standing behind the desk, had to wonder if that was a compliment or an expression of surprise. She wasn't sure how to react, whether to say anything in response, but then the man took the choice away from her. He abruptly turned around and left the office, receipt in his hand, and a few moments later he had zoomed away in his car.

"That was rude," she said, more to herself than to anyone else.

"Don't give it a second thought, Trina," she heard behind her. She turned and saw Richie emerging from the kitchen, crutches supporting his thin frame; the cast appeared to weigh more than the rest of him. Still, it was nice to see him up and about; that was progress, wasn't it? He'd just finished his morning coffee, something Trina had learned he couldn't live without. For that he'd race across the parking lot in two casts.

"But what did that mean—everything was clean?"

"The motel business is transient. One customer checks out, another checks in."

"Not according to the reservation book," she said, staring down at an empty page.

"Place like the Solemn Nights, we specialize in drive-bys. Weary drivers needing a quick refresh, they see a word like *solemn*, it suggests rest, the blinking neon sign calling to them. They turn in and so does someone else, and next thing I know, most of the rooms are booked. You just have to be patient in this line of work. You'll get the hang on it."

"I hope not," she said far too quickly, wishing she could take it back.

"Why not take a break? Carmen is here cleaning the rooms. If I need anything she's easy to reach."

"Richie . . . I'm sorry, I didn't mean . . ."

"I understand, Trina. You've barely been away from the property since you got here," he said. "Go on out and see the village, spread your wings. It's beautiful outside this late in November, and it's still warm. Odd for us; usually we've got a foot of snow at this point."

"You trying to get rid of me? We were going to go shopping later."

"I have no doubt you'll be back in plenty of time to take me. We're low on coffee."

"You're sure you can wait?"

"Go have a cup at the Five-O; Sara will take care of you."

Trina agreed, if for no other reason than to give Richie a break from her. She retreated to her room, where she fixed up her hair and dabbed on a bit of lipstick and a light jacket, deciding at the last moment to toss a scarf around her neck. You never know, the weather could turn cold without warning. With a glance in the mirror, she pronounced herself good enough for public viewing, and then set out on foot, leaving behind her car. Downtown Linden Corners was only a half mile away, and the walk, like it had the other night she'd ventured down to George's Tavern, would do her good. She walked against oncoming traffic, if it could even be called that, with barely a dozen cars passing her in either direction. It was the Saturday after Thanksgiving, with December just a week away, and indeed she was surprised by the fact that she'd worked up a sweat during her walk.

Her mother, Pamela, had warned her about going to Linden Corners, telling her that once she arrived she might not thaw out until April at best, and then wished her well.

Pamela was now retired and living in Florida with her third husband and had long ago shipped the man who played the role of Trina's father from her life. But while Pamela might easily dispense with the men in her life, Trina, despite not growing up with Richie as her father and as such barely knowing him, knew that blood was thicker than divorce. When he'd called and asked her if she could help him after his accident, she knew that doing so went against every fiber of his being. Richie Ravens had never before asked his daughter for anything.

And so here she was, in Linden Corners.

In fact, at this very moment she'd entered the downtown area, much more visible in the bright sunshine than it had been three nights ago when she had snuck out for a quick reprieve at the bar. She saw it down the road but knew such a place could hardly be her destination now. It might be five o'clock somewhere else in the world, but here in Linden Corners it was barely eleven in the morning. So instead she made her way toward the ironically named Five O'Clock Diner, but not before coming upon an old Victorian-style house, a sign on the front lawn announcing this was a place of business: A DOLL'S ATTIC, it read. A curious name, Trina thought, contemplating going inside for a look-see but opting for that anticipated cup of coffee at the diner. Also, it would be nice to have a conversation with someone she knew other than her father.

She opened the front door, the fresh-brewed smell of coffee drawing her inside, like she was under some kind of spell. Taking a round, cushioned seat at the counter, she gazed around and saw that the place was half-filled. Several of the booths against the wall were occupied with young families or with older men who were leisurely sipping away at coffee while enjoying the day off from whatever business they had. Two other men, who seemed not to be together, based on their lack of communication, sat farther down the counter. She also saw two women at a back table engaged in conversation, so much so that they looked lost in their own world. Just then, the door that led to the kitchen swung out, a woman Trina guessed as being between fifty and sixty emerging.

"Morning, hon," she said to Trina. "Coffee?"

"If it tastes as good as it smells, please," she said, realizing her remark sounded a bit like that customer at the motel this morning. "I mean, yes, and keep it coming."

The woman grabbed a ceramic mug, placed it in front of Trina, then poured.

"You new in town?"

"Oh, uh, sort of. I'm, really, I'm just passing through."

"Hmph, seems I've heard that before. Guy who said that ended up living here."

Trina didn't know how to respond, so she took a sip of coffee. Warmth spread to her insides as caffeine rushed through her bloodstream. She felt instantly awake, alive. "Wow, I don't know how you do it, but that's maybe the best cup of coffee I've ever tasted. Sara was right."

"Sara? You're just passing through but yet you know one of my girls?"

"Oh, she's my . . . I suppose you'd say she's my cousin-in-law. I'm Trina."

"Oh sure, Richie's girl. Name's Martha Martinson, honey, and this is my establishment. Your father and I help each other out a lot. I serve visitors a meal, he gives them a pillow to place their heads, and we both benefit. Sorry to hear about his accident, but that's real nice of you to come and help him out. Truth be told, I never knew Richie had a kid and I've known him a lot of years . . . Oh, I suppose that wasn't so good of me to say."

"It's fine, Martha. I'm well aware of the strained relationship my father and I have."

"Yup, guess you would be. So can I get you anything else?"

"Right now, this is perfect. Is Sara around?"

"She was here earlier but I sent her home, despite her protests. She's plumb tired and that baby's ready to burst. Well, nice to meet you, Trina, but I gotta get my butt back to the kitchen. I'm short staffed and the lunch rush is coming. Gotta get my chili ready."

"Need help?"

"Excuse me, hon?"

Trina found herself surprised by her own offer. Maybe it was the coffee fueling her, but she felt right now like she could walk several miles and not suffer any ill effects. "Richie's not expecting me back until three at best, and I've got nothing else to do. So I could do refills, take some orders. You don't have to pay me."

"Ever waitress before?"

"College. The local pub. Frat guys pinching my butt."

"Well, don't imagine that happening here, though you may want to avoid Chet's table."

She pointed to the booth where the two older men were chatting. One of the men lifted his empty coffee cup, beckoned to Martha for a refill. "I think I can handle him," Trina said, and that was that. Martha brought her around the counter, handed her an apron and a pad, and set her off with a fresh pot of coffee, telling her any tips she made were hers to keep. So she poured refills for the man named Chet and his friend, and then she emptied a table of dirty dishes while Martha handled the young family's bill, served a couple of omelets to a couple who'd just arrived and who couldn't wait till lunch. As Trina zoomed about the busy diner, she felt her adrenaline pulsing through her body and a constant smile present on her lips, and she realized she was having the most fun she'd had in . . . well, a while.

"Hi, ladies. Can I get you refills?" Trina asked as she approached the two women at the back table.

"You're a godsend," one of them said. "Poor Martha's been run ragged all morning."

"I'm happy to help her out, and Sara."

The other woman looked up at her. "How do you know Sara?"

"She's my cousin . . . er, cousin-in-law. Mark Ravens and I are first cousins."

"Well, Mark and Sara are good friends of ours. I'm Nora; this is Cynthia."

"Hi, nice to meet you. Trina."

"You just moved to town?"

"Yes, about a week ago."

"Just you?"

Trina wasn't sure what they meant by that. "Excuse me?"

"Husband, boyfriend . . . kids?"

If this was a multiple-choice quiz, she'd go with answer D. "None of the above."

"Well, Trina," Cynthia said, "you may think we're crazy, but you seem like the kind of woman who rises to a challenge—I mean, you came in for a cup of coffee and next thing you know you're serving it to all of us customers. Seeing what happened here just now, we couldn't help but be reminded about a friend of ours having had a similar thing happen to him—walked into a business as a customer, emerged an employee not an hour later. You broke his record."

"I'm not sure what you're getting at," Trina said.

"Would you like to meet him?" Nora asked.

"Meet him? Are you asking me if I want to go out on a date?"

Both women exchanged conspiratorial looks with each other before gazing back up at a visibly surprised Trina. The one named Cynthia then said, "As a matter of fact, yes."

CHAPTER 4

BRIAN

It was nearly the end of a warm November, a Sunday morning that found Brian Duncan mixing a bowl of pancake batter—his and Janey's usual weekend breakfast treat—the sizzle of bacon coming off the pan filling the kitchen with mouth-watering, run-down-the-stairs smells. Usually Janey was at his side by now, wanting to flip the shriveling slices of bacon before they got too crisp, but she was nowhere to be seen. He hadn't even heard her stirring upstairs. He'd better make sure she was awake before he set the batter on the grill; cold pancakes did not reheat well. So he put down the whisk and turned off the burner where the bacon crackled and made his way to the bottom of the staircase.

"Janey, breakfast is nearly ready. Sweetie, are you awake?"

"Be down soon," he heard, though the sound was slightly muffled. He heard the creak of her bedroom door, then, more clearly, "Don't overcook the bacon."

He smiled, not just at the sound of her voice but at the fact that he knew her so well.

"Already turned off. I'm about to put the pancakes on the griddle."

Her happy acknowledgment was cut short by the ringing of the telephone. Nine o'clock in the morning; who would be calling this early, and why? He hoped nothing was wrong. Back to the kitchen, he grabbed the receiver on the third ring, said hello.

"Brian, it's your mother."

This was the second time she'd phoned in the last four days, might be a record since he'd come to call Linden Corners home. The ever-proper Didi Duncan hadn't exactly approved—nor made her disapproval a secret—of her son's new pastoral lifestyle, throwing away a promising career in New York to care for some woman's child she claimed Brian hardly knew, all in some rinky-dink town that even time forgot existed. Not that Didi knew anything about Linden Corners. Neither of his parents had yet to visit, not in two-plus years of invitations. Yet her announcement on Thanksgiving evening had unexpectedly set the clock ticking to reverse that truth. The idea of their visit instilled more than a hint of fear in Brian, though he hoped on this morning it wasn't evident in his voice.

"Hi, Mom."

"Brian, dear, I know we kind of surprised you the other day, with our announcement."

"It's okay, Mom. The holidays can be emotional. It's okay if you're reconsidering."

There was hesitation on the other end and Brian had to guess he'd hit the nail on the head with his assertion. The very idea of Kevin and Didi Duncan, perpetual world travelers during the holidays, forgoing their usual cruise with their friends the Hendersons for a country Christmas had been a crazy one from the start. Though a small part of him was disappointed, he felt relief settle his nerves. Phone up to his ear, he turned toward the batter to resume stirring, and that's when he saw a still-bathrobe-clad Janey turn the corner and pad her way into the kitchen. He smiled over at her as his mother said something, and as a result he thought he misheard his mother's reply.

"Wait, Mom, what was that?"

"I said, on the contrary. Your father and I are very much looking forward to seeing you. Your . . . farmhouse, do you call it? We think it needs something more than you and Jane, a shot of family." She paused. "And speaking of Jane, my goodness, she must be growing so."

"Yeah, that she is," he said, quickly noting his mother's continual refusal to call Janey by the name she preferred. Like it was Didi Duncan's decision what a young girl she barely knew should be called. "In fact, Janey's right here with me, getting ready for breakfast. Oh, I forgot to heat the grill . . . wait, Mom . . . hang on . . . ," he said, turning back around to flip the switch on the grill while batter congealed like a blob on the griddle's surface. He scraped it off, stirring the pancake batter again, nearly dropping the phone. "Oh, crap . . . I mean, darn . . ."

He heard a giggle escape Janey's lips. Yes, he'd said a bad word. He shrugged her way.

"Brian, I can hear you're very busy. We can talk later. But I wanted to let you know to expect us around the fifteenth of the month. Is that okay? I assume you have room for us at your, uh, what do you call it?"

"It's a farmhouse, Mom. But usually we just call it home."

He was amazed he could get such a dig in at her, still reeling from the fact that they were arriving on the fifteenth. That meant they would be staying here under the same roof for at least ten days, more if they stayed through New Year's. He hadn't spent that much time with his parents in years, probably not since he was still in high school—half his life ago. An odd concept, he thought; they were his parents but he wondered how much he really knew them as people, how much they knew him. He supposed he was going to find out. "Uh, sure, Mom, you'll arrive just in time for some of our big traditions—like cutting down the Christmas tree up at Green's Tree Farm and of course the annual tavern Christmas party that I throw in George's honor, the Christmas Eve pageant . . . you'll get more than your share of Linden Corners' cheer."

She paused, as though taking it all in. "We look forward to it."

You do? He was glad his surprised mind kept those words trapped and didn't filter them down to his loose tongue, lest his mother believe she and his father were not welcome. They were; he'd been extending an invite since two Thanksgivings ago, and they had yet to take him up on his offer. Until now, strangely. And if truth were known, he didn't recall extending a specific invite for this Christmas, having given up on them after this past Fourth of July. What was different now?

"Can you put Dad on? I just want to make sure he's not being blackmailed or something," he said, his tone light.

There was hesitation on the other end before his mother said, "He's resting."

Brian felt an unsettled feeling sweep over him. "Hey, Mom, is everything all right?"

"Of course, dear," she said in her usual toneless way. "Why would you think otherwise?"

Because Dad was resting this early in the morning; hadn't he just woken? Kevin Duncan was a big man, in both size and personality, and he wasn't known for his "napping" at any point in the day. But Brian decided not to return her volley. He figured he'd find out soon enough what was going on, just two weeks to prepare the house, and even more so, prepare himself mentally. "Okay, so it's settled.

Janey and I will see you both on the fifteenth. We can't wait to show you around town," he said. "And just think, you two will finally get to see the windmill up close."

Didi Duncan had already hung up, leaving Brian wondering if he'd heard her good-bye while he'd been speaking of his beloved windmill. He knew his mother had never understood his decision to forge a new life in Linden Corners, even before the tragedy that had taken Annie from their lives. It was the ever-present spinning sails of the windmill that kept her spirit alive and, as such, kept Janey's and his bond as tight as could be. As he replaced the receiver, he stole a look out the kitchen window and caught sight of the old mill, its sails gently turning. For a moment he thought back to the secret surprise Christmas gift he'd received last week, hidden away inside the windmill until December twenty-fifth, as the card dictated. Looked like that unforeseen gift wasn't the only surprise this holiday.

"What do you think of that, Janey, my parents staying with us for two weeks?"

He realized he was speaking to an empty kitchen, as Janey was nowhere to be found.

Pancakes were bubbling up on the griddle and the bacon was now soggy with grease.

"Janey . . . ? Hey, Janey . . ."

He turned off the sizzling griddle and went into the living room, it, too, empty. Had she gone back upstairs, maybe to shower? But why not tell him? He took the stairs two at a time, feeling like his feet barely touched the creaky wood. He found the door to her bedroom closed, so he knocked, waited patiently for an answer. There wasn't one, so he tried again. And again, no response.

Uh-oh, he thought.

If he knew one thing about Janey Sullivan, it was this: if something was bothering her, she closed up tighter than an alligator's mouth. Her bite could be something fierce too. But he'd also learned not to let these infrequent bouts of withdrawal linger, so he turned the knob of her door and entered her bedroom. Her room, but he was the parent. He found Janey lying on the bed, fisted hand giving her chin a place to rest. She was staring at the head of the bed, her eyes zoned in on her stuffed purple frog, which sat upright on her pillow. He eased himself down on the edge of her bed, resting his hand against her back.

"You want to tell me why you ditched breakfast?"

"You were busy."

"I was multitasking, yes."

"You don't do that well," she said, and while it was true, the comment wasn't meant to be funny.

"Are you okay with my parents visiting? You haven't said much about it since I got the call on Thanksgiving."

"It's okay. I know you've been wanting them to come visit."

"Yes, that's true. And I'm going to need your help."

She paused, turned away from the frog, and looked up at him. "Why me?"

"Well, this is your home. You have to make them feel welcome."

"You live here too."

"Yeah, but you came first."

Her eyes darted toward the far end of the room, Brian's eyes following them. Hung up on the wall were Christmas presents from last year, portraits of both Annie Sullivan, her mother, and Dan Sullivan, her father, the former of whom she remembered every day, the latter of whom she'd lost at such a young age she barely knew anything about. Brian had discovered the portraits inside the drawers of Annie's studio inside the windmill; Annie had of course been the artist behind them. The fact that Janey's gaze fell upon them was not unusual, especially since here was Brian, thirty-six, fortunate enough to still have his parents part of his life, while Janey did not. Sometimes life was unfair. Sometimes he was amazed at Janey's resilience. This moment wasn't one of them.

"Tell you what. I'll make a fresh batch of breakfast; then we'll eat," he said. "And don't forget, today is Sunday, and that means we get to spend the entire day together. Mark's got the bar tonight."

"Um, do you think we can change those plans?" she asked.

"I guess. Why? What's up?"

"I want to go see Cynthia and little Jake," she said.

Brian nodded. If that was what she wanted, that was fine. The Knights' big announcement about moving hadn't received much play either in the last few days, Janey barely saying a word about it. Like she didn't believe it, and Brian didn't blame her; he wasn't sure he did either. A great new job for Bradley was on offer, a chance of a lifetime for them all. Those were all the pat words expressed Thanksgiving night, but with everyone around, Brian hadn't had a chance to get the real story. Cynthia Knight leaving Linden Corners was like the wind no longer coming to visit, rendered impossible by nature itself. But all that could wait. Janey could have her day with them and he could get some repairs done down at the tavern, recalling the creaky wood floor. But he told Janey that he expected her back for dinner and she easily agreed. Brian left, returning to their spoiled breakfast, doing what he could to rescue its charred remnants. Janey arrived at the table not five minutes later, her familiar purple frog dangling from her hand. She set it on one of the place mats before she went digging inside the cabinet, withdrawing a bottle of maple syrup.

"Let's have the real stuff today," she said. "You know, the

kind we bought in Vermont on my birthday weekend last month."

He looked down at the fresh order of pancakes, turned one, satisfied with its brown coating but little else. "Sounds like a plan," he said, his tone not unlike his mother's.

He'd gone cold with worry about Janey and ran through all that had happened already on this day. Portraits of her departed parents acknowledged, check. Stuffed purple frog she'd had forever clutched close to her, check. Mention of her recent birthday, check. Janey was sending out signals Brian could hardly miss, reminding him that while he was her guardian, her surname was indeed Sullivan, not Duncan.

Brian had learned a lot about little girls in the two-plus years in which Janey Sullivan had been in his care, and the most important one was when she needed the attention of a mother figure. So when she grew silent around him and then moments later passed up their usual day together and asked to see Cynthia, he didn't put up an argument, nor did he feel slighted. Brian Duncan knew the need would only grow exponentially as she stretched toward her teen years, and he realized he'd have to find a new role model for her.

Cynthia Knight wouldn't be around every day like she had been.

Even without this supposed move, little Jake would grow up to be big Jake and he'd need Cynthia's attention, and that was if they didn't add to their family with another child. Perhaps it was a good thing his parents were coming to visit; perhaps Janey and his mother could establish a bond both could benefit from. Janey had a way of warming even the iciest of personalities, the thought leaving Brian with an image of Didi Duncan on one of the cruises she enjoyed.

Iceberg, meet ocean liner. He laughed it off, knowing he was being too harsh.

After dropping Janey off at Cynthia's, he'd driven to downtown Linden Corners, done some needed shopping at Ackroyd's Hardware Emporium, and then stopped at the Five-O for a tuna fish sandwich, wishing it was a BLT; he'd already had some bacon today, burned as it was. He forewent eating at the counter, not really in the mood for Martha's twisted humor, and took his food to go, crossing the street and unlocking the front door to George's Tavern, where, between ˙ ˙tes, he screwed in the fresh lightbulbs he'd just bought. It was still an hour before the bar was set to open for the night, and even so, it was Mark's shift at the bar, as Brian always spent Sunday with Janey. Except today, and so to fill the empty time he wiped down the bar and mopped the floor and got the beer taps gleaming underneath the new bulbs, deciding the wood floor required a major investment. A soft glow caught his eye and he suddenly found himself thinking about Christmas lights. He usually waited until the first of December—now just days away—to put up the holiday lights around the perimeter of the building. He had them in the back of the truck, along with the staple gun, leaving him to realize he could get started now.

But he wasn't feeling very full of holiday cheer, and besides, the afternoon had started to grow darker with each passing minute. By the time he got the ladder up and began the work, the sky would have embraced night. Last thing he needed was to fall off the ladder and end up like poor Richie Ravens down at the Solemn Nights. So instead, Brian did an unusual thing. He opened early by turning on the outside lights and flipping the CLOSED sign to OPEN. He grabbed one of his freshly laundered aprons and tied it around his waist. Might as well make some money; nothing else to do. Maybe he'd call Cynthia and see about having Janey stay for dinner after all. He could call Mark too, and tell him not to rush back from his waiter job down at the resort in Hudson.

He was about to place both calls when the front door opened and in stepped an unlikely but welcome patron.

"Nora, what are you doing here?"

"I think I could ask the same of you. It's Sunday, right?"

"Yes. Which means I'm not supposed to be here. Let me guess—you come in when I'm off to drool over Mark like all the other girls in town.

"Hardly. Things were super quiet at the store," she said, "and I saw the light go on and thought a glass of red wine might be nice. Even the red wine you serve here."

"Always nice to be appreciated," he said.

He went around the bar, poured her a glass of merlot, set it before her while she sat on one of the round stools. She swiveled around on it, checking out the otherwise empty, silent bar. He'd forgotten to plug the jukebox in, and it stood quiet in the corner, ignored. He noticed her look back at him, her expression filled with judgment.

"Penny for your thoughts," she offered.

"With tips like that, I think I need a new profession."

"You do anyway, Brian," Nora said. "You need a whole new life, in fact."

Okay, that cut deep, he thought. "So glad you came by."

"Sorry. It's just . . . well, Janey had other things to do today. But not you. You're in a rut."

"You want to explain that one?"

"Do I really need to?" she asked, her green eyes wide open.

"I could say the same for you."

"Uh-uh, my issues are so last year. Travis and I came

home to Linden Corners, even if it was the last place I wanted us to come to. But the transition has gone well enough—the business is fine, and Travis has adapted nicely to his new school. We've even managed to not put on any extra weight despite living with my mother."

"And you have a new relationship to boot," Brian said.

She drank deeper from her glass, the usual firewater he served in place of decent wine suddenly like top-shelf champagne. "I thought we were talking about your life, or lack thereof. Where's Janey today anyway? Don't you two usually spend the whole day together? I bet that big field of yours is littered with leaves."

"The raking can wait," he said, "since there's no snow in the forecast again. Tomorrow's supposed to be a high of fifty."

"Happy holidays," Nora said with a raise of her glass.

"Anyway, Janey is with Cynthia."

"Not surprising, considering all that's going on with the Knights," she said. "You know, I spoke with Cynthia yesterday; we met for coffee across the street at Martha's. And we were introduced to the most charming young woman, actually. You'd like her."

Brian was half listening while he poured a bucket of ice into the large sink before him, readying it for the case of warm beer at his feet. He stopped, bucket in midpour and some cubes missing their target, and looked up at his friend. "I'm sorry, what did you say? Wait a minute—is that what you meant by a new life? Nora, please tell me you didn't . . . uh, initiate anything."

"Of course I didn't," she said.

"Good. That's the last thing I need . . ."

"Cynthia did," she said, an amused look crossing her face.

He set the bucket down, leaned over the bar. His fingers

toyed with the stem of her glass, the thought of polishing it off within easy reach. Yet, aside from one beer he'd had two summers ago, Brian Duncan hadn't touched a drop of alcohol since before his bout with hepatitis a few years back. It was an illness that had started him off on this journey, and while he was physically fine, its yellowing effects lingered long in the mind. He'd moved on from that life in New York, from Maddie Chasen, whom he'd once loved until her betrayal, and found a new life in Linden Corners. And now that carefully constructed foundation of his was seeing its first crack.

"Cynthia did. How interesting," he remarked. "Is that what the two of you do when you get together? Talk about my love life?"

"It would be a quick conversation if we did," she said with an easy laugh. "And, no, Brian, what happened all came about innocently enough. We were simply talking about her and Bradley's big announcement. I mean, this is a whopper, a whole new life change for them."

"One Cynthia really didn't want to get into much after Bradley told us all."

"Maybe it hasn't sunk in with her yet," she said, "though we're going to have to face facts, Brian. They are leaving, first of the year. Cynthia's been a rock for Janey and someone's going to have to pick up the slack. And you know that I'll do what I can, and so will my mother, but Cynthia's different; she knows her so well, and she also knew . . ."

"Annie," Brian said. "I know, Cynthia was Annie's best friend, Janey's last link to her past."

Nora emptied her glass, pushed it forward for a refill. Brian took care of her, then poured himself a glass of seltzer and splurged by dropping a slice of lime into the bubbles. "So you think the solution to this dilemma is to find me a new mother for Janey, and this supposedly charming young woman you met at the Five-O is the answer to my prayers?"

"We're certainly not planning a Christmas wedding—we did that last year," she said. "Nor are we looking to replace Annie in Janey's heart. But, Brian, when's the last time you went on a date?"

"When was the Truman administration?"

"You're hardly that old," she remarked.

"I know, that's why I asked you."

"Ouch. Brian Duncan takes off the gloves," she said, amusement in her voice.

"Look, Nora, I appreciate you two looking out for me, but conspiring to set me up just isn't what I need right now—and it's not something Janey needs either," he said. "Why is it that people in relationships always think everyone else should be in one? Look at you and Nicholas."

She drank her wine again. Brian knew this was her way of avoiding not just his question but also providing an answer. He'd sensed something was not totally right between them on Thanksgiving, and he had to wonder if it was Nick or Nora. Knowing his friend, it was probably her, as Nicholas was as open and friendly and unassuming as anyone. Nora Connors, formerly Rainer until her divorce had come through last spring, held things tight, though, her thoughts, her emotions. The last thing she'd been looking for was a new man, but Nicholas Casey, whom she had met during a holiday mystery last year, had proved too good to be true, a Renaissance man who appreciated the arts as much as he did a football game.

"Sorry, sore spot?"

Nora was saved having to answer as the front door swung open and Mark Ravens, the relief bartender, who worked three nights a week, entered, out of breath. "Oh man,

Brian, what are you doing here? Hey, Nora, sorry, didn't mean to burst in like this, but I mean, it's just four o'clock now, time to open, I would have been here sooner, but . . ."

"Relax, Mark. Why not go upstairs and freshen up? I meant to call you, but someone"—he paused, eyes darting Nora's way—"distracted me."

"I could take my business elsewhere . . ."

Mark nodded and said thanks, running up the stairs to the apartment he'd been renting out for the last two years with more energy than Brian could recall ever having himself. Guess when you were working two jobs and expecting your first child, you ran on adrenaline more than artificial fuel. As he waited for Mark to return, he saw Nora wander over to the jukebox, plugging it into the wall socket. She pulled out a dollar and slid it into the machine. The dulcet tones of Sinatra filled the room: "Luck Be a Lady."

"Funny," Brian remarked.

"Come on, Brian, you're a good guy. What's the harm?"

Just then Mark bounded down the stairs. "What's going on?" he asked.

"Nothing," Brian said emphatically.

"Oh, there's this cute new woman in town. Cynthia and I told her about Brian."

"Hey, that's cool, Brian on a date. Though I still bet on it snowing first."

Nora laughed. "We'd all take that bet."

"Ugh," Brian groaned. "See what I mean about people stuck in relationships? . . . And he's worse; he's married. Forget it, both of you. I'm not going on a blind date."

"Brian Duncan, I don't believe that for a second," Nora said. "You have to go."

"I agree," Mark said, easing around the bar. "So who is she?"

Nora smiled at both men and then said to Mark, "Your cousin, Trina."

A wide smile stretched out his scruffy cheeks. "Hey, that's a great idea . . ."

Brian looked up sharply. "Wait a minute, did you say Trina? I've already met her."

"That's perfect, then; it won't be blind after all."

Brian had a feeling even if he continued to say no he'd get nowhere with either of these two. All he could hope for was the date getting snowed out, but this season, it didn't seem likely at all, and for a moment Brian thought rather than Christmas looming in the air, Saint Valentine had blown in for an unexpected visit.

CHAPTER 5

CYNTHIA

From the moment Janey arrived for her afternoon visit, Cynthia Knight had been walking on the proverbial eggshells, and now, hours later, the elephant in the room still went undiscussed. And while she knew she was mixing her metaphors, that was the least of her concerns. Janey's wellbeing was paramount to anything else today, and so she'd tried several times to broach the topic, each time Janey expertly changing the topic, or just plain walking away, claiming she was going upstairs to play with Jake. Cynthia let it go for now, but avoiding the issue wouldn't change the fact.

Why had she let Bradley make the announcement like he had?

Didn't Brian and Janey deserve more consideration, or advance warning?

For the past month or so, she'd known the move was possible. But she'd said nothing, keeping it to herself, even at night while Bradley slept peacefully and she was left staring at the ceiling, considering the fact it would be a different ceiling that would hold her attention soon enough.

Subtlety wasn't her husband's style. He couldn't help it—he was a corporate lawyer, and a frustrated one at that these days, hence the pursuit of something new. He'd been relegated to boring tax law while all along he'd desired courtroom action. That's where the drama happened, he always said, and it hadn't helped having Nora Connors in town, a former defense attorney who had awakened Bradley's ambition. So whenever he got the chance to address a crowd and make a pronouncement, he grabbed it. And that had been the case at Thanksgiving; while everyone else had given thanks for all they had, he'd chosen that precise moment to tell them what the Knights would have after they moved far from Linden Corners. Family, a future. Far indeed, all the way to Texas, where a great new job awaited him, and where they'd be closer to his side of the family. Jake would get to see his grandparents regularly, as well as his cousins. Cynthia, like Annie, had been an only child; it was one of the things they had bonded over. Bradley, though, was one of four children—two boys, two girls—and his siblings were all married, all had a couple of children, and all lived within a few miles of their parents. And now so would they. She knew she should be happy for their entire family because this was a chance to reconnect and give Jake a strong foundation, a connection to his bloodline.

But at what cost to others?

Indeed, the downside was leaving her de facto Linden Corners family. Foremost among those she would miss was Janey Sullivan, the little girl whom she'd met on the day of her birth, whom she had held when she thought she couldn't have her own child, and whom she'd helped care for after the passing of first her father, Dan, then her mother, Annie. Something no child should have to endure. To not be around her and watch this special girl grow up—it had left Cynthia with many sleepless nights since she and Bradley had made the final decision.

Now, sitting in the kitchen with a cup of coffee long gone

cold, she felt a mix of sadness and frustration overwhelm her. With Bradley out running errands and Janey upstairs hovering over Jake like always—though perhaps this time with a bit more cuddliness, as though she were trying to bank a lifetime of hugs—Cynthia wondered if this was how she would feel in her new home. Out of sorts, feeling alone, her heart as empty as Texas was big. But no, she had a feeling her in-laws wouldn't allow that, nor would her sisters-in-law, who had already expressed interest in helping her get settled.

The ringing of the phone stirred her from her musings.

"Hi, Brian," she said, the caller ID giving him away.

"How's Janey?"

"Quiet. Playing with Jake."

"So she's not talking?"

"Not about anything, you know, important."

"Janey's like the wind, fickle, choosing its own moment to rear up, changing speed and direction on a whim," he said.

"Well said," Cynthia said. "And appropriate."

"Maybe with the night approaching, you can convince her to go out for a walk," he said. "She tends to open up more when the sun has gone down. Like darkness is better to reveal her private thoughts."

"Got it. You on your way?"

"I'm at the tavern, got a good crowd, so I'm helping Mark. I'll see you after dinner?"

"Janey will eat with us and then I'll bring her back home. See you then."

Cynthia put down the phone and got up, made her way up the staircase to the bedrooms, where she found Jake asleep and Janey staring at the purple frog she'd brought with her. Cynthia had noted its presence earlier, thought it strange but ultimately let it go. Janey might be ten and growing fast, but that didn't mean an insecure little girl couldn't still be hiding inside her.

"Hey, what are you doing?"

"Just hanging out, watching Jake sleep. He's so peaceful."

"He's been cooped up inside all day. I think he might be bored. Come on, let's go for a walk."

"A walk, now? It's getting dark out."

"Then we better hurry before it swallows us up," she said. "What do you say, let's take Jake down to the windmill; we'll see how things are turning."

The mention of the windmill always did the trick, Janey bounding off the bed and racing downstairs, her shoes on before Cynthia even had a chance to wrap Jake inside a warm blanket. Soon the three of them were ready for their adventure, the stroller leading the way as they left the confines of the Knights' farmhouse, an old structure not unlike Brian and Janey's and one that might be difficult to sell, given the amount of work—fresh coat of paint outside, maybe a new roof—it needed. Cynthia started to lead them down the driveway intentionally, even though it was in the opposite direction of the windmill.

"Hey, where are we going?"

"Oh, I want to check the mail."

"It's Sunday."

"And yesterday Bradley and I were so busy, we forgot."

She hoped she sounded believable. Regardless, she continued to trek down the blacktop, her reason for the change in course creeping up in the dying light of the day. With Janey's hand in hers, she noticed that a bit of wind had started up across the open field, and she stole a look down at a content Jake, who stared back with eyes wide.

"He's awake," Janey remarked.

"You know he loves his walks. Seeing the big, bright world."

"It's not very bright now. The moon is going to rise soon."

"So we'll walk by moonlight. That's just perfect on a walk like this; it will guide us."

They came to the edge of the driveway and Cynthia made an effort to check the roadside mailbox, even though she knew Bradley had retrieved the mail yesterday. She snapped down the door and dug her hand inside, feeling nothing but air. A second later she pulled out an empty hand.

"Know what that means? No bills."

But Janey was no longer paying attention, her eyes having focused on the metal sign that was staked to the front lawn, just a few feet from the mailbox. It was bending in the wind, like it wanted to be swept away to somewhere beyond reality. FOR SALE, it read, and below named a Realtor in nearby Hillsdale, two phone numbers included. Cynthia knew that coming here had been manipulative, but she wanted to get Janey talking and this was all she could come up with. Janey turned her face back to Cynthia, her nose scrunched up.

"Come on, you said the windmill," she stated, pointing her finger west. "It's that way."

So much for outsmarting a ten-year-old. Cynthia resigned herself to another tactic, perhaps another day, and let Janey lead the way, even allowing her to take command of the stroller as its wheels traveled over the low field of grass. She noticed too that Janey had slipped her free hand back into hers, leaving her heart swelling and a tear leaking from her eye.

"That wasn't very subtle of me, was it?" she asked.

"Not very. I mean, I saw the sign when Brian dropped me off."

Of course she had.

"If it's any consolation, I'm still not used to the idea."

"Why? Don't you want to move?"

Wow, this kid didn't pull any punches: she went right to

the core issue. "Sweetie, it's complicated, and of course a big decision—one of the biggest I've ever made. But, yes, as much as I don't like the idea of leaving, I know it's something that will mean good things for our family. Jake will meet his cousins and Bradley will see more of his parents, who are getting on in years, and I'll get to bond with his siblings and their families."

"Then that's what you have to do," Janey said matter-of-factly. "Ooh, the hill is steep; maybe you should take the stroller back. Jake needs you now."

Janey handed over the reins, breaking her connection with Cynthia. Which told her a big shift had occurred, Janey's seeming acceptance of the situation burrowing deep underground. So she knew she would have to force the issue even more. She steeled herself for when Janey's tightly controlled emotions erupted. The three of them circled around the edge of the Knights' property, beyond the old silo, which was no longer in operation, and toward a copse of trees that acted as the border between their land and that of the Sullivan farmhouse. A gurgling stream cut through the land, water bubbling over rocks; sometimes it flooded out over the land when the snow melted, but that was hardly a problem today with the ground so hard. A stone-cobbled bridge that curved upward allowed them to cross the stream, and they did so, and at last they reached the top of the hill. Coming into view was the windmill, its sails turning more fiercely than usual in the growing wind. It was like a new storm was making its way toward Linden Corners, but with the warmth blowing past them it could only mean rain. Still no snow.

"Cynthia, can I ask you a question?"

"You know you can ask me anything."

Janey stopped, looked up at her with serious eyes. "How come I don't have any family?"

Cynthia's grip on the stroller grew stronger, the question so filled with emotion. "Family comes in many forms, Janey. You have Brian, and you have me . . ."

"I know all that, and I'm lucky to have all of you," she said. "But what you said about all those people in Bradley's family . . . I mean, wow, siblings and cousins, nephews and nieces . . . Hey, that makes the two of you aunts and uncles. Sounds like Christmas could be lots of fun, but also a very full house."

"Well, that's not something we have to worry about this year," she said.

"It's not?"

"Janey, we'll be here for Christmas."

"Oh, okay. I like that."

"But that hardly answers your question," she said.

They had begun the downward journey toward the windmill, the dark night enveloping them deeper. In the distance she could see a dim light emanating from the kitchen of Janey's house, but she knew it was just a safety light, not an indication that Brian had returned. This discussion and its result were all on Cynthia. They continued walking and talking, the windmill's power drawing them ever closer.

"I don't have any aunts and uncles, do I?" Janey asked.

"Why are you asking me?"

"You knew my mom the best; you were her best friend."

"That's true, Janey. Which makes you and me best friends once removed."

She scrunched her nose over that one. "Mama never had any brothers and sisters. I guess neither did my dad, not that I've ever heard. Don't you think that's kind of weird? I mean, you'd think one of them would have, right?"

"Actually, Janey, it's what they bonded over. The fact that both were only children."

Janey grew quiet, as though considering such an idea. "I

guess I never thought about that or anything like . . . a bond."

"Well, they loved each other."

"Like you love Bradley?"

"Yes."

"And you made a baby, like my parents made me."

Cynthia had to wonder where this was going. "Well, that's how it works, Janey."

"I wonder if I might have had a sibling, you know, if my father . . ."

"I know this for a fact, Janey Sullivan. Yes, they wanted more. They didn't want you to have the same experience growing up as they did."

"But that's what happened."

"That's the thing about life, Janey. You can't predict anything," she said. "You just have to live with your heart."

"I think I would have liked having a brother or sister."

"Well, the way you are with Jake, you would have made an excellent older sister."

"Do you think I still can be? You know, if Brian gets married and they have a child?"

"Oh, Janey, I think that's a long way off." Cynthia, though, found herself laughing aloud despite the seriousness of the conversation. She knew Brian had dated and even been engaged a couple of times in his life, but since he'd assumed guardianship of Janey he'd practically been a monk. Not that she wasn't trying to change that, and for a moment she wondered if trying to set him up on a date was for him, or for her, or even for Janey. "Come on, it's getting late and dark and I need to put some dinner on the table. Let's say hello to your mom and then make our way back. Jake's starting to fuss."

"Okay, but can I ask one more question?"

"Sure, sweetie."

"Since I don't have any grandparents either, do you think Brian's parents will let me call them Grandma and Grandpa? They're so . . . formal."

Cynthia smiled, tousling her hair. "Now, I know you think I have magic answers for everything, but I think that's one you're going to have to check with Brian about. Remember how you struggled with the decision to call him Dad?" She paused and then said, "Are you worried about them coming for Christmas?"

"It sure will be different. Christmas, wow," Janey said, altering the subject only slightly. "This year will be our third, me and Dad. I think we've used up all the good gifts."

"Oh, I don't think so. I'm sure Brian has something special up his sleeve."

A smile lit Janey's face, and that was when she suddenly took off across the field, her legs pumping as she laid open her arms as though she were about to take to the gusting wind. Down the hill she ran, the windmill looming up before her. Cynthia did her best to keep up with her but had to consider the uneven terrain and the wheels of the stroller. As she eventually made her way toward the base of the windmill, Janey was running circles around it, trying to keep up with the sails, laughing as she did so, her arms reaching up as though wanting to touch far beyond the sails and into the windswept sky that threatened to close in around her.

"Hi, Mama," Janey said, her voice deep with emotion. "I brought Cynthia and Jake to visit, but they won't be able to stay for long because they're going to leave Linden Corners, and even though it's a good thing for them and I'll miss them terribly, I know that you're always here whenever I need you, just like in my dreams."

Cynthia fought back another tear as she thought about the idea of dreams.

She and Bradley were working toward fulfilling theirs, moving their family to a world of opportunity. Their dream— a new home and a new life; that was their dream as much as Jake had been, all of it a new reality. For Janey, though, her need for Annie was still as strong as ever; it always would be no matter the unconditional love Brian had for her, and that need would have to remain encased in dreams. Because for Janey Sullivan, reality was sometimes harsh, and even though all those around her had all seen her through these difficult times, there was no getting around the fact that this girl was alone in the world.

Finally, an exhausted Janey dropped to the ground, her eyes staring up at the sky.

She pulled the purple frog out of her pocket and held it tight to her chest.

Cynthia hadn't even seen her take it with them on their walk, and she had to wonder, just what was behind this new connection to an old friend?

Dinner dishes drying in the sink, Bradley relaxing in front of the television with Jake in his arms, a quiet Janey lying nearby, Cynthia decided it was probably time to get Janey back home. On the screen, a stop-motion Rudolph had arrived to save the day, his red nose able to cut through any storm Mother Nature could throw at them, according to a suddenly rotund Santa Claus, who moments ago had threatened to cancel Christmas on account of the fierce storm outside. Good, the holiday special was nearly over. She was just waiting for the Bumble and Yukon to make their surprise appearance and next thing you know, Santa and his sleigh would be taking to the storm-laden sky.

Janey had stayed later than expected; it was nearly nine o'clock. Tomorrow morning was the start of a new school week and she needed her rest, not only because of the long walk they had taken but also because of the myriad emotions that seemed to be swirling inside her. Cynthia knew they'd only hit the tip of the iceberg, her move and the arrival of Brian's parents just symptoms of a bigger issue. When Janey was ready to tell more, Cynthia hoped she'd be around to help.

As she made her way into the living room, she realized what a perfect picture this was.

Her husband, a young girl, a baby boy. The ideal family unit.

Not that she would ever deny Brian his rights as Janey's legal guardian, but Cynthia had to wonder—and not for the first time—how things might have been different if Brian had never come to Linden Corners. The terrible storm that took their beautiful Annie from them was as inevitable as nature, her fate written on strong currents of the wind, and without Brian, who would have been there to care for Janey? No doubt Janey would have come to stay with her and Bradley. If that was the case, would they have tried so earnestly for Jake, whose appearance after too many years of trying had taken them by happy surprise? Things happened for a reason. Look at them: They were selling their house and moving from the home they'd known for nearly fifteen years, ready to embark on a new journey beyond its borders. If Janey had been a part of their family, she'd be leaving too, and Cynthia wasn't sure the young girl could endure another loss of something so close to her heart: the windmill. She sure didn't expect to encounter one in their town outside Austin.

"Uh, Cyn, you okay?"

"What? . . . Oh, sorry, I was just waiting for the program to end."

"It already did," Janey said, "with gifts in their arms, the elves dropped out of the sky with umbrellas to help them fly. It's kind of a silly ending. How do they fly back up and reunite with Santa? Anyway, I think I'm ready to go home. Tomorrow's a school day."

"I was just thinking the same thing."

Janey gathered up her belongings, running upstairs to Jake's room, where she claimed to have left something. It turned out to be her constant companion, the purple frog, and as she went to stuff it into her bag, she changed her mind and went over to Jake, who was awake and fidgeting in Bradley's arms.

"The frog wants to say good night," she said, leaning the animal forward until its sealed mouth pecked Jake's cheek. He squirmed happily.

"He's looking a bit raggedy, your frog," Bradley said.

"That's because I've had him a really long time," Janey suddenly said.

"How come he doesn't have a name?"

Janey paused, gazed down at her stuffed friend. "He's just always been . . . the frog."

Cynthia said that was enough chatter for the night, and so they packed up the rest of her stuff and headed outside and into the Knights' SUV. A few raindrops were beginning to fall on them. As they made their way down the dark driveway and onto Crestview Road, the headlights hit the FOR SALE sign one last time, like a tease at Janey. The young girl said nothing, though, and soon they were pulling into the gravelly drive of the Sullivan farmhouse, where they found Brian sitting on the front step. A lone light shone down from under the porch, illuminating him in the newly falling rain. In his hands he was holding a box, wrapped in shiny blue paper with a silver ribbon around it.

"Hi, Dad . . . Hey, what's that? A Christmas present?"

He looked up, his expression a mix of surprise and guilt. "Yes, I suppose it is."

"You don't know?"

"Well, yes, it's a gift. I'm just not sure from whom."

"Brian, what's going on?" Cynthia asked.

"It's the strangest thing," he said, rising from the porch, still examining the package. "I found this waiting for me on the porch when I got home a few minutes ago. With the same message as before, 'Do Not Open Until Christmas.' But there's no clue who sent it, or why."

"What do you mean the same as before?" Janey asked.

Brian looked at them both and said, "Seems someone's playing Secret Santa with me. I received a similarly wrapped gift last week, found on the porch of the tavern. I put it in the closet inside the windmill and honestly forgot about it . . . until now. Until this."

"That's very strange," Janey said.

"Someone has a secret admirer," Cynthia added with a hint of a smile. "Are you going to do as asked? Wait until Christmas? I don't think I could stand the suspense."

"Me too. I'm curious," Janey said.

"We'll just have to wait," Brian said. "And see if there are any more to come."

"I like this game," Janey suddenly decided. "Maybe we should all do it."

Brian laughed, rubbing the top of her head. "Let's go, young lady. Christmas dreams will have to wait. For now it's bedtime."

Janey had always been agreeable about knowing when it was time to let the day end, so she started to make her way inside, but she turned back. "Dad, you're not going to put that gift in the windmill now, are you?"

"I wasn't planning on it," he said.

"Good, I don't want you to leave me."

With that, she headed inside, her footsteps on the staircase to the second level echoing in the silence she'd left behind. Brian turned back to Cynthia, a stunned expression on his face.

"What was that all about?"

Cynthia felt a knob of emotion constrict her throat. "I think that's my fault."

All that people did was leave Janey—parents, loved ones, and those whom she had known her entire life. Now Cynthia was added to that list, and she gave Brian a quick recap of the day's events before telling him they'd talk soon. She then drove back to her own home just as the sky opened up and the rain began to fall in earnest. Her house looked empty against the dark sky, a place she'd known for years, a place that in two months would exist only in her memories. Change was coming, but for just one night, she wanted a normal life. She made her way upstairs, where a lone light shone in the bedroom and where Bradley was propped up against a pillow, glasses on, a book resting against his bare chest. Quickly slipping into her nightgown, she slid under the covers, snuggling in close to her husband.

"You okay?" he asked.

She didn't meet his eye and instead stared out the window as the rain beat heavily against the shutters in need of repair. They weren't the only things, she thought, her heart wounded by the idea of change. Absently gazing at her husband's strong chest, oddly comforted by the thick hair that covered it, she let out an exhausted, contented sigh. Like his masculine presence served as her protector, albeit a preppy one.

"My mind is thinking, thinking, thinking. Can't shut it down."

"Thinking about what?"

"About Janey, and the fact that I need to do something special for her this Christmas. She had an idea, and I for one think it's perfect. The kind of surprise she'll adore."

CHAPTER 6

TRINA

The signs of Christmas had begun to crop up everywhere she looked, colorful lights brightening the downtown area, wreaths of holly with red bows and jangling bells displayed on almost every front door and business, the smiles on the faces of the residents of Linden Corners indicating they were in the mood for all this holiday cheer. All that was missing was the snow. To Trina Winter's knowing point of view, it looked more like Christmas in sunny Florida than in cloudy Upstate New York, the lack of palm trees notwithstanding.

The rainstorm that had swept through the region two nights ago had blown tree branches bare, leaving in its wake the final swath of fallen leaves lying along sidewalks and curbs. It had also taken the warm weather with it, and finally a cool breath filled the air to the point where she could see a misty spray of her own breath. Surely that first snowfall was just around the corner; it would infuse this town with a much-needed final piece of scenery for their rumored Christmas celebrations.

She'd spent most of the afternoon at the Solemn Nights Motel, but feeling like the walls were closing in on her, she'd asked Richie if it was okay to take a break. So he hobbled over and took command of the front desk, staring aimlessly out the window, watching for any traffic that might slow down at the sign of the motel. She had a sense that's how Richie spent most of his days, waiting to serve the needs of transient travelers whose names he would learn only if they were paying by credit card. Otherwise, guests could jot down any name, pretending to be whomever their fantasy dictated. Was that what occupied his mind during those lonely stretches of time, trying to imagine the lives of the people who came to and went from his rooms? From what she could gather, it was mostly businessmen and truckers, though the night of the storm had seen three families stop in the course of one hour as nervous mothers convinced their husbands to rest rather than risk driving in the pouring rain.

She bypassed the Five O'Clock Diner this time, her one-time volunteer stint successful but not something she was eager to repeat; no matter, peeking through the windows of the diner she could see her cousin-in-law, Sara, carrying a couple of plates toward hungry patrons. My goodness, her belly was large enough to balance a plate on. Lights adorned the outside of Martha's diner, creating an impressive ring of color that could be seen far down the highway. Hers blinked, no doubt intended as a way of attracting further attention. One of the families to seek refuge at the Solemn Nights had mentioned how they had dined there and been sent over by the owner, so she guessed Martha and Richie indeed had a good thing going.

Across the street, George's Tavern was also decorated with a rainbow of lights, but as it was only three thirty in the afternoon, the place wasn't yet open for business. She directed her attention down the street to the village park, complete with a gazebo blazing with light upon the expansive, still green lawn. It was a comforting image, Rockwell-like, and she supposed with a coating of snow and icicles perched on the side of the roof, it would look even more ideal. It almost put her in a Christmas mood, something she would have not thought possible. Holiday times for her were days spent at the beach. But she swerved away from a visit to the gazebo at the last minute, darting across the street to the local grocery store, named Marla and Darla's Trading Post. She might as well pick up some basics like milk and eggs, since the fridge at Richie's was running low on supplies. As she approached the store, she noticed two dogs lazily hanging out on the front porch, both of them golden retrievers, near twins. The smaller snouted of the two cocked its head and gave her a curious look.

"Hey, pooch," she said.

"That one's Baxter," said a voice, seemingly from nowhere.

Trina turned to see a large-framed woman standing in the doorway, holding it open either in greeting or fore-warning; her bland, humorless expression didn't reveal much.

"And the other?" Trina asked.

Before the woman could reply, another woman who looked exactly like the first one loomed. From their hair-styles, if you wanted to call them that, to their blue-gray flannel shirts, these women were exact matches. The dogs weren't far off, each with a red bandanna tied around its neck. Should call this place Noah's Trading Post.

"That's Buster, his father."

"Oh, well, hello to both. So, uh, are you open?"

"Need milk, chips, that kind of stuff?" the second woman said.

"Or some nice trinkets, postcards, that kind of stuff? Got Christmas cards in finally."

It was like this was a competition and Trina's business the prize. Trina wasn't sure at the moment what she wanted. "Perhaps I'll have a look around, thank you."

"I'm Marla," the first woman said.

"So that makes you Darla, I suppose."

"Could be," she replied.

This definitely had to be the strangest encounter she'd endured since arriving in Linden Corners. Why hadn't Richie warned her about the eccentric twins? They seemed well versed in how to react to what the other was saying, jumping on the next sentence like they were playing a continual game of one-upmanship, with Trina their token game piece. No matter, she wasn't going to linger long, so as the door opened wide to let her enter, she found Marla's—or was it Darla's? she was all confused now—eyes watching her every move as she looked around.

One side of the store was a basic convenience mart, with a dairy case, soda cooler, bread and cheese, the essentials you tended to run out of more than other household items, and it was certainly easier to stop in here than traveling miles down the highway to the big grocery chain over in Hillsdale. Or was it? she thought, catching Marla or Darla staring at her and rethinking her need for milk. Richie liked it in his morning coffee, and so she grabbed a quart and a few other items that sprung to her mind, bringing them to the counter.

"You're not even going to look at the other side of the store?"

Trina turned around to see one of the two women pointing toward the rack of postcards that seemed to act as a divider between the grocery store and the so-called trading post, whatever that really was. Looked like other people's junk, she guessed from this distance, like a perpetual yard sale. Just then she saw an older man emerge from the shelves in the back, shuffling along the floor with a scrape of his shoe.

"Oh, don't let them get to you, my dear. They played this same game with me last year."

Trina attempted a response and found she didn't have one. Instead, she reached into her purse for cash to pay for her purchases, hoping to make a quick exit.

"Name's Thomas Van Diver," he said, "and I'm guessing you're Trina Ravens."

"Uh, oh, actually, it's Winter. Trina Winter. How . . . how do you know me?"

"Well, Nora described you to Gerta, and Gerta and I were sharing stories at the Edge."

Who was this Gerta, and what was the Edge other than that rocker who played for U2? "Really, Mr. Van . . . Diver, was it? I'm not sure I'm comfortable discussing . . ."

"Ha ha, yes, I see that. You'll be perfect, then."

"Perfect how?"

"Well, for your date."

"My . . ." Her mouth fell open so far, she half expected her teeth to fall to the floor.

"Now, don't be shy. Brian's a fine man. Has an easy way about him."

"That's not my concern . . . How do you know . . . I mean, there's no date."

"Oh, that's not what Nora told Gerta, and she told me. And, well, Elsie too, down at the Edge."

"The Edge?"

"Edgestone Retirement Center, down the road a piece. Where us old folks live."

"And you've been discussing my . . . love life?"

"More Brian's. You're just the happy by-product."

"I'm not sure that's a compliment. Besides, who is this Gerta woman?"

"Nora Connors' mother and one of Brian's closest friends," he said with a wily twinkle. "Only thing better than her instincts is her pies."

Flustered now, Trina paid for her purchases, bagged them herself while Marla or Darla counted change, and then with barely a nod in anyone's direction, made her way out into the welcome darkness of late afternoon. She took a deep breath, letting go of the claustrophobia that had threatened to consume her inside the store. Well, she knew she'd never return there. As the door clacked loudly behind her, she thought she could hear a laugh coming from inside, but instead the noise came from Buster—or was it Baxter?—who appeared to be grinning while the other dog's tail was slapping against the porch.

"You too?" she asked before fleeing far from Marla & Darla's Trading Post.

The solitude of the Solemn Nights wasn't looking so bad now, and she was thankful it was found on the outskirts of the village proper, where hopefully they weren't drinking the same water as these strange folks.

"You're quiet tonight," Richie said, taking a forkful of the chicken dinner Trina had prepared.

"Hmm," she replied.

"Not quite a word, but I suppose any sound is progress," he said.

Since returning to the motel a couple of hours ago, she'd unpacked the groceries, checked on Richie, and then retreated to her room, where, lying on the bed, she relived the exchange at the Trading Post, her thoughts landing squarely on the idea of a date with this Brian guy. She was aware of him—well, she was after talking with Cynthia and Nora that morning at the Five-O, learning he was the uptight proprietor of George's Tavern, not that she let on that she'd met him or even shared banter with him. No sense encouraging something that wasn't going to happen. She'd barely given him, or this supposed blind date, a thought since then. She'd come to Linden Corners to help her father's recovery and maybe begin to repair their relationship; finding a new relationship, and a romantic one at that, was not in the cards. After dismissing the entire afternoon, she'd returned to the kitchen, made dinner, and was sitting quietly at the table while she pushed around the food enough to make it seem like she'd eaten.

"Waste of food, that's what that is."

"What? I've eaten."

"You'd have had to open your mouth to do that," Richie remarked. "Something bugging you, kid?"

Trina looked up at the man who'd given her life, his sudden use of the word *kid* taking her back to her early years, when he was still around. He had called her kid almost from the moment she'd been born. She'd once learned it was her pet name while in utero. As far as she could recall, she hadn't heard it again since, not even this past week. Richie Ravens and Trina Winter had kept a respectful distance when it came to their feelings, leaving any lingering hurts to the past, but not forging any new feelings to make them disappear.

Setting down her fork, she gazed at her father and said, "I remember you used to call me that. I was Kid Ravens."

"Like a boxer," he said with a laugh. "Your mother said you had a good kick."

"Let's not talk about Mom."

He nodded. "I can remember when you called me Dad."

"Richie . . . let's not get into this."

"People make mistakes, Trina. Maybe there are second chances. Like you being here."

"Someone had to come and help you. I mean, look at you, Richie. You can barely walk beyond the front desk." She stared at her plate, wondering why she'd made Brussels sprouts. She'd never liked them, and then she noticed not only was his plate empty, but so was the dish she used to serve the vegetable. Did she remember him liking them? "Besides, my being here is not a big deal. End of the year at my job, things were slow, and a leave of absence was no problem. I had a lot of vacation time saved up."

"You put your life on hold for me. I can't ignore that."

"You first have to have a life to put it on hold."

"You know what I remember most about you?"

"What's that?"

"How you used to run . . . like your little legs were the wheels of a steam engine, powering you to wherever you wanted to go. We had that big backyard and you would run circles around us, with Summer bouncing after you."

"Oh wow, I'd forgotten about Summer. He was a good dog."

"That dog sure followed you around like a lost . . . well, like a lost puppy." Richie allowed himself a rare smile, which brought a hint of redness to his sunken cheeks. "There were a few good times, with you and your mother. But not everything can last."

"Why didn't you ever remarry?"

"Didn't ever happen," he said with an aimless shrug. "Guy like me, unlike most people who make the same mistakes over and over again and never seem to learn from them, when I try something and fail, well, I accept those failures and move on. I go the opposite way of others, and instead of looking for answers I go in search of different challenges. One day I found myself stumbling upon Linden

Corners and I liked it. It had this innocent charm to it . . . but darned if back then I couldn't find a place to crash. Thankfully it was summertime and I set up a tent in the woods just beyond the old windmill; used to watch that thing turn for hours." He paused, his eyes glazing over as though transporting him back to those years. "The cold weather came soon enough, as it does in this neck of the woods. So I needed warmer lodgings."

"So that's why you bought the Solemn Nights? So you had a place to stay?"

"Bought it? Why, I built it," he said, the first sign of pride she'd seen in him.

This man sitting before her, with his leg broken in three places and with a cast signed by few, who lived alone and seemed happy with that, was a sudden surprise to Trina, and she felt remorse wash over her. Perhaps she'd let her mother's opinion of her ex influence her too much, hearing her refer to Richie as a "crazy old coot who wouldn't lift a finger for you."

"Trina, this is real nice, us talking. I'm glad you've opened up a bit, because you've been, well, tight-lipped since coming to stay with me. More nurse than daughter . . . and . . . No, no, before you protest, just know that I understand. We're strangers, you and I. And while I'm sure as heck curious about why you took me up on my offer to come to Linden Corners and help me, I'm not going to push the issue. You've got decisions to make about your life. I can see that. No one goes on a leave and takes vacation; it's one or the other, and I'm thinking you're here because you don't have that job anymore—which you don't need to confirm or deny, not now or not ever." He paused, reaching out a hand to where it lay atop hers. "Whether you're running to something or just plain running from someone, let me give you a piece of advice."

Trina picked at her food, taking a bite of the chicken and deciding she'd used too much lemon pepper seasoning. It had a tartness to it that made the back of her mouth pucker. Or was that because of what Richie had on offer tonight? Fatherly advice, a rare thing indeed.

"People spend their entire lives looking for their personal grail."

"Many people aren't satisfied."

"That's my point," he said. "I arrived in Linden Corners, and the strange thing of it is, I, Richie Ravens, found satisfaction. And while this crumbling old motel might not be much, for more than twenty-five years it's served me well. I meet strangers who need a bed for a night or two, and when they leave, they're still strangers, and that's just how I like it. Guess that makes me a loner of sorts, but when I feel the need, there's this whole crazy village nearby. There are times when I'll partake of some of the events in town, but always at my choosing. No one asks why, and if I show, I show. My life on my terms." He paused again, this time staring down at his leg. "Until this. Darn reminder of my own mortality."

"Is there a point to this life lesson . . . ?" she asked, stopping the word that nearly emerged from between her lips. *Dad.* Too soon for her to come around, if at all. He'd always been Richie to her from the moment they'd reconnected after she'd graduated from college. She remembered the card he'd sent her, now thinking it was actually a postcard— of a windmill—and right now she laughed at the idea of his having bought it down at the Trading Post. "Look, I appreciate learning about the World According to Richie Ravens, but I'm not getting the correlation."

"It's Wednesday night, good stuff on the television," he said.

"No, thanks."

"I wasn't inviting you. That was my way of giving you the night off."

"And what do you propose that I do with my time?"

"Girl like you, pretty and all, if a bit reserved, if you're going to hang around town, you might as well make some friends your own age. It's not the Ravens way, but of course, you're more Winter than Ravens—your mother and Charles made darn sure of that. And I'm not saying that to make you feel bad or to speak ill of the folks who raised you. . . . It's just fact."

Trina was still questioning where this conversation was leading, and rather than prompt it she opted for silence again.

"There's a nice tavern across from the Five-O. You'd probably meet some people your age."

"You too?" she blurted out, unable to hold back her words or her thoughts.

"Aha, so she does speak," he said. "Even a recluse like Richie Ravens has his network in this village, and word travels fast in a place like this. Let me tell you something about this Brian Duncan fellow. He is a lucky son of a you know what because he lives in the shadow of that old windmill, and to this day I still can't imagine a more poetic spot in this mixed-up world. Ask him to show you, Trina, and I think you'll start to feel some of the magic of Linden Corners."

If nothing else, a return visit to George's Tavern would allow her a chance to relax a bit, knock back a shot like she'd done last week, and as a side benefit she'd be able to have a quick conversation with this Brian guy and tell him that despite his efforts to get the entire town to do his handiwork in asking her out, she could bring about a fast resolution to this rumored date. So she quickly cleaned up the remnants of their dinner, helped get Richie settled down for a couple of hours, telling him to call her cell phone without hesitation.

"Those newfangled things work in Linden Corners?" he asked.

"I'm serious, Richie. I'm here to take care of you, not the other way around."

He allowed another smile. "That so?"

Trina rolled her eyes and retreated to her room. She left fifteen minutes later, just before nine o'clock, not bothering to comb her hair or put on a spot of makeup. There was no way she would even give this guy an inch of hope. What was the purpose anyway? It wasn't like Linden Corners was any kind of permanent home for her. This was a mere visit, extended as it was, to help get Richie, literally, back up on his feet. Come the removal of his cast and the New Year, she'd have that silly windmill in her rearview mirror.

As she made her way up to the front steps of the tavern, she took a quick gaze inside. There were about ten people there, some at tables and others on the stools in front of the bar, and, yup, behind the counter was the bartender from the other night. This Brian guy. She steeled herself for strength of character, then opened the door and made her entrance, her bit of drama managing to catch the attention of two men at the far end of the bar. One was that old guy, Chet, from the Five-O, and next to him was a sourpuss of a man, probably fortysomething. She was glad she hadn't done herself up; she didn't want to encourage anyone.

"Trina!" she heard.

Coming back from the jukebox was Sara, a friendly face if ever she needed one.

"Hi, Sara. What are you doing here?"

"Mark's working down at the restaurant tonight and I was hanging out upstairs in our apartment, bored stiff. I mean, the baby was resting, and I really can't do much around the house but sit around. So why not come down here and join the conversation? Besides, the baby likes the music, he—or she—has been kicking up a storm since I got here. But I could ask the same of you. Is Richie okay?"

"Gave me the night off."

"Good, you need a night out," she said. "Come on, let's get you that drink. I'll introduce you to Brian."

Trina paused, giving her cousin-in-law a suspicious look. "Why?"

"Um, because he's the bartender and that's who you get drinks from."

Which made her wonder if Sara was not in on this date thing, hoping that was the case. It would be nice to have a friend in her corner within Linden Corners. As they headed toward the bar, Trina noticed Brian pulling at the tap, but when he saw her, his gaze locked to the point that the beer flowed over the top of the glass. The overflow caught him by surprise and he pulled his hand away, the glass slipping out of his hand and falling with a crash behind the bar. Having caught the attention of the entire bar, Brian turned away, Trina thinking he was embarrassed by his lack of focus. But he recovered quickly enough, getting Chet his refill without further incident and then reaching for the bottle of Dewar's on the shelf behind him. By the time Trina had bellied up to the bar, he'd poured her shot.

"You remembered," she said.

"A good bartender has special powers," he replied.

"And slippery hands," she said.

"Yes, that takes talent." He paused and smiled at her, then said, "Welcome back."

"Wait, you two know each other?" Sara said.

"Long story," Trina said.

"Long night," Brian answered.

Silence hovered inside the bar, nearly palpable between

her and Brian. Even the jukebox knew to remain quiet, she surmised, when in reality it was merely changing songs. Some wise-ass customer had chosen Annie Lennox's "Walking on Broken Glass," which managed to garner big laughs from the rest of the patrons.

As the laughter subsided, Trina found all eyes on her as though the gossip network had reached each and every one of them and they were waiting to see what was going to happen next. That was when this clumsy but charming guy named Brian Duncan said, apparently for all to hear, the strangest thing, a compromise.

"I will if you will," was what he said.

CHAPTER 7

BRIAN

"Dad, who do you think left you those shiny presents?"

"I have no idea."

"Do you think it was this Trina woman?"

Trying to stifle a laugh, Brian couldn't help but let it out, wondering in what way Janey was going to work this first-ever date she'd known him to go on into their conversation. "Uh, I hardly think so. She doesn't know me, and I don't know her. It's a bit early for gift giving."

He was standing before the floor-length mirror inside his rustic, country-style bedroom, staring first at the stranger he saw, then back at the little girl who watched him get ready. Brian could see a confused look upon Janey's curious face. He waited patiently, almost expectantly, for the next jewel of wisdom to come from her, mostly because he'd lost patience with the tie he was attempting to wrap around his neck. Once upon a time he'd worn one every day, but after two years he was out of practice. Ties were not exactly standard uniform in the country.

"If you don't know her, why are you having dinner with her?"

"To get to know her. That's how it works."

"You mean dates?"

"If you want to call it a date, sure."

"That's what Cynthia called it."

Brian was hardly surprised by that admission, as an amused Cynthia continued to spread the news about his burgeoning relationship, all while ignoring the subject of her impending move halfway across the country. He had to wonder if this wasn't part of some master plan concocted on her part to ensure that not only would Janey be well provided for after their departure, but Brian would be too. He had a feeling the Knights were also the ones behind the Secret Santa gifts; nothing else made sense. "Cynthia of all people should know. She's the one responsible for . . . this night."

A newly arrived, cool December Friday night was here, three days since Brian and Trina had agreed to go out while the rest of the tavern patrons looked on, their reason for agreeing to it a common one—to get their friends and families off their backs. They'd spoken on the phone once since that night at the tavern, and they'd decided dinner was the ideal option, leaving Brian to confess to not having had any other ideas. Just where in Linden Corners did one even go on a date? Not the greasy counter at the Five-O, not the postcard rack at the Trading Post, and while Brian had been joking when he'd suggested the latter place, Trina, dead serious, replied, "Please, not Marla's or Darla's or whatever that store is called." To escape prying eyes, out of town they would venture.

"How about RiverFront?" she'd asked.

The resort-slash-restaurant down in Hudson. "You sure? That's where Mark works."

"Won't he be tending bar at your tavern that night? Isn't that why you're free?"

He liked the wily way Trina thought and instantly agreed.

Turning now to Janey, he said, "So, you okay with Sara coming over again to babysit?"

"I really don't like that word."

Ah yes, independent Janey Sullivan, ten years old and no longer in need of a babysitter. He let it go, knowing a reply was the last thing she expected. Instead, she moved toward his bed, where he'd laid out his suit jacket. She looked at it, then back at him.

"Too fancy," she announced.

"Really?"

"I suggest blue jeans, a nice shirt, and this jacket. That's what's modern."

"And how do you know what's in style these days?"

"I've never seen Mark wear a suit and definitely not a tie, and look at him."

Interesting turn of dialogue, he thought, deciding to see where she went with this. Like she was done with Cynthia and was already turning to the young Ravens couple for insight into the world. "So I should take fashion advice from him?"

"Not fashion advice, dating," she said, obvious exasperation in her voice. "He won Sara's heart and they got married and I've only ever seen him wearing jeans. Oh, and he doesn't shave often but that's okay for him; you look better without whiskers."

"Janey, not everyone who goes on a date gets married."

She pondered this before quickly adding, "Then why go on it?"

They'd gone far enough, he thought, and thankfully the ringing of the doorbell saved him from having to explain the rites and rituals of the complex world of dating. As Janey dashed out of the room to see to the person at the door, Brian stared back at himself, reflecting both on his appearance and on his romantic life. It was just two years ago

when Janey had heard stories of two of Brian's previous relationships, both of which had led to engagements, though
neither had led to actual marriage. Thirty-six years old now,
still unattached, now an unlikely single father going out on
his first date in . . . he wasn't even sure how long. Certainly
Trina Winter was his first since Annie, but his relationship
with Annie hadn't really been traditional—dates in the old
sense hadn't really occurred between them, their time together more as friends who quickly slipped into deep commitment. A dangerous word, *commitment*, and one far from
his mind right now. He just wanted to get through this night
with the right outfit, one that would allow him to relax and
signal to Trina that this was just as they'd agreed upon, casual, no strings, a night out meant to appease their friends
more than them.

"You look great," Sara said moments later when Brian
made his way down the stairs.

He'd gone with the jeans-and-blazer look.

"Janey's suggestion."

"He almost wore a tie," Janey stated, disapproval evident
in her voice.

"If it's any consolation, Brian, Trina called me three
times."

"Grown-ups are weird," Janey decided. "Come on, Sara,
let's see what's for dinner."

The two of them ventured off to the kitchen, allowing
Brian to escape their clutches—and further judgments—
and he headed out into the dark night to his truck. He
stared at it, realizing it was the most ridiculous vehicle to
show up for a date with; it was old and the engine rattled,
and truth be known, it had been Annie's and he really didn't
feel right about taking it out for a spin on the dating wheel.
His old Grand Am lay idle in the barn, but it was at least
more appropriate for such an excursion. Going back inside

the house for the keys, he couldn't help but overhear an exchange between Janey and Sara.

"It's going to be a house full of Duncans," she said.

"That will be wonderful, Janey. Family is important, especially around the holidays."

"But they're Brian's family, not mine," she said. "I mean, I don't even know what to call them."

"But I'm sure you'll get more gifts."

Brian slipped back outside, carefully avoiding detection and wishing he'd just driven the truck. If he had, he wouldn't have heard what Janey said, comments that tore deep at his heart. True, Didi and Kevin Duncan were his parents and not her grandparents. And she had referred to him just now as Brian, not Dad, as they had established two years ago after an episode that had threatened their trust. Maybe his parents' imminent arrival was more impactful on Janey than he had thought—or than she was letting on. He made a mental note to sit down and talk to her again without distraction. But that would have to wait.

For now, he had a date.

A word that sounded even stranger to him than *Dad*.

RiverFront Restaurant and Resort was located at the western edge of the city of Hudson, just a twenty-minute drive from Linden Corners, a combination four-star hotel and spa, as well as an upscale restaurant that overlooked the banks of the city's eponymous river. It was where Mark Ravens' primary job was, his main source of income as a waiter and occasional host, which afforded him the chance to provide for his wife and soon-to-arrive child. His job at the tavern was supplemental, the commute unbeatable. His job here also provided him with connections, so the staff had been alerted to the fact that Brian Duncan and Trina Winter were to be treated like family.

"Good evening, Mr. Duncan. Ms. Winter," said a tuxedo-clad gentleman with silver hair and a smile, standing tall behind the check-in desk. "Your table is ready if you are—and it comes with a lovely view of the river."

"How nice," Trina said.

The maître d', with his slicked-back hair and bow tie making Brian feel underdressed, led them across the floor and to a table for four that provided them with room to spread out. Dim lighting cast a hush over the dining area, which meant that even though a few tables were occupied with diners near them, they were encased in their own private corner, and true to the man's word, the mighty Hudson was seemingly within reach.

"Again, how nice," Trina said, gazing through the reflective glass at the river.

Night was in full bloom, with moonlight streaming across the currents like waves of light.

"Mark's doing, no doubt," he said.

"Mark speaks very highly of you, Brian," Trina said, pushing her hair back from her face. She wore more makeup tonight than Brian had seen her with before, and a lone gold necklace dangled from her neck. "He told me that without you he wouldn't have had the guts to get his life together. It was the relief bartender job that allowed him to get to know Sara so well—and we know how well that turned out." She paused, seemingly using the river view as an excuse to collect her thoughts. "If you want to know the truth, it wasn't your friends Nora and Cynthia who convinced me to come on this date; it was Mark."

"Nice to have an independent's endorsement," he said.

"I don't know Mark well. I mean, how could I, since I barely know my own father? I'm not exactly comfortable with the Ravens side of the family."

"What do you say we get a drink before we, uh, delve into our lives?"

"Sounds perfect."

A waiter arrived and took their order, a seltzer with lime for him, Trina asking if they had Johnny Blue, her face lighting up when the waiter confirmed they stocked it. He handed them menus and left them to peruse their choices. Silence settled over the new couple, leaving Brian wondering if the lack of conversation was acceptable. Was it a good sign they were comfortable not filling every single moment with conversation, or a bad one, the fact that they were out of topics before the first drink?

"So, Brian, you really don't drink?"

"Haven't touched a drop in three years. Well, except once."

"Fall off the wagon?" she asked.

"Voluntarily. In tribute."

"Care to share?"

This one was easy, Linden Corners 101. He told her about kindly George Connors and how he had taken a wet-behind-the-ears Brian under his wing at his bar, then called Connors' Corner, and by doing so helped initiate Brian into village life. While the story's ending was sad, it was inspiring too, with Brian adding, "I don't think I would have remained in town if not for George. When he passed away quietly just moments after pouring that one last beer, I did as he'd intended and I drank it down. I might have taken over his bar, but never again did I take a drop from the taps. Those are for my customers."

"That's a sad story, but a lovely one."

"Welcome to Linden Corners," he said. "We rise from the ashes."

Their drinks arrived and they cheered the phoenix, drank, and then studied their menus.

"So," he said, realizing it was the ideal transition word. "How's your father doing?"

"Ah, Richie," she said.

"You call him Richie?"

"It's complicated," she said, again pushing her styled hair back over her ear, keeping the strands from covering her face. "I didn't grow up with him. We've only been in touch . . . recently, the last few years or so. I had a stepfather who was always there for me."

"Had? Sounds like past tense."

"My mother is on her third husband."

"Always in search of the next ex-Mr.?"

"She's a fickle woman."

Brian laughed. "So I'm learning—about fickle women."

"Who would that be?"

"Janey. Confession time? I almost wore a tie tonight. I was advised against one."

"Janey is your daughter."

"My . . . yeah, my daughter."

"Sounds like another story."

"Parental relationships can be complicated," he said. "Which, by the way, you didn't tell me how Richie's doing."

"Richie is ornery."

"Well, we all know that."

"When he fell from the roof of the Solemn Nights, he broke his leg in three places. As you've no doubt heard, he's in a cast and of course can't get around much. Once it comes off, it will be weeks, maybe months, of physical therapy until he's back to normal. It also leaves me as the manager of a roadside motel outside a rinky-dink town that seemingly can't wait to celebrate Christmas."

"Have you put up lights around the motel yet?"

"Richie doesn't partake."

Brian nodded. "So I remember. It's always a pretty dark

stretch of road there no matter the season. You know, you could change that this year, and I can help put them up if you want. Keep Richie off of ladders, right?"

"Um, we'll see. I don't want to come here and change things."

"I think you already have," Brian said, suddenly feeling a rush of blood to his neck, making him blush. Where was that tie when you needed it? "Uh, anyway, you know, I stayed at the Solemn Nights when I first came to Linden Corners."

"Let me guess, you first had lunch or dinner at the Five-O and Martha sent you over."

Brian raised his glass in acknowledgment. "How long have you been in town?"

"Long enough, apparently."

He noticed she hadn't taken him up on the Christmas lights offer. "You make it sound like your being here is temporary."

"It is," she said, far too quickly. "I do have a life elsewhere."

Brian quieted down at that point, the string of questions in his mind suddenly tangled. He could make no sense of her, and even if he asked her more, was he confident in Trina's answers? He wondered just what he was doing on this date. A date with a woman who had no intention of sticking around town beyond the terms of her obligation. But as he reminded himself, this was an appeasement date. Dine, relax, go home—separately—and then the next day tell your friends she's/he's nice, but nothing to pursue. No spark.

Except he wasn't sure that last part was entirely correct.

Thankfully the waiter returned and took their dinner order, handily distracting them from their staccato-sounding back-and-forth dialogue. She would have the salmon, he the skirt steak, and she also put in an order for a second drink, and then the waiter was off, far too quickly for Brian's comfort. He imagined that he was fast losing Trina's attention, as there were lots of topics touched upon but he'd found no common ground between them. Maybe he'd spent too much time consumed with Janey's problems and insecurities, to the point where he no longer knew how to carry on a conversation with an adult, not counting Cynthia and Bradley—they were his friends—and Nora, whom he'd gotten to know only last year and had flirted with only to decide they worked best as friends. Other than that, his dating opportunities were relegated to his memory banks. Memories filled with early promise and ultimate demise.

"I have an idea, Brian," Trina suddenly said.

"Uh, okay?"

"I know what we agreed upon, but it's pretty clear this is a real date."

"Yeah, guess it feels like one."

"And a first one, at that."

"So what do you propose?"

"Just two people having dinner. Takes the pressure off."

"An interesting proposal," he said.

"I mean, this can't lead anywhere. I'm not staying and you're not leaving."

"Good point."

"You're a nice guy, but I'm not looking for any kind of guy."

"Fair enough."

"Plus, you have a kid and I don't want a kid."

Okay, that revelation shook him, and he wasn't sure how to respond. "That's . . . honest."

"Sorry, I didn't mean that to sound so . . . harsh. Look at my life, Brian," she said. "My parents had me and then divorced when I was three years old. My mother remarried, an older guy named Charles Winter, and not that I had any choice in the matter, but he adopted me, hence my legal last name. Bye-bye to Richie Ravens and any link to my actual family. Charles, whom I always called Dad, also had two children—both sons—from a previous marriage, which meant we were like a modern-day Brady Bunch, truncated for sure, and without the quick thirty-minute resolution to our problems." She paused before drinking her scotch. "Trina Winter in a nutshell. Your turn."

Seltzer water seemed wholly inappropriate at the moment, so he ignored his beverage and leaped into the deep end of the pool she'd taken them to. "After my fiancée's betrayal, I moved away from New York City and ended up in a small town called Linden Corners, where I met a woman, fell in love, and after she passed away in a freak accident, I was granted guardianship of her at-the-time seven-year-old daughter. She's ten now, and while I don't know where the time has gone, she's the absolute center of my life and I couldn't imagine waking without knowing she was there for me, and I for her. My best friends and Janey's support system just announced they are moving away, and to top it all off, my frosty parents, who haven't exactly approved of my life change, phoned me on Thanksgiving to say they were coming for an extended holiday visit—their first ever to Linden Corners."

She dangled her drink before him, and he wondered if it was a tease or an offer. "Okay, Windmill Man, you win that round. I just have to deal with Richie's eccentricities, and even he gives me a night off like tonight to knock back a few," she said with a surprising laugh, one that allowed a natural smile to cross her lips. He thought at that moment, with her mix of humor and sympathy, that she was as attractive as he'd seen her. Candlelight highlighting her eyes, she was a far cry from the desperate woman he'd met that night at the tavern.

Dinner arrived then, and they dug in heartily, happy for the distraction. They switched to the safety of small talk, his life down at the tavern, her experiences at the motel, the two of them finding common ground in the fact that both businesses tended to attract the transient. Brian admitted that when he'd left New York, setting out on the road for where he didn't know, he'd envisioned ending up much farther from New York City than the Hudson River Valley.

"I ended up less than three hours away from the city."

"Where do you think you'd have gone?"

"At that point in my life, I think Alaska wouldn't have been far enough."

"She hurt you a lot. This old girlfriend."

"Fiancée," he corrected, as though such a label added weight to the betrayal. "Let's just say I never expected what was going on. Big-city ambitions make you appreciate a place like Linden Corners. As George said, there's a simpler way of life here, where your neighbors are your friends, not strangers. When you ask for help, they ask how—not that you ever need to ask; the residents here just seem to know when someone is in need. Like tonight, Trina, I'm actually enjoying myself."

"Gee, a girl loves compliments like that."

"No, it's not about you, and I'm sorry if it sounded that way," he said. "It's hard to be selfish in Linden Corners, and I think that for the past two-plus years I've been on autopilot. Caring for Janey on a daily basis, caring for George's bar, back and forth between home and the tavern, I just do, act, respond. If Gerta needs something, I'm there. Same with Cynthia, Nora."

"Meaning you've put Brian Duncan on hold?"

"How could I not? The situation I found myself in, I'm the last person who needs help."

"Your friends think otherwise," she said.

"You're in the same boat, taking on the role of caregiver, which means you've put your life on ice too."

"Look at that, something in common."

Silence again fell between them, Brian noting it came tinged with an uneasiness he could remember from early dates with his old high school flame, Lucy, and even with the alluring, sexy Maddie, whom he was convinced he'd fallen in love with their first night together. He was feeling a connection suddenly with Trina, and whether it was the bright flicker of candlelight that danced in her eyes or the distant sound of waves upon the shore, it was a magic word that neither had consciously recognized. This newfound awkwardness meant a shift had occurred tonight. Two people, both vulnerable, feeling the pressure of responsibility, had been given the gift of a night off from their lives and a chance to explore something beyond their daily routine. For a moment Brian Duncan considered a breach of his tightly held self by ordering an after-dinner drink.

But Trina spoke up before he could address the waiter, and the moment passed.

"What do you say we get out of here? I for one could go for a walk along the river."

A romantic gesture, he thought, one that froze him in his tracks.

Not because he wasn't attracted to Trina, not because he feared intimacy.

It was the location, along the banks of the Hudson River. It made him think of Annie.

*   *   *

"You've grown quiet. Was this a bad idea?"

Brian had indeed gone silent, afraid if he spoke his tone would give him away.

They had left the restaurant and at Trina's suggestion ventured beyond the chains of the parking lot and into the accompanying park. The park was closed for the night; the swings were silent and the wind grew as quiet as Brian. Bypassing the park benches and continuing up a grassy slope that Trina hoped would afford them a beautiful view of the river, Brian wondered just how to answer her question.

"Are you afraid of heights, Brian?"

"No, it's not that . . . ," he said.

"Then what's wrong? Why the hesitation?"

"Nothing," he insisted. "Here, take my hand; it's a little slippery from the recent rain."

Brian reached out in the darkness, feeling Trina's hand connect with his. It was the first act of physicality between them, and he wasn't sure how he felt about that. Her touch was warm, and as he guided her up the last few feet of the hill, he caught her expression in the moonlight, she as relaxed as he'd seen her. Not that he knew her well at all, but he sensed that beneath her cool exterior was a gentle, generous soul. Someone who traveled all these miles and put her life on hold to care for an injured father she barely knew certainly had more to her than a brusque manner. If only she had chosen a place other than the hills above the river to end their first date.

At last they emerged at the top of the hill, Trina scoping out a large rock with a smooth surface on which to stand and stare down at the languid waters of the Hudson. He too gazed out at the way the river merged with the distant horizon, backlit by the glimmering moon. To say the setting was romantic was an understatement, and he was about to suggest they make their way back to avoid this going any further when Trina heightened the romance. He felt her lips upon his, soft and tentative. Like she too wasn't sure this was the right thing to be doing, her mind telling her one thing, her heart acting independently. She didn't pull back, their kiss lingering, while above them came the squawk of a soaring seagull.

Brian gazed up at the bird, unable to determine whether the bird approved.

She must have sensed his distraction, as the kiss suddenly ended.

"Sorry," she said. "You weren't ready."

"Trina," he said, "one word that should never follow a kiss is *sorry*."

"You want to tell me what you're thinking about?"

"You know, I think I'd rather save that for another time."

"Well, that's encouraging, another time," she said. "I thought this was a onetime thing."

"A kiss like that—did that seem like the end of something?" he asked.

"No, no, it didn't. Brian, tell me what's wrong."

"It's . . . it's just this place, this setting. It's too close to home."

"We're miles from Linden Corners."

He smiled, but his smile was tinged with sorrow that left her staring hard into his eyes. "Not in my mind," he said. "In fact, in the distance I think I can see the windmill."

"You too with the windmill?" she asked.

"What's that supposed to mean?"

He could imagine his face had grown darker from the derision in her voice.

"I don't mean any offense, Brian. It's just, the other night, Richie was going on about the windmill and how it inspired him when he first came to town. He told me it's one of the primary reasons he stayed. And he'd made a friend—as much as Richie can do—with the windmill's owner."

This was news to Brian. "The owner, who was that?"

"A man named Dan Sullivan," Trina said.

Brian thought about Richie Ravens, who had come to town more than twenty years ago; Dan would have been only a teenager. Having arrived a broken man, Richie forged a new life, only to become, as the years progressed, more of a recluse. Was that a scenario Brian wanted for himself?

Brian grew so quiet he wondered if he was still breathing. He thought about the portraits hung upon Janey's wall, and not just the one of Annie, whom he'd known and whom he'd loved and who continued to swirl around him like a windblown, loving spirit, but the portrait of her father, Dan, who continued to hover over his life like a spectral force of another kind.

"Brian, are you okay?"

He turned back to her, and this time he was the aggressor, as he planted a fresh kiss upon her lips. She responded in kind, their kiss growing deeper, longer, so much so that not even the squawking, high-flying bird or the moonlight that glided behind a cloud could stop them. Brian, tasting her, wrapping his arms around her and feeling an embrace he'd not allowed himself to know for too long, sensed his soul had been released, as though for the first time since Annie had left them he allowed himself to think there was another life waiting for him somewhere out there. Or maybe not somewhere far, but with someone close.

CHAPTER 8

CYNTHIA

Cynthia Knight was watching the front door to see who else might be joining the rest of the villagers for this impromptu meeting, pleased already at the turnout of nearly two dozen people but knowing they were still missing some key residents of their fair village. From her seat on the makeshift dais at the Corner Community Center—the CCC, as it was dubbed by the locals—she could see many elderly folks from Edgestone, the retirement center down the street, including Elsie Masters, whom she knew she could approach and ask who else from town to expect. Elsie knew things, having for decades run her antique shop on the main road until selling it last year to Nora Connors and choosing the life of a retiree, aching knees and all. With her was Thomas Van Diver, looking as dapper as ever with his trademark bow tie and his twinkling blue eyes, which somehow cast calm over a rising storm. And just now walking through the door was the reliable Gerta Connors, who made a beeline for her friends.

Cynthia checked her watch, saw that it was just past seven in the evening.

She'd chosen a time that ensured more of the local business owners could attend. It was Saturday night in Linden Corners, and if you weren't home watching television or partaking of a drink over at George's Tavern, there was little reason why you couldn't show up for a gathering that would set in motion this year's village Christmas plans. Leading the charge, armed with the knowledge that this was quite possibly her final Linden Corners Christmas, Cynthia was eager to make it the most special celebration they'd yet produced, a tall order considering last year's red-and-green pageant down at the gazebo. Golden luminaries in the snow had lit their way toward a joyous wedding as they witnessed the culmination of a decades-old holiday mystery that had seen its resolution achieved with hours to spare before Christmas arrived.

Cynthia was flying solo on this project, at least for the moment. Back home was Bradley, caring for not just Jake but Janey too. Janey had asked to accompany her, but Cynthia wanted all the plans set before telling the young girl that she'd been the inspiration for this year's event. In fact, Brian had really set the ball in motion when he'd spilled the beans about the mysterious Secret Santa gifts he'd been receiving. Before she could tell them, first she had to rally the town into accepting her idea. It was important to Cynthia for everything to go off without a hitch, and only after signs and placards were made and hung around town would their celebration become official.

She was waiting still on Nora and Martha, mostly, and when she noticed Sara Ravens enter the center, she got up from her seat and made her way to the pregnant young woman.

"Cynthia, hi . . . what a turnout; this is great. But what's it all about?"

"You'll see," she said. "But while we have a chance, any word from Trina and Brian?"

"I didn't talk to her all day. You?"

"Brian dropped Janey off earlier, but all he would say was that they had a good time," she said. "Typical male. We go to all that effort to set them up, and what does he do? Gives us nothing. Makes you appreciate girlfriends; they know how to spill details."

Sara, rubbing her belly, sighed. "So glad I'm not in the dating pool anymore."

A fresh burst of air swirled inside the room, Cynthia turning to see Nora arrive, Nicholas Casey at her side.

"Speaking of, there's one happy couple," Sara said.

Cynthia thought otherwise, noticing the less-than-thrilled expression on Nora's face. She waved in her friend's direction, Nora departing Nicholas's side, but not before he reached for her hand and readied a kiss. She turned slightly, so the kiss landed awkwardly somewhere between her lip and her cheek, Cynthia watching the interaction with growing interest. Not that Nora had said anything—nor was she inclined to—but a romance that had blossomed after last Christmas seemed to have lost a bit of its shiny glow.

"Hi," Cynthia said as Nora approached. "Thanks for coming."

"Like I had a choice."

"And you brought Nicholas."

"I repeat, like I had a choice."

"Nora . . ."

"Sorry, forget it, it's not important. But from the look of things here," she said, sizing up the growing crowd filling the community center, "something else is. What's up?"

"Christmas," Cynthia said, "and it's all my doing, though I have to say I did run my idea past your mother."

"A big Linden Corners celebration—which I'm assuming this is about—without my mother's input would be considered sacrilegious."

"Where's Travis?"

"With friends. Where else is a thirteen-year-old on a Saturday night?"

"Leaving you free for date night?"

Nora frowned. "Tell you what. Let's finish this meeting and have a drink at George's."

"What about Nicholas?"

"He can hang with Brian; they're chummy."

"Perfect. Because there's something I need your help on. Professionally."

That raised a curious eyebrow on Nora's part. "You mean, A Doll's Attic kind of work?"

"Absolutely. I need help fulfilling another childhood memory," she said. "I'll fill you in later. For now, let me get this going."

And she did, calling to order a fair representation of the village's population, asking them to take their seats. With coffee provided by the Five-O, the residents did as instructed, Cynthia noting that among the newly arrived guests were Marla and Darla and the sourpuss Chuck Ackroyd, a man who put not just the *bah* but also the *bug* in *bah*, *humbug*. In the back row was Father Eldreth Burton of Saint Matthew's Church, whom she'd specifically called to be here. Assembled in the front row were Gerta and Thomas, Nicholas and Nora, with Elsie, Sara, and Martha directly behind them. Missing were many of the men of Linden Corners, Brian and Bradley, Mark Ravens, and Richie too. She also noted that Trina Winter was nowhere to be seen, which distracted her for a moment. She could think it was curious that neither Trina nor Brian was here one night after their date, but she'd already checked that Brian was working the bar. Still, it was a great turnout and an indication that the town thought of itself as a collective, and she had every confidence that all would embrace her idea.

Rising to the podium, she tested the microphone, received temporary feedback.

She took a step back from it, then spoke without incident.

"Thank you to everyone in Linden Corners for turning out," she said. "Now, I realize the holidays are fast approaching us—I mean, what am I thinking? Thanksgiving is gone a week and a half already, which means Christmastime looms ever closer. Not that you'd know it from the lack of snow on the ground, but rest assured, Christmas is coming."

"So is this little guy," Sara said, referencing her extended belly. "About the same time."

"Right, which means we need to act fast," Cynthia said. "As many of you have heard by now, my husband, Bradley, and I—and of course little Jake—will be leaving Linden Corners at the start of the New Year, and know that we do so with great regret but also with great promise. As we leave behind our old life, know that we take with us the very spirit of Linden Corners and hopefully a chance to spread its sense of community to our new home. You are all our friends, neighbors, and we have known each other for so many years and you've seen us through tough times. But nothing suggests Linden Corners more than our celebrations, and so, for this year's annual Christmas pageant, I suggest something new . . . something we can all participate in."

"Another wedding?" Martha asked.

"Unless someone here has a surprise for us, I don't think so. We wouldn't want to repeat ourselves, now, would we?" Cynthia paused, gazing out at the crowd, her eyes landing on Nora, who appeared to want to slide under her chair.

Her cold stare of daggers told Cynthia to continue, quickly, and so she did, saying, "This village is accustomed to the notion of giving, and so what I propose is an all-out, full-participation game of Secret Santa. I'm calling it 'The Secret of Linden Corners.' "

"You mean, giving everyone gifts? In this economy?" Chuck said, rising from his seat.

"Hardly, Chuck," she said, not surprised he was the lone dissenter in the group. "Secret Santa—which some people may know as Kris Kringle—simply means you pick one name and keep it secret, then surprise that person on Christmas Day with a special gift. Or you leave them a series of smaller gifts, almost as a tease, a guessing game of whom their Secret Santa might be. For any of you who are concerned with cost, we will of course impose a spending limit."

"Oh, I think it's a splendid idea," Gerta said, clapping her hands.

Gerta's reaction had been rehearsed over the phone, Cynthia and Gerta having planned for an unofficial "second" for the record. Just then a buzz erupted amidst the group, as questions of logistics emerged, *when*, *why*, and *how* filling the room. Cynthia tried to quiet them down to little effect, and it was only when Gerta stood next to the podium and asked them to quiet down did they do so.

"My goodness, such a ruckus among you," Gerta said. "Now, I know you have concerns, so if you'll listen, we will explain how this will work. For the next week, a large Santa hat will be placed inside the gazebo in the center of the town. If you wish to partake in our village-wide game, just write your name down on a slip of paper and put it in the hat. Our drawing will be two Sundays from now, plenty of time for everyone to join in the fun, and we hope you'll all be there. Only those who put their names in the hat will be able to draw a name, which will keep our event organized and ensure no one is left out."

"Thank you, Gerta. Now to the exchange of gifts . . ."

"I don't want some stranger coming to my house on Christmas morning . . ."

"Marla, I'm not sure even Darla would dare do such a thing to you, and she lives with you," Martha said, laughter arising from the group.

Her joke managed to settle everyone down, and so they all focused back on Cynthia. She filled them in on the final details. "As you know, Saint Matthew's Church offers up both its vigil mass at five o'clock and the midnight mass on Christmas Eve, so, with Father Burton's blessing, our gift exchange will take place between them, after the annual children's pageant and our new tradition of the esteemed Thomas Van Diver reading 'The Night Before Christmas.' Only one thing will be different this year, and it's the location of our pageant."

"It's not the church?"

"No," Cynthia said.

"The gazebo again?" asked Sara, who last year had been married under its snowy roof.

"Now, what place in this town of ours can accommodate a large crowd but represents the spirit of our village? It will be lit, as always, with a thousand white lights that can blind even the sun and the stars above." She paused, letting the idea sink in among them, but then she went in for the final impact when she said, almost reverently, "The windmill."

"Nice delivery, Cyn."

"And nice idea," Nicholas said, sitting with Nora and Cynthia at a table inside the tavern. "But did you run that idea past Brian?"

"Run what idea past me?"

Brian had approached their table unbeknownst to them. Cynthia found his eyes zeroing in her, not surprising since Nora and Nicholas were also staring at her. Like she was the creative force behind whatever idea she'd yet to inform him about. Wasn't she?

"I'll tell you later, Brian. Trust me, you'll love it," Cynthia said.

"Oh, you mean about the Secret of Linden Corners celebration and the pageant ending at the windmill?"

"How . . . ," she said, and then gazed over at the bar, where she saw Chuck nursing a beer.

"This is Linden Corners; word travels faster than Martha's chili."

"Hey, I heard that," came a voice from a neighboring table.

It seemed as though half the residents had retreated to George's Tavern after the meeting. Martha, sitting with Marla and Darla over a round of tequila shots, nodded their way. Cynthia, red faced, confessed that she'd meant to talk to him earlier, but time got away, and besides, "you got home late last night. I trust all went well?"

"Changing the subject won't help you," he said.

"Really, Brian, this is about Janey . . ."

"I know, and of course I don't mind. But, as you said, we'll talk later. Got a full house."

"Speaking of," Nora said, "Nicholas, do us a favor and get us some wine. And then hang with Brian at the bar."

"I think I've been dismissed," he said with a scrape of his chair.

He also didn't look happy to have been sent away. Still, he left like a dutiful boyfriend, returning a moment later with their drinks in hand before settling back on a bar stool between the unfortunate choices of Chet and Chuck. Poor

Nicholas, Cyn thought, he was a good guy caught up in a relationship with a woman who still had her past to deal with. With one hand on the stem of her glass, Cynthia reached out her other hand and placed it over Nora's.

"What's going on with you two?"

Nora took a drink. "You said you had a job for me?"

"Fine, I'll go first," Cynthia said. "But, Nora Connors, I am not letting you out of here tonight without an explanation as to what's wrong. Nicholas seems like such a great guy—he's smart, educated, charming, and the way his curly hair curves over the collar of his shirt gives him this sexy vibe . . ."

"Cynthia Knight, if Bradley could hear you now!"

"Again, changing the topic," she said. "Okay, back to business. This job I've got for you. It concerns a frog."

Nora took a sip of her wine and grimaced. Cynthia wondered if it was the frog or the wine that didn't agree with her. "A frog, really? How does that relate to A Doll's Attic?"

"You found Thomas's rare-edition book last year, right?"

"Actually, Brian found it . . ."

"Regardless, Nora, you find things. Old things that help people understand their past, or just learn to appreciate it more."

"Sometimes it's not the toy you remember but who gave it to you, the intent behind it."

"Exactly my point," Cynthia said, taking a sip of her white wine. She too pursed her lips. "Ouch, guess I know why the bar does such good business with beer. Anyway . . . I'm not sure if you've ever noticed that Janey has this stuffed pet frog; it's purple and has no name."

"I haven't," Nora said.

"She's had it as long as I can remember, even back as a baby."

"Must be kind of ratty after ten years," Nora said. "How can I help? Are you looking for a new one?"

"No, I want to know the frog's provenance," Cynthia said. "Somehow it's important to Janey, a piece of her past . . . a connection to her birth parents. We all know that Janey remembers Annie; she was old enough to share so many experiences with her mother. But it's Dan Sullivan who is a bit of a mystery to her, and I think the frog holds some kind of importance to her. Why else would she be carrying it around all the time these days? It's the equivalent of a security blanket."

"Maybe she's scared; kids act that way," Nora offered. "I remember how silent Travis grew after his father and I split," she said. "Only after we came to Linden Corners did he remember how to speak. And I credit more of that to his grandmother than to me, and I suppose, somewhat, to Nicholas. He's a good influence on Travis."

"Just not on you?"

"We're still talking about Janey."

"Right, sorry," Cynthia said. "So what do you say? Will you look into it?"

"I'm not quite sure what I'm looking for. I'm guessing this is a secret mission?"

"Just go over to Brian's. Don't you and Gerta have dinner with them on some Sunday nights? Ask to see the frog, or I don't know . . . you'll think of something."

"Why tomorrow night? What's the urgency?"

"Because I want to know the story of that frog before Christmas," she said.

Nora rolled her eyes. "Here we go again. Last year Thomas and the book, this year . . . a frog."

"Speaking of, so Nicholas . . . is he one, or a prince?"

"You don't let up, do you now?" Nora asked.

"That's what friends are for."

"I'm sorry, when are you moving?"

"Ha ha," Cynthia said. "Now who's changing the subject?"

Pausing, staring over at Nicholas as he engaged in small talk at the bar, Nora sighed. Cynthia watched her friend, wishing she could help but also knowing that Nora was a complex woman, one some found a bit too icy on the surface. But once you got to know her, you sensed the little girl that dwelled inside her, a forty-plus woman with a teenage son, divorced and living with her aging mother and dating a man who lived on the wrong side of the border between New York and Massachusetts, all while overseeing a shop that embraced an adult's misty-eyed sense of yesteryear. Nora wasn't the type to reveal much, and it was only when a second glass found its way to them—courtesy of Nicholas, who quickly slipped back to his place by the bar with barely a word—did Nora finally speak her mind.

"Nicholas has asked me to move in with him," Nora said.

Cynthia of all people could understand. Moving out of Linden Corners meant a return to reality, to the real world, and why would anyone want to do that when inside the borders of their little town spun a wondrous, time-worn windmill whose sails reminded them that while some people only managed to dream their dreams, those who lived here got to live them.

CHAPTER 9

TRINA

Word of the Secret of Linden Corners Christmas celebration and its game of Secret Santa eventually made its way to the Solemn Nights, even if it took two days. Trina Winter had immersed herself in busywork to the point of making up jobs like straightening up the files and replacing the coffee-maker on the side cabinet, helping to distract her from the ups and downs of her frustrated patient, not to mention her own thoughts about a man named Brian Duncan, two men linked by the unlikely source of a windmill. She and Brian had spoken once since their date ended with one last kiss when he dropped her off at the motel, where they had said all the appropriate things about how nice a time they'd had over dinner, discussed plans to get together again, but ended the call with only a tentative agreement of "sometime in the coming weeks."

"Before my parents arrive," Brian had promised.

"See, look at that, spending the holiday with parents. More in common."

She wasn't sure why she'd said that, probably just a way to fill the silence.

After that, they'd ended the call, neither of them talking

about the stolen kisses up on the banks of the river, as if by not speaking of them they could pretend they hadn't actually happened. Suddenly Trina had conjured all this work that needed to be done around the Solemn Nights, and so it was only when Martha Martinson appeared in the door of the front office on Tuesday afternoon bearing two brown bags filled with lunch did Trina get pulled back into the world of Linden Corners.

"Have you put your name into the big Christmas hat yet?" Martha asked, setting the bags down on the counter.

"I'm sorry, what's that?"

"Surely you've heard about our village-wide Secret Santa game."

Trina blinked, her mind absorbing what she'd just heard. "Everyone?"

"Well, most everyone. That's the way we do things here in Linden Corners, population seven hundred plus, give or take a plus," she said. "In fact, I think we even convinced that grump Chuck Ackroyd to put his name into the hat, and if anyone in town could play Scrooge, it's him. Old Chet convinced him, telling him it was probably the only gift he'd likely receive this year. Mean, but perhaps truthful. So what about you, Trina?"

"Me? I hardly know anyone in town. To pick a random name and have to shop for them, I wouldn't even know what to get." She hesitated, pushing back her hair like she did when she was uncertain. "And I doubt Richie would partake either; I don't see that as being his cup of tea. Like daughter, like father."

"You leave Richie Ravens to me," Martha said.

"Let me guess: you've brought lunch over to bribe Richie."

"Martha's tuna salad never fails," she said. "How's he doing, anyway?"

Trina shrugged with indifference. "He's Richie, as enigmatic and stubborn as ever. Talks when he wants to, watches television the other times. See for yourself."

"That I'll do."

Martha barreled her way past the office counter, her sizable frame entering the apartment at the back. Trina followed, where she saw Richie dozing, his head back against the edge of the sofa, his left leg outstretched, the plaster cast no more colorful than it had been last week. That's how few visitors came to see her father—Mark had checked in a few times, sometimes Sara at his side, but otherwise, no one else. She recalled a time as a kid when she fell off her bicycle and broke her arm, and when she got back to school nearly every one of her classmates and teachers had signed the cast, turning the white plaster into a rainbow of get-well wishes. Kids tended to have large networks of friends, and Trina had to wonder what it was about adults that saw their worlds shrink. First Martha's comment about that Ackroyd guy, now Richie. Just how did a man like Richie Ravens end up a recluse, with so few friends, and seemingly nothing to his life beyond this motel and this sparse apartment? His choice, or life's?

"Look at you, lazy bum, sleeping like the sun ain't worth your time," Martha said while standing over him, her shadow more imposing with her hands set against her hips.

Richie's eyes flickered open, and when he saw who hovered above him, his mouth turned down in a grimace. "Well, look at what the cat dragged in," he said.

"Yeah, and I also brought you some lunch, so you better wake up."

"Speaking of cats," he remarked.

"Nah, that was our special, ran out early. Brought you tuna salad."

Trina saw a hesitant smile cross Richie's lips.

Martha pulled up a seat and plopped down with a thud, where she leaned in close to her friend. "So Trina's taking good care of you," she said, more statement than question. "Must be nice to have a caring daughter willing to spend her days tending to the likes of you."

Richie didn't have anything to say, but he did gaze over Trina's way. Martha followed his eyes there.

"Trina, if you want, I'll hang with Richie for a couple hours if you want to take a break."

"Oh, I should stay, really, there's actually a couple of midweek reservations and I'm not sure what time they're scheduled to arrive."

"Ah, how hard can that be? Take a credit card, hand over a key."

"Trina, it's okay, Martha and I got some catching up to do," Richie said, "Gotta tell her that it was her greasy French fries that caused my slip."

"Now, don't you go telling tales, Richie Ravens," she said with a laugh.

Trina supposed he was in good hands and so went to gather her purse and coat, hearing a bit of laughter coming from Richie's apartment, an actual sound of happiness that made Trina's heart tug. She'd been doing her best with a man she barely knew, asking questions about his life but really wanting to know more about his regrets. Had he missed out on raising her, or did he just accept it as his lot in life and move on, putting, like he said, failure behind him? She wondered if a man so used to independence even believed in regrets. Weren't they reserved for those people who missed out on their dreams, people who should have done more to ensure their coming true rather than sitting around and waiting for them to happen? Trina herself should know that answer; she'd run out of her own dreams long ago, her life now a series of missed opportunities.

Mark had said on Thanksgiving that life was better when you had something to look forward to, but she in turn knew she had a tendency to live in the moment, chasing nothing but empty tomorrows. Maybe she was more her father's daughter than she'd originally thought.

"Now, Martha Martinson, you know I wouldn't partake in such a thing."

Trina laughed. She was not someone who "partook" of things.

"The entire village is doing it," Martha said.

"And as I always remind you, the Solemn Nights is purposely outside the village limits."

"Richie Ravens, you've been an ornery one since you arrived here in Linden Corners."

"And I'll be an ornery one when I leave it."

Trina made her exit before she overheard too much, not wanting them to discover her and think she'd been eavesdropping. She wished that she'd left sooner and not heard his flippant remark about leaving, questioning whether there was any truth to it. He'd never said anything to her, and she had to wonder, did he have a plan, or was it just a shapeless idea that lived inside the back of his brain? And for that matter, if she wanted to examine the dark space between truth and speculation, just what was her exit strategy for Linden Corners? Richie's cast was expected to come off just a few days before Christmas, which would mean his physical therapy would begin shortly after the holiday. He'd get stronger, more mobile, his reliance on help—meaning Trina—less with each passing day. Then it was back to his old life, fending for himself.

And back to her old life too.

"Oh joy," Trina said to no one.

In her mind flashed an image of Brian Duncan, he pulling her up the last few feet to the top of the hill, and she remembered how his touch felt, his arms locked around her as they shared a kiss. While that initial kiss had been her doing, she had worried that she'd made the wrong move and brought ruin to their night. When he kissed her back, she let her fears take to the cool wind. The moment was all that mattered.

And at this very moment, she had no idea where she was going.

The idea of the windmill sparked her mind, because she had been wondering why not one man, but two, had a certain fascination for something most would consider a relic. Should she head over there and experience it for herself, or was it the kind of place where only an invitation produced its magical effect?

A few minutes later, Trina was still uncertain where she was going. Being relieved of her duties was unexpected, and she thought about hopping in her car, traveling to get her nails done, or to go shopping . . . anything to distract her mind. Just like the busywork she'd created at the motel had. But the day was so beautiful, with a sun-drenched blue sky painted with fluffs of white clouds floating high above her. If Christmas was just three weeks away, you wouldn't guess it from the breath of fresh air Mother Nature was swirling down on this little town. In a way, Trina Winter felt gypped by the weather because, despite her ironic name, she'd never really experienced a blast of Northeast winter, where snow and ice buried the area in deep drifts and created slippery sidewalks. She'd missed out on times when you sought refuge from the cold with blazing fires and hot toddies, that warm someone to share them with. Wasn't that how Christmas was supposed to look up here? Here she was in a town that embraced Christmas, its heart worn on Santa's sleeve, and Trina had to be cooped up with a Scrooge.

Forget her nails or a new pair of slacks, Trina once again found herself walking toward Linden Corners, determined footsteps taking her fast into the small downtown area. As a yellow school bus passed her, she realized the day was winding down and even with the lack of snow on the ground, it was still December and that meant darkness would creep up on her quickly. She found her feet had directed her to the front steps of A Doll's Attic, Nora Connors' store, and without hesitation she opened the door to the jangle of bells.

"Hello?" she asked, not finding anyone behind the counter.

"In the back, be right out," she heard, only to see Nora emerge from the stacks toward the rear of the store moments later. She wiped away flecks of dust, which no doubt came with a job where the past came back to life. She smiled when she saw who her customer was. "Trina, what a nice surprise."

"Thanks, good to see you too," she said, gazing around at the organized clutter of the consignment shop. "I was just passing through, so I thought I'd finally check out your store."

"Feel free to look around. Is there anything in particular you're looking for?"

Trina was silent a moment as she saw a shelf of games she remembered playing with her older stepbrothers. She couldn't imagine ever wanting to roll those dice again, with those competitive boys or with anyone else for that matter. What was the point? You couldn't recapture the moment or the feeling of closeness; it was all just manufactured nostalgia. But she supposed it was best to keep her mouth shut. Her philosophy didn't exactly jibe with Nora's business model.

"Oh, no, just thinking about Christmas," she offered. "Been a long time since I've bought Richie a gift and I'm fresh out of ideas."

"What does he like?" Nora asked.

"Close your eyes, what do you see?"

"Ah," Nora said with a nod. "For the man who has nothing."

"And proud of it."

"Have the two of you put your names into the Secret Santa exchange?"

"No, and I don't see us participating," she said. "It's not Richie's bag, so to speak, and I guess it's not mine either. What about you? Your cup of tea?"

"When your unstoppable mother is one of the organizers and you have a thirteen-year-old child who counts his gifts, you go with the flow," Nora said. "Otherwise . . ."

"I thought I sensed a kindred spirit."

"Speaking of tea, I was about to make some. Care to join me?"

"No, really, I was just stopping in mostly to say hello and . . ."

"And over tea you can tell me about your date with Brian."

Trina allowed a small smile to let Nora know she saw right through her friendly offer. "Then definitely no tea."

"We're only looking out for our friend, Trina. We don't mean to be . . . pushy."

Both women were saved from further posturing by the opening of the door, the jangle of bells announcing a shift in the air. Trina spun around to see who had spared her further grilling, saw a young girl bounce inside.

"Hi, Nora."

"What a surprise! Hi, Janey. What are you doing here? . . . Are you alone?"

"A bunch of us were playing over at the gazebo after school, but I needed to see you."

Trina felt her heart lurch, and her eyes darted nervously

Nora's way. She knew the name and now she had a face to go along with it. This little girl was clearly Brian's daughter—who else went by such a name?—whom Brian had spent so much of their dinner talking about, almost to the point that Trina had thought she could imagine her. But here she was in the flesh, and not even Brian's effusive description matched the energy coming off the girl standing before her.

"Sorry to interrupt, Nora, but I need your help."

"What about your Dad?" Nora asked.

"He can't know."

"Oh, sounds like our game of Secret Santa has inspired you."

"Sort of."

"And Cynthia can't help either?"

"Definitely not. See, I need to order something, and . . ."

Just then, Trina cleared her throat, not meaning to cause a break in their conversation but also not wanting to intrude on whatever secret business Janey had. "Why don't I leave you two to your very important business? Nora, thank you for the offer of tea . . . another time."

"Wait, don't you want to . . ."

But Trina was already halfway out the door, breathing more easily once she'd returned to the outdoors. She could imagine both of them staring after her, perhaps lulled back into business by the ringing of those annoying bells again. Trina knew she'd acted in haste, and not at all like a mature woman, but meeting Brian's daughter . . . she wasn't ready for that, and even so, like the windmill itself, if Brian wanted her and Janey to know each other, it was best arranged through him. Imagine poor Janey realizing the woman in the store was the woman with whom Brian had gone on his date. She hoped Nora had the good sense to keep quiet.

As she continued down the street, she noticed the light

had begun to fade in the sky, and she thought perhaps it was best to return to the motel. Having not accomplished what she'd set out to do, she forged onward, and eventually she made her way to the Linden Corners Memorial Park, where she saw a dozen or so kids running around, those two golden retrievers from Marla and Darla's store chasing after them with enthusiasm. Underneath the gabled roof of the gazebo, she saw the Christmas hat Martha had referred to, and watching over it were two older women.

"Hello, have you come to put your name in the hat?" one of them asked.

"For my father I was going to, yes," Trina confessed.

"But not for yourself?" the other asked. "Every young woman loves gifts."

Trina politely acknowledged them. "It's better to give than receive," she said.

"Well, dear, I'm Gerta Connors; this here is Elsie Masters."

"Nice to meet you. I'm Trina . . ."

"Why, of course," the woman named Elsie said. "You're Richie's daughter. I should have known."

Trina wasn't sure how to receive that comment. "Uh, yes, I am," she said. "I'd like to put his name in."

Elsie eyed her warily. "Does he know you're doing that?"

"Of course," Trina said. "He'd do it himself, but with his leg wrapped in a cast . . ."

"Elsie Masters, leave the poor woman alone; let her enact her own bit of holiday cheer," Gerta stated. She handed Trina a piece of paper and told her to write Richie's name on the front, then fold it up and drop it into the hat. About to do as instructed, Trina hesitated, wondering if she was doing the right thing. Would Richie be mad at her, or did he secretly wish for inclusion in his home's new twist on an old tradition? Only one way to find out, she surmised, and so she scribbled his name before changing her mind and dropped it deep into the warm confines of the red hat. She noticed that the words LINDEN CORNERS had been written across the white border in gold glitter so that it resembled the stocking she'd had as a child.

Perhaps it was that conjured memory, or maybe she just figured if Richie was forced to partake, so was she. She asked for a second piece of paper and this time she wrote down her own name. "In for a penny, in for a pound," she said, and then stuffed the second slip inside. She felt it drift from her fingers toward the bottom of the hat, secure, unable to be taken back.

"Thank you, ladies."

"Welcome to Linden Corners, Trina. I'm sure Richie is pleased to have you here," Gerta said. "Be sure to show up for the drawing this coming Sunday afternoon at three, and if you can, it would be nice if you brought your father along. I know he's been cooped up for a few weeks, might do him well to get out in the world."

Trina allowed another smile, realizing how genuine Gerta sounded.

"I'll see you then," she said, and then started away.

Though she hadn't voiced it, she had ascertained that Gerta was Nora's mother, and so no doubt the kind old woman also knew about her date with Brian, and she wanted to escape before it occurred to the kind woman to ask about it. She'd also heard the name Elsie and knew she was a bit of a town gossip; maybe that was why she thought she should have known Trina, and her not knowing it said more about her network than it did about Trina. The world of Linden Corners was closing in on her. Everywhere she went she was reminded of Brian Duncan. First a surprise run-in with his daughter, to whom she'd narrowly escaped an awkward introduction. Then only to turn around and be in the rosy glow of sweet Gerta Connors, whom she knew had been George Connors' wife and good friend to Brian and Janey, and before them, to Annie Sullivan.

One thing Trina had promised herself in agreeing to come care for her father, and that was not to get involved with the locals. And look at her now, running from people and confrontation both physically and emotionally all because she'd stupidly agreed to a date. A date that had ended with a kiss. What had she been thinking? Her life in Linden Corners was just a passing fad, a stopgap until she could figure out her next step. Richie's accident, not something she would wish on him, had nonetheless come at an opportune moment in her life.

A quick check of her watch indicated it was fast closing in on four o'clock, which meant not only was it getting darker, but it was time for Brian to make his way to the tavern for the night. She beat a hasty retreat from Memorial Park and past George's Tavern; the lights were still off and Brian's truck was not to be found in the parking lot. Good, she'd managed to get on her side of town before he arrived, and with a strong determination continuing to force her feet back toward the motel, she saw from across the street young Janey Sullivan come out of A Doll's Attic. Trina looked away as the girl began skipping down the sidewalk, waving her arms wildly in the air, and that's when she heard the rumble of the engine.

Brian's truck had arrived at the tavern, and with it of course was Brian. Trina watched as the young girl paused, looked both ways, and then dashed across the street, calling out "Dad, Dad." Then she leaped into his arms and he twirled her around as though she were the living embodiment of the town's landmark windmill.

"What do you say we toss our names into the big old hat Gerta's got," he said.

She laughed aloud and said, "I've already done it, Dad."

"Yours and mine?" he asked.

"Who else would it be?" she said.

A pang of regret struck Trina.

Here was Brian Duncan, not Janey's biological parent but happy to be called Dad. How natural the two of them seemed with each other, and for a moment Trina pondered the twist of fate that had brought them together. On the other side of the parental spectrum, fate had played another cruel hand, as Trina had known her father all her life but had lost or been denied their connection. She tried the word *Dad* on her lips, but it wouldn't emerge and her regret sank deeper inside her. She retreated again into the darkness of the falling day and away from the happy scene unfolding before her. She hoped Brian hadn't seen her.

She might not be ready for a second date, after all.

Except she wondered, all the way in the back of her mind, why that scene between father and daughter had struck such an unsettling nerve with her. Was it something she'd missed out on, or was it something she wanted?

CHAPTER 10

BRIAN

Time plays with the calendar, life moves when you don't realize it. Suddenly what you looked forward to was part of the past. So it was on this Friday, Brian Duncan wasn't anxious to get home, because to do so would mean the clock had turned past midnight and the next day's sun loomed ever closer, and with it would come the long-awaited arrival of Kevin and Didi Duncan to the land of the windmill. So the one night of the year Brian was willing to wait out his last customer to the bitter end, even if it meant staying until one, two, three o'clock in the morning, at eleven thirty the usually reliable Chet Hardesty was knocking back his last beer and announcing it was time to get home to the missus. Once he was gone, Brian would have the bar to himself.

"You never talk about your wife, Chet."

"Right as rain, Brian, and the wife never asks where I'm going, even if she knows," he replied. "Makes for a happy relationship, one that's kept us going on forty-six years now. Kids are grown and moved out, she likes to get up with the sun, while I've always been the night owl of our day-night romance. Now that I'm not working, I can stay up as late as I like."

"Then why are you leaving so early tonight?"

"We've got some holiday plans tomorrow, visiting Hester's sister in East Syracuse."

"Ah, gotcha. Family's important, Chet."

"So the good folks in this humble town of ours say. We'll be back on Sunday in plenty of time for the name drawing. I trust we'll see you there."

"Like Janey would let me miss that," he said.

"Well, you get on home to that little girl of yours, close up early."

That was the last thing Brian wanted to do, and besides, it wasn't like Janey would be there to greet him. First of all, she should be asleep at this hour, and second of all and perhaps more important, she wasn't staying at the farmhouse tonight. With all they had scheduled tomorrow, Brian had asked Cynthia and Bradley to take Janey for the night, and of course they'd agreed almost as quickly as Janey had. That's how it worked with them. He had to make sure she was comfortable with the arrangement, and if not, he made adjustments. With the Knights leaving town, the time Janey could spend with them was dwindling, so why not make the most of it?

This left Brian with a rare case of empty-nest syndrome, and while he knew he should take advantage of it, he'd never enjoyed having the farmhouse to himself. Like everything about his life in Linden Corners, the house was inherited, and when the darkness swirled around him, he felt like an imposter in his own home. The farmhouse had originally been owned by Thomas Van Diver's family, who'd sold it in the 1940s to the Sullivans. Now they were gone from Linden Corners, leaving the property and the windmill Brian's by tragic default. The tavern had belonged to George and had been in the Connors family for decades, and it was after his passing that Brian was first given the job of overseeing the business before being gifted the deed to the building by Gerta. And last, but certainly not least, there was Janey herself, whom he couldn't have even dreamed of ever being a part of his life, and now look at her: she was his life. But she wasn't really his.

The special charms of Linden Corners had done so much for Brian in the wake of the upheaval of his previous life, and now he realized it was his turn to impart its brand of magic to people who unsuspectingly were making their way here. Yes, tomorrow was at last the fifteenth of December, and Kevin and Didi Duncan, his parents, would soon be among the amiable folks celebrating Christmas within their borders, and inside the warmth of the farmhouse, traditions old and new would be acknowledged. It was going to be a strange clash of cultures, and as much as Brian was looking forward to seeing his dream of showing them the windmill come to fruition, he felt a knot in his stomach. As Janey had said, dreams existed where we wanted them, with reality bringing its own harsh wake-up call.

Earlier in the week he'd expected his mother to phone and say there'd been a change in plans. She had called, but only to confirm their arrival date of Saturday. The call had lasted not two minutes, and again he'd spoken only to his mother. Not that his father liked to talk on the phone normally, but this broken connection was beyond odd. He supposed he'd have to wait for Saturday for answers, now just minutes away according to the clock.

Midnight near, Brian realized he'd been daydreaming. But even while he was lost in his reverie, no new customers had come into the tavern.

He crossed the creaky wood floor, guessing he might as well turn the lock, clean up, and head home. As he approached the door, he gazed through the panes of glass to see if a customer was turning into the lot, headlights a signal that business was coming his way. No such lights were visible, and so he did what he'd come over to do: he flipped the bolt, heard its echo in the quiet. He thought back to that night before Thanksgiving when, after he'd closed, a surprise customer had appeared in the form of Trina Winter. He hadn't known her then, and he still didn't know her well, despite the night out with her last week.

In a way, he kind of hoped she'd show up tonight.

He hadn't seen her recently, and they hadn't spoken other than the day after their kiss.

Tentative plans were discussed, none made, and neither of them followed up. Was that an indication of disinterest on her part—on his?—or the sign of busy lives made crazier by the onslaught of the holidays? Truth of the matter was, Brian was confused, since he and Trina had agreed to go out if only to quiet their pushy friends, only to end up on a romantic stroll along the banks of the Hudson. A stroll that had ended with kisses that tasted of promise. And today, a week later, her kiss had dissipated like sand during a storm.

Brian flicked off the overhead lights, and the dim glow from the bar guided his way as he cleaned up. Unplug the jukebox, gather up empty pretzel bowls, and retrieve Chet's pint glass. Not in the mood to wipe down the bar or mop the floor, Brian hefted himself atop the bar, his legs dangling over the edge. From his perch, he gazed out over the room at the empty tables, his senses heightened. He felt he could hear every creak in the floor, every whisper of wind as it hit the building's side. As his eyes darted about, they settled on a box sticking out from underneath the pool table.

"What the heck?" he asked, jumping off the bar.

Before pulling it out from its hiding spot, he considered how carefully it had been set. Not quite hidden, as though whoever had placed it there had known just what he or she was doing. He took hold of it and then set it on the green felt of the table. Just like the first gift he'd received, it was a simple brown box, sealed with thick tape. He slid a finger beneath the tape and the flaps popped up. From inside he withdrew another gift, this one wrapped in shiny red paper. He possessed a gold one, a blue one, and now this third red one; the silver-colored ribbon was the same as on the others too, as was the message on the card.

DO NOT OPEN UNTIL CHRISTMAS

"This is getting ridiculous," he said aloud. His voice echoed, almost as though others were here and agreed with him. He thought about who might have placed the box under the pool table at some point tonight, running through the faces of the customers who'd stopped in. He'd still been thinking Gerta was the guilty party, yet he hadn't seen her tonight, nor had she given any indication—not a sly smile or a dropped hint—that she was behind this. Poker was not her game, so he eliminated her as a suspect. It could be Nora, but why? They were friends, that was all, so if this was some kind of romantic overture, he doubted Nicholas Casey would have approved of Nora's holiday flirting. Was it Cynthia's doing, guilt over leaving driving her? If so, why was she planning the village-wide Secret Santa?

He took a step back, eyes narrowing as he examined the gift, trying to decide if all three were the same size. He thought yes, and then he thought maybe he should shake it, glean a clue from whatever sound it made. But what if it was precious, irreplaceable? Last thing he wanted was to damage what was inside. But whoever his Secret Santa was, he or she hadn't written *fragile*. At last, Brian decided he'd enough of these games; he was going to open it. He went for the flap on the side, where a few strips of tape had sealed it closed.

Then he paused.

Should he really open it? And if he opened this one, what of the other two? For certain the gifts were linked, and to open one would spoil the whole game. Just then, Brian realized exactly what he was going to do. With the bar closed, Janey with Cynthia for the night, there was only one destination in mind: the windmill. By the time he could drive over and make the trek across the darkened field, he would have made up his mind about whether to store this gift with the others and abide by the rules of his mysterious friend, or end the mystery by opening all three. He could talk with Annie, ask her advice, and not just about the gifts he'd received but also about those Janey would be expecting.

With a renewed spring in his step, Brian ran behind the bar and reached for his keys and coat, flicking off the lights at the last second. As he turned to leave, that was when he saw the shadowy face emerge from behind the front door. He held his breath for a moment before he realized who it was, and then he allowed his smile to grow. He turned the lock and opened the door, and along with her amused grin came a cool blast of wind.

"Don't you ever stay open late?" Trina asked.

"Don't you ever call first?"

She shivered while standing on the porch, her arms hugging her. "Are you going to let me in or watch me freeze to death? In case you didn't know, it's gotten cold outside."

"Winter's first blast, just like you've been asking for. See, dreams do come true in Linden Corners," he said.

"Brian?" she said, her tone losing its playfulness.

"Sorry, yes, do come in, Ms. Winter."

"Funny boy," she said, entering the bar with a soft tap of her hand against his cheek.

Smiling widely, he closed the door behind her and turned the lock again, this time unsure why. While it was true he hadn't wanted to close, and only the lack of customers forced his hand, now he was loath for anyone else to show up. Now that she was here, it was possible others might have some last-minute thirsts that needed satisfying. Should he turn the lights back on, or was the mood ideal for their sudden rendezvous? He opted for the soft lights over the bar and kept the lock as it was, securing just the two of them inside, safe from the chilly elements. Making his way back around the bar, he turned to her as she settled on the same bar stool she used her first night.

"Déjà vu?" he asked.

"Nah, nothing French," she said. "How about a scotch?"

He liked the way she played with words. Heck, he just liked having company, someone to talk to, and the fact that it was Trina feeding those needs . . . even better. Reaching to the top shelf for the bottle of Dewar's, he retrieved a glass and poured her a healthy amount. He set the bottle on the bar for easy access. She took a sip, let out a sigh of relief.

"Just what I needed."

"Tough day?"

"Tough . . . few weeks. Want to know something, Brian?"

"What's that?"

"I snuck out tonight, like a delinquent teenager."

"And why is that?"

"Because Richie Ravens is an infuriating man."

"And you came here because I'm less infuriating?"

"No, because you run a bar."

"Ah, so you're seeking refuge in a bottle?"

"The drink I needed, yes, but it was the company I wanted."

Brian felt himself flush, glad the lights were dim. "Sorry, it's been a busy week . . ."

"Brian, I'm not looking for excuses. Whatever happens . . . it happens."

"Is that your life's philosophy?"

"It is . . . now."

Brian nodded. Clearly something was bothering her. "Want to tell me about it?"

"About what—me, or Richie?"

"Either, both, neither."

"Well, if I'm going to discuss either of those first two, you may want to pour yourself a glass. And no, I don't want to hear your protests, Brian Duncan. Have a drink, it won't kill you, and besides, I hate drinking alone."

"You didn't seem to mind the other night."

"Which night?"

Even though Brian ran a bar, he didn't want to encourage her. "Trina, we don't have to stay here. We can go for a walk, you can talk . . ."

"Desperate times, desperate measures. Pour, Windmill Man. And don't forget yourself."

He reluctantly smiled while he poured her refill, two fingers' worth, which he hoped satisfied her. But what would he have? With the bar separating them, he took a step back and gazed at the varied glasses on his shelves. Wine, beer, cocktails of varying sizes and shapes, and with nearly three years' bartending under his belt now, he knew just which glass to grab for whatever the customer ordered, but now that he was faced with making a decision for himself, it wasn't the glass stopping him; it was his choice. He could have told her that he didn't submit to peer pressure but figured she wasn't in the mood for platitudes. He grabbed a pint glass, poured a Saranac lager, setting it before himself but not drinking from it. He stared at the amber liquid until his eyes blurred, the foamy top and hoppy scent like strangers. It was not unlike him and Trina, and while he had tasted both and had felt his heart zing at forgotten memories, he wasn't sure if there was enough attraction building inside him to take the next step. To her, or to the beer. His eyes flicked upward to hers.

"Cheers," she said, raising her glass.

Brian lifted the glass and let it clink against hers, and then set it against his lips. He took a small sip before setting it down. "Okay, Ms. Trina Winter, tell me your life story."

"What do you want to know?"

"What do you want to tell me?"

"Brian, we'll get nowhere if all we do is banter around questions," she said, spinning in her chair as she took another drink. He'd have to watch her alcohol intake; he wasn't sure if she had driven over, thinking it unlikely since she seemed to enjoy midnight walks. Which meant he might have to drive her home.

"What's that?" she asked, pointing to the gift on the pool table. "You're getting ready for Secret Santa already?"

"More like the other way around," Brian said.

"I thought names were going to be picked on Sunday."

He explained the strange gifts and how this had been going on since the night they'd met, and how the arrival of the second gift had inspired Cynthia to come up with a town-wide Secret Santa. "It was actually Janey who made the suggestion."

"Janey, she's adorable."

Brian had lifted his glass to take a drink, happy for the diversion. "You met her?"

"Not officially," she said. "She stopped by Nora's store the other day and I happened to be there."

"Janey was there, why?"

"From what I heard, a Christmas surprise," Trina said. "I didn't stay to find out what."

Brian had no idea why Janey would be turning to Nora for something. Unless it was her way to move beyond her dependency on Cynthia. Which just reinforced the idea that both of his friends had—that Janey needed a woman in her life. The questions was, did Brian too? He stole a look at Trina, busy knocking back her scotch.

"Barkeep, how about a refill?"

He paused, looked at her empty glass, his full one. She was up two to none. "Last one."

"Brian Duncan, you are too good to be true," she suddenly said.

"What's that supposed to mean?"

"Do you ever get tired of looking out for people?"

He shrugged. "Guess it's in my nature. The people of this town have been good to me, so I like to return the favor."

Ignoring the fresh pour sitting before her, Trina hopped off the stool and came around the bar. Brian wasn't sure what she was doing, but he didn't have long to wait to find out. Like the other night at the river's edge, she leaned in and kissed him, this time wrapping her arms around his neck and pulling him toward her. Her lips pressed deep against his before releasing them.

"Maybe it's time you do something for yourself, Brian Duncan."

He paused to find his voice. "I'm not sure what you mean."

"Yes, you do."

He blushed again, and this time the color went deep on his face. "Uh, you do realize that Mark and Sara live upstairs?"

She slid her hand into his and smiled. "Brian, you do realize I run a motel."

Whether her remark inspired him or perhaps just set fear afire inside him, Brian Duncan reached for his beer, and he drank.

* * *

Snow had begun to drift down onto Linden Corners in the last half hour, a heavy wet snow that was sticking to darkened roads and sidewalks. Conditions were deteriorating fast, making it less than ideal for walking and worse for driving, but Brian figured it was only a half mile to the Solemn Nights Motel and less than two miles the other way back to the farmhouse.

Inside the truck, the heat was blasting but he still felt a chill rip through him.

It wasn't the outside cold affecting him but a rushing mixture of fear, apprehension, and something he hadn't felt in too long, desire. As a result, he felt that every move he made, every word that popped into his mind, would just add to his nervousness. So he just stared forward, flicked on the wipers, and concentrated on turning out of the parking lot. He went left, driving toward the Solemn Nights.

Trina was at his side.

Neither said much of importance during the short ride, thankfully the arrival of winter's first storm of the season distracting them. Trina admitted that the sight of snowflakes as they caught the beam of headlights was what had been missing from her Linden Corners experience, and Brian stole a look sideways, seeing the wide smile on her face. She'd grown up in Florida, and so the classic image of Christmas was just that, an iconic portrait she'd seen only in pictures and television shows. Branches of the surrounding trees were quick to grab the falling flakes, almost as though they were craving them, holding them tight and asking where they had been all season. Nature spoke its own language, both outside among the trees and here, inside the confines of the cab, where two people silently anticipated the complex clutches of warmth.

Brian pulled into the parking lot of the motel, dousing the engine just outside the office. Turning off the headlights, he was blinded by the blinking, teasing neon of the VACANCY sign. Taking a quick survey of the lot, he saw only two other cars parked in front of doors.

"Number seven and number ten," she said, answering his question before he'd voiced it.

"Oh, uh, oh," he said.

Yeah, better to keep quiet.

She took hold of his hand again and squeezed it, and he felt the warm touch of her skin. With her key already out, he realized this was the point of no return. Should he make his excuses and return home? But return home to . . . what? An empty series of rooms? Or he could follow the intent of that key, giving entry into a new room, a new world. Hesitation finally losing out, he got out of the truck, watching around him as she quickly slid the key into the lock and turned the knob. The door swung open and she waited for him to step in first.

"See, now I get to invite you in," she said.

Brian had been inside the rooms at the Solemn Nights only once before, three years earlier, when he'd first come to Linden Corners. After just a few nights' staying here, he'd secured more permanent lodging at the apartment above the tavern, now rented out to Mark and Sara. In an odd twist of fate, Brian entered a building owned by his tenant's family. The room, he saw, was sparse, with the expected furnishings and little else that spoke of Trina's individuality. Hadn't she been here for a few weeks? It didn't look very cozy at all, not in a way that would make her feel like it was home.

"I spend most of my waking hours at Richie's apartment," she explained, again before he'd asked the question.

"Oh, uh, oh," he replied.

She slid up before him, wrapping her arms around his waist. "You're nervous."

"Trina, I haven't been with anyone since . . . since Annie."

She kissed him, and he returned the kiss. He enjoyed her touch, realizing it had been so long—too long—since he'd been in the arms of a woman. Sure, he had his friends and he had Janey, whose hugs filled his heart in other ways, but Trina was different. She was an enigma, one minute seemingly annoyed at the world, the next ready to tackle it. He wondered which one he was getting now. Gazing into her soft eyes, he detected someone else entirely, a hint of the person he'd met on the banks of the river. He recognized in her sweetness, softness, and a warm, welcoming light that drew him close to her.

"Someone once told me that you're not living unless you have something to look forward to," she said. "Looking back only causes pain, but living beyond today has its share of dangers too. No one knows how long they have on this earth, but yet so many still put off today thinking they'll wait for another time. Not me. I subscribe to living life in the here and now. It's a good place to be. Here is a good place to be, with you, Brian."

He took hold of her hand and led her to the bed. As he bent down, a flash of light flickered in his eye, momentarily distracting him. He noticed that an open slit in the curtains was allowing in the glow coming from the parking lot. Trina had seen it too, and she got up from the bed and peered out. Brian then heard the unmistakable sound of car doors opening, then closing.

Trina couldn't help but laugh. "I do believe I have some late-night arrivals."

"Hourly?"

"Not from the looks of them," she said with a laugh. "It's an older couple. Brian, I'm sorry, but Richie is asleep and this is why I'm staying here. Let me get them checked in and then I'll be right back. Fear not, I'll give them room nine, far away from us."

Trina grabbed her keys and made a fast exit, closing the door behind her. Brian sat down on the bed, stretching out his body, surprised at how comfortable the mattress was. As he stared up at the ceiling, he couldn't believe this scenario, nor could he have expected it. But had the stars not aligned on this night? Janey was taken care of, his customers had left him alone early, and his nosy friends had pushed him and Trina together, to the point where he accepted that they enjoyed each other's company. And now he was here in her bed, as if it was meant to be.

He thought it was also too soon.

The door opened a few minutes later and Trina returned, her face as white as a sheet.

"Something wrong?"

"Uh, Brian, are you expecting company?"

"Here, at the Solemn Nights . . . ?" he asked, confusion on his face. "I don't understand . . ."

"The people who just checked in—they gave their names as Kevin and Didi Duncan."

$\mathcal{I}$NTERLUDE

She felt the warm, soothing touch of the woman she had known her entire life, wishing never to have it pulled away from comforting her. Wishing time could somehow stand still and the two of them could remain as together now as they had been in a time people referred to as the past. She was only ten, so the concept of the past was strangely foreign to her, memories not yet buried in her mind, and instead lying so very close to her heart. Which was why when night fell and her eyes closed to the image of snow drifting down from the darkened sky, she grabbed tight hold of a frog with no name and wished she could see her. That was when her dreams began in earnest.

"Sweet dreams, my sweet," she heard, a fading echo in the room.

She snuggled deeper into the tangled mix of blankets, protected against the cold that had, almost without warning, swept down over the land of the windmill. Her worry over not having a white Christmas had been for naught, as a soft coating of snow began to cover her home. That didn't mean her other worries were placated. Christmas was fast approaching, and so much was changing, so much to get done. This year's celebration would mean saying good-bye to friends, and it meant welcoming new folks into *their pine-scented world of decorated trees and glittering tinsel, and not for the first time did the little girl begin to feel like a stranger in her own home.*

Even when she wasn't there. Like tonight.

An inner fear washed over her and she stirred in her sleep. Her dream had darkened further with the thought that her desired visitor wouldn't know where to find her. The frog she nearly strangled, her need for security, safety, deep. If she couldn't come see her tonight, she would cling to that which best represented her, the first gift given to the little girl. Tonight would have been the ideal time for a visit, and she began to speak softly in the darkness of the room.

"Mama, I'm not home, Mama. Do you know that? Can you see me here?"

The wind howled its answer, and that's when her sleepy eyes darted wide open, in time to see the willowy shape take form inside the room. A glow illuminated her face, wonder spreading wide over her features.

"It's time for you to join me again, Janey. There's another story for you to know."

"I'd follow you wherever," Janey replied.

But again such an unknown journey wasn't necessary, because, much like the first time, the windmill was their inevitable destination, and only the story would be different.

Janey felt like she was floating on air, carried beyond the confines of the Knights' home and toward the mighty windmill, and perhaps she was, since she saw no footprints in the fresh snow. The white blanket that had fallen from the sky in the last few hours remained as pure as when the clouds released it and gravity took hold.

Gravity had no such lock on her, and soon she was cresting the hill and through the thicket of woods that separated one property from another. She could hear the gentle gurgle of the stream and saw the stone bridge that enabled mortals to cross from one side of the bank to the other. At times, like when the snow melted and the season changed from cold to spring beauty, the stream would spill over and flood the land. It was one of the reasons for the building of the windmill, but practicality had not been the sole reason in the mind of its creator.

At last the little girl and the woman she called Mama emerged into the clearing, and the windmill loomed like a twirling giant on an empty landscape. The sails spun, slicing snowflakes that came into its path, the reconfigured flakes like confetti falling from the air. Janey, nearing the windmill, wondered why she wasn't cold. With her tongue she tasted the snow, and when it melted seconds later, she knew she was surrounded by a force of great warmth. That was because her small hand was connected to the spirit guide and she could feel the steady pulse of their bond, Annie's hair flowing behind her like wings able to keep them afloat.

"What story from the past are you going to tell me this time?" Janey asked.

"Why should it be a story from the past?" she asked.

"Isn't that where all stories come from, from experiences already lived?"

"Some stories are yet to be written," she said. "And others, well, their time is now."

"Mama, you never used to speak in riddles," she said.

"Where I live, all riddles have answers."

"Do you see Dad?"

"Which one?" asked the willowy spirit, and she would say no more.

The windmill awaited them, and suddenly Janey found herself standing before the door. It opened without assistance from her, and she stepped in. Darkness surrounded her, and she realized she was alone. Not a single light shone inside the old mill, and not outside either. Sudden worry washed over her. Why, with Christ-

mas ever so close, had Brian not done as he had the past two holiday seasons and adorned the windmill with its endless rows of lights?

Brightness called out to her from upstairs, that same glow she'd seen inside her room.

"Mama?"

"I'm here, Janey, always. But know that this is not a place for doubts, so you must leave them outside your dreams."

Janey knew this was a test of faith, not just of Annie, not of Brian, but of herself. Trust in yourself, *she thought, and moments later she was magically transported to the second level of the windmill, her eyes immediately glancing over at the closet, the door closed. Despite its being a place known for hiding Christmas gifts, temptation just a turn of the knob away, Janey knew not to look. This was another test, one of truth. So she turned her back to the door, and that's when she saw a flickering light coming from outside the window. A sail passed by, then a second, a third, a fourth, and with each revolution that beckoning light flickered more, drawing her to its flame.*

She saw a scene before a fireplace widening as fast as her eyes.

She knew the room; she recognized the photographs on the mantel and the red and white stockings that hung from it. This was her home, and it was magically decorated for Christmas. But which one? She had to wonder, expecting to see her mother and her father emerge from the shadows and enact another Christmas memory. But hadn't Annie said tonight wasn't a night for yesterday, and if not then, and if not tomorrow . . . then where was this scene supposed to be taking place? Time was making little sense to the little girl, and as was often the case, confusion set her nose scrunching.

"Mama . . . ?"

It wasn't Annie who answered, but Brian. He'd called out her name, or she thought he had. She peered deeper into the magical window.

"Janey, we're ready for the final touches," he said.

He wasn't speaking to her from inside the windmill, but rather from within the scene she saw through the window. A blurry image before her caused her to blink, and as she opened her eyes again she saw green tendrils come into focus. Branches of a tree, that's what they were, and she knew then it was their Christmas tree. But still time eluded her. Which Christmas was this? Who else was there? Just she and Brian, as it had been? Or . . . and then she saw them.

She knew them, the two figures who stood before the tree, admiring its beauty.

"That's Brian's parents," she said aloud.

But they weren't here yet, she thought. Then she remembered tomorrow . . . if time's laws still ruled in this dream-spun world, tomorrow they would arrive, and so this must be how the present Christmas would occur, Brian and his parents and Janey . . . wait, where was she? He'd called to her but she'd yet to appear.

From a square box that suddenly appeared in his hands, Brian withdrew an ornament of shiny blue glass with silver lettering on one side of it. She could not make out what it said, but she didn't need her eyes; her memory knew it spelled out his name. This was Brian's precious name ball, a family heirloom, and she watched as he hung it securely on a high branch. His mother, dressed in a cardigan sweater, with a string of pearls around her neck, took hold of another of the ornaments, hers golden in color and the name "Didi" written across it. She chose a branch and seemed very satisfied with it. At last came Brian's father, a man seemingly as large as the tree itself. He pulled out a red ball that read "Kevin," and it reflected off the flame in the fireplace. The glare caught Janey's eye and she blinked away glittering spots and missed where he placed it; either that or her gaze didn't reach that high. When she refocused, she saw the three of them each taking a turn with another ball, this one blue, and as Brian's mother placed it on the branch nearest hers, she clutched at her pearls and allowed her husband to embrace her.

"Remember Philip," she said.

"So many years since our ornaments have hung together on one tree," his father said.

"The Duncan family, together."

"Almost," Brian added.

Yes, almost, Janey thought, nearly screaming those words inside her mind. Me, I'm not there, even though you called out for me. Why hadn't she joined them, and where was her name ornament? If this was indeed the Christmas of now, where was Janey Sullivan and where were last year's gifts that she would hang on the tree? Ornaments that sealed two families as one?

"Mama . . . Mama, where am I?"

The scene before her faded like smoke, and the windmill again went dark.

All she felt was the warmth of her mother's hand, even though she could not see it.

Early dawn broke, the sun still hidden behind clouds. Snow still fell and cold began to creep in through the cracks of the old farmhouse. The little girl stirred, opened her eyes. The room was unfamiliar to her, and for a moment she felt fear strike within her heart. Fallen to the floor was her purple frog, a dust bunny on one of its arms. She scooped him up and brushed at him, then returned him to her grip.

She was glad to see the light of morning, no matter how dim.

The Knights' house was silent; not even Jake's morning wail had begun.

Pulling back the covers, Janey padded her way to the window. Snow was everywhere, on the tree branches and all across the wide stretch of land. No school today, she thought, and then remembered it was Saturday. And not just any Saturday, but Green's

Tree Farm Saturday, where she and Brian would go to chop down the tree that would make their home glow for the season. They would take it home and they would decorate it and they would adorn its thick branches with the ornaments that made their past two Christmases so special.

Just she and Brian, like it was supposed to be.

Except that wasn't how this Christmas would unfold. She'd seen it, maybe in her dreams or maybe not; maybe it was as real as the snow that blanketed the region. A blast of wind blew by, rattling the old house. She shivered and hid back under the blankets, hiding even her eyes from the light of the new day. Sometimes only the chill could embrace your heart, no matter the warmth you desired. Sometimes not even purple frogs that conjured memories of old could save you. Sometimes the notion of tomorrow represented your only escape, and whether you ran to it or hid from its unknown promises decided the wonders that awaited your life.

PART 2

THE DUNCAN FAMILY

CHAPTER 11

BRIAN

Brian Duncan learned two things about his mother that Saturday morning, the first of which was how skilled she was at deception, the second her powers of observation. The first he discovered when Didi Duncan phoned at ten o'clock that morning and announced that she and his father had just seen their first mile marker for Linden Corners, "only five miles away, Brian," she said without a trace of guile to her voice, and the other he didn't ascertain until after they'd pulled into the driveway and he saw the way his mother studied the battered old truck they had parked beside.

He didn't say anything about her fib, nor did he offer why his truck might have been in front of a motel room past midnight, not that she even asked about it. No matter, the truck had not remained there for long, not after the abrupt and surprising arrival of his weary parents to the Solemn Nights Motel had killed the mood. Partly reluctant, partly relieved, Brian Duncan had extended his apologies to an understanding Trina before sneaking off under cover of the snowy night. Now morning had arrived and so had his long-awaited reunion with his parents, and it was going as expected; his mother's cool reserve might have breathed a fresh sheen of ice over the freshly fallen drifts of snow. It was almost like an understanding quickly existed between them—she knew what he'd been doing there and he knew what she'd done and didn't we both get along so much better when we buried our suspicions?

"Hello, Brian, dear," his mother said, embracing him as he stepped out onto the porch.

"Hi, Mom," he replied as they parted, as expected, quickly.

"Look at you, son, lord of the country manor," said his father as he took in the spread of land in which the farmhouse stood. His father, usually so larger than life, with a booming voice, seemed reduced somehow, though it could have been because in Linden Corners all seemed to be done on a smaller scale. He was thinner, Brian thought, or maybe that was a result of seeing him in something other his usual business attire. And while he wore no tie and his jeans were loose, his mother's signature pearls hung around her collared neck, tightly strung, not unlike the woman who wore them.

"The rural, rustic version, but yeah, that's me. Welcome, Dad."

Brian accepted a surprising, warm embrace from his father, recalling that Kevin Duncan was known mostly as a handshaker. But as father and son reunited, Brian kept his eyes focused on his mother as she gazed over the property, her narrowed eyes returning to the old truck. He was thankful that the snow had continued to fall last night, leaving the hood of the vehicle partially unrecognizable.

"Where is that young cherub of yours?" Kevin asked with a clap of his hands. "I thought for sure she'd be first out that door and running a blue streak fast as her little legs could take her. Straight into my arms. Ha ha."

"Oh, Janey stayed overnight at Cynthia's," Brian offered, carefully watching his mother's coiled expression as he revealed he'd not needed to be home last night. Further evidence for his snooping mother. "And she's not so little. She's grown a lot in two years."

"Has it been two years? My, how time flies."

"Yes, girls do grow up faster than boys," Didi added. "Physically and emotionally too."

"Is that supposed to mean something, Mom?"

"Oh, Brian, don't go looking for messages where there are none. I'm just observing that it's best that a girl of Janey's age have a strong woman's influence in her life. From what you've told me about Cynthia, she's the closest the poor girl has to a mother. It's important they retain that bond."

Brian decided now was hardly the time to discuss the Knights' upcoming departure from Linden Corners and their lives. Instead he changed the subject by suggesting they come inside for a cup of hot coffee. Winter had definitely announced itself.

"I thought for sure you'd first want to show us that charming windmill," Didi said. "We must have missed it on our drive in. Brian, you said it was on the side of the road as you came into town. I hardly think we would have missed such a sight, if as you say . . ."

"It's everything I've said it is, and more. Trust me, you can't not see the windmill," Brian said, obvious pride filling his voice. "But we have to wait for Janey to return home; otherwise, I'll never hear the end of it."

"Dear, you still haven't learned much about raising children," she said, a comment that to her was a throwaway one, but to Brian was a cut right through his heart. "You don't let them control the flow of events. Have a plan, stick with it."

"Didi, don't start with the boy . . ."

As amused as Brian was by his father's description of his son, what happened next surprised him more, and it made him wonder less what was wrong with his father and more what was wrong with his mother. Because Didi Duncan just capitulated to her husband's request without further argument, saying, "I suppose you're right, Kevin, all in good time. We're here to relax, after all, and enjoy the holiday. Now, I suggest we get inside where hopefully it's toasty warm and take Brian up on his offer of coffee. Oh, Brian, do you have tea? No caffeine?"

"Uh, sure," he said, growing uncertainty leading the way.

He led them down the snow-covered walkway, apologizing for not having had a chance to shovel a clear path yet. Once inside, he led them to the kitchen and offered them chairs at the round table in the center of the room, watching his parents' expressions as they took in the details of the country-style room. Red gingham curtains, simple wood furnishings, and of course on the wall the windmill clock that indicted only ten minutes had passed since he'd heard the crunch of their tires against gravel. Felt more like ten days already. Still, they offered up kind words about his home, gentle compliments about how homey it all felt. Brian nodded silently as he set about making tea.

"It's pretty much unchanged from when Annie ruled the kitchen."

"Still so sad what happened," Kevin said with a shake of his head.

Brian didn't want to go there, not now. "So, you must have gotten an early start if you're here, uh, so early," Brian said.

"We left Philadelphia yesterday," Kevin said, "drove up the turnpike and spent the day in Manhattan, saw the tree at Rockefeller Center . . ."

"You know, to put us in the holiday spirit," Didi said.

"We left after dinner, made our way up the Taconic, only to find ourselves in the midst of this unexpected snowstorm," he said. "At Didi's request, we found ourselves a roadside motel, not realizing just how close to Linden Corners we were."

Uh-oh, here we go, Brian thought.

"Yes, the Solemn Nights," Didi said. "Do you know it, Brian?"

He was trying to determine what she really knew and what she was guessing at. Had she seen him depart, the noise of his engine causing her to look out the window? No matter what she thought, he decided it was more fun to keep her guessing, watching her sly grin turn to a grimace as he said, "Of course, who in town doesn't know the Solemn Nights? It's the only place near Linden Corners to stay. As a point of fact, I stayed there when I first came to town. Looks like we're on similar paths. Next thing you'll tell me you had breakfast at the Five-O."

"I'm sorry, the what . . . ?" Kevin asked.

"Our local diner. You'll get there soon enough. Anyway, why don't I phone over to Cynthia's and get Janey back home? We've got a big day ahead of us."

"Oh, I hope not one too taxing," Didi said. "We need our rest."

"Didi, relax. We're here, and we're ready for the true Linden Corners experience. Just as Brian has been promising us all this time."

His mother's expression read differently.

Brian considered the string of evidence that was laid out before him, detecting a strange phenomenon occurring. His tireless mother had never needed a midday rest in her life; she wasn't wired that way. And as for his father, a nap in the afternoon, according to his philosophy, would mean a loss of potential earnings that would bring about a noticeable depreciation in his portfolio. At least, that's the way his father used to talk, today just nodding as if he was agreeing with his wife. Why did his father need a rest in the middle of the day, and worse, why was he so easily accepting of it? But Brian let it go; there would be endless stretches of days ahead of them and no doubt awkward silences for them to fill. For now, he wanted Janey at his side to greet her . . . her what? With all that had been going on, he hadn't given further thought to what Janey would call his parents, the idea having popped into his mind when he overheard her and Sara discussing it. Brian racked his brain to remember what she'd called them during the trip two years ago to Philadelphia for Thanksgiving, and while he came up empty, did those names even apply today? Back then he'd been Brian to her, and now he was Dad.

About to pick up the phone, he heard the front door open, and in walked Janey. She was not her usual boundless self, keeping her energy on reserve. Brian had to think her behavior was partly Cynthia's doing, who was thankfully coming in behind her. No doubt they'd both seen the additional car with the Pennsylvania plates in the driveway.

"Well, look at who decided to return home," Brian said.

His parents turned to see who it was, setting down cups of tea. Kevin's face lit up at the sight of Janey. His mother held her smile tight, not out of dislike or disapproval; it was just her way. It was probably how she'd greet Jesus if he magically appeared before her and turned her tea into fine wine.

"Janey, my dear, why, look at how big you've grown," Kevin said with a warm smile, rising from his chair. Two years ago Janey had charmed him so, and Brian supposed that glow either hadn't worn off or had been given fresh life from anticipation. Kevin held out his arms and Janey allowed herself to be wrapped into the embrace of the large man, Brian watching as she was nearly swallowed up. Maybe he'd been wrong about any changes in his father, since Janey was the one who had grown.

As the sweet reunion ended, Janey then turned to greet

Didi, who bent down and allowed Janey to peck her warmly on the cheek. "It's lovely to see you again, Jane, and I do find myself agreeing with my husband. You have grown a foot, it seems, if you've grown an inch."

"Well, I sure grew more than an inch," Janey pronounced.

"There you go," Didi said.

She'd actually grown six inches, but the compliment still made Janey beam, the smile conjured despite the anxious fact that Didi had referred to her as Jane. His mother had detested the singsong nature of the childish name when first she'd heard it, and clearly her opinion remained the same. *Oh, this ought to be fun,* Brian thought, *two weeks with all of them suffering identity issues.*

"Dad, why didn't you call and tell me your parents were here?"

"Don't blame him. We just got here and only now settled in for some tea," Kevin said.

Cynthia had been hovering by the doorframe while Janey enjoyed her reunion, and only now did she step forward, her hand outstretched. "Mr. and Mrs. Duncan . . ."

"Sorry, that's my bad," Brian said, assuming control of the introductions. "Kevin and Didi Duncan, this is Cynthia Knight, our neighbor and best friend, my confidante and most of all Janey's savior. And oh, I don't know, she's lots of other things."

Cynthia blushed over the string of compliments he'd tied together, waving them off with a sheepish smile. "Mr. and Mrs. Duncan, you've raised a very kind son," she said.

"Well, Cynthia, we've heard a lot about you, and we certainly do thank you for all you've done for Brian," Didi said. "And please, call me Didi. And he's Kevin."

Brian couldn't help but notice she hadn't offered the same option to Janey.

Janey had called them "his parents."

He'd have to nip this one in the bud, once he settled on how best to approach the topic.

"Are you ready for a big day?" Janey asked.

"We keep hearing about plans but haven't heard anything specific," Kevin said.

"Welcome to life with Janey. She'll keep you on your toes," Brian explained.

"You'll need to keep your toes all bundled up," Janey said, her smooth transition catching his mother's attention.

"And why is that, dear?"

"Because we're going into the woods to cut down our Christmas tree!"

"That sounds like a marvelous plan," Kevin said.

"We'll talk about it," Didi countered, all too quickly.

Janey's face deflated at the thought of a possible change in plans, causing Brian to spring into action by suggesting Janey go upstairs and get ready while he helped get his parents settled. Maybe it was his tone, maybe it had been his mother's lack of enthusiasm, but Janey did as asked without complaint, and soon she disappeared upstairs. Cynthia too said her good-byes, telling them all to enjoy the day and saying she hoped to see them soon.

"I'll walk you out," Brian stated.

He followed her, neither of them speaking until they'd stepped out onto the front porch and out of earshot. Brian wrapped his arms around himself against the cold.

"Wow, you were right about your mother," she said.

"That's not why I'm cold," he said, and then grinned. "Sort of."

Cynthia laughed. "How long are they staying?"

He didn't want to think about it. "Long enough. How was Janey last night?"

"Last night fine, this morning . . . a bit odd."

"How so?"

"Quiet."

Brian nodded as though he'd been expecting to hear such an answer. He'd known Janey long enough to know her moods, and her silence was a classic Sullivan move. When something was bothering her, she handled it by clamming up. Annie had made him suffer so on several occasions, and apparently she'd handily passed the trait down to her daughter. Brian would have to pay careful attention and ensure that Janey felt as included as possible with all he'd planned for his parents' visit. For too long they'd passed quiet judgment on his newfound life in Linden Corners without knowing a thing about it other than his stories, which had grown fewer and fewer each time they spoke. It was clear they lived on different planes, and while they believed there was an indulgent fantasy to his life, the reality was far different. Caring for a ten-year-old girl who'd lost both her parents before she'd turned eight was not without its challenges. Yet here Kevin and Didi were to see it firsthand, and at last he would get to show them around, and they would experience for themselves why he'd fallen in love with a town that had fallen in love with him.

And it would begin today where it had all begun for him and for countless others who had happened upon the windmill along the roadside and been transformed by its majestic beauty, Annie not least among them. To the windmill they would go, and the sooner the better.

Magic happened there, and Brian had to hope its glow would rub off on the new visitors to Linden Corners. Skepticism ran rampant in the Duncan family, and even Brian had once been a cynic lost in the panic of New York. Until he'd taken a leap of faith and stumbled upon a town just a few hours away from his previous existence, a place that was worlds apart from anything he'd ever known before.

Would it have the same effect on those who had borne him?

"Mom, grab hold of my hand; the footing gets a little unsteady at times, and with all this snow on the ground it's even worse," Brian said.

"Which means I better take your hand, little lady," Kevin said to Janey, following behind.

"Oh, I know this path like the back of my hand," Janey announced.

"Well, then, I suppose you better hold on to mine," he said. "Because I don't."

Janey gazed up at the imposing man, trying to assess his motives before locking her small hand into his, hers nearly being swallowed up by his large fist. Then she started leading them along the snow-covered field, the two of them making fast progress, quickly overtaking Brian and a cautiously stepping Didi. Brian had to admire the sneaky way his father handled Janey, turning the tables so that she thought it was she helping him.

At just after eleven that same morning, Brian had suggested they take a quick visit to the windmill before leaving for Green's Tree Farm, and so they were now clomping through snow eight inches deep. It was slow going for the four of them. Kevin remarked on the breadth of land Brian owned and asked how much an acre in this region cost. Brian had to laugh inwardly, his concerns about his father's seeming change in priorities taking to the wind. He was the same old businessman he always was.

"Dad, I'm not selling if that's what you're thinking."

"Sectioning it, maybe tilling the land or building or . . . I don't know, something."

"I like it as it is," Brian said.

"Me too," Janey said, "because then I can run as far and as fast as I can."

As if on cue, she broke free of Kevin's hold, her feet fighting against the sinking depths of the snowdrifts. She forged her way to the crest of the field, turning back as though to prepare herself for liftoff. Here the land and horizon produced an illusion that made it appear the edge dropped into an endless void, but then upon approach you saw the land reappear, and with it rose the windmill, its sails stretching high into the bright blue sky as though they could paint patterns on the clouds.

He watched in delight as Janey ran for those same clouds. Oftentimes during the long, cold winter, when he and Janey craved precious Annie time, he plopped her on the toboggan and sent her on a thrilling ride down the steep hill, the sound of her joy filling the countryside all around them, and sometimes, as the sled exponentially picked up more speed, he zeroed in on the giant sails of the windmill, imagining them spinning faster and faster, as though the power of her descent won out over the wind and fueled their growing speed. Today she needed no such sled; her natural enthusiasm to show off the windmill was all she required.

"Jane, be careful . . . ," Didi said, calling out.

"Mom, she's fine. Just watch her go."

The three of them did, reaching the crest of the hill. That's when the windmill came into view, almost like the floating clouds suddenly dissipated, leaving in their misty wake the image of the wooden, shingled tower and its large, latticed sails, and that alone. The windmill itself never shied away from admiration, like it was a living, breathing ornament, sensing that first-time onlookers had arrived to gaze upon its majesty. It stood more proud as it dominated the landscape, leaving Brian feeling not unlike how the wayward Don Quixote must have felt upon discovering the giants he needed to conquer.

"My goodness, it's really real," Kevin said, surprise spread across his face.

"It is . . . magnificent indeed, Brian. How it must have captured your dreams at that confusing time in your life," Didi said, a gentle nod unable to stop her smile.

"You can see it from your room," he said. "Its sails will lull you to sleep."

For once Brian was transfixed by something other than the sight of the windmill, focused instead on his parents' expressive faces, and it was the newfound wonder that lit their eyes that caused his heart to swell. For the first time since he'd gotten word of their visit, Brian Duncan allowed himself to breathe a bit easier, until he felt the tension drain from his shoulders. Perhaps out in the real world doubters existed and cynics ruled, but here in Linden Corners, where an old windmill spun fantasies for all, once you witnessed its allure you couldn't help but be drawn in by its beauty and by its energy and by the wishes it enabled you to send out upon the whirling wind. If the sight of the gently turning windmill wasn't enough to capture his parents' closed hearts, no doubt the snapshot of a young girl dancing around its base and swirling to the rhythm of its moving sails would.

"Hi, Mama," Janey called out. "Look, we've brought you new friends to meet."

Brian urged his parents forward, Kevin eagerly taking the lead.

But like the wind, nothing lasts, and in blow new storms. Sudden concern crossed Didi's face when she said, "Is that healthy, Brian, Jane talking to her mother? I mean . . . it's not like the poor woman is here. Jane, dear," she called out, not bothering to wait for a reply from her son, "why don't you help me down the hill. I'd like to see the mill up close."

Janey hadn't heard the earlier remark, and so she reacted with a beaming smile, charging back up the hill as fast as she could. Brian, though, felt a stabbing inside him.

"Mom, if you're going to be here for a couple of weeks, her name is Janey."

"Nonsense, don't the people here have nicknames for you, Mr. Just Passing Through?"

He was surprised she knew such an odd detail about his life off the top of her head, causing him to wonder whom, if anyone, she had been talking to. Had they had breakfast at the Five-O after all and introduced themselves as his parents?

"Actually, some people now call me the Windmill Man."

"Different names, and as such, different bonds. To me her name is Jane, her birth name. Honestly, Brian, how do you expect her to enter college and the workforce saddled with such a childish name?" she asked, her tone indicating she didn't expect, or want, an answer. "I think I've arrived just in the nick of time; the poor girl needs a strong woman in her life."

Janey arrived, out of breath from her climb up the snowy hill, her presence putting an end to a conversation he didn't want. He let it go, just happy to see Janey's warmness to his parents, especially to his difficult mother. As the two women, young and old, clasped hands and Janey led Didi down the remainder of the hill and toward the shadow of the spinning sails, Brian turned to his father. They'd only been here two hours, but Brian's exasperation was evident.

Kevin just shrugged. "You know your mother."

True, but that wasn't ultimately what was bothering Brian—you couldn't suddenly turn an animal with spots into one with stripes. What struck him more was his mother's remark about arriving just in time. How long were they planning on staying?

Brian decided it was best not to question too much, because he'd learned one more thing about his mother this morning, and that was the fact that her cool exterior extended inward, and only by experiencing a winter in Linden Corners would her heart begin to melt. Magic did exist in this world and in other worlds they couldn't see or comprehend, worlds that allowed departed spirits to ride the passing clouds for a visit and to speak to them, even if they did so only through the whims of the wind and the gentle spins of an old windmill. His mother would learn.

After fifteen minutes during which Brian gave them a tour of not just the outside of the windmill but the inside as well, both his parents begging off climbing the winding iron staircase to the second floor, it was decided time was slipping away from them.

"We have a tree to chop down, and we better hurry before they're all gone," he said.

"Silly Brian, Mr. Green has plenty of trees."

"Then we don't want Travis getting the best one, right?"

"Who is Travis?" Didi asked.

"Nora's son, Gerta's grandson. It's kind of a tradition; we all go tree chopping together."

"Oh, we get to meet the famous Gerta Connors already?" his mother asked.

Brian wondered why his mother found that idea appealing.

He suggested they all remain at the windmill, as it would be easier for him to bring the truck around the roadside than to have them trek all the way back.

"Just give me a second. I have to retrieve the ax from the barn," he said.

"Don't forget the saw too, Dad," Janey said, turning her rolling eyes to Didi and Kevin. "He's not very good with the ax."

Brian watched his mother visibly blanch.

She didn't like the name Janey, and now he had a feeling she didn't like the name Dad.

Green's Tree Farm was located fifteen miles north of Linden Corners, a quick ride into the snow-capped mountains that bordered New York and Massachusetts. The makeshift Duncan family had all snuggled into the front cab of the truck, a small backseat able to fit Janey while the adults sat up front. As the truck rattled around on slippery country roads, Kevin suggested Brian upgrade soon before this "pile of junk" on wheels stranded them in the Berkshires, Didi nodding her head in agreement.

"Not a chance," Brian said.

"This was Mama's truck," Janey explained, and that said it all.

The inside of the cab grew quiet, but soon enough the turn for Green's Farm arrived, and Brian pulled in, the engine coughing once before going as silent as the rest of them. There were a few other cars in the lot and some folks wandering down the worn path, having already claimed their prize trees. Brian helped his mother out of the truck, and Janey took hold of Kevin's hand again, just as a rotund, red-faced man emerged from under a protective wooden structure.

"Aha, I remember you, young miss, though I must say, you're growing in leaps and bounds," the man said. "Pretty soon you'll be taller than my trees."

"I doubt that," Janey said. "Not even he's that tall."

She had indicated Kevin.

Brian laughed, shook the man's hand. "Merry Christmas, Mr. Green."

"Albert, please, for my regulars. What does this make, three years in a row?"

"You have a remarkable memory," Brian said.

"And you've brought some new friends," he said.

"My parents, Kevin and Didi Duncan."

"Aha," he said with a jovial smile, and then turning to Janey said, "Grandparents visiting for Christmas, huh? Nothing finer."

They were saved from responding by the sudden arrival of Gerta's car, Nora behind the wheel. As quickly as they parked, Travis was leaping out to join them, his grandmother and mother not far behind. Introductions were made, polite smiles and handshakes exchanged, and then as they all stood in a small circle waiting for a natural transition, Travis broke the moment.

"Janey, let's go find our trees," he said, taking off so fast Janey could barely keep up.

"Well, he's an eager boy," Didi said. "Nice Janey has someone around her age."

Nora smiled. "How I wish. Travis is nearing fourteen."

"And Janey is just fine the age she is," Brian added.

"Listen to the two you. If kids didn't grow older, the human race wouldn't get very far."

Gerta allowed herself a smile. "Can't even remember being a child."

"Enough chatter. It's cold out here; let's say we get started," Kevin said.

As they began the trek up the winding hill, Brian took hold of Gerta's arm, she reciprocating with a warm pat of support. She of all people knew how difficult his mother could be; he'd told her enough tales. But now she would get to witness it firsthand and know he'd not been exaggerating. "You'll be fine, Brian," she said.

Kevin, carrying the sheathed ax and pretending he was the embodiment of Paul Bunyan, was making fast strides since the snowy pathway had already been packed flat from other tree hunters, and he pulled ahead, determined to catch up to the kids, Didi issuing forth a warning to "be careful." He waved away her concerns, which amused Nora, and soon she was at his side and the two new buddies were off on a tree-hunting excursion. Which left Didi without an arm, and so Brian slipped his free arm into hers, and suddenly he was flanked by his mother and by his surrogate one, and if the sight was one he couldn't possibly have imagined until today, he felt a burst of warmth spread throughout his body. Not even the saw that dangled from his side could cut this kind of umbilical cord.

Far into the white-covered hills they went, green trees stretching out before them as far as the eye could see, and beyond, high into the lush Berkshire Mountains. Occasionally they would stop and admire a particular tree and test its branches, and for one reason or another pass on it, eventually taking a path where they could hear the gleeful sounds of the kids, both of whom pronounced that they had found the perfect tree. As Gerta and Nora went off to inspect Travis' choice, Brian led his parents over to where Janey was bouncing up and down.

"This one, this one . . . it's tall and full and it smells so fresh."

"It's very nice, Jane. I think we have our first one."

She scrunched her nose as only she could. "First one? How many trees are we getting?"

"Two," she said. "We always have two."

Brian grew silent, his face suddenly as white as the untouched snow. So many years had passed since he had celebrated Christmas at his parents' house, the memory of certain traditions only now coming to the surface as his mother raised the issue. Growing up they had always had two trees: one of them set up in the den, decorated with colorful lights and tinsel and an odd array of ornaments, and the other in his mother's more formal living room, that one adorned only with white lights and a string of silver garland. He remembered now how that second tree sparkled on Christmas Eve, the lights glowing in the window and reflecting off the snowdrifts blown up against the side of the house.

"Mom, I'd forgotten . . ."

"That's ironic, Brian," she said, "considering what I always called it."

"The Memory Tree," he said.

Kevin moved in, sliding an arm over his wife's shoulder. "Didi, this is Janey's Christmas and we have to honor her traditions, not to mention the ones she and Brian have created. I don't see that we need to overcrowd their house with yet another tree. We have all the memories we need, and we of course brought from home what's important."

"Did you bring your Christmas name ornaments?" Janey asked.

Didi Duncan, usually so reserved, was silent a moment as she fought off whatever buried emotion was emerging, and then said, "Yes, Janey, we most certainly did bring them, and I cannot wait to hang them on your tree."

"Our tree," Janey said, and that's when she threw herself around Didi. "I have one too. It's red. What color is yours?"

"Gold," Didi said, "just like your smile."

Brian nearly had to turn away, amazed by the generous spirit that lived inside his mother, wishing too that she would show it more often. He had the sense that Linden Corners was already beginning to work its magic on her; on his father too, who with a warm smile was taking the ax out of its sheath and preparing to chop down their tree.

"If this is the one Janey wants, then that's the one we'll have," he said, lifting the ax over his shoulder.

"Don't even think about it," Didi said, causing the big man to stop in his tracks.

"Didi, don't start . . ."

"Dad, I've got it. Really, the saw is easier."

Soon Brian had cut through the base and the tree crashed down into a puff of snow. With string provided by Mr. Green, Brian and Kevin wrapped it up and hefted it down the hill to the parking lot. Didi and Janey followed them, hand in hand. As they loaded it into the back of the truck, they caught sight of the Connors family with their own tree. Brian put it into the back of his truck also, Travis helping. Then Brian and Nora went to pay Albert Green and receive his usual booklet of how to care for their trees during the season. As they returned to the group, Gerta announced it was time to return to Linden Corners, where hot cocoa was waiting for them back at her house.

"With tiny marshmallows?" Janey asked.

"Would I have it any other way?"

Janey wrapped her arms around the old lady and said, "You're the best, Gerta."

As they piled back into their vehicles, Brian pulled his mother aside for a quick moment.

"You okay?"

"Jane . . . Janey, she's quite close to Gerta."

"That's not what I meant," he said, but then wondered if the display of affection between Janey and Gerta had unsettled his mother. Or was she putting on a brave face in light of the mishap with the second tree?

"Brian, I'm fine . . . Your father is right. Christmas is for the children anyway."

"That's where you're wrong, Mom. At least, that's not the way we do it in Linden Corners," he said, a growing smile widening his face. "Trust me, Mom, you'll get your memory tree this year, and it will be the most spectacular one you've ever seen."

CHAPTER 12

CYNTHIA

At least their Secret Santa drawing would be alive with wintery atmosphere, Cynthia thought. How empty Memorial Park and the gazebo had looked the other day without a coating of snow, the holiday bunting that hung from the gazebo's roof and brightly beaming lights looking forlorn without their frosty accoutrement. But the storm the other night had taken care of that issue, and so today's event would imbue them all with the holiday spirit, adding to the drama of half the town showing up to find out whom they would be playing Secret Santa with. The drawing was only an hour away at this point and she was running late; she had to get down to the gazebo and attend to the finishing touches, not wanting to stick Gerta with, no doubt, last-minute entrants.

"Bradley, are you all set?"

"I'm just trying to put Jake into his new snowsuit and boots," he said from atop the stairs. "It's not easy. This kid is squirming big-time."

"That's because he's never worn it before."

Cynthia smiled, the image of her son bundled up like an inflated snowman reminding her to pack their camera. As she dug into a drawer in their first-floor office for the digital camera, a feeling of sorrow washed over her, as she realized starting next year she would have to share photographs of her growing boy via e-mail and social media. Gone would be the days when she could rush over to the farmhouse and show Janey and Brian the latest googly face he had made. This move across the country might as well be taking them to the other side of the moon, but of course, that was why she was spending so much time and energy on this Christmas. She wanted to leave Janey with so many memories, all wrapped up with the kind of embrace they expected in Linden Corners, a warmth to melt away the bitter cold the young girl would be feeling on moving day.

"Hey, you okay?" Bradley asked.

She hadn't even seen him approach and now welcomed his hands on her shoulders as he massaged her. "Oh, don't stop. Can't we just stay here?"

"Do you mean Linden Corners? Not move?"

She sighed, thinking how nice that sounded. But no, she knew that wasn't possible, not anymore. The job was his, the house was on the market, her life was changing. "No, I mean here. Just you and me and Jake and a relaxing afternoon."

He kissed her on the cheek. "Come on, girl, this Secret Santa mess is all your fault."

"Humbug," she said.

It wasn't that she really wanted to remain home, but sometimes when the little moments in life sprung up on you, you wished for time to stand still. She saw Jake in his seat, squirming to escape, beginning to cry, and despite the noise the image brought a wide smile to her face. So much for that wished-for relaxation; her little miracle was anxious to get going. "We've got one stop to make; then it's off to the gazebo."

"What's Brian having you doing now?"

"What makes you think Brian's involved?"

"I heard you on the phone with him earlier," he said.

True, Brian had phoned her this morning, asking for what he termed a "huge" favor, and once he'd explained what that favor entailed, she was on his side. "I'll tell you on the ride over."

They left the house and got into the car, packing Jake into his child seat in the back. He squirmed again until he grew unusually fussy; Cynthia imagined he was uncomfortable being strapped in while wearing that bulky snowsuit. She told him it was only a quick trip, but those words did little to soothe an eighteen-month-old, and so they dealt with a crying Jake while Bradley drove the short distance to the Duncan farmhouse. As he was about to pull into the driveway, she told him to continue down to the end of the road and head to the windmill.

"Another windmill surprise?" he asked.

"Bradley Knight, you love that old windmill as much as anyone," she said. "Didn't you and Dan Sullivan hang around there?"

"More like the stone bridge between our properties," he said with a wistful laugh. "The stream would keep our beers cold while we talked the night away. Wow, I haven't thought about those days in a long time. What made you think of Dan?"

"Guess he's been on my mind, he and Annie. You know . . ."

"We lost our best friends, both of us."

"And now Janey is losing us."

Bradley pulled to the side of the road, and Cynthia found him looking at her. "Okay, you want to tell me what's really going on?"

"Bradley, I just want to make sure Janey has a wonderful Christmas."

"So she doesn't forget you?"

"Bradley Knight, if you make me cry right now . . ."

"Fine, to the windmill we go," he offered, continuing until he had at last turned onto the main highway, pulling over to the shoulder a half mile down. "Okay, I see . . . one, two . . . that's it . . . no, wait, there's a third person. Let me guess—those are Brian's parents alongside him and you're here to relieve him of his mother and keep her busy in town while he busily decorates the windmill for the holiday. How am I doing so far?"

"Not bad, Detective. Your story is a little incomplete," she said.

"Ah, more guessing—you want me to stay behind and help him."

She leaned over and kissed him. "That's why I love you so."

"So the menfolk stay here and work, while the women-folk go into town to organize the biggest shopping spree this town has ever seen."

"Jake's coming with me," she said.

"Ah, to be coddled by said womenfolk."

"Bradley Knight, you're more evolved than that."

"Sorry, just practicing my Texas macho routine."

She punched him hard in the arm. "No more reminders of our move, not today, please. Let me enjoy Linden Corners one last time."

"Oww," he said, rubbing his biceps.

She laughed. "So much for macho."

The two of them trudged through the snowy field en route to the windmill, Jake happy again to be released from the constraints of his seat. Brian welcomed them with a friendly wave and then introduced his parents to the men of the Knight family.

"So what are the Knights up to today?" Brian asked, pretending this visit was unplanned. Cynthia didn't find his tone very convincing, and she noticed a hint of skepticism toying with Didi.

"Brian Duncan, you have a terrible memory," Cynthia said, playing along and hoping she was doing a better job. "Today we draw names for the village's Secret Santa celebration . . . Why don't you all join us? Surely you've put everyone's name in the hat?"

"What's this, the entire village is playing?" Kevin asked.

Cynthia nodded. "Only those who want to; we can't force everyone, but at last count we had over three hundred entrants, and I suspect we'll get a few dozen who have been on the fence suddenly tossing their names in before the drawing begins."

"Sounds like a huge undertaking," Didi commented.

"As much as I'd like to go, I've got some work to finish here at the farmhouse," Brian said. "Janey will be there. She's been at Gerta's since late morning, helping Nora and Travis set up their tree. Janey said she would pick mine and promised not to look at who I got . . . unless I can get this work done beforehand and join in on the fun. Hey, Mom, Dad, why don't you go on with Cynthia. It'll give you a chance to meet more of the folks in town."

"I'll stay behind, Brian, keep you company," Kevin said. "Didi, go on ahead, sounds like a fun afternoon."

Bradley then piped up and suggested he remain behind too and help, saying, "Maybe that way we'll get done sooner and be able to join you for the end of the drawing."

"Uh-oh, Didi, I think it's the men versus the women here."

"Yes, so it appears," Didi replied, her lips pursed.

So the group agreed upon the plans, with Didi set to accompany Cynthia—who insisted Jake come with them—for an afternoon in downtown Linden Corners. As they prepared to leave, Didi grabbed Brian by the arm and told him he was as subtle as a frozen snowball, and then with Cynthia grinning and tossing her friend an amused look, they started down the field.

"Brian," Didi said, turning back, "don't let your father do any heavy lifting. No ladders."

"Didi . . ."

"That's okay. I've got Bradley for that," he said.

Even Cynthia partook of the laughter, and the two women, joined by a wailing Jake, who still wasn't happy about being in his snowsuit, got into the car and drove off toward the village, where the official start of the Christmas season was set to begin. The Secret of Linden Corners celebration was under way.

"The two of you are terrible actors," Didi remarked.

"Trust me, Didi, what Brian's doing, it'll be worth it. Brian's pretty good at surprises."

Didi allowed herself a small smile. "Of course he is. Where do you think he got it from?"

The crowd gathered around the snowy Memorial Park was impressive, all of them milling about while nearby parking lots overflowed with cars. And while it was only three in the afternoon and the light of day hadn't fully descended, downtown was held in a glowing halo of color emanating from the roofs, sides, and porches of the neighboring businesses, from Marla and Darla's Trading Post to Ackroyd's Hardware Emporium, the Five O'Clock Diner and George's Tavern, and even a bit farther down, at A Doll's Attic, the local Hudson Valley bank, and a Realtor's office. Cynthia wondered where she was going to park, not even having thought about that problem, but then she saw Nora waving to her from the sidewalk near the entrance of the park. She pulled over.

"We've got a spot saved for you at the tavern; you'll see Mark there holding it for you."

"Thanks."

"My goodness, how everyone looks out for their neighbors," Didi commented.

"Welcome to Linden Corners," Cynthia said.

"Yes, an oft-used phrase," she said. "Like we've stumbled upon Brigadoon, here for just a short time before disappearing for another hundred years."

Cynthia grew sad at the prospect, realizing the old legend held a kernel of truth for her.

"Are you okay, dear?"

"Your comment makes me realize just how much I'm going to miss this place."

Didi held out her arm, locking eyes with Cynthia. "Brian has told me you're leaving here early next year. While I know it will be difficult for all involved, perhaps for Jane the most, you have to pursue your dreams. Time waits for no one."

"I worry about that girl so much," Cynthia said. "But not because of Brian. He's great."

Didi thanked her, then suggested they put such talk on hold, since it appeared the entire town was waiting on her arrival. They parked, with Mark Ravens playfully directing them into the reserved spot like a valet. At his side was Sara, obviously pregnant beneath her long coat. More introductions were forthcoming, Didi smiling widely as a scruffy-faced Mark welcomed her to their humble village, telling her how much Brian had helped him and his wife.

"I mean, Sara and I fell in love because of him, and we found a home together because of him, and we got married thanks to his efforts," Mark said. "We owe him our future."

"My goodness, Brian certainly is an industrious man about town, isn't he?"

"When we lost Annie after that awful storm," Sara said, "he became our heart. The way he restored the windmill, what he really did was help restore an entire village. But you'll see that for yourself soon enough. In the meantime, I think the natives are restless, eager to see who they have to go shopping for. Personally I hope I get someone I know . . . I mean, I know that's not the point, but picking out gifts is hard enough. To get for a stranger . . . how about you, Mrs. Duncan? For you I suppose we're all strangers."

"Oh no, I'm not participating," she said. "My goodness, I've only been here little more than a day."

"Come on, babe, let's get you settled at the park. So many people here—Cyn, do you think we'll be done before Sara goes into labor?"

As the Ravenses walked off hand in hand, Cynthia took hold of Jake from his car seat, then took out the stroller and got him settled. Didi asked if she didn't mind if she pushed it. It had been a long time since she'd played the role of grandmother, she explained. "Brian's sister, Rebecca, has a son, Junior, and we barely see him now that he's living with his father, but other than that, nothing."

"What about Janey?"

"Oh, well, yes, I suppose . . . Cynthia, may I be honest?"

"Of course."

"I haven't always approved of Brian's choice, having become a parent the way he did."

Cynthia nodded. She knew. She'd heard Brian talk enough about his frustrations with his parents over his new life in Linden Corners, but now she held those secrets on her tongue, not wishing to embarrass the woman. From what Brian had said of Didi Duncan, admitting to such a truth must have been difficult, and Cynthia was all too happy to listen. Perhaps she could help heal the rift. Perhaps she could get Didi to think of Janey as a granddaughter. Family was not all about blood; it was about bonds. And she'd never before seen the kind of bond that existed between Brian and

Janey, almost like destiny had dropped Brian down in the land of the windmill for the express purpose of raising a girl who'd suffered her share of storms, a girl who, through the generosity of those around her, strangers and friends alike, would live to again see sunshine.

"Then I'm glad you're here now," Cynthia said. "We do Christmas right, and you'll see just how special Brian and Janey are together."

At last the two women, with a sleeping Jake before them, came up the plowed pathway of the park, where they went directly to the steps of the gazebo. Residents were milling about, saying hello, drinking coffee provided by the Five-O, but all knew that Cynthia had organized this event and so her arrival must mean they were about to get started. All the seats were filled, and the rest of the villagers remained standing, all of them encircling the gazebo. Didi told her to attend to her business; she'd look after Jake. As Cynthia took the steps, she saw Janey come running up from behind and drop down into the snow, staring at Jake but not disturbing him. *Let him sleep, please.* Janey ended up on Didi's lap, the older woman left with a surprised expression on her face.

Cynthia imagined that Didi was already getting comfortable in that grandmother role.

The image gave her the fuel to carry on, and so it began.

"Hi, everyone. Welcome to the first and hopefully not last Linden Corners Secret Santa drawing," Cynthia said, addressing the crowd. "I know you're eager to get started, so let me explain briefly how this is going to happen. Gerta and I have the master list of all those who have already put their name into the hat, so when you come up we'll cross your name off the list and then you'll get to draw a name. And please, while we obviously cannot police this, no switching names with other people, and don't tell anyone whom you picked. If you're not certain what gift to get your person, don't ask your friends; search your heart."

"Oh, and one other thing," Gerta said. "On the odd chance you pick your own name, let us know and you can draw again. So let's start with those who are sitting, and those standing, you can fill those empty seats. Folks, this is a truly great turnout, and it means that our annual Christmas pageant will be the most special one yet—which is really saying something. Shall we form a line and begin the drawing?"

A general consensus of agreement erupted among the large crowd.

"Wait, wait one more moment, everyone," Cynthia said. "I'd like to ask if there's anyone here who has not already put their name in the hat and would still like to participate. Last chance to join in the celebration on Christmas Eve. This is your last chance. Remember, the pageant leaves from my house at the northern edge of Crestview Road and goes through the woods and over the stone bridge until we arrive at the windmill. Any last-minute Secret Santas?"

A couple of people came forward and jotted their names down. While they did, Cynthia looked over at Jake, who was still sleeping, and at Janey, who was whispering something into the ear of Didi.

Cynthia paused and then saw Didi's hand go up. She held up two fingers.

"I'm very happy to see that, Didi. Folks, for those of you who don't know, visiting us this holiday season are Brian's parents; his mother, Didi, is right over there," Cynthia said to the crowd. She turned to watch Gerta write down two names: Didi Duncan and Kevin Duncan.

With the new entrants' names tossed into the oversize Santa hat, Cynthia felt energized. She got the line organized and began to guide the residents one by one. First came many of the folks from Edgestone Retirement Home, with Elsie leading the way and an unsteady-on-his-feet Thomas Van Diver, who told Cynthia he wouldn't have missed this for anything, especially since his birthday fell on Christmas Day.

"It feels like one big party for a man soon to turn eighty-six," he said.

"Just wait until you see all the lit candles," Cynthia told him.

Thomas then stepped into the gazebo, thrust his arm down inside the hat, and pulled out a slip of paper. He gazed at it, nodded, before he moved along.

After the older folks departed came a burst of youthful energy, with Travis Connors stepping up, a bunch of friends lined up behind him. Gerta crossed their names off, and they chose their names and moved on, each of them teasing the others into trying to guess whom they got and who wanted to switch. Not much Cynthia could do about that. Soon came Martha and Sara and Mark, and even Chuck, who pulled out a name and grimaced when he read what was written on the card.

"Can I try again?"

"Chuck Ackroyd, you play nice," Gerta said. "And whoever it is, no hammers from your store. You really have to shop."

He moved along with a grumble. Behind him were Marla and Darla, and one of them—Cyn was still never quite sure which twin was which—stepped up and repeated the process everyone else had gone through. As the first one pulled the name out, she announced that she'd chosen her own name, and Cynthia checked it and laughed.

"Well, maybe you did, maybe you didn't."

The card read Marla Devine.

Her sister came up and saw it and announced, "That's not you; that's me."

"Regardless, put it back and try again."

The twins finally moved away, seemingly satisfied with their choices. The line continued for another half hour or so, moving at a steady, continuous clip, all while around them darkness had begun to settle over the village, a cold wind blowing through the park causing some people to head indoors. After Mark and Sara chose their names, they left, she to help Martha serve the dinner rush at the Five-O, Mark to open the tavern, as Sunday was his usual night. The crowd was dwindling and the Santa hat was nearly empty.

At that point, Didi started up the steps to the gazebo, Janey at her side.

"You go first, Jane."

So the young girl did, digging down as far as she could and pulling out a name. She held it tight against her small frame, repeating the process while proclaiming this one represented Brian's pick, not even wanting to look at either until she was safely out of sight of others. She stuffed one of them into her pocket, avoiding the temptation of discovering who Brian had. Now, there was a girl who took the game seriously, Cynthia thought, but of course this game had really been Janey's idea, so her actions came as little surprise.

"Didi, I believe it's your turn?"

"I don't know why I raised my arm," she said.

"I do," Cynthia said, but said no more. No further explanation was required.

Didi chose one, then a second for Kevin, and she did just as Janey had done.

As she started back to baby Jake, Didi nearly collided with another woman.

"Oh, my apologies . . . Oh, hello . . . you're the woman from . . ."

"Trina Winter," the woman said. "From the Solemn Nights. Hello, Mrs. Duncan."

Cynthia could see Didi giving the woman a lingering gaze. Why did Didi find Trina so interesting? She wondered if Brian had said anything about having had a date with the woman. She rather doubted it, since Brian was reluctant to discuss it even with his friends.

"Trina, I'm so glad you made it. You almost missed your chance."

"I almost didn't come."

Gerta looked over her list, flipping pages until she came to the end. "Actually, I've only got two names remaining. Yours and Richie's. Did he come with you?"

Trina shook her head. "Guess I'm picking for him. No doubt shopping for him too."

So Trina removed the two remaining slips of paper from the large Santa hat and without bothering to read them, stuffed them into the pocket of her jacket. She offered a quick good-bye, her eyes darting about the park while she started down the path. Nearly ready to chase after her and ask what was wrong, Cynthia realized she couldn't fix everything, and even if she wanted to, the ringing of her phone stopped her.

"Hey, sweetie," she said as she saw Bradley's name pop up on the caller ID.

"We're done, and ready for the unveiling."

"We're just finishing up, so we'll be there soon," Cynthia said.

"Brian said you should bring Gerta and anyone else you think is appropriate."

Cynthia smiled as she watched a retreating figure nearly being swallowed by the falling night. Someone who needed to be shown the light. "A better idea I've never heard."

CHAPTER 13

TRINA

First she arrived a stranger to Linden Corners, and now, weeks later, and in this very moment, she felt even worse. She felt like an imposter.

Trina Winter knew that the people of this village sought out the windmill and its inspiring ever-turning sails, hoping to send out wishes upon the wind, and ironically, Trina found that her wish would be to be anywhere other than in the windmill's looming shadow, especially now. She'd yet to even lay her own eyes on it, and now with her friendship-plus with its owner, Brian, this wasn't how she wanted to be introduced to it, in front of his friends and family. But Cynthia Knight wouldn't accept no for an answer, much like she hadn't when they first met at the Five-O Diner, insisting that Brian was someone she needed to meet. While Trina was loath to admit to anyone besides herself that she enjoyed Brian's company and found him sweet, warm, and handsome, taking this deeper step into his personal life for the night's annual lighting of the windmill was pushing the relationship a bit too far. He didn't even know she was coming, and she didn't want to blindside him. In a way, she felt coming to this setting was much more intimate than any-thing they might have shared that night in her motel room.

Something she was glad had been interrupted, and by his parents no less.

At this confusing time when her life was uprooted, when her future remained unwritten and her messy past some-thing even she hated to discuss, getting involved romanti-cally with anyone, much less a man with a motherless child, was an exercise in poor judgment. No matter how good a sweaty night of passion might have felt that night, the next morning she would have awakened with that pesky emotion called remorse. It's funny that you could give your body to another person in the dark of night, only to feel shame and embarrassment when facing him as the sun rose.

"Trina, are you with us? . . . We're here."

She hadn't realized they'd arrived at the farmhouse, Cynthia's voice barely registering in the backseat.

"What? . . . Oh, sorry, I must have drifted off."

"It's not that long a drive, dear," added Didi, who'd been sitting in the front.

Trina looked over at Jake in his car seat, sleeping so deeply it was like he wouldn't wake till morning; how she envied him his innocence, the easy look of contentment writ-ten across his face. Still, he offered her a good excuse for being distant.

"Guess the little guy inspired me."

Cynthia gathered her son up, Trina following after her down the driveway when a second car pulled in behind them. Nora, Gerta, and Travis emerged from within, and last, but certainly not least, came Janey Sullivan, the little girl tossing Trina a curious look. Wondering just who she was, no doubt, and why she was here. As the group gathered to make the trek down the hill, Trina again found herself saddled with an uncertain feeling that had her dragging her feet. As though she didn't belong, not with this makeshift family, not in this picturesque setting, where she'd been told of a woman who had lived fully and died bravely and whose spirit reportedly still rode the wind. Trina knew she was being ridiculous; she should just go up and introduce herself to Janey.

The little girl beat her to it.

"You must be Trina," Janey said matter-of-factly, scrunching her nose.

Trina looked for an accusation in her tone but found none. How strange that a ten-year-old could put her at such ease. She exhaled and said, "Yes, I am. And of course you're Janey. I hope you don't mind that I've come tonight; Cynthia insisted."

"Cynthia just wants my dad to be happy," Janey said. "Do you make him happy?"

This kid was smart; she knew how to play the game by keeping her opponent off balance, thought Trina, blushing slightly. "It's a little too early for such a pronouncement," she said, "so why don't you just think of me as another friend of the family. One who hasn't yet seen the windmill."

Her eyes widened. "You haven't?"

"Not all of us are as lucky as you, Janey, having such a beautiful object in your yard."

Their conversation was halted by Didi, who was waving in Janey's direction.

"Oh, Jane . . . Jane, please take my hand and help guide me down," Didi said, standing near the edge of the driveway.

Janey looked like she wanted to remain at Trina's side, hesitating slightly. But then she rejoined Brian's mother, and the two of them began the long walk across the field. Travis did the same with his grandmother, leaving the three women—Cynthia, Nora, and Trina herself—the former two circling around their new friend and coaxing her to join them.

"That wasn't so bad," Cynthia said. "Janey is very resilient."

"I think she was more the grown-up than me," Trina said.

"You wouldn't be the first," Nora added, her tone flippant. "Shall we get this over and done with so we can warm up?"

"What's with you, Nora?" Cynthia asked.

Nora looked apprehensive, almost like she didn't want to talk in front of Trina.

"Nothing, it's . . . nothing."

"Where's Nicholas? We haven't seen much of him lately."

"Like I said, it's nothing."

Trina tried to think of something to say but failed. Who was she to offer up relationship advice?

"Sorry, I didn't mean to push," Cynthia said.

"Let's go; it's cold."

Indeed, at five in the afternoon, the winter's night had fallen deep over the region, with a chilly wind blowing past, heightened by the open field behind the farmhouse. Glad she had brought a long scarf, Trina wrapped it around her neck in an effort to stave off the frigid air, then joined the ladies as their feet crunched through the snow. With the time spent at the gazebo amidst Christmas lights and assorted holiday wreaths and the fresh scent of pine, now headed toward an old-world windmill for its annual lighting, Trina was definitely feeling the crush of the season. She wondered if she'd done the right thing in participating in Secret Santa. And whether including Richie was a good idea. Despite how much he loved this little town, he joined in on its celebrations only on his terms and his alone, and he probably wouldn't like Trina pushing him into something he wouldn't normally choose. No going back now, she thought, and realized that applied to her current situation. Cynthia had dragged her here, so she supposed the season was one of adaptability for the Ravens family.

At last the three of them crested the hill, providing Trina with her first ever look at the windmill. With only a smattering of stars and a half-moon lighting the sky, the landmark was more shadow than structure, and so she felt rather deflated. That was the thing about buildup; it was often laced with disappointment. Or maybe she just didn't have that special gene that made life in Linden Corners so special, perhaps the appreciation having skipped a generation. Richie spoke of the windmill's simple beauty and had said he'd even spent time living near it, in these very woods, which tonight looked like skeletons dancing in the wind.

What she could see were half a dozen people mingling around the windmill, staring up at its dark hull, as though waiting for inspiration to strike them. The Connors family had already arrived, and joining them was the elderly Thomas Van Diver, whom she'd met that odd day at Marla and Darla's store. Didi had taken up beside her husband, Kevin, whom Trina recognized from the other night at the motel, and then there was another man, tall and blond, whom she had to assume was Cynthia's husband. Whom she didn't see was Brian himself, and that made her final few steps toward the windmill that much more awkward for her. The one person she shared any kind of connection with, and he was nowhere to be found.

But then a light from inside the windmill caught her attention. As she drew ever closer, she saw that a catwalk lined the second level of the windmill's tower, one of the windows revealed to be an actual door, a cutout in the wood of the tower. As the door opened, the soft light cast a glow upon the snow, managing also to catch Trina in its path. Brian emerged from inside, his hands resting on the iron rails of the catwalk as the latticed sails spun past him. His smile already wide, it grew wider still when he noticed Trina. She wished she could talk to him first and explain why she was here, but that wasn't possible. To interrupt the flow of the evening now would only make her presence here more awkward. Might as well get on with it, and to the point, she saw in his hands a switch, his finger itching to turn it on. First, though, he spoke.

"Thanks, everyone, for being here," he said. "Tonight is a special one, and not just because it's the annual lighting of the windmill but because of who's here among us. For the past two and a half years, I've been fortunate to call Linden Corners my home, and to live right beside this old windmill with a girl whose indomitable spirit keeps its sails turning. I don't remember what made me think of lighting the windmill that first Christmas, only thinking that I wanted to do something so special for Janey she'd remember it forever, and what better place to do that than here, where she and I first met. Little did I realize that I was inspiring not just a young girl's dreams of her mother, but filling a town with its own hopes for the holidays. Last year it was another person who helped fuel the windmill's sails, a man who knew this land as a child, only to lose it. Of course, knowing me, I went too far last year by stringing so many lights I ended up blowing out the power. The windmill lay dark more nights than made me comfortable, and only on Christmas Eve did it light up again."

"Just in time for Santa to find us," Janey announced, her infectious joy creating a ripple of laughs amidst the small crowd.

"And it would have provided such good light for me to read the story of Saint Nicholas to the children," Thomas added, "though the gazebo served me just fine too."

Even Trina grinned at the refreshing innocence of both young and old, as she waited for Brian to continue his story. "When last year's pageant had to be moved to Memorial Park, I sent out my own wish upon the wind, hoping Annie would hear it, and seeing you all here, I can only think she spends her days not just hearing them but granting them. Now another holiday season has come to Linden Corners, and we have so much to be thankful for—new friends who are seeing the windmill for the first time, other friends who may not see it lit for some time, as their lives are taking them far from our borders. For them, for us, and for the entire community, this year's lighting of the windmill is all the more special because of the celebration it will host on the eve of Christmas. If I learned anything during my life in Linden Corners, it's that time is precious, and it's fleeting too. It ticks endlessly toward the future, held close by our memories. Traditions here are important, and the thing about traditions is they can be from long ago or the recent past, but they have one thing in common: a rich desire to see them fulfilled. Tonight the traditions of many families come together—three families for whom the power of the windmill has become a part of their fabric. For the Van Divers, who came first and built it, and for the Sullivans, who still imbue its mighty spirit, to the Duncans, who restored it and now help carry its treasured past on shoulders it made strong . . ."

Brian paused, another of the windmill's giant sails swinging past him, another still. Like the building was a living, breathing entity, knowing it was the star of tonight's show.

"So without further ado and with all of our friends gathered tonight, let me present to you the Linden Corners Memory Tree."

Trina found herself holding her breath, realizing everyone else was doing the same. Not a sound could be heard, and only the chilly mist of their breaths gave away any hint of breathing, fading into the air like nearby memories. Standing a few feet back from the rest of the group, her hands clasped like those of a little girl anticipating that first gift on Christmas morning, Trina watched as Brian suddenly flicked the switch in his hand. She blinked, and in that split second of blindness what she saw was a flash of light and what she felt was an immediate warmth that spread deep inside her, and at last she opened her eyes and saw what everyone else saw, the color of magic.

It was like the sky had journeyed down to them from above, stars like raindrops dancing in front of them. The windmill sparkled gold, adorned with so many white lights they lit the open field and cast a gleaming coat of ice upon the snow. The oohs and aahs that followed were like those heard on the Fourth of July, and while the spectacle set before them was of a glowing white, inside her mind were explosions of vibrant color, red and gold, blue and silver, and all were shiny, like wrapped gifts under a tree.

"Oh, Brian," Didi said, her eyes filled with wonder. "It's magnificent."

"I'm not done yet," he said, quickly disappearing into the windmill again.

Trina was already impressed, yet waited eagerly to see what Brian had up his sleeve. As she waited, she saw Bradley and Cynthia snuggled close together, Jake's eyes glistening in the glow of the lights; Janey stood between Didi and Gerta, with Nora and Travis and Kevin Duncan nearby, and with a tear slipping down his cheek, the man named Thomas Van Diver. How close they all were, how strong their bond. Again, Trina felt like she didn't belong, wishing she could slink back to the motel, but even then it wouldn't be far enough away. Richie was there, and like the sight before her, he was a reminder of all she'd missed out on in life.

The glow emanating from the windmill, though, wouldn't release her from its hold. Even if she were to leave now, she would do so with all eyes watching her escape. So Trina stood there, alone amidst family. Brian at last returned to the catwalk, and Trina saw his eyes fall upon hers. As though by doing so, he was letting her know she belonged. He was glad she had witnessed this night.

Without further word, another burst of illumination lit the night sky. A glowing white star had been placed atop the windmill, its five points spinning in the wind like an iron weather vane, changing direction, as fickle as the sweep of the wind. Trina once again felt warm all over, and this time she attributed it not to the beam of light but to the wondrous generosity of the man still positioned along the catwalk. As he gazed upward at his last touch, Brian Duncan announced to the crowd, "Now, that's a memory tree."

"You certainly have a flair for the dramatic, Brian Duncan, Just Passing Through," Trina said. "Can you tell me about the genesis of the memory tree?"

"For that story you're going to have to ask my mother, and no offense, but I think Didi Duncan has affected one of our nights already."

"Affected? Is that a euphemism?"

"Ruined?" he asked with a noticeable grin.

"Ah, now that's honest."

Everyone else had cleared out from the field, some of them returning home while others had retired back to the farmhouse for hot chocolate and Gerta's famous strawberry pie, leaving Brian and Trina alone amidst the lights. He had suggested they take a walk on this cold, dark night, and with the glow of the windmill guiding from behind them, she found him leading them far from its power, like magnets reacting negatively. At last they came to the edge of the woods, where Brian helped her up the sloping ramp of the stone bridge, the two of them coming to rest at its crest. They leaned against the thick rail while the stream ran noisily under them, cascading over ice and rocks.

"Like the sounds of your bar," she said.

"Sorry, I don't have a small bottle of Dewar's with me to warm you."

"I don't mind the cold. I did ask for it, a traditional Upstate New York winter."

"Ask and you shall receive."

"Is that what the windmill advises? It seems to grant your wishes," she said.

"It's a special place," he said.

"Is that why you led me away from it?"

He paused, looking away. "Sorry, this is all new to me . . . you, us, whatever this is."

"And the windmill was Annie's."

"Truth of the matter, Trina, is everything in Linden Corners reminds me of her. Her house, her windmill, her . . ."

"Daughter."

"Her life, not mine, yet she's not here and I am."

"It's okay, Brian," she said, "and I totally understand my role."

"What do you mean, your role?"

"Everyone who loses someone has to eventually move on. There has to be a first one."

"I'm not using you, if that's what you think."

She reached over and took his wrist, feeling the heat of his pulse even through the glove. "Definitely not," she said, a hint of regret spoiling her expression. "That's not how I meant it to sound. You and I . . . we've become victims of our own availability and vulnerability, with your friends thinking they were doing you a favor. And who knows, maybe they were, and not just for you. Like I said, some lucky girl has to be the first you date after Annie's death, and you've certainly honored her and grieved her a long time. If either of us has anything to apologize for, it's me. For the night I barged my way into George's—call my motives premeditated, call it happenstance, but there's no denying I wanted you that night. I wanted to feel your arms around me and I wanted to be comforted. Dealing with Richie is not easy, since his mood changes . . . ha ha, with the wind, and he just sits there . . . letting life slip by. I'm guilty of that too; it's what I'm doing in Linden Corners. Hiding. Waiting for some sparks to get my life restarted. But it gets lonely in such a close-knit community, and I guess . . . well, I liked you; I liked your honesty."

Brian was quiet after her speech, gazing into her eyes while moonlight bathed them. It cast a fiery glow inside them, and he felt drawn to their power, their heat. He leaned over and he kissed her, a gentle touch of his lips upon hers. When he pulled back, he said, "Guess I'm not the only one who's good at making speeches."

"Was that your way of silencing me?"

"No, that was good, real good to hear you speak," he said. "I think I learned more about you just now than I did on our first date."

"And I learned so much about you tonight too, Brian," she said. "The way you so fully embrace this holiday and honor your family, it's a special gift, Brian. Better than anything you could wrap up or buy. And I know you've said your mother can be difficult . . ."

"She makes Richie seem like the Prince of Linden Corners," he said with a rueful smile.

"But you affected her tonight, I could see that, with your memory tree."

"Are we really back to talking about my mother? Have we come full circle?"

"Well, actually, I think that means we should call it a night."

He nodded. "Janey's probably finished all the marshmallows by now. She puts so many in her hot chocolate she may as well label what's in her cup melted marshmallows with cocoa sprinkles. Come on, I'll drive you home."

"That's not necessary . . . Oh," she said, her voice trailing off, remembering she'd arrived at the gazebo on foot and come to the lighting of the windmill via Cynthia, who was home tucking in Jake. So she accepted his offer and the two of them departed from the stone bridge, emerging from the trees to a starlit night made even brighter by the twinkling windmill in the near distance. Again they put the view in their rear mirror and returned up the steep hill, bypassing the sound of laughter and music coming from inside the farmhouse.

"You sure you don't want to join us?"

"That's sweet, but I think I've intruded enough for one night," she said.

"Trina, you're not intruding . . ."

She took his hand, squeezed it. "Brian, it's Annie's house, as you said, and I can imagine a ten-year-old who may not be ready for her dad to welcome a new woman into its kitchen."

"Janey adapts well—"

She cut him off and said, "I don't."

Inside the truck they went, with Brian having to turn the engine twice before it caught. On the road, it was a quick trip through a darkened Linden Corners, the only sign of noticeable activity at the tavern. They didn't stop there, Trina saying no to a shot of scotch, and soon Brian was turning into the parking lot of the Solemn Nights, its flickering VACANT sign seemingly redder in the wake of the bright-white spectacle glowing off the windmill. As Brian set the truck to park, Trina paused, uncertain of her next step. They'd been here before, just two nights ago, and had they not been interrupted, who knows what would have happened inside her room. Was she ready for a second attempt, or was the near miss the other night a masked signal?

"Brian . . . ," she said, only to be silenced again, and again in the same manner.

His kiss was more urgent, and she returned it with zeal, their exchange heated to the point that the windshield grew fogged, like two teenagers were locked inside the cab. His touch was sweet, tender, and she felt pulled in by his strong arms, his comforting presence. With the cold locked out of the front cab of the truck, she felt as though she could melt right into him, and if only they could keep the cold at bay while they made it to her room, she might just give in to temptation. She knew, though, that the moment she ventured into the night, the passion would dissipate like her misty breath, and her heart would freeze up. As they pulled away from each other, she felt Brian's fingers caress her cheek.

"I don't object to rushing things," she said. "Who knows what our lives have in store."

"But," he said.

"But what I don't want to do is rush tonight."

"Right. My family is waiting for me," he said.

"You have a little girl to tuck into bed."

"She's growing up; she's exercising her independence," he said.

"No more distractions, Brian Duncan," she said. "For us to share something so real and so personal, so intimate, neither of us should be just passing through."

He nodded with an appropriate smile, but not before leaving her with a single last kiss and a personal invitation to the annual George's Tavern Christmas party "next Saturday.

Trust me, the whole town turns out and Gerta serves up a feast of food and pies that will lure even your father to the bar. I'll see you then."

"Not if I see you before," she told him, and then watched as the truck pulled out and the taillights disappeared down the darkened road, until not even their red glow lingered in her eyes. Trina Winter hadn't expected to be gone from the motel for so long; it was just supposed to have been a quick trip to the gazebo, pick two names, and then return home. Pulled into the ceremony of the lighting of the windmill, lulled into the woods by her handsome suitor, she felt like tonight had been part fairy tale, part dream, complete with twinkling lights and a promise of brighter tomorrows. No glass slipper, though, just a pair of wet boots that helped her trudge through deep snowdrifts.

Inside the motel office, she took a look at Richie, asleep on the sofa with the television still flickering puppets on the walls, shadows in the dark. She made her way to her father's side, and, instinct overriding any conflict that existed between them, she gently kissed his forehead. Then she pulled from her coat pocket one of the names she'd taken from the hat and set it on the table beside him. Still, she didn't look at the name, and instead turned off the television.

Back in her room, she at last took out the second slip of paper and read the name of whom she'd be playing Secret Santa for. Her smile continued to light the room, even as she slipped under the covers. She turned out the lamp beside her and drifted off to a deep sleep that was alive, surprisingly, with dreams.

CHAPTER 14

BRIAN

Brian awoke that Monday morning to a cacophony of sounds, so much noise he imagined his life in Linden Corners had existed as one long dream, and now he was finally waking to the constant noise outside his Manhattan apartment. Garbage trucks doing battle with cabbies for ownership of the street, with horns blaring and the crush of recyclables winning out over all, sleep included. But as he opened his eyes, the familiar sights of his bedroom warmed him, even as he slipped the covers off and his bare feet stepped onto the cold planks of the floor. This had of course once been Annie's room, and before that hers with Dan; it had taken months for him to even begin to think of it as his room, some nights giving up on sleep and retiring to the sofa down in the living room. Imposters had no place taking possession of other people's homes.

And down the hall slept his parents, the takeover by the Duncan family of the Sullivan farmhouse in full assault mode. He'd been worried about Janey's reaction to his parents' arrival, but so far all had gone well, though Brian was first to admit he'd kept them all pretty busy this first weekend together, to the point that no one had time to think about the consequences of all living under one roof. The start of this week and the looming holiday would certainly test their mettle, and as worried as he was about his parents—his father, in particular, given his mother's cryptic warnings—Janey was of course his first priority. She was still the child, this was her favorite holiday, and no matter how many new traditions they had established the past two years, he knew she remembered the little details from past ones that spoke of Annie's influence. Not so with Dan, who had died in a car crash when she was so young. In truth, Brian was the only Dad she ever remembered.

A loud thud caught his attention again, reminding him of what had woken him.

Wrapping a thick blue robe around his shorts and T-shirt, he opened his door and listened for the direction of where the noise was coming from. He waited, heard nothing, instinct taking him to Janey's room, where behind the closed door he found an empty bed, one freshly made. Only one aspect was different; her stuffed purple frog could not be found resting atop the pillows per usual, and he had to think Janey had it with her, much as she had the past few weeks. He nearly called out her name but remembered his parents were sleeping down the hall.

That's when he heard the thud again, and this time Brian looked upward.

The attic.

What was Janey doing in the attic on a Monday morning? It was only seven.

He padded midway down the hall and opened the door to the attic, its squeaky hinges no doubt announcing his presence. Upstairs he ventured, where he found Janey sitting on the dusty floor amidst a series of cardboard boxes, a few of the lids tossed aside. No surprise, there at her side was the purple frog with no name. What did surprise him was the fact that she hadn't heard him, her head practically stuffed inside one of the boxes.

"It has to be in one of these," she said, apparently to the frog.

Its sealed mouth kept it from answering.

"Janey, what are you doing up here, and at this hour?"

She lifted her head from the box, her mouth clamping shut at the sight of him. She gazed down at the mess she had created, making a fast move for her frog, clutching him hard to her frame. "You scared me," she stated.

"And you woke me . . . and maybe my parents. I repeat, what are you doing up here?"

"It's for my Secret Santa gift," she said. "So I can't tell you."

"Why not? You didn't pick me, did you?"

"Silly, of course not. Gerta would have made me put it back in the big hat."

"Then why can't you tell me?"

"Because those are the rules. Cynthia said no trading and the only way to avoid doing that is not to know who people have," she said, her familiar exasperation and complex answer hardly hindered by the early hour. "Aren't you following the rules by not opening those gifts you keep getting? The person said you have to wait until Christmas Day to open them, right? You haven't unwrapped them in secret, have you?"

"No, I haven't."

"See? Rules."

Brian sighed, settling down onto the floor. He was constantly surprised by whatever her mind figured out next, knowing silence was often the way to get to the heart of whatever she was thinking. Janey eventually came around to reveal what was bothering her, and he had to think now was going to be one of those moments. So much had been happening this holiday season, from the unexpected Thanksgiving announcement from Cynthia and Bradley to his surprise date with Trina to his parents' arrival in Linden Corners; it was a lot of upheaval for a girl who'd seen too much of it already in her young life, making Brian feel like he'd lost control of the stability he ensured during the remainder of the year. Waiting on her, he reached out and shook the frog's limp hand. Staring at the frog, he wondered what secrets it knew.

"Brian?"

His connecting with the frog seemed to have opened the floodgates.

"Do you know the story of how my parents met?" she asked. "I mean, where they were and what made them want to talk to each other?"

Brian admitted he didn't. "Your mom, she didn't speak much about him to me," he said, the truth. He'd heard plenty of other stories about Dan Sullivan from others in town, including Bradley, and also from the surly Chuck Ackroyd, who had reason to dislike him, and if the stories were to be believed, Dan hadn't been the prince Janey imagined. Ironically, Dan Sullivan might have been more frog. But none of the rumors concerning the last months of Dan's life were Janey's to know, not now and hopefully not ever. "All I know is that you were all that your father wanted, you and Annie and your lives together."

"I see him sometimes, in my dreams."

"That's perfectly natural, Janey, and I'm glad that you do," he said, intrigued by where this conversation was going. "Especially since his portrait is the last thing you see every night before you fall asleep, his and Annie's. So your mind pictures them while you sleep. I'm sure they tell you tales of their lives."

"Mama speaks in riddles," she said.

"Does she, now?"

"Yes, when she comes to me in the dark of night and takes me to the windmill," she said. "You know, when I'm sleeping."

Brian smiled at her, smoothing down her hair and hoping it brought her comfort. He knew Janey spoke to Annie often, running to the windmill to tell her about her day at school or a special art project she'd made, telling her she hoped one day to have the same talent her mother displayed, and while it wasn't realistic to think Annie responded, there was something about the sails of the windmill, as though their endless spins grabbed hold of those words and transported them to places where Annie could hear. He would never deny Janey this fantasy world, because he knew she still needed her mother and that she always would, on simple days when the rain fell or on future days when she had something to celebrate, a graduation, a wedding, a baby of her own.

"Will you come with me for a moment?" he said. "I want to show you something."

"Can I bring my frog?"

"Of course. He needs to hear this too."

"Before we go, can I tell you something else?"

"Anything."

"I'm thinking the frog needs a name."

"Okay, that's a good idea. What have you come up with?"

"Nothing."

"Well, calling him 'Nothing' is almost like not having a name at all."

Janey rolled her eyes with obvious amusement. "Silly, Brian." Then she put her hands to her mouth. "Oops, I mean Dad. When you act all silly, it makes me think about when we first met and you did the silliest things . . . You know, when you would fall in the snow and make an angel . . .

That's when you were Brian to me. Names are weird, I think, because they can help you get to know people better, while other times they keep you from getting to know them. It all depends on what name you use."

"That's very insightful, Janey. I never really thought of it like that," he said, imagining this had something to do with his parents and how to refer to them. "While I ponder that, are you going to join me downstairs? It's almost time for you to get ready for school, and you need to eat and get dressed first."

"What's downstairs?"

"Well, first of all, everything."

Janey considered his words, scrunching her nose in classic fashion. Only after they were halfway down the attic steps did she laugh and tell him she'd just got his little joke, and she called him silly again. Their fun banter kept them occupied until Brian led the way into the living room. With the curtains closed and the lights of their Christmas tree switched off, the room was dark, not yet awake on this early morning. Rather than draw the curtains, Brian bent underneath the tree and pressed the switch. It came alive with color and a shiny glint that lit their eyes.

"We never turn the tree on in the morning, unless of course it's Christmas morning."

"I want to show you something, and what better way than with the lights on," he said.

They had decorated the tree Saturday night, Brian and his father setting it in its stand and the four of them stringing it with many lights and hanging on its branches a wide assortment of ornaments found inside the boxes stored in the attic, finishing it off with a string of garland and two boxes of silver tinsel that caused the tree to glisten with reflective light. The final touch had come when each of them, in turn, hung their name ornaments on the best branches.

Janey's was a shiny red, and it settled on a branch halfway up the tree, and not far from it hung gold and green ornaments, each with the name of one of her parents written across its front. They had been gifts from Brian for last year's Christmas, and so this was the first opportunity Janey had to hang them for the entire duration of the holiday. He remembered the wide-eyed joy on her face as she welcomed Dan and Annie to a tradition that Brian had introduced her to. His own ornament was on a higher branch, not far from Didi's, and on the branch closest to the angel atop the tree was Kevin's, but that's because, as Janey said, "he's the tallest."

"Have a seat, sweetie," Brian said.

Janey sat upon the sofa, legs dangling, her gaze still locked on the shimmering glints of the tree. Her unnamed frog that just might get one for Christmas remained in her tight embrace. "What do you want to show me?"

"You asked about how your parents met, and I told you I didn't know."

"Right. What does that have to do with our Christmas tree?"

"Because, Janey, sometimes life's mysteries remain that way, and we never know how or why certain events occurred, just that they did. While we can't know the past, the present shows us unequivocal proof of it having happened, and you are that proof."

"Unequivocal? Even that word is beyond me."

"Meaning there's no denying that you exist," he said.

"Well, I am right here."

He smiled at her genial innocence, her quiet understanding of complex issues. "What I'm trying to say is that even though you can't know what drew your parents to each other, the fact is something pulled at them and they created you. While they may be gone, they live on through you, and there is no better example of that than the ornaments that hang on those tree branches. They are part of you, which makes them part of us and part of our Christmas."

"And not just this Christmas, but every future one we celebrate."

"Right. And what other ornaments do you see on the tree?"

"Mine, and yours!"

"And . . . ?"

"Um . . . your parents'."

"Right, so we have a tree that is equally divided—three Sullivans, three Duncans. Two different families, and now we're one, sharing the holiday together."

"Wow, I never thought about that, Brian . . . Dad. Why do I keep doing that?"

"I think you're having trouble with a lot of names these days," he said.

"You mean the frog?"

He paused, wondering if he should go where his mind already was. It was early and the start of the week and she had a full day of school ahead of her, but in the end he couldn't let this opportunity pass him by. "No, Janey, I mean my parents."

She grew silent, looking around the room as though it could offer her someplace to hide. But not with the bright lights of the tree illuminating even the darkest corners of the farmhouse, and so she finally gazed back at Brian. "They're very nice, Brian, and they've been good to me, and even your mom decided to join in the Secret Santa game at the gazebo, which surprised me and I think her too. But . . . I just don't know what to call them."

"What do you want to call them?"

"I call Gerta by her name and Thomas too, and they're even older than your parents."

"So you want to call them Didi and Kevin?"

"That doesn't seem right, though, especially since I call you Dad . . . when I remember to," she said, with a slight giggle to excuse her slipups this morning.

"You don't have to decide right now, Janey. But I want you to know you can talk to me about this anytime. For now, why don't you go on upstairs and get ready for school, and maybe I'll make you a special breakfast . . . French toast this morning?"

"That sounds good," she said, and as she got up from the sofa, she stopped and embraced Brian until he felt his heart might swell so big it could force tears from him. "I love you, Brian Duncan."

"I love you too, Janey Sullivan."

She ran to the stairs while Brian started toward the kitchen, but when he looked back he found her still standing there. She wasn't done talking. He knew her so well sometimes, but he could only guess at what her mind was churning over now.

"You know something?"

"I know many somethings," he said with a smile.

"Brian, I'm being serious."

"Sorry, Janey, go ahead. What something would you like me to know?"

"I'm ten years old, but I've never ever in my whole life called anyone Grandmother or Grandfather," she said, and then before Brian had a chance to respond, she went dashing up the stairs, closing the door behind her with a sound as loud as the one that had awakened him. He had a feeling that sound would finally stir his parents from their slumber. It was time to begin the day, and if Janey's thoughts were any indication, it would be a day that continued to reveal, and revel in, its holiday surprises.

Brian realized she'd left behind her purple frog. He picked it up.

"What name would you like to be called?"

Of course it remained silent, just as it had since being given to Janey all those years ago.

Several hours later, Brian found himself settled in the backseat of his parents' gleaming black Mercedes, his father in the unlikely role as passenger while his mother concentrated on the road ahead of them. Not that there was much traffic as they headed into downtown Linden Corners on this early Monday afternoon, but his mother took all of her roles seriously—wife, mother, driver, protector of the family.

"Kevin, I thought you were going to remain back at the farmhouse," she said.

"Brian has to set up his bar, and I want to see him in action," he said. "Don't you?"

"Another time," she said, her tone indicating that Brian's job was the least interesting part of his life here. "If we're going to participate in the village Secret Santa event, I may as well get some shopping done while the weather remains decent. And before you suggest going with me, I'll take care of your gift too. Brian, you said the best places are up in Albany?"

"They have actual malls up there," he said.

"Fine. I'll use the GPS."

"Make sure you're beyond our borders before you use that; the one thing Linden Corners fails to embrace is technology."

Didi pursed her lips, Brian able to see them in the rearview mirror. She stated that her jaunt would take only a couple of hours, so why didn't she pick up "Jane" at school and the two of them could go over to Cynthia's and discuss

Christmas plans, especially as Kevin insisted he remain with Brian down at the tavern. They would rendezvous later for dinner, and so, plans set in motion, Brian and Kevin were dropped off in the parking lot of George's Tavern, Didi pulling out moments later and disappearing down Route 23. Brian imagined his mother's desire for a shopping excursion had more to do with her needing a break from small-town life, which he was fine with; it gave him some one-on-one time with his father.

Maybe he'd just get to the bottom of why they'd chosen to spend their holiday here.

"Dad, let me show you George's Tavern, formerly Connors' Corner, where I spend most of my time when I'm not with Janey," he said, stepping up on the porch and taking out his keys. "It's not much, but it's mine."

He noticed his father checking out the structure's durability, remarking that the outside needed a fresh coat of paint, with Brian assuring him it was in the plans for whenever spring decided to rear its bounty in this neck of the woods, as was replacing the floorboards, "so before you say anything about how loudly they squeak, I'm well aware of it. George's here has a rustic charm, and that's partly what keeps the regulars coming. That, and the fact it's the only drinking establishment in town."

"Still, it can't be that profitable," Kevin said. "I don't know how you make ends meet."

"Dad, don't start. I'm content," Brian said.

"Content is just a fancy substitute for happy, and not as convincing," he said. "How you left a high-profile job in Manhattan to sling drinks for the local folks, I'll never know, and before you start to judge my capitalist ways, Brian, let me state that I'm very proud of the strength of your convictions. Many men would have run from the tremendous responsibility you've been thrown, but the way you are with Janey . . . so natural, and with all of the folks in this town. The life you've created here is quite remarkable. And truth be told—and don't let your mother know I said this—I'm envious."

"You, Kevin Duncan, envious of another person?"

"People change, Brian; they evolve," he said. "You, my son, best illustrate that."

Brian liked the way this discussion was going; he just might uncover what his parents were hiding. With that in mind, he opened the door to the tavern and was affronted by the faint odor of stale beer and sawdust, and before he took off his coat he moved to the windows and thrust them open, letting in the cool winter air to swirl around and clear it out for a fresh week. He flicked on the overhead lights, went over to the cash register, and depressed the lever to open the drawer. He made a quick perusal of last night's receipts, deciding it wasn't so bad. The bar did well on nights that Mark bartended, usually drawing a younger crowd that seemed to drink a bit more. Funny to think that at thirty-six Brian was the elder statesman of the bar.

"What do you think?"

Kevin sidled up to the bar, grabbing a seat on one of the stools, and gazed around.

"I like it, rustic indeed. But I see the appeal. I can't imagine there's much stress."

"Only on nights when I can't get Chet Hardesty to leave," Brian said, stepping behind the bar and grabbing a handy glass. "So, stranger, what'll it be?"

"Your mother would tell me coffee."

"You want coffee, the Five-O Diner is across the street."

"What are you having?"

"My usual, seltzer with lime."

"Still not drinking?"

"I stopped for health reasons. Don't see why I should start up again."

"I'll join you in that seltzer."

Kevin Duncan, businessman, entrepreneur, was known as much for enjoying a glass of whiskey as he was for his portfolio, and often meetings that affected the latter were done over healthy shots of the former. Before him was a different Kevin Duncan. Shorn of his pin-striped suits and rep ties, he was dressed in jeans and a flannel shirt, like an older, taller version of his son. For the moment Brian let the anomaly pass, pouring two glasses of the harmless bubbly, dropping wedges of lime into both. He slid one glass toward his father, who picked it up and took a quick sip.

"You charge for this swill?" Kevin asked with a laugh.

"Don't try the wine," Brian replied.

Kevin told him to go about his business, he was just going to hang out and watch, and so Brian set about his daily routine, mopping the floor and washing down the tables and chairs, the soft yellow lights above the bar coming on. Sometimes he forgot to turn them on as night fell, so it was part of his routine. Brian felt self-conscious as he worked, the manual labor so far from anything his father had done, and in point of fact so far from the world he'd come from in New York. He'd once worked in an office where faceless cleaners came in during the night to make pristine his workspace by the next morning. Now that world was gone—Maddie Chasen, his coworker and fiancée; Justin Warfield, the boss who had screwed everything, Maddie included.

Despite it all, Brian had never been happier in his work environment.

"You really do like this," Kevin remarked. "It's not just face-saving when you call."

"Dad, nothing about Linden Corners is false."

"So it seems," he said. "Tell me again, about George. How you came to meet him."

Brian smiled at the memory, finally putting down his dishcloth to face his father. "From the moment I walked in, I had this sense that I would be spending a lot of time here, an ironic thought considering at the time my doctor had advised me not to drink. But here I was, my first night in Linden Corners and staying at the Solemn Nights Motel down the road, when I realized I was bored. Imagine a restless New Yorker so accustomed to bright lights and a city that never sleeps, suddenly in this town where even the owls turn in early. So I came to the only place that was open, Connors' Corner."

"So you strolled into a bar and asked for a seltzer?"

"Actually, it's what put George's trust in me," Brian said, "the fact I didn't drink."

"And then he passed away?"

"Only months after I'd arrived. He was a good man, one of the best I've known."

"Of a heart attack?"

"Right here at the bar. He poured a beer—the last he ever would—and then he was gone."

Silence fell between them, Brian searching for words that would keep the conversation moving forward. He felt that this was the moment of truth and that there was a reason that their talk had gone down the path it had.

"Dad, are you all right?"

Kevin paused, stared at his drink before speaking. "I had a heart attack, three months ago."

Brian felt his own heart leap, irrational fear striking him. He thought of George, gone in the blink of an eye, and here was his father, alive, present, but having suffered the same problem. He wasn't even sure he'd heard right, and his father's continued, eerie silence only served to confuse him further. As though, like his bloodstream refused to absorb the bad stuff he served here at the bar, his mind refused to acknowledge this danger to his father.

"Dad . . ."

"I'm fine. I'm here, aren't I?"

"No wonder . . ."

"I'm surprised you didn't pick up on this before, the way your mother hovers."

"I suspected something was up," Brian said, "the way she called and announced you were coming here for Christmas. I asked to speak with you but she said you were resting."

"Your mother would be happy if I were always taking it easy."

"Dad, she doesn't want to lose you. Heck, I don't want to lose you."

"The fool doctor in Philly says that I'm fine; the attack was mild. But he's advised me to . . . what was his phrase? Oh yes, I should slow down, take better care of myself, to avoid any further complications. So here we are in Linden Corners, relaxing."

"Can I do anything?"

"Yes. Don't tell you mother what we discussed," he said.

Brian crossed his arms. "Besides that?"

Before he had a chance to answer, the front door opened and in stepped the first customer of the day, and of course it was his new regular, Chet Hardesty. What was odd today was the package in his arms; usually the only thing Chet carried with him were some bills, and of course the baggage of unemployment. A cardboard box led him to the bar, where he set it down.

"This was on the front porch, nearly stumbled right over it."

"Not another one," Brian said.

"What's that, son?"

He gazed at the package, at his father, then back.

"Well, before I say, let me be sure," he said, and went about removing the duct tape from the flaps. They popped open and Brian withdrew another package, this one wrapped in shiny green paper and the same style silver ribbon. Once again the message was all too clear, written in a bright red marker:

DO NOT OPEN UNTIL CHRISTMAS

Brian stood staring at the fourth mystery gift for so long he didn't hear Chet clearing his throat until the third time.

"Uh, Brian, how about you look at your pretty gift later. A man's thirst comes first."

It was what happened next that truly surprised Brian, because he saw his father spring into action by going around the back of the bar, dropping an apron around his neck. He sidled up to the taps and pulled out a glass, then said to Chet, "What'll it be?"

CHAPTER 15

CYNTHIA

The week before Christmas had finally arrived, and it was shaping up to be a busy one. Nothing like the complications of uprooting your lives during the busiest time of year, and, as Bradley had said, "tacking on the additional duties of the annual Christmas pageant." On this Monday afternoon Cynthia Knight had the last of many errands to run before she was scheduled to return to her disheveled home, where large moving boxes were beginning to resemble makeshift furniture. Not that those were her concern today; only thirty minutes remained before company in the diametric forms of Didi Duncan and Janey Sullivan was expected at her home. While it would be rude to allow them to arrive first, especially since Bradley was still at work—his final week—she had to figure time was still on her side. She was only two miles from home. So she pulled into the parking lot at Nora's store, A Doll's Attic, and after gathering a sleepy Jake in her arms, she made her way up the stairs and into the musty consignment shop.

"Hang in there, slugger. Mommy's almost done."

He didn't stir, good toddler that he was, on his best behavior. It was warmer today, so she hadn't bundled him up in his snowsuit.

As she walked through the front door, her cough provided much more of an entrance than the ringing of the bells. No matter how much Nora opened the windows to air out the contents of the store, its inherent, musty link to the past was far stronger.

"Cynthia, hi. What a nice surprise," Nora said, emerging from behind the busy counter. She held an old book in her hands, and from the looks of it, she hadn't gotten very far. Either it was a recent acquisition, or she'd just started it, or her mind was elsewhere. Cynthia assumed the latter. "I was just thinking I needed an afternoon pick-me-up. Can you join me for some coffee at the Five-O?"

"I'd love to, but I'm short on time. Jake's been patient enough with me."

"Okay, so then this is a business call?"

"Hate to be so brusque, but yes, and I'm due back at the house soon," she said. "Janey will be there."

Nora nodded. "And you want to know if I've made any progress on her stuffed frog?"

"Are you going to pull a Christmas miracle a second year in a row?" Cynthia asked, her tone as optimistic as her smile was uncertain.

"I wish," Nora said with a shake of her head. "I realize how important it is for you to find out why Annie and her husband gave Janey that stuffed animal—trust me, I've dug all over the place—eBay of course, some old catalogs, other connections with shops across the country I've made over the last year, toy manufacturers, a whole network of Beanie Baby aficionados, the works. But Janey's frog, while unique to her, doesn't seem to be jogging the memory banks of any collectors. What I surmise is that Dan or Annie found it at a local flea market or perhaps a craft shop. I'm guessing it was made by hand rather than factory, and as such there wouldn't be any record. Sorry to say, there's no way of tracing its provenance."

Cynthia nodded. She understood, even if she was disappointed by the outcome.

"We've got a week till Christmas, so I'll keep digging. I just don't want you to get your hopes up."

"I guess that's one story that doesn't have a happy ending," Cynthia said.

"Janey doesn't get many of those, does she?"

The remark wasn't intended to sound harsh, but still the truth of those words stung, creating a fresh burning inside Cynthia's heart. It was like she was losing a part of herself, knowing this was her final Christmas in a town she loved with a little girl whom she adored. She felt like she was breaking a promise to always help look after Janey, and now she was just weeks away from a new home in a new town, somewhere west of the life she'd known these past fifteen years.

"Nora, don't stress over it. What happens, it happens. You've done more than I could have asked," Cynthia said. "Look, I really appreciate your efforts and I hope you'll send me a bill . . ."

"Don't be ridiculous, Cynthia."

"Please, send me a bill. You are running a business, and I hired you."

"We'll discuss it later," Nora said, sounding as though she never wanted to hear another word about it. "Who knows, maybe I picked your name for Secret Santa."

Cynthia laughed. "What are the odds? Ha. Okay, look, I've gotta run . . . Everything else okay with you?"

Nora looked away suddenly, her saddened eyes replacing the amused ones she'd flashed earlier. She didn't appear to want to discuss anything beyond business and Cynthia de-

cided to respect that, at least for now. She really was running late. "Fine, Nora, I won't pry. So, I'll see you Saturday
night at the annual tavern holiday party, yes?"

"You will indeed. I'm helping my mother with the food
as much as she'll let me."

"So you're a spectator?"

Nora laughed. "Thanks, I needed a laugh."

"This is the holiday season; it's supposed to be special.
Problems can wait till the New Year."

"Which means what?"

"Bring Nicholas to the party and just enjoy yourselves,
hang with me and Bradley if it will help ease some of the
tension," she said. "You can figure out the rest of the stuff
when January rolls around. That's what it's there for, resolu-
tions and all that pabulum. Okay, I've gotta run before
Janey gets there first. Wish me luck—Brian's mother is joining us."

"Yikes."

Cynthia leaned over and gave her friend a hug.

"Thanks, Cyn," Nora said. "Now, go. I'm fine."

Cynthia emerged back into the light of day, only to see it
begin to fade in the sky. Time was fast running away from
her, on preparations for the upcoming pageant, on Christmas Day, but mostly on her remaining days in Linden Corners. As she drove through the tiny downtown area, she
mused about all she saw and all she would miss, her eyes zeroing in on the gazebo, the site of so many past Christmas
celebrations, Memorial Day picnics, and Independence Day
fireworks, all of those holidays heightened by memories of
people, of good food and laughter and special times. Driving like an old lady headed to church on Sunday, she ab-
sorbed it all like she'd never see it again, even watching it
from her rearview mirror as it grew more distant. Only her
arrival at Crestview Road returned her to the present, and

instead of taking the turn up, she continued on and pulled to the side of the road beside the windmill.

Brian had lit it before leaving for work at the tavern, its powerful beam of light beginning to dominate the landscape as the sun dipped beyond the horizon and the night took shape. With Jake asleep, she got out of her car, leaned against the passenger door and just stared forward. She watched as the sails spun, ever so slowly in the nearly nonexistent wind. All around her a gentle quiet had settled in, on the roads and in her heart too, until she imagined she could feel every beat, hear the constant thrum. This visit to the windmill was unlike her, she more of a realist, and so seeking inspiration from its knowing sails was beyond her. She knew the windmill was a constant source of energy for Janey and for Brian, and for once she felt its spark. It was beautiful, no doubt, and the sparkle it gave off on this early night filled her with an inner warmth that mixed with regret.

She supposed only now was she appreciating what the old windmill did for others.

What it was doing for her now.

It was this land, this sight, that first drew a wanderlust-struck Annie to Linden Corners, where she met the first man she would fall in love with. But what really filled her days after moving here was the windmill itself, so much so that she was dubbed by the locals the Woman Who Loved the Windmill, and it was because of her it still stood; she had saved it once from being torn down. Had she done so out of her sense of loss for her husband, her dedication to all his family had done to preserve it? Given Dan's missteps in the final months of his life, she gathered Annie had done it for herself, and for Janey.

"Annie, I guess it's all going to turn out okay. I'm sorry we have to leave . . . but Janey is in the best hands possible. But you knew that, didn't you?" she asked aloud, feeling empowered by a fresh whipping wind that blew past her, "and besides, I know she will always have you looking after her. It's like those sails are loving extensions of your arms, and she comes here to feel your embrace. I feel it too, Annie, my best friend who I miss so much."

Cynthia knew she was officially running late, but she couldn't leave just yet.

Jake was sleeping, as though understanding his mother's need for some alone time.

Time that, for her, moved ever so slowly, like the windmill's sails.

She thought of the day she had first met Annie. It had been the height of summer and all around her nature was painted in vibrant, verdant colors, and she'd heard this joyful exuberance coming from the field that separated the two properties. She had gone to investigate, and as she'd stepped over the stone bridge, she saw a woman dancing around the base of the windmill, Dan Sullivan standing just feet from her. She then ran to Dan and leaped into his arms.

"Whoa," he called out, "not even the frogs in the stream can leap like that."

And then he spun her around till her legs took to the sky, and then they kissed and they laughed like nothing else mattered in the world. Cynthia thought she had never before witnessed a more romantic scene, and now as the memories flooded her mind, her eyes began the gentle flow of tears.

She was late, having arrived back home at nearly four thirty that afternoon, the headlights of her car flashing onto another one, already silent in the driveway. Thankfully, though, neither Didi nor Janey had needed to wait in the car or on the porch, since Janey knew where they hid a spare key. When Cynthia walked into the house she heard the sound of guests making themselves comfortable, the smell of fresh-brewed coffee luring her to the kitchen.

"I'm so sorry I'm late," Cynthia said. "Time can get away from you."

"Think nothing of it. We were a few minutes late as well," Didi said.

"Hi, Cynthia . . . hi, Jake," Janey added, her lips coated with the remains of hot chocolate.

As though they'd been here far longer than Didi was politely letting on.

Jake was wide awake now after enjoying a good nap, and he gurgled at the familiar sight of a smiling Janey, who went up to him and started playing with his tiny fingers. It wasn't long before she had taken Jake off Cynthia's hands, bringing him upstairs to play with his array of toys. Cynthia was relieved at the chance for some peace and quiet in her kitchen, but any chance of that would have to wait, as she saw Didi pour one cup for Cynthia, then a refill of hers. She had a feeling Didi's inviting herself over this afternoon was anything but a social call.

Kevin might be the businessman, but Didi was far more imposing.

"Successful shopping day?" Didi asked.

"Mostly," she said. "Bradley is impossible to buy for, so I usually just get him new dress shirts. But not this year."

"What's different this year?"

"You have heard we're moving," she said.

"Yes, and far away, I hear. A major decision in life."

"Life is about opportunity; you have to seize it," she said.

"Your husband's words?"

"Excuse me?"

"Well, dear, it's just you sound like you're trying to convince yourself, not me."

Cynthia held the mug close to her lips, hoping to hide

her faltering expression. She needn't have bothered, her eyes like open windows to her troubled soul, which allowed Didi a chance to peek in. "Brian was right. You're very direct."

"Honest," Didi said. "Otherwise I find that conversations can get diluted, sidetracked."

Cynthia set down her cup, the taste of bitter coffee on her tongue. It was almost as if the aroma's scent had lured her into a carefully orchestrated scene, Didi's agenda conducting itself. Cynthia steeled her nerves and straightened her back, her arms set forward on the table as though she were about to be interrogated. She eyed Didi carefully and decided they might as well get this over with.

"Fire away, Mrs. Duncan."

"Please, dear, call me Didi, and I didn't mean to make you uncomfortable in your home. Which, I must say, despite all the boxes strewn about, is quite charming. Much more modern in its conveniences and furnishings than the farmhouse, as Brian insists on calling it. So, please, relax, I only want to ask after a few things. Call it a mother's concern."

"What would you like to know?"

Didi didn't even hesitate. "Do you think Brian is truly happy?"

"I think Brian is a man who makes other people happy," Cynthia said.

"Now, that's hardly the same thing, is it?" she asked. "My goodness, his father and I have been here barely three days and already we've gone and chopped down a tree, decorated it the same night, attended a village-wide Secret Santa drawing, then watched as Brian lit practically the entire countryside with the windmill, and now on what should be a quiet night he's off for a spell at the tavern. Don't mistake me, the beauty of those lights on the windmills—and his intent behind it—is not something I'll soon forget."

"I know I won't," Cynthia said.

"But you do see my point, don't you? Is Brian always so busy?"

Cynthia considered her words. "You left something out."

"What's that?"

"All that he's done, he's done for Janey. And to an extent, the two of you."

"I'm not sure I get your point, dear."

"Brian's put his life, his own priorities, on hold, or so he keeps informing me," she said. "Sure, every few months he'll announce a plan in which he's going to figure out his future, but before he takes two steps he gets distracted by our daily lives here. It may be a small town, but he's got big issues to consider. The upkeep of the farmhouse, the property—he's the keeper of Linden Corners' legacies, and he wears his responsibility well. But his biggest concern is Janey. He'll do anything for her peace of mind, for her happiness," she said, realizing her tone was bordering on the defensive. She felt her voice begin to quake. "If that means overdoing it a bit at Christmas, so be it. Janey's still only ten years old, and she's endured worse than people five times her age have. What I see, Didi, and not just during this season, but year-round, is your son's utter devotion to that little girl. Her happiness is what makes Brian happy."

"Except now you're not going to be around to see her grow up."

"Mrs. Duncan . . . Didi, I believe you said you believed in being honest. Why now are you dancing around whatever issue you wish to discuss?"

Didi pursed her lips before speaking. "Fair enough, Cynthia."

Cynthia waited while the woman collected her thoughts, sipping at now-cold coffee.

"Who is this Trina woman?" Didi finally asked.

Brian was right about his mother: she didn't miss a trick. The only problem was, when it came to Brian and Trina, Cynthia knew very little. No doubt Didi had become intrigued when Trina was invited for the windmill lighting, the fact that Brian had staged a disappearing act with her shortly after everyone else had gone back to the house for pie. Cynthia herself was curious to know just what she'd created between Brian and Trina, but so far, neither was talking, at least not to her, and apparently not to Didi either. Their lack of knowledge about Brian and Trina's relationship gave them common ground.

"I'm not sure what you're getting at . . . I mean, they're friends."

"Hmph. How long have they been . . . dating?"

"I'm not even sure you can call it that," Cynthia said. "Trina's new in town, the daughter of one of our longtime residents," she said.

"She works at a motel," Didi said with a sniff of disapproval.

"Actually, Richie Ravens, her father, owns it, and he's recovering from a fall. She's here to take care of him and help run the business."

Didi considered this, clearly not happy that her rush to judgment was unfounded.

"How did they meet?"

"Nora and I thought we were responsible for pushing them together, but it turned out that they'd already met. Trina had been to the tavern. I think she just popped in late one night and I guess they got to talking. I think they were already intrigued with each other before Nora and I suggested they might want to . . . you know, go out."

"So she's Brian's girlfriend?"

Cynthia looked amused. "I wouldn't go so far as to say that," she said.

"But you admit you had that in mind when you put him up to the date," Didi stated.

"Brian's been alone a long time . . ."

"And now with you leaving town and shirking your responsibility to Jane, you thought you'd simply marry him off to ease your guilt?"

"I think that's oversimplifying the situation. Seriously, I think you're reading too much into this," Cynthia said, her mind blown. Conversations like this just didn't happen in Linden Corners. "I'll admit it would be great to have Brian settle down, and it's obvious Janey will need a mother figure in her life as she gets older. And I'm not saying Trina is that woman . . . I mean, they've only just met, so I wouldn't go buying a dress anytime soon."

"Except you don't know Brian's pattern."

Cynthia did. They'd had long talks about life, love, things like satisfaction and happiness and settling, on quiet summer nights when only the chirping crickets were privy to their secrets. But she figured she'd let Didi fill her in. It would be interesting to hear the perspective of a mother who simultaneously sneered at her son's choices and did little to help encourage him. As she waited for Didi to continue, she wondered just where Bradley was, why he wasn't rescuing her from this bit of awkwardness, or for that matter, where Janey was too. Had she fallen asleep upstairs with Jake? Not that she wanted Janey to overhear any of this conversation, but her bright smile would be most welcome, a reminder that Cynthia was indeed home in sweet Linden Corners and not in some staged melodrama starring an overbearing mother.

"Brian falls in love at the drop of a hat," Didi finally said.

"He did in high school, and he did again once he arrived in New York, and he did a third time, right here in Linden Corners. Lucy Walker was his childhood sweetheart and they dated not just in high school but all through college. Only after he got the job offer in New York did they part, since Lucy didn't want to move there—she's married to a doctor now and I think they have more homes than children. Anyway, after a while he met that Maddie Chasen woman—a cold fish, if you ask me, and before you go thinking whatever your mind is conjuring, I know I too can be a tough cookie. I wasn't disappointed when I learned of her . . . corporate machinations with the boss."

She'd slept with the boss to get ahead was what she'd done.

Cynthia knew it had devastated Brian, the original reason he'd set out on his journey.

"And then there was Annie," Didi said.

Cynthia had had enough of this; she wasn't going to hear her friend's name minimized by this woman's ill-formed generalities. Squelching anger, she said, "Mrs. Duncan, if you dare compare Annie Sullivan to those other women, I will have to ask you to leave my home. You never met Annie, and despite the way you wish to lump all of the women in Brian's life into one category, Annie defies it. He was going to marry her, and they were going to be happy, and they should have been. He and Annie and Janey—they were a family with everything to look forward to. When she was taken from us, your son stepped up and helped out a little girl who was so lost, she might have given up on any hope of any of her dreams coming true. Each and every day, Brian does that for her, and you know what? She does it for him."

"Yes, dear, your words are very impassioned, and your loyalty to your friends admirable," she said, "and I appreciate your vehemence, your honesty, even if you feel the need to take it out on me. But let us finish this topic with one indisputable fact: Brian was engaged to each and every one of those women—Lucy, Maddie, and yes, Annie—but something happened with each relationship that made marriage impossible."

"Yes, Mrs. Duncan, but in Annie's case, it wasn't fear of living in the big city or not having enough homes, and it certainly wasn't because she climbed the corporate ladder from the bedroom." Cynthia paused, trying to catch her breath, her tone filled with an overriding sadness made more so by her recent epiphany in the shadow of the windmill. Then she said quietly, with reverence, "Annie died."

Didi nodded quietly, and then said with unflinching honesty, almost as if she hadn't heard Cynthia, "And how will it end with Trina?"

CHAPTER 16

TRINA

In a small town like Linden Corners, solitude had a way of finding you. Sitting at the front desk of the motel, Trina Winter was surrounded by silence, realizing for the first time since her arrival that she had the motel to herself. Midweek, there were no guests staying, and Richie was at his doctor's appointment having his cast removed. She could have gone all the way up to Albany for the procedure and in fact had planned on it, when her cousin Mark showed up and offered her a choice: take Richie to the doctor or hold down the fort here.

She chose the motel, and so Mark had taken his uncle the thirty-minute trek to the state's capital. It wasn't that Trina was shirking her responsibilities; she'd done all that was expected of her and more since her father had called with his reluctant request for the favor. On her downtime, during the time when there was a lack of customers and when Richie was found napping, she'd gotten to work, and the motel hadn't looked more spotless in years. Even Richie had noticed, remarking the other day when a bright sun happened to be shining through the plate glass window of the office. In truth, Trina had been cleaning like a madwoman for the past several days, and she knew why. With the leg cast coming off, Richie was well on the road to recovery and thus would have more maneuverability, more flexibility, in not just getting around this motel but his schedule as well. His need for assistance was waning, reduced to physical therapy appointments and exercises back home, and that knowledge had begun to seep out of Trina's subconscious. Watching Mark help Richie into the backseat of the car and drive off, Trina felt the bond she'd begun to establish with him slip back to the way it had been. Distance defined them, and not just in miles.

Her days in Linden Corners were numbered; that was what she told herself.

But then again, just what was she going home to? An empty apartment, the occasional dinner out with friends, or worse, an invitation from her mother to stay for the weekend in Coral Gables with her new husband? Did she even want to return to her job? Being an office manager was hardly inspiring. Another idea appealed more to her, one that allowed her to just hop into her car and cruise down the open highway, destination unknown, not unlike what had happened to Brian. Maybe there was some windmill of her own to discover, to conquer?

Now, where had that scenario come from? she asked herself.

The Sunday night lighting of the windmill and her subsequent non-date with Brian; that was where. For days she'd tried—and failed—to deny the obvious attraction developing between them, even as she knew there was something deeper. The ease with which he lived his life was enviable. He just accepted life as it came, never plotting in advance, never dreaming beyond the realistic . . . the achievable. Was that even in her? She always wanted things to be better, lacking only the resources, the resolve, to seek those

changes. How wounded Brian must have been to leave behind his old life. Had he even known where he was going or
what was in store for him? Probably not. All he knew was
that he had to remove himself from the confines of New
York and leave behind bitter memories.

The difference was, Trina wasn't bitter. She was just
uninspired.

Life in Florida—sunshine, heat, year-round, and at times
so expected it grew boring.

Which was why she'd come here, not just for her father
but in search of winter too. When you watched the seasons
change before your very eyes, it encouraged you to do the
same. The frigid blast of wind, the falling snow that lined
tree branches and buried the earth underneath a white blanket, the notion of fireplaces crackling; these things spoke to
her more than she'd expected they would. Yet today it was
neither sunshine nor snow that held her attention, but a
steady drizzle outside, gray clouds hovering even as the afternoon stretched on quietly. Indeed, that was all she heard,
the persistent patter of rain against the roof, droplets creating runaway streaks on the window. Like Linden Corners
was mirroring her cries over leaving. This town had a way
of embracing new people, taking them into its homespun
hold. Like her day at the Five-O Diner, serving up coffee as a
way to help Sara, Martha. Like the Secret Santa drawing . . .

"Oh no, I forgot," she said, this time her thoughts given
voice.

In the craziness of caring for Richie, she'd completely
forgotten about having to buy the gift for the town's Secret
Santa game. *Wait, slow down*, she thought, *you have time still.
Christmas is six days away, the pageant and Secret Santa celebration in five.* With Richie out of his cast, it would free up
more of her time in the coming days, enabling her to complete her shopping. And not just hers, but clearly she'd have

to buy Richie's gift as well. He hadn't exactly been thrilled with Trina when he woke to learn that she'd entered him in the village's new tradition—the card with the person's name on it remained ignored and was later found in the trash can. She'd retrieved it and stuffed it in her purse along with the one she'd chosen.

Headlights suddenly caught her eye, and she watched as a car pulled into the lot.

The rain had become a torrent from the sky, and so when the man came dashing from his car, he was soaked by the time he entered the office.

"Afternoon, may I help you?"

"Yeah, I guess so," he said, wiping droplets from his brow. "I was thinking I could make it all the way to the Massachusetts border, but this rain is picking up and I'm not a fan . . . So the outside sign says you've got rooms?"

"We do indeed," Trina said, happy for the distraction of work. "Just one night?"

"I think that's all I'll need, yes. Truthfully, I got a little lost on all those county roads and just stumbled upon this place. It's like I've arrived in the middle of someone else's story."

"Motels all have their own stories, most of them short, like the stays."

He nodded appreciatively as Trina set the ledger before him, watching as the man, probably late thirties and nice looking, respectable in a business suit, jotted down his name. She asked for a credit card, "or will that be cash?" and he said, "No, that's fine, credit it is," and so she ran the card and had him sign the receipt. She watched the looping flair with which he signed his name: Jonathan Parker.

"Mr. Parker, I hope you'll enjoy your stay at the Solemn Nights," she said, handing over the key to Room 10. "Free coffee early in the morning but otherwise if you're feeling hungry I suggest the Five-O Diner just a half mile down the road. Great food and reasonable prices, you can't beat it. There's also a nice tavern across the street from the diner that will keep you occupied in the night hours, about the only thing in our town that will."

"Many thanks," he said. "Ironic in the rain, but all I can think about is a shower."

She laughed, watching as he returned to his car and grabbed his lone suitcase, trying his best to protect himself from the rainfall. Then he was gone from sight, headed to his room for a respite from the demands of his regular life. She recalled what Richie had told her about the transient nature of the motel business—people checked in, they checked out a day or two later, and they were off on the remainder of life's journey. Was that her too, with this motel just a stop in her life, a time-out from what she should be doing?

Moving out from behind the counter, Trina secured the door open and allowed the mild air to sweep inside and clear the cobwebs from the corners of the motel's office and from her mind. Christmas might be days away, but the rainstorm was doing too good a job of melting the snow, leaving the highway wet, the snowy drifts darkened with soot and the entrails of passing traffic. It was not very picturesque, and she had to hope that by the time Christmas Eve arrived a fresh batch of snow would have fallen over the region. Otherwise the storm from earlier this month served as nothing more than a tease of winter's promise, and she wasn't sure she could deal with such a thing.

Another set of headlights caught the reflective glass of the office, almost blinding her.

"Busy day for the Solemn Nights," she said, but then she realized it wasn't a new tenant but a familiar face. She recognized the truck, since just the other night she'd been inside it. Her heart thumped, nervousness and anticipation washing over her.

"Trina, hi," Brian said, dashing through raindrops but still getting wet during the quick jaunt to the protective covering over the office. He shook his head to release excess rain, producing a smile when he looked at her. "Lovely day, isn't it?"

"Don't tell me you've come looking for a room. Need an escape from your parents?"

His eyes darkened in the cloudy day. "Don't joke—you're not far off. And not *parents*."

"Ah, parent," she said. "Let me guess, your mother."

"I don't even want to get into it . . . ," he said.

"Okay, so you're not here to complain."

"Actually, I was out running errands and was going to see if you were free for coffee at the Five-O. But from the looks of it, you're here by yourself."

"Holding down the fort," she said, using Mark's words, and then explained the particulars of her day.

"Well then, I won't keep you. But while I'm here, I just want to double-check that you're coming to the annual tavern Christmas party. This Saturday night, remember?" he asked.

"You mentioned it the other night . . . in passing. What, no printed invitations?"

"Just a personal one."

"Brian, you could have called."

"I could have," he said.

"But . . ."

"But how about I didn't want to call."

"You weren't out running errands; you drove here right from the farmhouse."

"I wanted to see you."

"How did you know I was here?"

He smiled. "Because Mark texted me about an hour ago and said he was running late for his shift at the tavern tonight. The doctor's office was backed up and he wasn't sure when they would return."

"So you came to town to open up for him?"

"I guess so."

"Where's Janey?"

"With my parents. Having a night of getting-to-know-you."

Trina nodded. "Lucky them," she said.

"Not sure Janey feels that way," he said. "My mother . . . she has a way of arming people."

"And you, Brian Duncan, you're very disarming," Trina said.

"If we keep talking, the conversation is going to circle back to my mother again."

"So you don't want to talk about her."

"No."

"What do you want to talk about?"

He paused before saying, "Nothing."

She decided just a shake of her head was answer enough.

That's when Trina closed and locked the door of the office and took hold of Brian's hand, leading him down the pathway in front of the motel, stopping before her room. She felt his eyes focused only on her, and they were glassy, perhaps wet, and not from the falling rain just inches away from them. Twisting the knob, she guided him inside, closing it quickly behind them.

"Don't you have to open soon?" she asked, her tone playful.

"I'm the boss. I can open when I want."

"What about your regulars?"

"Chet Hardesty's liver could do with a break."

She nodded, smiled. "Can I get you, uh, anything?"

"Trina Winter, I think our window of opportunity is closing. Time is not our friend."

"So let's make it stop," she said.

They came into each other's arms in a burst of heated passion, kisses deep, forceful. She felt his lips kiss her neck, the scrape of whiskers sending fresh sensations washing over her. Hands in his hair, she pulled him tighter to her, leading him to the bed. This was crazy, her mind was screaming at her. Just a moment ago she was checking a complete stranger into one of the motel's rooms, and now she was taking into her bed a virtual stranger, this man she knew as Brian, whom she liked and whose presence in her life was as unexpected as anything she'd experienced since coming to Linden Corners—impromptu shifts at the diner, a whiskey shot in the dark, and the brightest display of lights she'd ever seen, all atop an unlikely windmill that captured hearts, thoughts, and imaginations. But none of those were a match for what she felt now, what she wanted, desired, and in another moment's time her world exploded with more lights than her eyes could take. She closed them, she felt, she touched, and she thrilled at the response of someone who made her body flush with heat.

"Oh, Brian . . . ," she said, her breath short, her voice soft.

The afternoon segued into early evening all while the rain continued to pelt against the side of the motel. Gray clouds swept down ever closer and the clock inched ever forward, until just one world existed, the one inside a room where memories were as fleeting as its guests, and where strangers who had become friends now became something deeper than friends.

"So does this mean you'll be my date for the Christmas party?"

In the enveloping darkness of the room, the two of them burrowed beneath an array of twisted blankets, the silence broken first by Brian's question and second, and more loudly, by Trina's laughter.

"Oh, so now you're asking me out on a proper date?"

"Our first night was a real date," Brian said, a smile highlighting his features.

"Yes, just how a girl likes to be asked—'I will if you will.' Very romantic."

"It worked," he said.

"So did your poorly staged invitation today," she said.

"I was that obvious?"

"You've got a bar to open," she said. "You didn't have time to dance around it."

"I still have a bar to open."

"Is that your exit strategy?"

He pulled her tight against his body, kissing her. "I'll stay all night if you want."

Trina returned the kiss and wondered if she would really want that. About what they had just shared, she had no regrets, and she was glad that Brian hadn't asked her if she did. The glow of their lovemaking hadn't even worn off; why spoil it with intrusive thoughts of the aftereffects? She rose from the bed, wrapping her body in a robe that hung on a hook on the bathroom door. As nice as the terry cloth felt against her skin in the stark coldness of the room, it was no match for the smooth, heated flesh of the man in her bed.

"I'll take that as a no?" Brian asked.

She sat upon the mattress, facing him. "Brian Duncan, we both know you have to leave."

He stole a look at the clock on the bed stand, her eyes following his.

"Yup, five thirty," she said.

"I'm late."

"Yes, you are."

"I guess that means I should go," he said.

"Brian, if you're trying to spare my feelings, don't. I'm fine . . . I'm great."

"Great?" he asked, a wide smile settling in across his face.

She laughed. "Good."

"It's been a while . . ."

"Brian Duncan, get out of that bed, get dressed, and get back to your life."

He did two of the three things she'd suggested, and as he stood in the center of the room finishing buttoning his shirt, he pulled Trina tight against his body. "How can I get back to my life when part of it is right here, in this room, in my arms?"

She allowed another kiss but then pushed him away.

"If Richie comes home and finds that I locked up the motel for a couple hours . . ."

"And if he sees the truck parked here. Two plus two equals . . . us. Just like my mother deduced the night she and my father stayed at the motel."

"Okay, that seals it. You're talking about Didi again. Time to go."

He laughed heartily as he departed, Trina watching from the door as the old truck pulled out of the lot and retreated back down the highway, disappearing even faster than a clear day would have allowed. The falling rain was still strong, and a shadowy mist had dropped low from the sky. She was glad for the cover of not just the night but also the swirling fog, hugging herself out of a natural sense of self-preservation. Down the parking lot, she saw that her guest, Mr. Parker, was not around, his car gone. Perhaps he'd gone for food at the Five-O, she thought, or was attempting to have a drink at the bar she had recommended, all while she was busy keeping the bartender from attending to his duties.

She smiled at the thought of Brian. He was sweet, and today he had been hesitant at first, but he'd come around, almost as though he and she, so alike, were lost in that desired stoppage of time, with nothing beyond the knowing walls of her room mattering. Returning to the room, she quickly made the bed, running a hand over the covering as though trying to absorb the memories spun from it. Only the sound of a car pulling into the lot stirred her to action, and when she saw it was Mark's car, she threw her clothes on as fast as she could, knowing while she fussed with the last buttons that Richie would know she'd not been in the office the entire time.

As she threw open the door of her room, Richie was hobbling out, still on crutches. But the cast was missing and what passed for a smile for him was plastered on his face.

"Did I catch you taking an afternoon nap?" he asked.

"I spilled coffee on my shirt; I went back for another one," she said.

The fact that she had to turn the lock on the office door spoke otherwise. Richie said nothing and just made his way beyond the office and to his apartment, dropping onto the sofa. He let out a heavy sigh. While he was doing that, Trina thanked Mark for taking him.

"How was he?"

"He was Richie," Mark responded.

"I'm sorry."

"I'm used to him," he said.

"I'm not."

"Stick around long enough, Trina; he'll get under your skin."

"You mean like a rash?"

"I heard that, missy!"

Mark laughed and told her good luck; he was off for a quiet, unexpected night off.

"Brian said he'd take the shift since he started it," he said. "Which means I'm free."

"Sara's not working?"

"Sara's about to pop," he said proudly. "Martha sent her home on Monday and said don't come back till the only thing in the oven is her Christmas turkey. I'm off from the resort, Brian took the bar tonight . . . I can't remember the last night my wife and I got to spend together."

"Enjoy it, because once that baby arrives . . ."

"Right, our little Christmas bundle of joy."

"The gift that keeps giving."

"And taking," Mark said, "for eighteen years. I can't wait."

Mark departed back into the rain, leaving Trina no choice but to return to the apartment. Richie sat with his eyes closed, but he could hear her for sure, because when she sat down he asked, "Any business?"

"One gentleman. I gave him room ten."

"Better than nothing," he said. "Business has been slower than normal this season."

"Like you said, Richie, it's a transient life."

"One you seem to be enjoying," he said.

She wasn't sure what he meant by that and really didn't want to get into anything with him. Yet she couldn't avoid all topics of conversation, and in an effort to deflect any talk of her growing involvement with the Linden Corners community, she said, "Richie, can we talk about Christmas?"

"What's there to talk about?"

Trina looked over at a bare corner in the apartment. "We don't even have a tree."

"I don't do trees," he said. "They're a fire hazard."

"Right, just like you don't do Secret Santa?"

"Trina Ravens, don't start with me," he said.

"It's Winter," she said, her words more hurtful than she intended.

"If that's the case, I don't know what you're doing here," he said.

"Richie . . ."

"Right. I'm Richie, not Dad, and you're not a Ravens," he said. "We're nothing to each other, Trina."

She felt on the verge of tears and wondered how life could hand her such a high as what she'd experienced this afternoon, only to turn the tables on her and sink her down to the lowest depths. She fought through them; she wouldn't cry in front of the man who'd given the little girl in her plenty of nights when tears lulled her to sleep. When her stepbrothers would wish their father a good night and Trina tried to enact the same reverential tone, usually failing and scuffling off to her room, she was reminded of just how much of a stranger she felt inside her own house. She felt that way now, and worse, since her room was the definition of temporary. She'd been living in a motel for weeks now, and only once had she felt alive inside it, only a couple of hours ago.

She didn't know what was bothering Richie, but she wasn't about to ask. It was like poking a wounded bear. In her mind she saw herself easily picking up right now. Pack her bags, get in her car, and go. Good-bye, Linden Corners; good-bye, Richie Ravens.

Running away was so the Richie Ravens way to do it. Failed? Don't fix, move on.

Which was why she remained right where she was, a tear in her eye.

Richie looked away, suddenly embarrassed. "I'm sorry, Trina, that was wrong of me. I'm just . . . frustrated. I can't imagine eight weeks of physical therapy . . . three times a week. I just want my life back."

"Time heals, Richie," she said, "or at least, it's supposed to."

"That doesn't excuse my lashing out at you. You've been here for me, always."

"Not always," she admitted. "Some nights I sneak out, like I'm some teenage girl."

He actually allowed himself a smile. "I know, you go to George's."

"Why, Richie Ravens, are you spying on me?"

"I told you, I know people in this town. People in this town talk."

"People in this town should mind their business."

"Just be careful, Trina. If you don't live here on your own terms, this town will suffocate you."

She was beginning to think she and Brian had much more in common than ever, not least among them parents with eyes in the backs of their heads. She decided to let it go, all of it, her anger at him and her frustration over her stagnant life. Wasn't Christmas Day right around the corner, and wasn't that what she'd really come for? Why couldn't she just enjoy it for what it was, a special time of year to be celebrated with friends and family? And the last time she checked, in Linden Corners she had both, and more.

"What do you want for dinner?" she finally said.

"How about the Five-O?"

"Fine, and now that you've got your cast off, we're going out to dinner."

"Trina Winter, don't try and change your old man."

"Why not?" she asked. "Isn't this the season for miracles?"

CHAPTER 17

BRIAN

After the all-day soaker from midweek had washed away the snowy remnants of the previous storm, Linden Corners was looking decidedly un-Christmas-like with two days remaining until the eve of the holiday. The soggy field beyond the farmhouse was a checkerboard of melting snowcaps and grime-encrusted ice, leaving the striking windmill the lone piece of beauty on its landscape. That would change. Local weather forecasters were promising a white Christmas, as a big storm that had already left upward of two feet of snow across Canada and the Great Lakes was sweeping its way across New York State, just in time to imbue the annual tavern Christmas party with a touch of sky-fallen magic.

At just after eight o'clock on this Saturday morning, with the lights doused and the wind silent, there was not yet any hint of the storm that was brewing. He'd been out back in the barn since before seven, digging out his party supplies and the extra folding tables that were required to accommodate the large crowd that turned out for the feast. He'd let his parents and Janey sleep, content to work alone. Knowing he would leave people happy, full, and filled with the holiday spirit was enough to keep him going. Of all the many yearly celebrations they shared in Linden Corners, Brian considered this Christmas tradition his favorite, not only allowing him to continue one of George's time-honored parties, but also seeing everyone gathered together was what he'd come to love about his adopted home.

And it made Gerta so happy; that was the icing on the . . . well, in her case, the pie.

After packing the back of the truck with various supplies—preparing for the first of several trips he'd need to make this morning—he snuck back inside a farmhouse awash with sleep, fetched a bag filled with presents he'd purchased yesterday afternoon. He hadn't had a chance last night to hide them inside the closet in the windmill, not after Janey had come bounding off the school bus just as he'd arrived home, thrilled that it had been her last day of school until the New Year. Now, as she savored her slumber before the anticipation of the upcoming holiday won out, he made his way across the soggy field, his boots splattered with mud by the time he reached the door to the windmill. Once inside, he ventured up the winding staircase and proceeded to open the locked closet.

"Oh, of course . . ."

He'd almost forgotten about the four gifts stored inside. He looked at them, all the same size, different only in the color of the wrapping: blue and green, gold and red, and for a moment he thought there was something familiar about how they looked together. Only the silver ribbon was the same, and of course, the message written on the Santa-adorned cards. He could have easily opened them right now . . . maybe just one? But he had waited this long. Why deprive his Secret Santa of his or her satisfaction? Besides, now that he was involved in the same game—this time as the gift giver—he could understand the anticipation of waiting until the gift was opened and the identity revealed. Avoiding any further temptation, he placed the plastic bag inside and locked it up fast, sliding the key into his pocket.

He left moments later, but not before taking a look back at the closet.

Whoever was playing this game with him, he was certain he knew them, and no doubt the person wore an excellent poker face. In the month since their dance had begun, not one person had tipped his or her hand, not a single clue had revealed itself to him. One gift had arrived, and then another, placed innocently on the porch of the tavern or the farmhouse, until there were four presents in all, all delivered with stealthy precision. With two days still till Christmas, he wondered if a fifth and final would be forthcoming. Speculation would have to wait until the day of revelation; for now, he had a party to finalize.

Fifteen minutes later he was on Route 23, headed toward downtown Linden Corners, the first to arrive at the tavern. Heck, it had been only a few hours since he'd closed up after a busy night, and while here he was again, this time pulling into an empty lot instead of out, he noticed someone else had beaten him. No surprise as he recognized Gerta's car. He saw the kindly old lady stepping off the porch. She waved to him in her genial way, which brought a smile to his lips.

"And I thought I'd be getting the worm," he said, getting out of the truck.

"Eaten and digested," she said.

"One of Martha's specialties?"

"Oh, you and your jokes, Brian Duncan. Good thing Martha didn't hear you."

He welcomed her warm embrace, more so than normal as he felt a decidedly cold wind sweep past him. Even Gerta shivered, wrapping her arms around her woolen jacket. The weather had already begun to shift. He walked to her car and retrieved a series of boxes that contained decorations like plastic ivy and silver bells and a sprig of mistletoe he would hang from the front entrance, as well as burners for the trays of food that would be on offer all day. Gerta had been cooking up roasts and other specialties all week, always trying to outdo herself.

"You look good, Brian. Everything okay with you?"

"Considering the stress at the farmhouse, yeah, I guess," he said. "I feel like I've barely seen you in weeks."

"Don't be ridiculous. I've been around. Plus, you've been busy with your parents."

Brian frowned. "Adopt me, Gerta Connors."

She laughed, and as they carried the boxes inside the bar she told him it couldn't be all bad, and that launched him into several tirades about his mother's actions and remarks, from her insistence on referring to Janey as Jane, to her raised eyebrows whenever she heard mention of the name Trina, and "oh, and then what she said to Cynthia the other night . . ."

"Yes, I know all about that one . . . Goodness, Cynthia told me and I thought she was going to pop a blood vessel. Brian, the thing you have to remember is this: parents are always looking out for their children, no matter how grown-up they are. Your choices aren't necessarily what they would choose for you, so if your mother is . . . acting out, or verbal with her opinions, isn't it better than saying nothing at all? Just let her speak her mind, and that gives you the right to respond with your opinion. And then be nothing more than your wonderful self."

"See, that's what I've missed. Down-home advice."

"Sure, you'll listen to me," she said. "Nora on the other hand has her own thoughts about advice from her mother."

"Trouble with Nicholas is what I hear."

"My daughter wouldn't know what's good for her if it asked her to dance."

"Nora is very stubborn," Brian said, adding, "She'd probably get along great with Didi."

"You can't choose your family," Gerta said.

"If that were true, Linden Corners would be a very different place."

Their smiles lingered until a sweeping wind forced them back to work, and inside.

For the next several hours, it was work that consumed them. As they set up tables and additional folding chairs in the large, open room, then set up serving tables and the wire tins for the food, time moved quickly. After a couple of trips back and forth to the farmhouse and to the Connors home, the noon hour arrived with most of the preparations in order, so that Brian and Gerta, with a helpful assist from the sturdy teen Travis—he doing the heavy lifting—all finally took a breather. Brian served up tall glasses of soda, and they sat down at a table and took in their handiwork. Christmas adorned the walls and the edge of the bar, and that sprig of mistletoe hung right over the main entrance.

"I do think we're ready," Gerta said.

"All we need now is the people," Brian added.

"And the food," Travis reminded them.

"Ah, speaking of, I promised you lunch, didn't I?" Gerta said to her grandson. "Shall we have a quick snack over at the Five-O before the festivities begin? Brian, would you like to join us?"

"I've got one more errand to run," he said. "I'll see you back here at three o'clock."

Brian watched as grandmother and grandson walked hand in hand across the main route that cut through Linden Corners, pulled inside the diner by the enticing smells of

Martha's cooking. As for Brian, he drove back toward the farmhouse, his mind conjuring similar images of Janey and his mother, trying to ascertain whether it was anywhere near close to reality. When he arrived back, he found the farmhouse was empty. He knew Janey was over at the Knights', leaving his parents unaccounted for. No note had been left. They were grown-ups and could do as they pleased, but no matter, Brian was glad he had this one last moment of the day to himself.

Once more he journeyed down to the windmill, feeling that fresh wave of cold air rip through his body. The weather was fast turning bad, which he thought could affect the turnout for the day's party. But Linden Corners was full of hearty folk, and it would take a beast of a storm to keep them from a tradition such as this. In the end, he realized he had no control over any of it, and so he ventured back inside the windmill and forged his way to the circuit breaker. He flipped the switch and saw a bright glow shower the gray covering of the day. Retreating outside, he looked at the results of his hard work, the flickering shadows of the turning sails already beginning to take shape on the field.

One Christmas he had forgotten to light the windmill, while another the power had failed.

This year he was determined there would be no such incident, no surprises, nothing but cheer and the joy brought by the season, goodwill toward man. And as if to grant his wishes, that's when the snow began to fall.

The tavern was filled with the hungry, thirsty residents of Linden Corners, who were all laughing, talking, and embracing in the true spirit of the holiday, playing a guessing game about who got whom for Secret Santa. Amidst all the frivolity, only Brian Duncan remained unsatisfied, continually watching the front door for the arrival of the obvious ones who were missing. By the time the first hour passed, chief among them were Kevin and Didi Duncan, not to mention a woman by the name of Trina Winter. Sure, Chuck Ackroyd was here, and Chet too, and a bunch of other regulars. Martha from the Five-O was enjoying one of her rare nights off, and the twins Marla and Darla had taken up residence at the corner of the bar, indulging in their annual tradition of too many tequila shots. The older folks from Edgestone Retirement Center had ventured out from the comforts and routine of prepared meals and the annual holiday concert from the high school band for the wondrous smells of Gerta's holiday roasts and a jukebox filled with Christmas songs. Elsie Masters and Thomas Van Diver and their usual breakfast gang had taken over one of the tables near the jukebox, lording over the song choices. Bing Crosby's "White Christmas" was playing now, perhaps its fifth go-round in the last hour. No one had complained about their hogging the machine.

Most of the kids had taken to the backyard, where the snow that had been falling all day had already left enough for snowball fights and angel making, though clearly by evidence of the thin snowman positioned by the side of the road, a few more hours were needed for him to come to life. One of the exceptions to the kids was Janey, who was hanging out with Sara, so pregnant it was easier for her to stay in one place, at the far end of the bar. The two of them nursed Cokes while they shared possession of Jake, who was nibbling at a bowl of Goldfish crackers. They were close enough to the door leading upstairs to Sara and Mark's apartment that if Jake grew tired or restless—or Sara did— they could easily slip out.

At another table were a rather subdued Cynthia and Bradley and Nora and Nicholas, and while they seemed to be chatting amiably enough, even from a distance Brian could tell not everyone there was at their happiest. It reminded him that he wasn't having the best time either, as he continued to keep a steady eye on the front door, waiting for the moment either his parents arrived or Trina did, but as the clock turned closer to five, they remained missing in action. He thought about calling his father to ask where they were, fear stabbing at him when he questioned whether their absence was health related. Had his father had another heart attack? Would they even tell him when they did show up, or wait until after the holidays, or maybe never, leaving Linden Corners behind without clueing him in to all that was going on?

At last Brian's day brightened, as Trina cautiously slipped inside the tavern, her arrival as stealthy as that of his Secret Santa gifts. Which meant he took quick notice, and, with a smile on his face, made his way over. Was she wearing more makeup than he usually saw her with, or maybe her cheeks were just reddened by the cold air outside? Had she walked over again?

"I'm sorry to be so late . . . ," she said.

"It's okay," he said, "as long as you're here now. Where's Richie?"

"In one of his moods. After two hours of trying to convince him to come, waiting for his inevitable change of heart, I gave up. But my goodness, I don't think you'd even notice if someone was missing, this place is so crowded. I trust no one has finished my scotch?"

"They haven't," Brian said, "and just an FYI, I do notice."

Taking her hand, he walked her over to the bar, feeling the eyes of his friends on him like snow sticking to the ground; they weren't going anywhere. He took her coat and hung it on the rack in the corner, returning to pour her a drink but finding Mark was already on it. She chatted with her cousin briefly, and then excused herself to see if Sara needed anything. Brian let her go, getting back to work with more than a spring in his step. He felt like paying forward his happiness, so, noticing his friends' drinks were running low, he poured a fresh round and brought them over, setting them down in front of them before clearing out the empties.

"You guys do know this is a celebration, not a wake?"

Bradley thanked Brian for the refills, took a healthy drink from his while the others went untouched. "I'm afraid we've got a somber crowd here," he said, pushing his blond locks from his forehead while offering up a sheepish smile. "Cynthia's acting like she's already in Texas, and these two . . . I don't know what's going on. But it's nice to see you and Trina . . . uh, getting along."

"Yes, Brian, tell us more," Cynthia said. "Give us some happy relationship news."

Brian ignored the gentle poking, turned his eyes to Nora. Nicholas was looking away.

"You two okay?"

"It's nothing. We're fine," Nora added. "Go and have fun, Brian."

"I'm working. It's you four who should be having fun."

Cynthia looked aimlessly toward her son while Nicholas acted like a newcomer who had sat down among strangers. Brian needed a quick fix, and so on his way back toward the bar he whispered into Thomas' ear, and the old man grinned, he too gazing over at the forlorn folks at the table. When the current song ended, a rousing version of "Rockin' Around the Christmas Tree" took over, encouraging a few folks to dance. Brian watched as Bradley coerced Cynthia to the designated dance floor, and soon he had her twirling around, a smile beginning to spread across her face. When Janey joined them with baby Jake in her arms, the four of them looked so natural, like a family should at the holidays. Even Nicholas had somehow persuaded Nora to get up, and soon the two of them were locked together, enjoying the dance if not eye contact.

Mission accomplished for now, Brian told Thomas to keep up the festive tunes, and soon enough the joyous atmosphere had spread throughout the tavern. The dance floor became the most popular area, with even a few happy couples sneaking kisses under the mistletoe. His regulars, though, remained glued to their bar stools, knowing the moment they got up they would lose them, and so Chet and Chuck and the twins did their best to groove to the music while sitting. Their best move was a finger indicating that a refill was desired. As one song ended, clapping filled the room, only to be drowned out by the sudden shattering of a glass. Chuck had knocked over his beer, it landing on the wood floor in splinters and shards.

"I'll get it," Mark said, coming around the bar.

Brian slid a fresh one Chuck's way and said, "You may want to slow down, Chuck."

He responded in the form of a sneer, followed by the downing of half his beer.

"I'll drink what I want, when I want, Windmill Man."

Brian just shook his head and walked away. He'd been dealing with the many moods of Chuck Ackroyd for as long as he'd been in town, the two of them far from best friends. Some people were just not happy until they'd made other people miserable.

"Keep an eye on him, Chet," Brian advised.

The next song was "I Saw Mommy Kissing Santa Claus," and for a moment Brian's mind took him back to his own childhood, thinking about his parents and how his father had been the jokester in the family, dressing up as Santa on Christmas Eve and eating the cookies they'd set out, even as his older brother, Philip, and his sister, Rebecca, watched with knowing amusement. Brian had been the youngest by several years, and at the time, he still believed in holiday magic. Which meant he wanted to sneak onto the stairs and see what happened when he was supposedly asleep. What he witnessed was his mother sneaking a kiss under Santa's flowing white beard, but hearing the familiar laugh of his father. He'd dashed upstairs and under his covers, his mind reeling. It was one of his first memories of the disappointment that can accompany life, and he was feeling it now, knowing it was once again his parents' fault. As if on cue, the front door of the tavern opened and in walked Didi and Kevin Duncan, she in her uniform of smart skirt and sweater, her pearls clasped around her neck, he in slacks and a cardigan sweater over a dress shirt. She was in reserved mode, keeping her distance, while his father seemed to be embracing the laid-back spirit Linden Corners represented.

"You're here," Brian said, walking toward them.

"We apologize, Brian . . . time got away from us," Didi offered.

"Where were you?"

"Don't ask questions so close to Christmas, young man," his father advised with an easy smile. "Well, this is quite the party, Brian, wonderful turnout, near about the whole town, it looks like . . . Say, I could use a whiskey—got anything good?"

"Kevin . . ."

"Geez, Didi, one isn't going to kill me."

Brian knew his remark was intended as a joke, but the echoing words didn't sit well with his mother. As he escorted them deeper into the bar, he made introductions to Father Eldreth Burton from Saint Matthew's Church, who was sipping wine while talking with a woozy Marla and Darla, trying in vain to get them to come to church on Sundays. He noticed Trina helping Sara get up from her chair, leading her to the door to her apartment; he guessed Sara needed a respite, and he was glad to have Trina vacate the bar, at least for now. He nodded her way, she smiling back as though she understood.

Brian got his parents settled on a pair of recently vacated stools. He poured his father his desired top-shelf whiskey— a Dewar's, just like Trina put up with—and served his mother a glass of red wine, watching the downward turn of her lips after the first sip.

"I'm sure it's an acquired taste, dear," she said.

"Just like Linden Corners itself," Kevin said, raising his glass.

The party grew busy again with the arrival of more people, so Brian had to return to his post behind the bar, and only occasionally could he sneak a look beyond the buildup of bodies at the bar. Outside, the snow continued to fall, thick flakes that showed no sign of stopping. A bunch of the kids gave up on the cold, finding the hot chocolate stand in the kids' corner at the far end of the tavern. Cookies and punch were set up too. Brian noticed that Janey had tired of caring for Jake and had joined the younger set, hanging with Travis Connors and her old friend Ashley, whom she rarely saw, since she'd moved to a new school in a neighboring town. He was glad to see Janey fit in so well with anyone she encountered, whether it be the toddler Jake, the adults like Sara and Cynthia and Gerta, or just kids her own age.

This was his favorite part of the party, taking a backseat to the action and watching who talked with whom, and what new connections in this tiny town were made. He saw his parents engaged in conversation with Gerta, she obviously filling them in on some of Brian's travails in town, as evidenced by smiles both tight and broad, from Didi and Kevin, respectively. He heard her telling the story of his taking Janey by sled halfway across town to make sure Gerta was okay that one Christmas morning. Noticing their drinks were low, Brian wandered over with a bottle.

"For me, yes," Didi said. "For him, he'll have seltzer."

Gerta caught Brian's eye as he returned with the drinks.

"I knew there was something special about him from the moment he arrived," Gerta was saying now. "I mean, one night my husband, George, comes home early from tending bar, unusual for him, and when I ask him why, he says he thinks he's found someone who will help him out. I had to find out for myself this man George was raving about. And while my George was the gentlest soul I've ever known, he could see a con coming a mile away. He had one rule when he ran this bar: no tabs." She paused and looked over at a familiar face at the bar and said, "Yes, I mean you, Chuck Ackroyd."

Brian thought Chuck looked bleary-eyed and whispered to Mark that he was cut off.

"Let him build back his tolerance," he advised.

"Anyway, Brian Duncan was a godsend at an awful time, and I count my blessings he came into our lives."

Didi was clutching her pearls when she said, "Brian was always conscious of others."

While Brian waved off the compliments with modesty, he'd sooner have heard more than witnessed what happened next.

"Brian Duncan is a self-serving jerk and I wish he'd never come to this town, damned Windmill Man," came a fresh voice to the conversation. They all turned to find Chuck, unsteady on his feet, facing them. Clearly he'd drunk more than Brian had noticed, and this didn't bode well. Perhaps being cut off had set him off.

"Chuck, why don't you and I get some fresh air," he suggested.

"Don't touch me. I don't need your help, Brian Duncan Just Passing Through . . . hmph, if only. You and that windmill and your precious Annie Sullivan, who you think was some kind of saint, but if she was, why then did her husband go straying with my wife? Those Sullivans, both of them hypocrites who didn't care about anyone but themselves . . ."

Brian shot a fast look Mark's way, and the muscular Mark was on it, coming up behind Chuck faster than the storm had arrived. Grabbing hold of him, Mark began to lead him outside into the cold—maybe throwing him to the snow would sober him up. But before he could get him out the door, Chuck turned around and said, "It's all Dan Sullivan's fault; he ruined everything. He was the biggest fake in this stupid town . . . hey, get off me . . . hey . . ."

His words were cut off when he was thrown to the ground.

He lay there silently, snow falling on him.

"Let him be for a few minutes," Brian said. "I'm sure he'll come to."

When Brian came back inside, he noticed that all eyes were on him. The bar had grown silent and the mistletoe hanging above his head seemed like a joke right now. Chet slid off his stool and said he'd see to Chuck and get him home, and as he left the music started up again thanks to Thomas, who was still manning the jukebox like a DJ. In a few minutes' time the party was back in full swing. Brian felt relief wash over him, glad to have nipped that problem in the bud, glad too that his mother seemed to have let it pass. Last thing he needed today was to get into the complicated history of Annie and Dan Sullivan, and that's when he noticed that maybe he hadn't escaped unscathed. Janey was staring straight at him, and while she didn't appear to be letting Chuck's words affect her here, he knew she'd overheard them and would no doubt bring them up sooner rather than later.

Damn Chuck Ackroyd, stealing Janey's perfect notion of her father.

It was everything Brian had tried to avoid. Now it was something he'd have to face.

"Brian, why don't you take a break? I've got the bar," Mark said.

"No, it's okay, I think work is good for me . . ."

"Fifteen minutes," he said.

"And if things get busy, I'll help out," Kevin said. "Just like the other day."

"Excuse me?" Didi asked.

Brian realized now was the perfect time to escape, and so he made his way outside to the front porch, where he saw only the imprint of Chuck's body in the snow. He'd have to comp Chet a few drinks some night in thanks for taking care of the problem. Appreciating the bracing cold against his skin, he watched with a settling sense of calm as the snow continued to fall on a land that had already seen about eight inches. He noticed that the wind had picked up big-time, now howling in the dark night. With the village adorned in bright lights that lined the main street, it was as perfect a scene as he could have envisioned: a winter post-card that Nicholas Casey's relative might have painted a century and a half ago. What continued to amaze Brian after so many years had passed was how unchanged was the human desire for the ideal Christmas, with only the people changing, traditions living beyond generations that time had claimed. His only worry was the people still inside the tavern, and he wondered if it might be better if he got them all home before the storm worsened during the long night.

Part of him pictured the bar empty save himself and

Trina, and the music continued and the mistletoe finally earned its reputation.

The sound of fun and frivolity won out, and Brian decided not to play Scrooge tonight.

Someone else was already trained in the role.

"Hi, Mom," he said, her familiar perfume announcing her presence.

Didi Duncan had put on her warm coat, which indicated to Brian that she wasn't here to bring him back inside.

"It really is quite lovely here, Brian. Just as you've always described it."

"I'm glad you like it," he said.

"Your father is quite taken with this village."

"Sorry about putting him behind the bar, but he enjoyed it."

"And he's enjoying it now; it's a change of pace for a man like him."

Brian paused, still concentrating on the snow, looking like rainbow-colored flakes as it drifted past the Christmas lights, dotting the sky with fireworks gone cold. He was glad for another white Christmas, and glad too to have family at his side. Christmas had always been an important holiday for the Duncans, from his mother's memory tree to the story of his brother, Philip, whose final gift to them had been the giving of the same name ornaments that continued to define their holiday. At last Brian turned and looked at his mother.

"I'm glad you and Dad are here," he said. "For Christmas."

"Duncans should be together at such a time."

"Speaking of, any word from Rebecca?"

He heard a sigh of dissatisfaction. "Your sister is, I believe, in Paris . . . no, Nice."

"International, huh?"

"Apparently she's run out of unsuitable American men," she said.

"What's this one's name?"

"Hard to keep track. I think Gustave. Or maybe Flaubert. Claims to be a writer."

Brian laughed at his mother's joke. "And Junior?"

"With his father, full-time," she said, her tone sounding like she didn't want to discuss it.

What Brian said next was an abrupt transition, but he didn't see any other way to force the conversation. "So why didn't you tell me about Dad?"

"You know I don't like discussing unpleasant topics," she stated.

"Mom, you could have told me up front rather than dropping hints," he said. "Don't let him on the ladder, no heavy lifting, don't let him use the ax . . . don't let him drink whiskey. I'm not sure you're aware of this, but Kevin Duncan doesn't take lightly to being told no."

"I've been married to your father for nearly fifty years," she said, as though such a statement said it all.

"He didn't go into details," Brian said. "Can you tell me what happened?"

"It was all quite unexpected, as these . . . things usually are," Didi said, a rare vulnerability filling her voice. "He wasn't feeling well that one morning back in September but he went to the office anyway. Far be it from Kevin Duncan to take a sick day. What kind of message did that send to the employees? Well, the message of being carried off by ambulance has a far bigger impact." She paused, as though her mind was taking her back to that day. "I'll never forget when the phone rang, the chill I felt when I realized it was his secretary on the other end. Of course I raced to the hospital as fast as I could and . . ." She paused, wrapping her arms around herself. "When I finally saw him, he was so pale . . . unlike himself. You know your father, so big, so full of life . . ."

"And he still is, Mom."

"Linden Corners has been good for him," she said, "the fresh air, the change of pace."

"I'm glad I could help. I still wish you had told me."

"You have enough on your plate," she said.

He had a feeling that was her way of tackling the Trina subject, but he never got to find out. From his view on the porch Brian noticed a spark of light against the sky, a sizzle in the air. The flash made him blink, and then he stepped off the porch to investigate. Had it been thunder and lightning? Not terribly uncommon with such a fierce storm, and the idea of it sent shivers of fear throughout his body. He thought of that summer storm two years ago and the burned shell of the windmill, their precious Annie. Storms like that were rare, and he hadn't seen another like it in all these subsequent months. Until now. The wind had picked up in the last fifteen minutes, and the snow was falling sideways, blowing across the road in willowy sheets. He stole another look to his left and he thought he could see the horizon come alive with an orange glow. It was faint at first, but then he smelled smoke.

And then he heard the whistle blow from atop the bank tower.

"Brian, what's that awful sound?" his mother asked.

"The fire whistle," he said, a sinking feeling taking hold of him.

Men came rushing out of the bar amidst a flurry of activity, racing across the street to the firehouse, retractable doors flung open. And in what seemed like mere seconds the gleaming red engine pulled out and began to race down the highway, its sirens overtaking the holiday sounds of Bing Crosby coming from inside the bar. Other folks began to file out of the tavern and into their own cars, some concerned about what had happened while the rest figured with the storm worsening, it was time to get their families home to safety. It might have been only seven o'clock at night, but the annual tavern party was crashing to a fast end, and soon only a handful of people remained, most of them his friends and family.

"Where do you think the fire is?" Nicholas asked. "Looked like the trucks went east."

"Whatever's on fire, it can't be good," Bradley added. "Not with this wind."

His comment silenced the group, and it wasn't until the door of the upstairs apartment opened and Trina emerged that the pieces began to fall into place for Brian. The direction the fire truck was headed, the nearby orange glow. There was only one place he could think of.

"What's going on?" she asked.

"Trina, we don't know. There's a fire, but no one knows . . . ," Brian said, trying to be calm.

Fear washed over her, her face going ghost-white. "The motel," she said.

"We don't know that . . ."

"Richie . . . where's Richie? Where's my father?" she asked.

She nearly fell against the wall, caught at the last second by Brian and a fast-acting Mark. That was when the phone inside the bar rang, Kevin grabbing it while the other bartenders were busy. He nodded once, and when he set it down, he said to everyone, "The Solemn Nights Motel is on fire."

Nearly midnight, and the fire had finally burned through its last ember, but even on this snow-ravaged night the damage had clearly been done. The fierce wind had been too strong, too wild, the flames hard to control, and so while the volunteer firefighters from Linden Corners and a couple of neighboring villages had fought valiantly, what remained along the side of the road where the Solemn Nights Motel had stood for twenty-five years was a burned-out husk, now coated with ice, like it was being preserved for a time when an angel could wave a magic wand and heal its frozen wounds.

Brian stood on the edge of the highway, arms around Trina in an attempt to soothe her. Neither of them felt the cold, even though they'd been here for the last couple of hours. From behind a protective barrier, they had watched Richie Ravens' dreams fall victim to violent flame. Ashes to ashes, fire claiming all in its path.

The fire chief, Stephen Wallis, a longtime Linden Corners resident who had been at the party but not drinking, finally walked up to them, calmly shaking his head. "I'm sorry, there was really nothing we could do. Sometimes fire wins."

"What about my father?" Trina asked.

"No sign of anyone . . . any . . . you know . . . You said there were only two guests staying at the motel; both of them are accounted for."

"Chief Wallis, can you tell us what exactly happened?" Brian asked.

"Downed power line, probably snapped under the weight of the snow and ice. My guess is it struck the roof," he said. "Old building like this, it was like kindling to a campfire."

They watched as the chief made his way back toward the scene, fire truck after fire truck packing up and leaving until only the soot-covered engine from Linden Corners remained. Brian heard footsteps approaching from behind, looked up to find Mark Ravens getting out of his car, the light from inside showing he wasn't alone.

He could easily make out Richie's form in the passenger seat.

"Where?" Brian asked.

"Chuck Ackroyd's place. Seems Uncle Richie drove himself over to the tavern when he ran into Chet, who needed some help getting the drunken Chuck home and sober. The three of them knew nothing of what was going on, not until Chet came back to the bar a short while ago."

Trina listened, even as she watched Richie struggle to get out of the car. She went racing over to him, her voice clear in the cold night when she exclaimed, "Oh, thank God . . . Dad." She embraced him as if it was the most natural thing in the world to do. Brian, out of respect for their privacy, turned away as the tears began to flow down Richie's cheeks, wondering if they were tears of sadness over his loss, or tears over what he'd just gained.

Brian Duncan realized that despite the acrid odor of loss swirling around them, on this stormy night, Linden Corners still had a few surprises left up its sleeve this holiday.

CHAPTER 18

CYNTHIA

Linden Corners was proving to be a place just like any other, where the notion of forever was nothing but a dream, and the Solemn Nights Motel was its latest piece of evidence to the fact. Yet while the loss of the only lodgings for visitors to town was gone, no one had been harmed and that in itself was cause for rejoicing. With Christmas now upon them, everyone in town had been relieved to know that Richie Ravens, ornery old coot that he was, had turned up fine and that the holiday wouldn't be marred by tragedy beyond the burned-down motel. Linden Corners would rise from the ashes and endure without the Solemn Nights, but it would hardly be the same without its eccentrics, Richie one of its longest tenured.

For Cynthia Knight, eccentric she might not be, but the village would miss her too.

Monday of a new week meant Christmas Eve had at last arrived, and the buzz emanating all over downtown Linden Corners was electric, like the residents themselves were powering the bright lights that kept the village sparkling all through the season. With Bradley out "taking care of business," as he had said, Cynthia had needed to run an errand over at Ackroyd's Hardware Emporium, and when she arrived with Jake in tow, it appeared she wasn't alone. The place was overflowing with formerly procrastinating shoppers in search of those last-minute items like tree stands, strings of lights, and those thin metal hooks used to hang ornaments that you still find embedded in the carpet months after the tree has been taken down. Cynthia was picking up a special order of votive candles that had arrived, and just in time. She thought she'd had enough, but realizing how grand her ambition was, she'd ordered a second box. She remarked as such to Chuck, who was standing behind a counter toward the back, sober now but no less surly.

"Told you it would arrive by Christmas," he said.

"Cutting it close, Ebenezer," she said. "We're depending upon these for the pageant."

"Like the windmill isn't bright enough," he remarked. "Now you go and add candles."

"Luminaries," she said, correcting him.

"Whatever," he replied, obviously uninterested.

Jake, who was securely tucked against his mother in a baby sack, was facing forward, but still Cynthia could see him stick out his tongue. Her son might be young and his reaction was probably simple fidgeting, but still, how nice it was to imagine her son playing the role of protector.

Cynthia smiled her friendliest, toothiest grin and told Chuck she would see him later, and when he harrumphed and said he doubted he could make the festivities, she reminded him that he had picked a name out of the Santa hat and someone else had picked his, "so there's no changing your mind this late in the season, Chuck Ackroyd, so you better be there. I don't know who you picked, but if it's a child, imagine their disappointment when they realize someone forgot them."

"Life's full of disappointments; it's good for kids to learn that early on."

That sorry comment reminded Cynthia of Chuck's drunken words from the tavern party. "You know, Chuck, what you said about Dan Sullivan . . . Janey was there. She heard everything."

He shrugged with obvious disdain. "And? Like I said, it's good for those spoiled brats to learn that no one's perfect . . . Dan Sullivan included, and you can throw that Brian Duncan into the mix too."

"Chuck, despite what your twisted brain thinks, Brian and Dan are not the same man, nor does Brian deserve to be the victim for mistakes made before he got here."

Chuck had no response to that, excusing himself to help another customer.

Deciding Chuck was one person she wasn't going to miss when leaving Linden Corners, Cynthia moved away from him with her package tucked under her arm, Jake suddenly curious about it. She was glad to have prepaid for her order, since she was now able to avoid the long lines at the registers; the ensuing small talk would no doubt steal precious time from her. Cynthia was a lady on a mission, and the countdown clock had started. Time was fast slipping away from her, and things had to be just perfect.

Once outside, she breathed in the bracing air, glad to be away from Chuck's surly nature. She felt sorry for both the person who was required to buy a gift for him and the person for whom he had to buy. Just where in Linden Corners did one buy coal anyway?

She returned home to find that company had arrived in the helpful form of Nicholas and Nora, and she was glad to see the two of them holding hands. But today was not a day for distractions, in the form of the line at the hardware store or whatever storm had been brewing between them, so she wasn't going to ask about it, figuring it had either passed or they were in the eye of it, calm for the moment. The holidays were supposed to be about togetherness.

"Am I late?"

"We just got here," Nicholas said, coming around the side of the car and taking command of the package. "What do you say Nora and I get started with the luminaries while you get Jake settled; then you can come and check on our progress."

"I have absolute faith in you. As for Jake, he's fussy because he doesn't like being put into his snowsuit. I guess he's going to like the heat of Texas." She paused, her eyes glistening with a sudden faraway look. "Um, where's Gerta?"

"Back at the house with Travis. The two of them have their hands full," Nora said.

"With what?"

Nora allowed a smile when she said, "With a Christmas present," and said no more.

"Enough of the town gossip, ladies," Nicholas said, "We've got a lot of setting up to do."

So Nicholas, with Nora in tow, started down the field, leaving Cynthia free to get Jake out of his winter constraints. The moment she did he began crawling around the boxes that were strewn about the living room, making way for the Christmas tree in the corner. It was like he'd been set free in the wild, and Cynthia watched him with a mix of amusement and sadness. He was growing up so fast, and as much fun as he seemed to be having now, she knew in his mind the memories of their last Christmas here in Linden Corners were fleeting, to be remembered only in photographs and, of course, in her heart.

The ringing of the phone brought her back to reality. She ran to the kitchen and answered it on the second ring, all while keeping an eye on Jake. It was Bradley.

"Where are you?" he asked.

"Home. You?"

"Near. I'll be there in five, ten minutes."

She could hear excitement in his voice, and when she asked him what was going on, he said she'd just have to wait until he got back, and suggested that she meet him at the edge of the driveway. Bradley Knight, good-natured, well-spoken, wasn't much of a man of mystery, but what he said before hanging up couldn't have surprised her more.

"Our future begins tonight."

"Would you care to explain that one?" she asked.

"I'll see you soon, and then you'll know soon enough."

He actually hung up on her, the sound of his laughter echoing inside her mind.

Perhaps her straightlaced husband was beginning to loosen up. This move to Texas was rife with opportunity, and his growing sense of anticipation had reached, for him, a feverish pitch. The boxes in every room showed he was anxious to get going, and part of Cynthia had to agree. Being in limbo, packed somewhere between yesterday's memories and tomorrow's promise, had its frustrations. The last items to be packed would be their Christmas decorations. They almost hadn't gotten a tree this year, relenting only recently, and even so the tree wouldn't last into January like usual. The moving van was coming for their belongings a couple of days after Christmas, meaning a quick week later they would be living in their new home, new lives ready-made for them. That was the plan, and if she knew anything about her husband, always so neat, always so organized, it was that once he set his mind to something, there was no deviating.

So she better be on time to meet him.

She hated the idea of having to stuff Jake back into his snowsuit, so she made a quick call to Nora on her cell, asking if she wouldn't mind coming up to the house and looking after Jake for a few minutes. Nora said she was down at the stone bridge and would be up in a minute, and in fact it was two, trudging through the snow making the trek difficult.

"Thought you could do with a break," Cynthia confessed.

"It's all good, Cyn. Nicholas and I . . . we've tabled everything until the New Year. I like him . . . it's just, he's asking too much of me right now."

"You'll figure it out. You two are great together."

"And if we don't, I'll have to call you long-distance," Nora said.

Cynthia gave her a quick embrace. "Anytime."

Cynthia tossed on her coat and made her way down the driveway, arriving just as Bradley did, his car pulling to a stop just off the road. She accepted a kiss and then asked him what the big mystery was.

"This," he said, pulling from the backseat of the car a metal sign.

It read: SOLD.

Cynthia felt disbelief wash over her as she watched Bradley attach the sign atop the FOR SALE sign, seeing the satisfaction on his face when he turned back to her.

"Well?"

"How . . . but . . . who?"

"All in good time," he said, pulling her tight against his body.

Cynthia just stared at the sign, her mind unable to absorb its implications. The past few weeks she had been living in a dreamland, where her days were filled with imaginings of a life in Texas, her nights dancing amidst the memories of Linden Corners. Neither seemed true, almost as though she were walking through fog. Here was the definitive proof that no matter the hour, no matter time or place or what her wishes might be, the hard truth of reality was staring back at her.

"It's really happening," she said, her voice barely above a whisper. "I don't believe it."

"Yes, you do, Cynthia, because today is Christmas Eve, a day when we all believe."

Night began to fall early, just after three, almost as if the sky was as anxious as the residents for this year's pageant to begin. By four o'clock darkness had settled over Linden Corners, except in the land of the windmill, where the bright lights of the memory tree soared into the clear sky. As the star above the tower spun in the ever-changing currents of the wind, it was as though its beam was putting out a call to points east and west, north and south, drawing people from everywhere with the allure of its golden glow. The villagers of Linden Corners had been assembling all afternoon, each of them bearing a gift for the town-wide Secret Santa exchange, setting beautifully wrapped presents and holiday bags beside the windmill. Sleds and toboggans had been set up around its wooden base, protecting the boxes and gift paper from growing soggy atop the wet snow. With gifts piling up two, three, four deep, it looked as though the windmill had been transformed into a giant Christmas tree, the bounty from all the residents representing the picture of generosity.

Spanning out in circular fashion away from the windmill were tracks of luminaries, with candles flickering inside the white paper bags, seemingly hundreds of them locked to the ground by small piles of sand. They cut a path through the field and wound up toward the stone bridge and beyond, to the Knights' farmhouse, where the children's pageant would begin its yearly procession. The final touch of the event would be the arrival of Santa Claus atop the fire engine, driven by fire chief Stephen Wallis; last year the truck had carried on it a bride about to be married, but this year something else was planned, a celebration of the many generations that kept Linden Corners the magical world it is.

For Cynthia Knight, all of her planning had come down to this, and she took a moment to admire how beautiful the field looked. Nicholas and Nora and a few other helpful volunteers had worked all afternoon to set up the luminaries and light them, and now, as she stood on the stone bridge, itself adorned with holly and lights on its arches, she imagined that bridge was the portal that would take them from one world into the next, one where promise lived, where memories were stored. Watching now how many people had showed up for the pageant and the exchange of gifts, she knew this one final Christmas in Linden Corners would be just perfect.

But she could enjoy the satisfaction of her achievement later; time had advanced and the pageant would wait no more, and so she returned to the farmhouse to hear the eager, joyful sounds of youth filling her home. Forty-one children in total, boys and girls both, were dressed in outfits of seasonal red and green—ties for the boys, crushed velvet scarves for the girls—Travis and an eager Janey among them. This year Father Burton had been chosen to guide them, and Cynthia now saw the kindly priest trying to organize them into a cohesive line, just as they had rehearsed earlier last week.

At last he had them lined up, placing Janey front and center at Cynthia's request. It was only appropriate that Janey lead them to the windmill.

"Ready, kids?" he asked.

They cheered their response, and at last, Christmas Eve in Linden Corners began.

"Let me get settled with everyone around the windmill,"

Cynthia told Father Burton, "so I can watch it along with them."

"Nonsense, Cynthia, you'll process with us," he said.

"No, this is for the children . . ."

"At this time of year, I believe we're all children," he said wisely.

She put up no further protest, and soon the kids began to walk, Janey leading the way like Rudolph did Santa's sleigh on that stormy night, or so she announced. Father Burton reminded them all of the solemnity of this night, and whose birth they were truly celebrating. Santa would have his moment later. It was a good reminder for them all.

"And remember, once we hit the outdoors, turn on those lights," he stated.

Rather than having the children walk with lit candles across an open field, where their light could be so easily doused, this year each child had been handed a glass Christmas ornament, the lights inside them of varying colors, and as they made their way out of the farmhouse and into the cool, dark night, they switched them on. In seconds the snowy field was bathed in the colors of the Christmas season, reds and blues and greens and golds, the flickering rainbow carrying them beyond the Knights' backyard and down toward the creek, crossing over the stone bridge and at last emerging between the lines of the luminaries.

Cynthia, rather than watching as the parade of lights approached, was able to appreciate it in a way she couldn't have envisioned, from behind, she and Father Burton bringing up the rear of the procession. Her arm was locked in his, and she felt rather like a princess being led to the ball. She steeled herself for the moment they crossed over the bridge, realizing that for the past several weeks, as much as she was looking forward to the celebration, she was wistful about what happened after. It would mean time had truly caught up with her, her inevitable move that much closer. With the windmill's giant sails coming into view, it began to dawn on her that time could never be stopped, even if she were remaining in Linden Corners; it would always turn, days would pass and children would grow and others would pass and the cycle would continue. So she knew that right now all she could do was enjoy the moment.

Her smile widened as they crossed over the bridge and emerged out of the clearing of the woods that separated the Duncan and Knight properties, and suddenly there was the windmill in full glory, its glow as bright as the starry sky, a beacon calling to her. The children forged ahead, almost as though the wind was pushing them forward, or perhaps it was the promise of a gift at the end of the procession that lured them. Through the path of luminaries they walked, like Dorothy on the brick road, this one more golden than yellow. A string quartet had been set up near the windmill, and they began the lush, lovely sounds of a song called "The Christmas Canon," the children's voices joining in and making the world around them alive with its lilting, angelic melody. The effect was reverential, uplifting, and the crowd grew hushed the closer the parade approached, and at last the children rounded the windmill and came to a stop on a carpet of pine needles.

The music ended and a gentle quiet took brief hold of the land, as though time really had stopped. Then the applause erupted, a thunderous cacophony of appreciation that seemed to fuel the spinning sails further. Cynthia was beaming widely as she saw all of her friends amongst the crowd, the happiness written on their faces filling her heart with deep satisfaction, as well as an inevitable sense of remorse. The twins Marla and Darla stood with their arms crossed, wearing matching jackets that further confused who was who, and near them, arms crossed in defiance, was Chuck Ackroyd and his drinking buddy, Chet Hardesty.

Nicholas Casey and Nora Connors were wrapped tightly in each other's arms. Gerta Connors was standing beside Thomas Van Diver and Elsie Masters. Near them were Kevin and Didi Duncan, the latter of which held her hand close to her heart, and right next to them of course was Brian Duncan. At his side was Trina Winter, and the truth of the matter was how happy that last couple appeared together, Cynthia knowing she had done the right thing in pushing two lost souls toward each other. A defining moment indeed, and if this was how Cynthia Knight went out in Linden Corners, she couldn't imagine a better scenario.

Except the night was about to go one better, the siren of the fire truck piercing the night. Everyone turned to watch its approach, Cynthia's mind flashing back two nights to when its siren had cried out for different purposes, and she stole a glance Trina's way, wondering if she too was thinking about the fire that had claimed her father's motel. Trina rested her head on Brian's shoulder, and she saw her wipe a tear away. Brian leaned down and kissed the top of her head. Was it possible her bit of matchmaking had worked, and that a future existed for them? She had to wonder how Janey felt about it all.

All romantic speculation would have to wait. The fire truck arrived, pulling to the side of the road, its red light swirling against the drifts of snow that covered the land. The fire chief was first to descend from the truck, helping several people down from the cab. In order, she saw whoever had volunteered to play Santa this year, followed by Bradley carrying baby Jake, and then she saw a dimpled Mark Ravens escorting his pregnant wife, Sara, and then she saw Martha Martinson helping a man who needed the assistance of crutches, realizing it was, of course, Richie Ravens. The small group came forward across the field, ending up standing right beside the children's parade.

Cynthia then stepped forward to address the crowd.

"Oh my, my dear friends and family of Linden Corners, it is with a full, and heavy, heart, that I stand before you on this glowing, glorious night we call Christmas Eve. When I first began to envision what our annual Christmas pageant would be like, I could never have imagined . . . this. The beauty here, in colors that dance inside our eyes to the wonder that fills our hearts, it's beyond special." She hesitated, her eyes focusing on Bradley and Jake, the former nodding his head in approval, in support, before moving onward to her friends. "As you all know, my family will be leaving Linden Corners in a few days, but I want you all to know that while we may be gone physically, so much of this place remains locked in our hearts and our minds and we will never forget any of you. Once upon a time I came to this town with a man who would change my life, who would love me for being me, and it was here that I met my best friend and her daughter, whom I've watched grow from infant to beautiful young lady, and so many others of you who have filled my life with so many memories and so much love. To see the many generations of our village celebrated on this night, from Richie, who shows that the past must be appreciated, to Bradley and Mark who inspire the present, to my precious son Jake who reminds us that a new generation already lives among us, and finally, to our radiant Sara Ravens, who carries inside her the eternal promise that Linden Corners will live on for all tomorrows." She paused, fighting back tears that won out anyway, and then said, "I think I've said enough, so I'll leave you with one last wish—you have all given me so many gifts, and it is my hope that the gift you are about to receive, whether it be from friend, neighbor, or stranger, is something you'll always cherish. So let the Secret Santa exchanges begin."

She watched as the residents began to pore through the

piles of gifts, finding their names written on cards, or discovering those of their friends, happily passing them on. Presents were exchanged and wrappings were ripped open by eager children, squeals of delight filling the night air. Even the adults exclaimed pleasure in what they received, Cynthia standing there with joy, forgetting that a gift waited for her. It was Brian who brought over to her three square packages that felt light in her grasp.

"From you, Brian? You were my Secret Santa?"

"Not me," he said shaking his head. "Now, how coincidental would that have been? No, I just saw that they were the only gifts that remained unclaimed. Come on, open them and let's see what you got."

By then a small group of friends and curious residents had circled around Cynthia, all of their faces anticipatory of what was to be found under the wrappings. Part of her didn't want to open them, because she knew that once she did it meant the end of all she had planned, the clock fast approaching when they should all be gathering at Saint Matthew's for the vigil mass, and after that the hands of the clock would hit midnight and Christmas Day would be upon them, Soon after, she would be leaving behind her friends, her home, a life that was so embedded in the fabric of the community. Some gifts, she thought, are meant to remain unopened.

Not so this one.

"Cynthia, open them!" Janey exclaimed.

"My goodness, we were only supposed to get one gift. This . . . this is excessive."

Still, she slipped a finger beneath the tape of the first gift, and the colorful paper decorated with snowmen fell away to the ground, revealing a white box. She opened it up and pulled out a shiny blue ornament, the name *Cynthia* written across it in a glittery silver script. Cynthia's mouth dropped open, even as she grew a bit unsteady on her feet. She knew she had to continue, because she knew, right then and there, what was inside the other two boxes, and also just who her Secret Santa had been. She repeated the process once, a second time, and when she was done, three gleaming ornaments were on display, Bradley holding his red ornament with his name written in the same style, Janey holding on to Cynthia's so she could appreciate the gold ornament dangling from her fingers, one that caught the lights emanating off the windmill and creating a glint across the snowy field. *Jake*, it read.

"I wasn't sure if it should say Jacob or Jake, but everyone calls him Jake like everyone calls me Janey, and that's what my ornament says."

"Janey . . . they're lovely. Perfectly lovely."

"Nora helped me order them; even Brian didn't know. I used my allowance."

"Thank you, thank you so much. But, Janey, these are your family tradition."

"They're Brian's, really, but he made them part of my Christmas, and I just wanted you to know you'll always be a part of mine, no matter where you are. Families can be together, even when they can't. And, I was going to give them to you on Christmas, but then, well, out of all those names inside the big Santa hat, I chose yours," Janey said, "and I couldn't believe it."

Cynthia smiled as she bent down and took Janey tightly into her arms. She felt like never letting go, as though by doing so she would be relinquishing her connection to Linden Corners. But that was silly, as Janey might say; their bond was too strong and memories were one thing distance could not claim. As they parted, Cynthia, wiping away tears that wouldn't stop now, cradled by her husband and son, said, "That's the thing, Janey, about dreams. If you choose to believe in them, they do come true."

CHAPTER 19

TRINA

"I had Mrs. McCluskey."

"Oh, she told everyone in earshot how much she loved her picture frame, saying it was just what she needed for her grandchildren's latest school photographs. And she told me she had Susie Anderson, who I think got new mittens that perfectly matched her coat. So thoughtful."

"Her husband, Milton, he had Bradley, I think."

"Did he get a board game?"

"Mr. Carducci gave me a feather pen and inkwell."

"I had Adam Carpenter, the guy who's taking ownership of the fruit stand from Cynthia."

"I—well, Trina really—actually picked Father Burton, and he received a new set of wineglasses. Though I suppose they're good for water too."

"Some young girl named Ashley gave me a delightful pair of earrings that had owls on them."

"Ashley's my friend, and she likes owls like I like my frog."

"And I received a gift from one Elsie Masters, a desk calendar with pictures of dogs on nearly every page."

So said, in order and with decreasing enthusiasm, Nora,

Gerta, Thomas, Nicholas, then Travis with the smart-alec remark about Milton Bradley, followed by Trina, and then Richie, who even though he didn't do the actual shopping was amused enough by what the priest had been given, and finally Didi, Janey, and Kevin joined in, the latter of whom, after mentioning his gift, received a stern look from his wife. The entire group was gathered inside the Duncan farmhouse sharing stories of the Secret Santa gift exchange, just hours after Thomas Van Diver had read, with twinkly-eyed reverence, "The Night Before Christmas" to eager children, filling all of their minds with visions of Santa flying over the rooftops in Linden Corners, and after the choral-filled vigil mass at Saint Matthew's. Now, as the adults sipped wine or tea, and the children—as well as Trina—indulged in hot chocolate, it was time to relax as Christmas fast approached. To Trina, it just felt right, a sense settling within her of how Christmas Eve was supposed to feel, anticipation winning out over expectation.

Suddenly all eyes turned to Brian, the only one of them who hadn't revealed who he had picked for Secret Santa, or who had him—turned out one of Janey's teachers did. When he finally did open up about who he had, he sounded like Charlie Brown on an altogether different holiday, Halloween, complaining, "I had Chuck."

"No way," Nora said, and then the whole room erupted into laughter.

All except Trina, who didn't know enough of the conflicted history between Brian and Chuck Ackroyd, a man whose reputation was suspect at best. In fact, sitting beside the mantel, where an orange fire crackled and gave off a warmth of healing rather than one of destruction, as it had while ruthlessly burning through her father's motel, she still felt an icy chill. Because in the span of the nearly six weeks since her arrival in Linden Corners, Trina Winter had gone from total stranger to imposter, and now in this most ideal holiday setting, sitting amidst new friends and convivial conversation laced with laughter, and with the Christmas tree shining brightly and carols playing softly in the background, she felt more like a full-blown intruder. Midnight—and thus the arrival of Christmas Day—remained mere hours away and, Richie aside, her connection to him based more on past regrets than fresh memories, she was in the company of people who were not her family, and pretending otherwise wasn't going to instill in her heart any basis for belonging. She witnessed the ease with which the Connors family was integrated into this house, and of course Brian's parents were more than welcome, here to celebrate the holiday with their son and his daughter. So, what business did the fractured Ravens family have in disrupting their traditions?

"Whatever did you get Chuck?" Gerta asked.

Brian paused, eyes mirroring the flicker from the fire, before saying, "A bottle of scotch, to encourage him to drink at home. Oh, and a handshake intended as an act of forgiveness."

"You're a better man than me, Brian Duncan," Nora said.

"But you're a woman," Janey stated matter-of-factly.

Her comment received a roomful of chuckles, and that's when Brian rose from his seat, informing his wise, grammatically savant young girl that Santa Claus didn't stop at houses where children were still awake. When she was finished rolling her eyes, she agreed that bedtime was a good idea, and so she bade good night to everyone and then trudged upstairs, Brian starting to follow after her.

"Brian, dear, perhaps I could tuck Jane into bed tonight?" his mother said.

Janey and Brian looked first at her, then at each other, and Trina could see that a silent message was being sent between them. It was Janey who finally responded. "I would like that very much on any other night, but it's Christmas Eve, and, well, Brian . . . well, he and I have our special tradition . . . Is that okay, uh . . . Mrs. Duncan?"

Didi's face held tight, not giving away her disappointment. "Traditions are important."

Trina noticed she wasn't the only one having issues with how to refer to people. Her own father she had called Dad only once on this visit, and that was after realizing he hadn't perished in the fire, and not that she wished him any harm, but the reason why she spoke that name she'd been denied all these years had surprised her. Instinct, perhaps a growing love, overrode history. When it came to what to call Brian's parents, Janey was clearly suffering the same dilemma.

"How about tomorrow night, and I can tell you all about my gifts. Just us ladies."

"Then I will definitely look forward to such a time," Didi said with a widening grin. "For now, tonight, it's you and Brian and, as you said, your special tradition."

Janey ran back and gave Didi a quick hug, tossing Kevin one as well so as not to deny him, and then suddenly she was dashing up the stairs with more energy than a child about to catch a night's sleep should have. Brian followed after her, winking back Trina's way, as though telling her not to go anywhere.

With their host momentarily gone, silence settled over the group, and had Richie not still been here, she might have said good night as well, though what did she really have to return to? Since the fire had destroyed the Solemn Nights Motel, she and Richie had been staying with Mark and Sara, and while their generosity was larger than life, their apartment was small, with a tiny second bedroom and a sofa that barely fit her outstretched body, much less Richie's; he had insisted on doing the fatherly thing by giving her the private room and sleeping on its worn cushions. Add in the fact that the apartment was on the second floor above the tavern, and Richie—with his crutches—had to climb up steep stairs. Moreover, she wasn't eager to get back and spoil their anniversary. Still, beggars couldn't be choosers, and at least Mark and Sara had put up a tree so Christmas wasn't a total bust, even if it was far from what Trina had expected.

She was about to suggest that she and Richie depart, when Richie broke the silence.

"In all my years living in Linden Corners, I've never set foot inside this house."

"Richie Ravens, you've called this village home for twenty-five years," Gerta said.

"I've never been inside your home either," he replied.

"Yes, but you and Dan . . . you were tight at one point, friends, weren't you?"

"That's a long time ago, even before I envisioned building the Solemn Nights."

His voice took on a hint of remorse, Trina realizing he was displaying more emotion now than he had since he'd watched his motel's demise. She wondered if she should change the course of the conversation or let him talk and get it out of his system. What he did next surprised her, getting up from his chair with obvious discomfort, grabbing for his crutches. The cast might have come off, but that didn't mean he was anywhere near healed.

"Richie, what can I get you?" she asked.

"Nothing, I'm fine. Just got to see a man about a horse," he replied with a short laugh.

He disappeared from the room, and small talk resumed, the Connors talking about their plans for the holiday, Didi and Kevin remarking how lovely Linden Corners was awash in holiday lights, how convivial everyone in town seemed, and Trina found her mind wandering. Feeling even more awkward without Brian or Richie in the room, she fidgeted in her seat, and then she started to gather empty mugs and glasses and, despite a protest from Didi, brought them into the kitchen. As she set them in the sink, she gazed out the window, where in the near distance she could see the light emanating off the windmill. It wasn't the only thing she saw, the glow coming off the horizon highlighting the shadow of her father as he hesitantly made his way across the field.

"Richie Ravens, what are you up to?" she asked aloud.

"Talking to yourself, I see. Do you do that often?"

It was Brian who had snuck up behind her, slipping his arms around her. He nuzzled her neck, the sensation so sweet, so unexpected, she felt herself melt against him. How strange was this, she and Brian inside this house, and upstairs slept Janey, a girl who'd lost so much but still believed in and dreamed of the perfect Christmas morning, where presents awaited her, all while in the other room was her extended family, their close friends. It was just as Christmas was supposed to look, one of those postcards found on the spinning racks inside Marla and Darla's Trading Post. The scene so perfect its unfamiliarity rang inside Trina.

"Janey asleep?" she asked.

"Not yet; she'll get there."

"Do you really have a special tradition?"

"We talk sometimes, and I think tonight she needed me."

"Your mother is . . . intimidating?"

"Why does our conversation always turn to her?"

"What would you like to talk about?"

"How's Richie doing?"

She decided not to say anything about his nocturnal excursion to the windmill. "Typical, not saying much about what happened at the motel."

"What do you think he'll do? Rebuild?"

Trina immediately shook her head. "That's not Richie's style. If I've learned one thing about Richie Ravens, it's once something is done, it's time to move on. Just as he did with his failed marriage, the notion of fatherhood. He abandoned both, leaving the ruins behind."

Brian nodded. "Seems to me he's coming around on the idea of being a father."

"He's trying, which is more than he did when I first got here."

She felt Brian's tender lips against her neck, reminding her of the one afternoon they'd spent together. Their one and only time. It felt so right being in his arms, but yet his next words reminded her that nothing was really real, nothing ever lasted.

"You know, you're both welcome to stay the night. We have plenty of rooms."

"Oh, Brian, that's so generous of you . . . but, no, we couldn't possibly."

"Your choice; the invitation is open-ended. It might be more comfortable . . ."

"Richie in one bedroom, and me . . . Where do I sleep?"

He paused, then said, "Yeah, okay, really soon. And maybe . . . confusing."

"For Janey."

He nodded. "And for us."

"Can you give me a minute? I'll rejoin the group soon."

"Uh, sure. Everything okay?"

She paused before saying, "What I think is that everything happens for a reason."

Brian kissed her on the lips this time, his tender touch lingering until she felt like she needed to lock it inside her heart. A kiss lasted only a moment, a memory far longer. As Brian disappeared back into the holiday warmth of the living room, she once again stole a look outside the window. Richie was long gone from view, yet the windmill was not done with its revelations of the night. What she saw surprised her so much she nearly called out to Brian.

Janey Sullivan, dressed in a thick overcoat, was crossing the field, not unlike Richie had done moments ago. She seemed to be hugging something, as though protecting it from the cold. Trina could not make out what it was.

What was the allure of the windmill, and on a night such as this?

Did Janey do this often, sneak out at night?

Trina had to imagine Brian wouldn't approve. She was ten; wandering off wasn't safe.

Taking matters into her own hands, Trina quietly snuck to the foyer, grabbing her coat off the hook, wrapping her scarf around her neck, and, after glancing back to ensure her escape had gone undetected, she slipped out of the farmhouse and into the cold night of an approaching Christmas. Stars lit her way, twinkling. She wondered what surprises awaited her.

"Oh, Ms. Janey, you surprised me."

"Sorry. I'm supposed to be sleeping. Or at least, I should be in bed."

"Yes, that's what I understand. And yet, here you are."

"I saw you from my bedroom window; you were walking toward the windmill."

"But that's not where I ended up, is it?" he asked.

"I prefer the windmill," Janey said. "It's where I talk to Mama when I need to."

"And what did you say to her tonight?"

"I didn't get there yet. I came right here. I followed your footprints."

"Very clever of you," he said.

"Why did you come here?"

"This bridge holds many memories for me."

Trina was listening from behind a tree, she too having trailed their footsteps with a stealth-like quality. She'd followed them and couldn't say why. Was it because she felt responsible for Richie, a sense that she was fulfilling the obligation that had originally brought her to Linden Corners? If that were true, she would have chased him the moment she saw his unsteady frame making its way across the wide field. It wasn't until she had seen Janey mirroring his actions that Trina had sprung into action, and even so, she didn't understand her motives. Why not just go to Brian and tell him about Janey's escape?

Fearing discovery, she opted to remain where she was, hidden behind the thick trunk of a tree. The old stone bridge was in easy view, and she was within earshot of both the swirling current from the stream and the conversation taking place. She didn't intend to eavesdrop, but she didn't want to discourage what truths were being laid bare tonight. Janey had come here for a reason; she'd admitted as much. She wanted to talk to Richie, and obviously, privately.

"You knew my dad?" she asked.

"Now, Janey Sullivan, you're a lucky girl; you've been blessed with two dads."

"Brian's great; he's the best," she said. "But I meant my other dad."

"Dan Sullivan," he said.

"I see him in my dreams, and for the past couple of months, ever since I turned ten, I've been wondering about him and my mama. Can you tell me about him? Do you know how he and Mama met, and why they got married, and then why . . . why they can't be with me anymore?"

"Well, that last question I cannot answer, and I doubt

anyone can. Life likes to hold on to its mysteries, young Janey. It likes to tease us with things like wishes and hopes. It's how you come out the other end that defines your character."

"I like wishes, and I'm always full of hope. But lately, my dreams confuse me."

"Christmas will do that, makes us think anything is possible," he said. "We experience so many emotions, we often don't know what we're thinking from one moment to another."

"Christmas is so wonderful, but really . . . it's just one day. When it's over, the lights dim."

"You're wise beyond your years, Janey Sullivan."

"That's what Brian . . . I mean Dad says."

"You have trouble calling him Dad?"

"Not really, just sometimes I slip. Sometimes I feel . . . disloyal, to my real dad."

"Dan Sullivan would have liked Brian. I'm sure he's happy you're in such good hands."

Trina wasn't sure she could hear more, this conversation between wizened old Richie and the wise-beyond-her-years Janey hitting far too close to home. Fathers and daughters should not miss out on moments, and here were two people who had lost both, the only difference being that Richie could turns things around. Trina herself had been given a second father, even though her first one hadn't died; he'd just . . . disappeared. He'd found a life beyond hers, and only after coming to town had she begun to understand what had made him leave. Perhaps she would gain further insight here, and so, despite the guilt she felt about overhearing them rushing through her system, she listened further.

"I met Dan right here. Did you know that?"

"Here, on the bridge?"

"Oh, he loved hanging out here; he liked to fish."

"Fish? I don't think there are fish in this stream."

"Well, he fished for things other than fish."

Trina heard a pause, imagining Janey trying to process such a dichotomy.

"How can you fish for something else?"

"See that stuffed animal in your arms?" he asked.

"Sure, he goes everywhere with me. He was my first-ever Christmas present."

"I'm not surprised," he said. "Because your father used to find frogs in the stream."

"He did?"

"Sure, he was . . . what, thirteen, fourteen years old when I met him. The same age that Travis is now."

"How do you know?"

"Because when I first came to Linden Corners, I kind of lived around here."

"How can you kind of live around . . . the bridge? Did you live inside the windmill?"

"No, I pitched a tent in the woods."

"Weren't you cold?"

"It was summer, and I used to fall asleep while counting the number of times the sails of the windmill spun."

"So you do like the windmill!"

"Of course I do. It's what made me stop. I wasn't supposed to. I just kind of . . . found it."

"Just like Brian!"

"And your mama before him."

"Mama loved the windmill."

"Did you know that it was because of the windmill your parents met?"

There was no response. Trina, crouching behind the tree, let out a sharp breath, hoping her sound hadn't alerted them to her presence. She hoped they thought it was the wind. She imagined that Janey was processing this information, perhaps shaking her head. It was Richie's voice that continued, as he told the young girl the story of her parents' first meeting.

Annie had been living nearby, he said, caring for an elderly aunt, and she'd gone out for a drive one afternoon when she came upon the windmill, and she had stopped to admire its beauty and its simple majesty, never thinking such a move would forever change her life, but that it did. As she walked ever closer to the spinning sails, she heard the joyful cry from nearby, and rather than run far for fear of being discovered, she advanced further toward the woods, eventually finding her way to the stone bridge.

"Dan was there, and of course this was years after I had first met him and settled into Linden Corners. He was a grown man by this point, saddled with the responsibility of running the family farm. His parents were gone already. So who could blame him, forced to grow up so quickly, holding tight to the things that reminded him of more innocent times. So there he was, grabbing frogs, and don't you know, he had just pulled one out when Annie showed her face. He turned to her, smiling at what he told me was the most beautiful woman he'd ever seen, and he presented her with the squirming frog in his hand, and what happened next defined the rest of his life. Rather than squeal at a big bullfrog being thrust at her, the woman reached out and took it in her hands. Dan told me that he would never forget what she said next."

"Which was?"

" 'Does that make you a prince?' "

The bitter cold of the night was insinuating itself beneath her jacket, chilling her bones, but at this moment Trina felt such warmth spread throughout her body. Not only was Richie's story magical in its truth, but the way in which he revealed its details was rife with drama and surprise, and she could imagine the joy spreading across Janey's freckled face.

"So that's why they got me a frog for Christmas," Janey exclaimed, "because that's when they fell in love, and after that they got married and Mama gave birth to me, and they lived here. All the while I thought it was the windmill they bonded over."

"This bridge was your father's," Richie said. "It's where he came to dream."

"Can you tell me more about him? What kind of dreams did he have?" she asked. "That mean man Chuck Ackroyd said bad things about him the other night at the tavern, and I've been thinking about them, mostly when it's nighttime and I'm supposed to go to sleep, but I can't. Like tonight."

"You, Janey Sullivan, were Dan Sullivan's dream," he said, "you and Annie."

"So his dreams came true?"

"For a while, yes."

"Nothing lasts," she said.

"If you know that, then you already know to appreciate it when you have it," he said, "and while life forces you to move on, it cannot lessen all your heart knows."

"Mr. Ravens?"

"Yes, Ms. Janey?"

"I'm sorry about your motel. I heard it was ruined."

"Thank you."

"What are you going to do now?"

"I haven't figured that part out yet. The world hasn't yet handed me a sign," he said. "So sometimes you just have to look to the stars and see how brightly they are shining."

"Or which way the wind blows," she said.

"Now, that, Ms. Janey, is very wise indeed," Richie said. "And I also think it's a fine way to end our philosophical discussion. I cannot remember one so rich, so filled with truth. Seeing you here, where you father dreamed and in the shadow of your mama's passion, it is no wonder you are the angel you are. Besides, from what Brian said, Santa Claus doesn't like to show up when little girls are still awake, and so we must get you back."

"Don't tell Brian I snuck out."

"He may not like it, but I bet he'd understand, especially on this special night. Janey, you have a chance tonight to live out your dreams as you wish them. Whether it's your wishes for the best Christmas yet, where gifts you didn't even expect to receive fill your life with renewed joy, or a perfect dream where you see your parents together, the sight of them bringing comfort to the memories your heart carries." He paused until only the blowing wind could be heard, before saying, "Like your friend here; he's your connection to your parents, and while they may no longer walk the earth, their spirits live on . . . right inside this purple frog."

"He's getting older," she said. "Like me. But he's still dependent on me."

"And you're not dependent?"

"Brian says I'm too independent."

"Can you tell me one last thing about your frog?"

"Sure, anything."

"Does he have a name?"

"No," she said, "although I've been thinking he needs one."

"A name will make him feel more alive," Richie stated.

"He's just a stuffed animal," she said. "He's not real."

"Oh, but, Ms. Janey, that's where you're wrong. He's stuffed with so much more than life. Dan Sullivan filled him with love."

Trina watched as Janey hugged Richie with tight, deep-felt affection, and then she went dashing off toward the farmhouse. Her little legs moved quickly, and soon Richie was alone at the stone bridge, and Trina was nearby, fighting the urge to reveal herself and do just as Janey had done, embrace the man she knew as her father. It was something Janey couldn't do. It was something Trina could.

She turned away, fighting tears, and she locked eyes with the turning sails of the windmill, her mind transfixed, her heart overwhelmed with emotion. First at the loving family that had once lived here and lived no more, then at the transition and tragedy this young girl had been forced to endure, and then at her bright spirit, which powered the windmill when the wind could not. Suddenly Trina Winter knew what she needed to do.

Family was everything, and if she didn't act fast, time could take it from her.

She edged her way out of the woods, coming face-to-face with her father.

"Trina," he said.

"Hi, Dad."

"What are you doing here?"

"I thought you'd like to share tomorrow with me."

He looked at his watch. "It's already here."

"Then let's stop wasting time. I think it's our turn to start tilting at windmills."

Midnight had arrived, which meant so too had Christmas Day.

CHAPTER 20

BRIAN

"What do you mean . . . you're leaving? Back to Mark and Sara's apartment, right?"

From her tone, he knew he was wrong. He knew the word held deeper connotations, of permanence, of loss. At least it did for him, because despite how her announcement sat with him, he could tell there was a glint of excitement in her eyes, noticeable even here in the dark of night. Still, the ache in his heart when she spoke rattled him.

"No, leaving Linden Corners," she said. "Me and Richie."

"When?"

"Today, now."

"Now? But it's midnight."

"Which most people see as the end of the day, when really, it's the start of a new one, and I see no better time."

"Slipping away when the sun can't catch you?"

He felt her hands to his cheek, soft, like the one time they'd been together. "You're always so poetic, Brian Duncan; it's one of the things I like about you. You're so open . . . and giving."

Brian didn't feel much like a poet, and, standing outside on the porch in the freezing cold weather, Christmas Day was beginning with something other than a gift. He hadn't brought his coat because he thought this was just going to be a quick good-bye. Maybe it was.

"Trina, at least stay for one more day. Haven't you been saying all along you expected a traditional holiday? Snow, gifts, lights, the crackle of the fireplace, and most important, family to surround you. It's the whole package. You've got it right here, with Mark and Sara and another Ravens to soon join the family. And to make things even more ideal, there's even a little girl who still dreams, who still believes in the magic this day brings."

"That's one of the reasons I'm leaving."

"Janey? I don't understand."

Trina hugged herself, and Brian could feel the distance between them growing already. In her car, parked in the driveway just a few feet away, he could see Richie Ravens in the backseat, no doubt stretching out his leg. He was healing but still had a long road ahead of him. It was an apt metaphor, Brian thought, and in that instant he knew that no matter what he said, his words would only bounce off her. Her mind was made up, and worse, so was her heart.

"Brian, I came to Linden Corners thinking I would help Richie . . . Dad, and maybe I'd get to know him a little better, understand why he chose the path he did. During my stay, something else happened. I got to know myself a little better, and in his stubborn way, I have him to thank, but I also have you."

"Me? All I did was pour you a couple of shots."

"You gave me a shot in the arm is what you did, Brian Duncan," she said. "I have a new chance at having a family—so before I jump into the deep end with a wonderful man and a young girl, as you say, who have the whole package—I think I need to take things a bit more slowly. I need to learn first how to be a daughter." She paused, her eyes moist. Brian's were too. "After the motel burned down, something inside me told me it was time to move on. As Richie will tell you, living in a motel is a transient existence, and once it's gone . . . well, what's left? The open road, and whatever adventures await us."

"You sound like me, a couple of years ago."

"Which is why you should understand."

"I do, Trina . . . but . . ."

"Brian, no more buts. Like we said during our first date, some woman had to be your first after Annie. There will be others too, and one day, there will be the one. I'm sorry it's not me. You're so special, the warmth you bring out in others, your generosity of spirit and time. What you've done for Janey after all she has faced . . . some woman out there is going to find herself the luckiest girl on earth."

Brian nodded, her words beginning to sink deep inside him. Perhaps he knew all along that Trina was a first step indeed, someone to help him begin to finally move on. She'd allowed him to walk more than one, and indeed one of those steps had led him into her arms, her bed. It was all so fleeting, their time together relegated to memories.

"What about Mark and Sara? They're family."

"Oh, I think they've always been among family," she said. "We'll call them to explain."

"So, you really were just passing through?"

"Sometimes words are truth; you just don't always know it . . . until you do."

"So now what?"

"This," she said, and leaned forward to plant one last kiss upon his lips.

Brian wanted to take her into his arms in a sweeping gesture of romance, and it would have been perfect, as the snow had begun to fall and glint off the dim light of the porch, but only one thing kept him from acting on it. It couldn't have been perfect, because Trina wouldn't allow it to be. When she pulled back, he knew he'd lost her for good.

"I hope you find what you're looking for," he said.

Trina looked back at the car, smiled. "I think I already did."

"Where will you go?"

"Brian Duncan, I'll say this in a way that only you can understand," she said, and then, with a smile that suddenly opened up the entire world to her, she added, with the hint of a poet's heart, "Wherever the wind takes us."

She was gone seconds later, not just from the porch but also from his driveway and, soon, from Linden Corners and finally his life. How long he remained on the porch he couldn't say. The Connors had already left for home, and his parents had gone upstairs, and Janey was fast asleep dreaming of Christmas morning, and once again Brian Duncan was awake and feeling alone in the farmhouse. Cold finally seeped deep enough inside him that he needed the fireplace, and so he turned to go back to the warmth found inside. A shiny object on the wicker chair on the side of the porch caught his attention. This time there was no cardboard box, just a brightly wrapped package in red foil and a silver ribbon adorning it.

There was only one difference, the message.

OPEN ME NOW

He did, paper wrapping tossed to the ground like he was a ten-year-old kid who could no longer wait, his eyes growing wide with surprise as he retrieved his gift. His mother's memory tree of yesteryear grew into focus and he said aloud, to himself and perhaps to the wind that knew of things from the past, "Teddy?"

* * *

Brian Duncan didn't know that it was possible to dream all night long when his eyes weren't closed. It was like living inside a world somewhere between the one he knew, of memories from the past, and a world to be found, the present pulling at each piece of time, battling the other. Both of them kept him from moving toward a future he knew could only be filled with uncertainty, and, he supposed, a fair share of loneliness. Another relationship had fizzled out, this time even before really catching fire. Was it any wonder he wished to remain just where he was, hidden under the warm comfort of blankets inside his bedroom? It might be Christmas morning, but nothing yet was stirring, and in a farmhouse this old, that could actually include a mouse.

His dream took him back into the farthest reaches of his mind, where the past lived. What he saw in unfolding, sepia-colored images was a child, maybe six, maybe seven years old, and of course that child was himself. He waited near the top of the stairs of his childhood home. Behind him his sister Rebecca cradled him, and taking up the rear, his older brother, Philip, clearly too grown up to partake in such an event, but traditions won out over everything. At the base of the stairs was a Labrador retriever named Teddy, and he was barking up at them. Teddy had never liked the open stairs, but clearly he wanted to be part of the gang, of the family. The three Duncan kids, with stockings filled with toys and necessities in their hands, were ready to descend on Christmas morning, down the stairs and to the array of gifts that awaited them all beneath a glistening Christmas tree. Yet his dream led him to a different room, one lit by golden light.

It was here he found the Memory Tree.

Every year after they'd exchanged gifts, their mother would remind them of one last gift, and so they would make their way into the formal living room, where Didi Duncan could often be found sipping a cup of tea while sitting upon her antique sofa. It was in this room she set up her yearly Memory Tree, awash in white lights. There were three gifts under the tree, one for each of them, and their mother would say, before they opened them, "Those are from your grandmother." This tradition continued long after Grandmother Locke was no longer with them.

Another set of images had the Memory Tree transforming itself into the windmill, alive like the tree with a dazzling display of illumination. There were gifts waiting there too, and not the ones placed by the residents of Linden Corners last night. No, these were gifts that were part of a bigger mystery, their appearance as uncertain, as confounding, as anything Brian had yet to experience. It had taken all his willpower to resist opening them, and his dream was letting him know that today the mystery would be solved, his Secret Santa exposed. Yet in his mind he saw empty boxes; it had all been a cruel deception, just alluring boxes wrapped with empty promises. The shiny red paper reminded him of a car's rear lights, and of course he had seen such a sight minutes before going to bed, with Trina disappearing into the night.

A ringing sound suddenly broke Brian from his reverie, and he realized it was the phone.

He was about to reach for it, but the ringing suddenly stopped. A moment later he heard a gentle knock at his door.

"Brian, dear, it's your friend Mark on the telephone."

"Thanks, Mom, I'll take it in here."

So he got out of bed and wrapped a robe around himself because it was cold in the house, picked up the cordless phone he kept on the bed stand.

"Mark, Merry Christmas," he said.

"That it is," Mark said, delight in his voice. "And I'd like to toast it later with a cigar."

Brian immediately understood. "Mark, congratulations. Sara?"

"Sara and baby are doing just fine. She went into labor last night, just after midnight."

Just as Richie Ravens was crossing over the border and out of Linden Corners, here came the arrival of a new member of the Ravens family to take his place. Life working its magic. Just then Janey came running into the room, jumping up and down with excitement, her purple frog dancing with her. He tried to hush her, whispering an aside that they could get their Christmas celebration started soon.

"Silly, ask him, is it a boy or a girl . . ."

Brian realized he hadn't asked, and also detected that this baby held much promise for Janey. Seemed a lot of responsibility was already being put on the newborn Ravens child, what with baby Jake soon to be making an exit from Linden Corners too, not unlike the child's great-uncle. He listened, and he nodded and then he sent his congratulations again. "We'll see you soon; later today we'll come by the hospital. Uh, Mark, have you talked with Richie, or Trina . . . ? Got it, yes." At last he replaced the receiver, and Janey was still bouncing like she'd gotten new batteries in her stocking.

"Well?"

"It's a boy," he said, "Harry Ravens, after Mark's father."

"Wow, they came up with a name so quickly!"

By now Brian's parents had joined them in the room. "What a lovely gift," Didi said.

"Come on, I think there's even more gifts that await us all, downstairs," Kevin said.

Janey went dashing over to Kevin and took his hand, and together they made their way down the stairs. Baby Harry would wait; it was Christmas morning and a ten-year-old

girl could wait only so long. Brian, though, remained behind, his mother too, clearly aware not all was right with
him.

"Something on your mind, Brian?"

"Trina left," he said.

She nodded. "I saw you two on the porch, and then I saw
her leave. I'm sorry."

"It's for the best. I guess I'm not ready."

Didi came over and embraced her son. "You always fall
so hard, so fast."

"I have to have one bad quality," he said, an attempt at
humor.

"Most women would find that rather appealing," she
replied.

Brian attempted a smile as he set the phone back down
on the table. It was there he noticed the red collar one would
put around a dog's neck, the one from inside last night's final
Secret Santa gift. The leather was more than weathered; it
was cracked with age. He took hold of it, showing his mother.
"It was you all along, wasn't it?"

Didi Duncan, when she allowed herself to smile, could
light a room.

"But . . . how?"

"With a little help from your friends," she said. "Gerta
mostly."

"Gerta? Remind me never to play poker with her."

"I phoned her before Thanksgiving and told her my
idea."

"Which is what? Why give me Teddy's old collar?"

"Shall we go downstairs and see about those other gifts
Kevin was speaking of?"

"Mom, where are you going with this?"

She slipped her arm into his and said, her voice quaver-
ing, "Eventually everyone has to move on from loss, and

while we all do so in our own time, I often find you need something new to focus on. I thought it was time you and Janey had something you both can share together. It's called having something to look forward to."

"If you've done what I think you have . . ."

"All I've done is brought a little more love into an already loving home."

As they journeyed downward to the living room and the first Christmas they had spent together in years, the scene before him made Brian realize he would have to wait a bit longer to uncover the real story behind the Secret Santa gifts. This moment was all about Janey, and she attacked her presents with zeal. Too many gifts from Brian, that's what Didi said, but she wasn't being judgmental, and besides, how could you not be drawn in by the sheer exuberance on Janey's face when the gift wrap was peeled away and revealed its secret. Clothes for her, clothes for her dolls, a tea set from Didi, and a laptop from Kevin, which Brian proclaimed was excessive.

"Nonsense, a studious girl like Janey needs the latest technology. You do have WiFi?"

"What about Brian? What did you get him?" Janey suddenly asked, looking up from her pile of spoils.

Kevin and Didi exchanged looks and said, "I guess it's time."

"Time for what?" Janey asked.

"I think we have to put on our boots and mittens," Brian said. "To the windmill we go."

Wonder crossed Janey's eyes as she pieced together the evidence. She dashed to the hall closet and immediately tossed on her coat and readied herself for a wintery trek down the hill, all while urging the three of them to hurry up. It was just a few more minutes, Kevin delaying the moment with a quick phone call. What was that about? Brian wondered. Then the four of them—as well as Janey's purple frog—stepped out into the frosty morning as a cold breeze swept across the backyard. Their feet crunched on frozen snow as the windmill's sails rose over the crest of the hill, like it was pulling them closer, and at last they were standing before the door to the windmill, the sails passing just overhead. On the walk down, Janey had explained how the past two Christmases they had opened gifts inside the windmill, and Didi said, "I suppose we'll be doing the same this year."

"It's a tradition!" Janey exclaimed.

Up the winding, iron staircase they went, Didi and Kevin settling on a small sofa in the corner while Janey eagerly accompanied Brian to the closet door. One by one he withdrew the four colorfully wrapped gifts, untouched from when they had first arrived, and set them on the floor. From his pocket he withdrew the red collar he'd received last night.

"What's that?" Janey asked.

"It was in the fifth box, which arrived sometime last night."

"Why did you open it?"

"Because the card said I could," he explained. "Now I suppose it's time to finally find out what's inside these, since today is Christmas Day. What do you say, Janey, do you want to take the first one?"

"Sure, I love opening up presents," she said.

"Before you do," Didi said, "would you look at the gifts, all together?"

Brian did so, wondering what his mother was getting at. One was red, and another was blue, with green and gold completing the holiday rainbow. The sunlight gleamed through the window, making each of them sparkle like Christmas ornaments . . .

"The name ornaments—they're the same colors."

"You mean, all of these gifts are from the two of you? But . . . why?" Janey asked.

"Because we wanted to bring some fun with us for the holidays, give Brian something to look forward to," Kevin said. "The wrapping was the clue."

Janey scrunched up her nose and said, "How did you know Brian wouldn't open them?"

"Yeah, how come?" Brian asked.

"Because we're your parents, Brian, and we know you are a man of honor. Even as a child you wouldn't sneak peeks at what we bought; you were always so patient. Go ahead, open them, please."

Janey took the red one, saying it was because her name ornament was red too, and when she pulled the flaps back, what she pulled out confused her. It was a round metal bowl. Another one was found beneath.

"Huh?"

"Keep going," Kevin said.

Brian took the blue gift for the same reason, and he quickly displayed a leash. Janey took the green one, and she discovered a book about dog training and a calendar for the next year all about dogs, and that's when her eyes began to widen with delight, her knees bouncing off the floor. She told Brian to hurry, and so he did, completing the gift opening by holding out a collar not unlike the one that had been inside the box from last night, but this one was shiny, new, and all it lacked was a dog to wear it.

They didn't have to wait long.

A barking sound could be heard coming from outside, and Janey got up and rushed to the window.

"Brian, look!"

He was right behind her, and what he saw was an eager young puppy, black with a spot of white on its chest, and it was flopping around in the snow. In the distance he could see a familiar car at the side of the road, where stood Gerta, Nora, and Travis. Janey wasted no time in running down the stairs and jumping out of the windmill with a squeal of having seen an old friend, and Brian had a feeling that's what they would be in no time. Brian watched as the puppy went running up to her and jumped up and Janey giggled and fell to the snow, allowing their new pet to lick her face.

As he watched, he was unaware that his parents had joined them outside, not until he felt his mother's arm in his. "That," she said, "is what we've done. He's been staying with Gerta the past couple of days, and I believe Travis was rather reluctant to give him up."

"It's why we were late to the tavern party; we'd just picked him up."

Brian didn't know what to say, so he just watched.

He had to admit it was a pretty amazing picture, and the ensuing scene only got better, as Janey got up from the ground and seemingly took to the wind, running around the field, laughing, dashing, darting, the dog following her every move, barking with delight, the two of them fast friends, who no doubt would be as inseparable as Christmas was from miracles.

"Okay, you've had all day to think of a name," he said.

"Mark and Sara had nine months," she said.

It was bedtime, and while the arrangement had been for Didi to tuck her in tonight, on this night when Christmas would shut its twinkling eyes for another year, Janey had requested that all of them join her in her room. *All* meaning Kevin, Didi, Brian, and a black Labrador retriever whom she had played with all day and who now rested on the edge of the bed, clearly exhausted. On the walls of her room, portraits of Annie and Dan Sullivan stared back, almost as if they too had received a special invitation. On her bed was her ubiquitous frog, looking a bit long in the tooth. Why not? Didn't he turn ten years old today?

"First I want to say thank you again. I can't believe it . . . Brian . . . Dad, wow, we have a dog."

"There's a lot of responsibility that comes with owning one," he said.

"Owning? We don't own him, Brian, he's . . . one of us, part of us."

"Family," Didi said.

"Just like all of you; you're my family." She paused and said, "So if the puppy is going to have a name, then so is my frog, finally, and trust me, he needs one after going all these years without one. I can imagine what that's like because, well, for the longest time I struggled over how to refer to . . . you, and you."

Kevin and Didi nodded with understanding. Brian realized he should have handled this a while ago and not have had Janey for the past two weeks awkwardly fumbling with their names or just clearing her throat when she wanted their attention, and now he was feeling guilty that it was a child who'd had to broach the subject. In the end, he supposed it was okay. Children had a way of filtering out the plain truth.

"I never had any grandparents, so I've never really had to say the words," Janey said. "And it took me so long to call Brian . . . Dad, and sometimes even today I slip up. So, if he's my dad and you're both his parents, do I get to call you Grandma, or maybe Grand?"

"Well, I don't see how Grand works; there's two of us," Kevin said. "Why not Grandma and Grandpa? I'd like that."

"As would I," Didi said.

Brian watched as Janey considered this quick solution, finally nodding her approval. "Wow, my family got really bigger today, and now that we have that settled . . . let's see about the dog's name. All day I've been torn between two names, and it's only now that I've decided. I liked both names, so I figured whichever one the dog doesn't get . . . the frog will."

"That sounds like a very smart plan," Didi said.

"Janey, are you sure you don't want to talk about this first, you know, just us?"

"Dad, don't be silly," she said with a roll of her eyes. "Although he usually is."

Kevin and Didi laughed at their son's expense.

"Okay, let's have it. I don't want to be calling out over the backyard 'dog.' "

"His name is Sully," Janey said, "and the frog's name is Dunc."

"Sully?"

"Dunc?"

"Yeah, as in Sullivan and Duncan, our last names. The frog is joining our family, so he becomes Dunc. And Sully . . . well, he has to know of his other family, and so when he's running around the windmill Mama will know it's okay to share things with him too."

Didi leaned down and kissed the top of Janey's head. "You're a very wise young lady."

"Perfect names, indeed," Kevin added.

"Wow, two pets, a dad, and grandparents, all together," she said, "and we'll be a family for as long as we can. Because I know once Christmas is over, Grandma and Grandpa have to go back home."

"Janey, we can worry about that when the time comes," Brian said.

"Not so fast, the both of you," Kevin said. "You don't get rid of us that easily. Christmas is over, there's the door?"

Brian spun around, his father's words surprising him. "What do you mean?"

"Your mother and I were saving one last Christmas surprise for you, Brian," he said. "I was wondering, perhaps you might need help down at your tavern. After all, if we're going to be neighbors, I'm sure there are nights you'll need off to help this little lady."

"And on nights you have to work, a woman's influence will do her good," Didi added.

Brian was thinking he should have gotten new ears for Christmas, because the old ones weren't working. "I'm sorry, did you say neighbors?"

"Yes, who do you think bought the Knights' farmhouse?"

It wasn't words that ended their day of holiday magic, because Brian could find no more, and as his parents left the room with a chuckle and the promise of more details later, Janey closed her eyes and with a sleeping Sully warming her feet and Dunc in her arms, Brian had the chance to concentrate on the sails of the windmill as seen through Janey's window, their endless rotations not unlike the passage of time. Brian realized that in the land of the windmill, there were fresh memories to be made and indeed, many things to look forward to.

EPILOGUE

Clocks turn even when you're not looking, the sun rises and falls as the passing days move gently into the quiet of night, and so time effortlessly glides by, unseen but ever present. For those with little to look forward to in life, time can drag on till it seems the earth has stood still, while for others the endless rotations of its axis move far too quickly, leaving them with a sense of time running out, always planning, seldom living. Time is universal, yet it represents so many things to so many, and while it can be enigmatic, even mysterious, it also represents one of the few constants in the universe. What no one has in common with time is how much of it they have.

In reality, the world marches on, and before anyone realizes it, time has flown by on the currents of the wind, with another day, month, and year having elapsed, leaving us all a little older, perhaps a bit wiser. And always wondering, Where has the time flown?

Sometimes people anticipate the arrival of a certain day, a birthday or anniversary, a trip that will take them to the far reaches of the earth, feeling it will never come. And then suddenly it's gone, whisked away by time's inevitable advancement, leaving in its wake those things called memories. Sometimes people wish

time would grind to a standstill, allowing them to forever trea-
sure a moment so hard to catch, like witnessing a falling star, the
first bloom of love, a long-planned wedding, only to realize that
time is a part of life no one can lay claim to—its hold on us strong,
our grip tenuous.

Time is always present, but it's remembered in the past,
thought about for the future.

"Remember that time . . ."

"Time will tell."

Time means everything and yet it ultimately means nothing,
leaving a place like the small village known as Linden Corners
somewhere between yesterday and tomorrow. For eager kids down
at Linden Corners Middle School, a year of studies can feel like
forever; for anxious adults in the simple act of waiting for a cup of
coffee down at Martha's Five O'Clock Diner, time can come to
mean impatience; and for the elderly folks down at Edgestone Re-
tirement Center, who have seen their lives fall behind them, time
taunts like an enemy. Even the iconic, majestic windmill that
looms over this countryside knows of time's unstoppable dance, its
spinning sails silently recording every step.

But then come those special times of year when folks dream of
better lives. Holidays are like time-outs from the rigors of daily
life, filling out days with Memorial Day picnics and Fourth of
July fireworks, these events like time caught in a bottle. At
Thanksgiving, we take time for our families and ourselves, giv-
ing thanks for all we have, all we share. And then of course there's
Christmas, which stretches the notion of time to extremes, for it is
not just a single day amidst a cold month, but something joyfully
referred to as Christmastime, one built on a giving spirit, on tra-
dition. And what is tradition but time told in reverse.

Only one thing in this world can halt the passage of time.

Only one thing in this world can transport you to another time
and another world.

That one thing is called a dream.

For one wide-eyed girl in Linden Corners, she with freckles on her usually scrunched-up nose, dreams were sometimes all she could cling to.

Once more in this fading, unforgettable year, the willowy shadow appeared in the dark of night, as though brought back to the little girl on the currents of an unseen wind. Shutters clacked, and the wind whistled, a homespun melody she knew by heart. As Sully slept beside her with his tongue hanging out, unknowing of the visitor, the shadow beckoned to her.

"Mama, is that you? Oh, I'm so glad you're here. There's so much to tell you."

"There's so much I already know, and so much of tomorrow still to be discovered."

Her golden glow was so like the windmill, still shining brightly as the New Year neared. As she rose from her bed, Dunc the purple frog fell over against the soft pillow, his sewn mouth seemingly upturned, unafraid now to be in the dark. Janey feared nothing either, and it was as though believing so allowed her body to float over the floor, and soon she was being transported across the field. The windmill drew her to its gently turning sails, and in moments she was back upstairs, just as she had been on Christmas Day, just as she had been during her two previous dreams, one that gave her a peek into the past, the other showing her just how wonderful her Christmas this year would be, and both had proven to reveal truths she'd shared with no one.

"Mama, what are you going to show me today?"

"Look through the window as before, Janey, and tell the wind all that you wish."

"Do I have to say it aloud?"

"Dreams defy voices," she said, leaving Janey thinking it was another riddle.

But she quieted down, enjoying the silence, the stillness of the world around her. That was when she closed her eyes, and inside her mind colors opened up before her. They may have been out of focus, yet also so blindingly bright, and she thought of things in this life she had and she thought of things in this life she didn't, and then she wondered if there was something missing in between . . . someone. At last she opened her eyes, and that's when the sails passed by the window and the images began to flicker, like a movie reel.

She saw a Christmas tree, and she saw people gathered in the familiar room. Stockings hung on the mantel, fire crackling beneath them. It was her living room, her home. She thought she could hear music, the lulling sounds of "Do You Hear What I Hear?" which Janey had learned only recently was one of her grandmother's favorite holiday tunes, and so that indicated to Janey that whichever Christmas was unfolding before her, Didi and Kevin Duncan were around, and indeed, that's when she saw them, almost as though thinking of them had willed them there. They were hanging their ornaments on the tree.

"Mama, this dream is just like the last one," Janey said.

"Just watch, Janey, and listen."

She waited, but nothing changed, perhaps her words having scared away the future.

Then she saw a dog bound into the room, his dark coat and white ruff just like Sully's, his red collar distinct. It was him for sure, but he appeared older, no longer a puppy. Chasing after him, Janey saw herself, and unlike in the first dream, when she'd been a baby, and unlike in the second dream, when she couldn't see herself, she was different too, somehow older. She blinked and suddenly she was gone from view, but she could hear her own laughter as she called out to Sully, whose bark Kevin shushed.

"Brian, when are you ever going to train this dog?"

"Sorry if I've been a bit busy."

Janey recognized Brian's voice, and she watched for him to enter the frame. There he was, and he didn't look much older, his hair still brown with no flecks of gray, so this scene couldn't be

*taking place too far into the future. Maybe it was only next year.
Janey decided that had to be the case, thinking the dream was
about to end because she'd seen all her family. She knew, however,
there had to be more to come; nothing different had really been
shown to her.*

"Brian, why don't I take the baby?"

*The baby? Janey wondered. Had Sara and Mark brought
their newborn over? Or maybe it was Jake, but then she remembered that Cynthia and Bradley had already been gone a few days,
and of course they had taken Jake with them. They were halfway
across the country by now. So, wait, who was this?*

"Mama, I don't understand. What are you showing me?"

*Janey was forced to look back, where she saw Brian hand over
a baby who appeared to be no more than one month old. One last
person entered the room, but she was blurry, and no matter how
hard the little girl who was not so little anymore tried to adjust
her eyes, no face was forthcoming, no identity would reveal itself.
But whoever she was, she had an aura about her, and Janey could
feel warmth spread all through her body, even as outside it had
begun to snow. Like somehow the chill of winter was fast dissipat-
ing, as quickly as the images she had seen through the windmill's
window.*

Time was advancing; a new season loomed over the horizon.

*"But, Mama, where did the pictures go? I want to see her.
Who is she?"*

*"That, my sweet and beautiful Janey, will have to wait,"
Annie Sullivan said, her voice an echo, as though the wind were
taking her far from home and everything she loved, to lands distant and unknown, a place that remembered the past and gleaned
the future. Her willowy shadow was no more, and Janey could
have sworn it was just the wind that spoke her mama's final
breath.*

"Another story for another time."

ACKNOWLEDGMENTS

My thanks and appreciation to Audrey LaFehr, Martin Biro, and the publishing professionals at Kensington, for caring so deeply about the world of Linden Corners. I never could have imagined I would write four books (and counting) about these special characters.

Also, the front of the house staff at Broadway's beautiful Belasco Theatre was especially supportive. Much of this book was written between shows at the 2012 revival of Clifford Odets' *Golden Boy*. The play's question of art versus commerce was not lost on me, and I hope I did its message proud.

Lastly, to the passionate readers who have reached out to me to express their love of my books, in particular the stories about the windmill, I am very, very thankful.

If you enjoyed *The Memory Tree*, return to
Linden Corners in Joseph Pittman's

A CHRISTMAS WISH

Turn the page for a special excerpt.

A Kensington trade paperback on sale now.

CHAPTER 1

If tradition dictates the direction of your life, then it was inevitable that my mother called me two weeks before Thanksgiving to ask whether I would be joining the family for our annual dinner. Every year she makes the same call, every year she asks in her deliberately unassuming way, and every year I respond in my expected fashion. Yes, of course, where else would I be? This year, though, so much had changed—in my life and in my parents' lives, too—that I had to wonder whether the notion of tradition belonged to a bygone era, appreciated only by thoughts of the past, no longer put into practice. How I answered my mother on this day proved that indeed change was in the air, a first step toward tomorrow. Because I informed her that before I could give her an answer, I needed to consult first with Janey.

"Brian, dear, that's very sweet, but you don't ask children what they want to do. You tell them," she stated matter-of-factly.

"No, Mother, Janey and I, we're a team. We make decisions together."

"Brian, dear, you have so much to learn about children."

Actually, I thought my mother had a lot to learn about her son.

I had been in the kitchen at the farmhouse, mulling over dinner. I hung up and was left to brood the remainder of the day while I cooked, even when Janey came home from school filled with an undimmed light that usually brightened me. I put on my best front as she busily talked about her day. We ate a bland chicken, turkey's everyday fill-in, and still I didn't bring up the idea of the holiday. I waited until bedtime to ask Janey her thoughts on the subject of the coming holiday.

"Thanksgiving? Away from Linden Corners?"

I nodded. "It's your call."

"Do you want to go, Brian?"

"I will if you will," I replied.

"That sounds evasive."

"Where did you learn such a big word like that?"

She rolled her eyes. Vocabulary had never been an issue with Janey. "See, evasive."

I laughed. "Okay, okay. Yes, I'd like to go."

"Good. Then I will if you will," she said, her smile uplifting. "Funny, I get to meet your family. I never thought about them before. That you have parents . . . do you have a big family? Where are they? Do they have a dog. . . ."

"Slow down, slow down. All in good time."

"I'm just curious. Up until now you've always been . . . well, you've been Brian."

"We all come from somewhere."

She thought about that a moment, and I feared it would lead the conversation down a path she wasn't ready for. I certainly wasn't ready for it. But then she just innocently stated, "I can't wait."

Her sudden pause had me wondering what else she was thinking. You could always see the wheels of her mind turning, almost as though they spun her eyeballs.

"Is your mom like mine?"

No, my mind said. I chose not to answer that one directly. "Everyone is their own person."

"Evasive," she said.

I couldn't help it, I laughed. "So, it's agreed, we go. You and me, hand in hand."

"Hand in hand," Janey agreed.

That's how it worked with us.

As night fell and Janey slept, I phoned my mother back and told her to add two plates to the Duncan family's dinner table, that the Linden Corners faction of the family would join them.

"You know how much this means to me, Brian."

Yes, I did.

And while accepting the invitation may have been a relatively smooth process at the time, now, as we turned the corner off Walnut Street in Philadelphia and were only two blocks from my parents' stately new home, anxiety and trepidation ran through me like a monsoon. Sweat beaded on my brow, nerves taking control once I'd parked. The trip had taken us six hours (with a dinner break), but really, it had been an even longer time coming. Nine months had passed since I'd last seen my parents, and during that elapsed time my world had drastically changed in a way none of us could have predicted, myself at the top of that list. I had quit my well-paying job as a thankless corporate drone, sublet my tiny New York apartment, and left behind the supposed woman of my dreams. Setting out on a journey of self-discovery, I had landed in a place that was not far from all I'd known in terms of miles, yet worlds away. I'd met Annie Sullivan and I'd loved her and then I'd lost her, we all had, and as a result I had been given the care of her only daughter, eight-year-old Janey Sullivan, a wonder of a girl, the true one of my dreams. Since then, I'd been very proprietary in terms of exposing Janey to new things. I hadn't allowed any visitors, not friends or family from beyond Linden Corners, wanting this time of transition between me and Janey to take shape without any further disruption. Even now I had my concerns about taking this precious girl out from the safe confines of her life, but realized, too, there was a time for everything, even for moving forward.

"Which house is it?" Janey asked, pointing out the car window at the long row of houses lining both sides of the dimly lit street. This was Society Hill, where both Federal- and Colonial-style town houses prevailed, these classic, restored structures adorning each side of the tree-lined street. It was a sea of brick and white lattices. I didn't blame Janey for being confused; all the houses looked the same. Still, I indicated the building on the far left corner. "With the porch light on."

"Good thing they have that light, since it's so dark. How else would we find it?"

"Well, Janey, I do have the address."

"Oh," she replied with a giggle that made me grin, a good thing right now. Settled my nerves to see how relaxed Janey was.

We had parked on a side street, left the suitcases behind for now. We had enough baggage with us already. So, with Janey's hand in mine, our unlikely team made our way toward the upscale residence of Kevin and Didi Duncan. For years they had lived in the Philly suburbs (in the house I'd grown up in) and then had just this past summer done the opposite of all their friends. They had gone urban, selling the old house and instead buying this very nice home in this very nice section of the City of Brotherly Love. Some investments of Dad's must have really paid off. I had yet to see it myself, thinking this was a good thing, there were no memories of past holidays awaiting me behind those doors. Neutral territory. Though you can never really escape your memories, no matter the walls you've built up, your mind can tear them down when it wants, prompted sometimes by the simplest of senses. As we reached the steps, I looked down at Janey's freckled face and asked, "Ready?"

"You keep asking that," she said. "I think the question is, are you ready?"

"And I think the answer is: Not really."

"Silly—they're your parents, Brian."

As if Janey's words were a magic key, the front door opened and a bath of light from inside illuminated us, sending our shadows retreating to the sidewalk. Yet we stepped forward to where my mother waited in the entranceway. She was dressed in a simple navy skirt and white blouse, a string of pearls dangling from her neck. Perfume wafted in the breeze. Her familiar scent. See what I mean about memories? I had the picture of my mother from years ago, tucking me into bed before she and my father went out to dinner. She smelled the same then, now. What had changed was her hair—she'd allowed it to go gray, and it was salon perfect. She wouldn't be Didi Duncan if not properly attired, even at this hour.

"Well, who have we here?" she asked.

"Your son," I replied, and then Janey said, "And me, I'm Janey."

My mother moved off the top step and gave me an embrace that felt more like an air-kiss before bending down so her face was level with Janey's. "Well, you're a pretty thing, aren't you, Jane?"

"Janey," I corrected her.

She ignored me, keeping her focus on Janey. "That's such a childish name, now, don't you think?"

"I am a child," Janey remarked.

"Nonsense, dear. You've grown tremendously the last few months, haven't you? Come in, come in, the both of you."

And we did, shutting out the encroaching cold behind us. We entered a hallway crafted lovingly with antique wood, and then were ushered down to the living room, where a warm fire was blazing in the large fireplace. My father, Kevin Duncan, sat beside the crackling fire in a wing-back leather chair, still dressed in his business suit, the tie still on, the top button to his shirt still clasped. That was the thing about my father. *Still* was a word that described him perfectly. He never changed. He was reading the *Wall Street Journal* and on the table near him was a tumbler filled with his traditional dry Manhattan, the successful entrepreneur in relaxation mode. When he saw us enter, he gently set the paper down on a nearby matching ottoman.

"Hello, son, it's good to see you," he said, shaking my hand with his strong, firm grip. His greeting was as efficient and businesslike as ever; it was just his way, all he knew. He was a tall man, six four and built strongly, and I imagined in his office, even if he hadn't been the boss he would still strike an intimidating pose. Yet a surprising feat happened on this evening. As Janey poked out from behind me, she craned her neck up high so she could see my father and that's when she exclaimed with wide eyes, "Wow, you're big." The stern businessman's face crumpled and a smile found its way to his ruddy face.

"What ho! Well, let's get a look at you, young lady," he said.

"You'd have to sit on the floor to do that."

Kevin Duncan was a big, barrel-chested man, with thick gray hair and a pair of glasses upon his nose, and right now the figure of the man who had always intimidated me actually laughed—something he wasn't exactly known for. Then, instead of bending down as Janey suggested, he lifted the little girl into those big arms of his and I realized that the impossible had been accomplished, Janey had softened the heart of a moneyed giant. I felt pent-up tension lea~~ing~~ shoulders and I realized then that maybe this T~~~~ us, wouldn't be so bad. My mother had f~~~~

witnessed the entire exchange between her husband and her . . . my goodness, I almost thought *granddaughter.* I would have to watch my words; Janey and I to this point had avoided all such labels, all such complications.

The four of us settled into the living room and talked genially, Janey enjoying a glass of apple juice and me a seltzer with ice, while my father and mother drank their Manhattans. Their attention remained focused mostly on Janey. They asked her questions about school and friends, nothing about her mother, Annie, or the difficult times this girl had already known in her life. There was no mention of the windmill that had brought us together. As they chatted, I sat on the edge of my seat, waiting anxiously for any misstep.

About ten o'clock, the excitement of the long trip and of Janey meeting my parents finally taking its toll, it was decided we had best get Janey to bed. I retrieved the suitcases from the car and attempted to get Janey settled into her room. She'd gotten her second wind apparently, so busy was she looking at the old photographs my parents had hung on the walls.

"Is that you, Brian?" Janey asked, pointing to a geeky teen posing for his high school graduation picture. I was seventeen. I looked twelve. When I told her it was, she laughed. "You look different now—better." As I thanked her, she pointed to the other two similarly styled portraits that hung above mine, one of a dark-haired, handsome young man, the other a young woman with eyes that dominated the frame. Again, high school graduation pictures. "Who are they?" she asked.

"Well, one is Rebecca; she's my sister."

"She's pretty. And who's the other guy? He doesn't look so . . ."

"Geeky? Like me?"

" ah," she said, with an impish smile.

 nswering her question, I stared at the photograph that was up for discussion, thought of the memories his rugged good looks inspired. For a second I looked around for the trophies and awards, the ribbons and framed citations that adorned his walls, and then remembered this was no longer his room. Not even the house he'd grown up in, any of us, actually. Suddenly I was surprised that the photos had been placed on the walls here, not packed away like other memories. I wondered how my parents had felt packing up the old house, saying good-bye to a room that had remained fixed in time. Then I answered.

"That's my brother, Philip."

Our conversation was quickly interrupted as my mother came brushing through the doorway. She cleared her throat knowingly. Photographs were not something she wished to discuss. When she saw what little progress I'd made in getting Janey to sleep, she summarily tossed me out.

"Honestly, what do you know about caring for little girls, Brian?"

My mother liked to ask questions, but she seldom waited for answers. Tonight was one of those occasions, despite the fact I could have answered her with easy confidence. Because I knew a lot. Janey had helped me in figuring out the curious mind of a growing child, oh she had helped me plenty. But I let my mother enjoy her fussing over Janey, said my good nights, receiving back a huge hug from Janey and a polite smile from my mother, and finally retreated to the other guest room. And as I fought to find sleep that night, I hoped that tomorrow and in the coming weeks I would be able to reciprocate the feelings behind Janey's warm hug. She was in a strange house, meeting strange people, and even though they were my relatives, being here couldn't have been the easiest thing. And it was only the beginning of the holiday season. How much she would need me nearly scared me. How much I would need her terrified me.

Brian and Janey's story continues in Joseph Pittman's

A CHRISTMAS HOPE

Turn the page for a special excerpt.

A Kensington trade paperback on sale now.

CHAPTER 1

NORA

"How come it's snowing . . . it's only October."

"Because, honey, we're in the thick of Upstate New York and in this neck of the woods they only have two seasons, winter and August."

"That makes no sense, one's a month and the other is a season."

No argument there. She nodded agreeably. "Welcome to Linden Corners."

The boy looked dubiously at his mother. "Am I going to like living here?"

Good question, she thought. Was she? Did she ever like it?

The drifting snowflakes falling all around the fire-red Mustang were only the first hint that she was nearing the tiny village of Linden Corners, but it wasn't until she crested over the rise in the highway and came upon the spinning sails of the old windmill that she knew she was truly home. Home, she thought, afraid to taste the flavor of the word on her bitter tongue. What other notion instilled such a juxtaposed sense of both comfort and failure? Being back here was reason enough to sigh, and not in a relaxed way. Her name was Nora Connors Rainer, and she wasn't pleased by any of this, not the snow and not the sight of that windmill, not to mention the idea of Linden Corners itself. Returning to the place of her childhood meant only one thing: Her adult life was an utter disaster, and given the fact that her car was overstuffed with her belongings—what some might call "baggage"—a jury would render a verdict within minutes of deliberating. Guilty, Your Honor, of grossly mismanaging her life, as well as that of her twelve-year-old son. She was a lawyer by trade, unable to even win her own case. How she wished she could just continue driving through the village, it was small enough it would only take a minute or so. A one-blink-and-you-miss-it kind of town.

There was also a sense of claustrophobia about the town, too, or so thought the worldly Nora, who had traveled the globe and seen many beautiful sights, now seeing the world spit her out from whence she originated. Just when she needed her street smarts the most, home was calling, the comfort and security and understanding that you could only find inside the walls of your parents' house, now just a mile away and creeping ever closer. No doubt a couple pieces of her mother's famed strawberry pie awaited them both. With the windmill now fading to small in her rearview mirror, Nora felt her heart beating with nervous anticipation. Home meant many things to many people, but at this moment Nora needed its sense of reassurance. Knowing those old walls came complete with a supportive mother to hold you tight and tell you everything was going to be just fine, her mind told her maybe all would be okay.

But then she knew it wouldn't be, not initially.

Her homecoming would no doubt be seen as an occasion for her mother. So she had to assume the house would not be empty, since the sweet-natured Gerta Connors enjoyed having company. And said company would ask questions, and said company would expect answers. Suddenly Nora saw a houseful of guests, all of them stuffing their faces with pie, their smiles sweeter than sugar, but digesting gossip at her expense.

"Please, do me this one favor and don't let her have anyone over, I can't deal with . . . this, not now," Nora said aloud. "Don't let her think my homecoming is a celebration."

"Uh, Mom, are you talking to me?"

"Sorry, honey, Mom's weirding out."

"No kidding."

Her son's sarcasm, which had been coming on strong in the past six months, actually produced a rare smile on her tight face. Normally she'd reprimand him for his tone, but not today. He'd earned the right to vent as much as she deserved its wrath, she'd turned his life upside down. Still, Nora knew her mother, just as much as she recognized the friendly confines of Linden Corners, both the good and the bad. Having grown up here, she was well acquainted with the village's quirky tendency toward parties and parades, the happiest of holidays and heart-spun happenings, her mother, Gerta, oftentimes at the center of planning the numerous, joyous celebrations. Heck, it was only the end of October and the fallen snow already had a layer of ice beneath this fresh coating of snow, no doubt the residents had a name for such an occasion. "Second Snowfall" or something cheekily homespun like that. Winter in this region came early, stayed often, and you needed the patience of a saint and good driving skills to navigate its literal slippery slope. This year, Nora herself would be like the ever-present season, setting up roost for some time to come, though even she didn't know for how long. She could one day decide to leave, then a storm inside her could erupt and she'd be trapped. Again. Nestled in the lush Hudson River Valley, cocooned from the outside world, she could easily lose herself.

That part she liked.

Of course cocooned was just a nice word for hiding.

Nora Connors Rainer and her one son, Travis, had left the flatlands of Nebraska five days ago, enjoying the long drive and each other's company, if not necessarily looking forward to their final destination. They could have easily flown to Albany, had the car shipped or just sold it and bought a new one when they arrived, but Nora wasn't ready to sell off everything from her past life. Call her shallow, but she'd worked too hard to buy her sporty red Mustang. Too bad she hadn't worked as hard at her marriage. But hey, a car allows you to just turn on the engine and steer it to where you wanted to go. A husband tended to have his own ignition, liked to drive by himself, go off on his own, embracing the unexpected surprises around winding curves. So then why was she the one on the open road, heading into the tiny downtown of a village whose future best existed in a rearview mirror?

Not that the village was all that empty at four o'clock in the afternoon. She recognized several stores like Marla and Darla's Trading Post—twins she'd gone to school with, inseparable then, business partners now, sisters forever—and guarding the storefront, under the porch and seemingly oblivious to the snow, were two golden retrievers who lay quietly, sleeping the afternoon away in that lazy, entwined way shared only by our canine friends. Of course, too, there was the Five O'Clock Diner, run by the sharp-tongued, quick-witted Martha Martinson, plus the reliable Ackroyd's Hardware Emporium and George's Tavern, which she had known her entire life as Connors' Corners. It was where her father had happily toiled for much of his adult life. She'd heard about the renaming in e-mails and phone calls and how that wonderful Brian Duncan continued to honor George Connors's traditions and she'd seen pictures of the new sign, but the sight of it now made her heart ache for the loss of her father, for her still-living mother who had to live with the daily memories of her late husband.

But the store that most caught Nora's attention was darkened, a CLOSED sign posted on the locked front door. The building was in need of a paint job, flakes peeling off its sides. Elsie's Antiques it was called and had been for the better part of her life. But that was about to change.

Even in Linden Corners, change occasionally happened.

"Hey, Mom?"

"Yeah, baby?" Nora said, her eyes drifting away from Elsie's shop with reluctance.

"You know what today is?"

"It's Thursday, I think. Wait, what day did we leave . . . ?"

"No, not day. Today. It's Halloween."

Nora looked out her driver's side window and wondered how she had missed them. Too focused on seeing the village her way, she failed to notice how her son's eyes would view it. Seemed the sidewalks of the village were currently peopled with tiny ghosts and goblins, witches with straw brooms, vampires with fangs and tight abs, bums (though, truth be known, that last one might have not been a disguise), all of them carrying orange plastic pumpkins, winter coats unfortunately partly covering their clever costumes. Adults accompanied them to ensure nothing untoward happened to their ghoulish charges, or that they got too cold while out trick-or-treating. The allure of Halloween had lost its appeal years ago, just another foolish pseudo-holiday. She remembered dressing up as a ballerina when she was a kid; but heck, it's not like she played the part of a ballerina. People today, they tended to embody their costume rather than just simply wear it. As though everyone was starring in their own movie, stopping at makeup before stepping before the camera. While Nora may not like it, Travis always enjoyed planning his costume.

"Sorry. You were gonna be Batman this year, right?"

"Nah. Robin."

"How can you have Robin without Batman?"

"Dad was going to play Batman."

Well, that comment shut her up but good. And she felt worse than before, a sharp pain stabbing at her empty gut. Not only was Travis missing out on one of his favorite holidays, but he was missing it along with his father. She hated disappointing her only child—taking him from his home and school and friends, all he'd ever known, to return to . . . here. She looked again at the kids dressed in costume, one in particular covered in a white sheet with two eyelets. Ghosts indeed, they were all around, and not just on the sidewalks, but in the trunk of her car and inside her mind. Oh yes, those phantoms never left, did they? They never needed the arrival of a single day of celebration to come out and haunt.

"I'll make it up to you," she said.

"What, you'll be Batgirl?"

She smiled over at him, relieved to see he still had a streak of sweetness underneath all that almost-teenage sarcasm. "I promise to make the next holiday real special, okay, sweetie? I know how much you like Christmas, too."

"Uh, Mom?"

"Yeah, honey."

"The next holiday is Thanksgiving."

She actually laughed, loud enough to rattle the windows inside the car. The sudden release felt good, and at last she allowed her shoulders to drop. For Nora Connors Rainer, this new life they were starting here in Linden Corners, it was going to be harder than she envisioned. Good thing her mother was there to help, and not just with Travis's expected adjustment. Nora knew she needed all the help she could get.

"Oh, and one other thing?" Travis asked.

She was concentrating on the snowy roads ahead, yet she managed to sneak a quick look at her young son. She felt an overwhelming sense of love, knowing she would do anything to ensure a happy childhood for him. She knew how lucky she was to have him at her side. It might have been different.

"Sure, love, what's that?"

"Can you just call me Travis from now on? All that baby, honey, sweetie stuff," he said, "it doesn't suit the man of the house."

Nora's easy laughter from moments ago dissipated, like she'd opened the window and let her joy grow brittle in the cold air. Now she just wanted to cry.

How was it that her son was growing up when she wasn't?

She turned off Route 20, which served as the village's main artery, and wound her way up Green Pine Lane, remembering each curve of the road as well as she knew herself. When she caught sight of the old house, Nora felt herself retreat back to Travis's age, a helpless twelve-year-old girl with brown pigtails and hand-me-down clothes from her three older sisters and a sour, uncertain expression on her face. Only the hairstyle and clothes had changed. Oh, and her age.

Forty and moving back in with Mom.

Good job, Nora, she thought.

"Mom, I know you're still talking to yourself . . . even if I can't hear it."

"This is hard, Travis. Just give me a moment."

She pulled to the side of the road, tires crunching in the

fresh snow. The house looked small, even though it had three floors, four bedrooms, and lots of space in the basement and attic. After all, her parents had raised four girls there—she the youngest, along with older sisters Victoria, Melanie, and Lindsay, so clearly the house had been big enough to accommodate them, big enough that if you wanted to hide you could. And Nora was a hider, even back then. Down in the basement or cuddled up on the old sofa, she could easily get lost in the fantastical world of whatever book she was reading, or the drama found in the pretend lives of her dolls. She wondered if her mother would insist that she take back her old room. Nora wasn't sure she could handle that, but also questioned where else she would hide. This was the first time she'd been back to the house since her father, George, had died, almost a year and a half ago. She took a deep breath. Yup, this was hard, harder than she'd anticipated.

"Okay, kiddo, you ready?"

"That's a new one."

"What is?"

"Uh, hello, kiddo?"

"Sorry, mother's instinct," she said. "Ready, Mr. Rainer?"

Travis just rolled his eyes.

"Got it, sorry, let's go," she said with another laugh; her emotions were a jumbled mess, there was no telling how fast her mood could turn. She guided them back onto the slick, snow-covered road, steeling herself for the final steps. It was just another three hundred feet before she would turn into the short driveway, their journey complete yet somehow also just beginning.

A blaring horn from behind caused her to slam on the brakes and that's when a loud smack jolted them forward.

"Shit," Nora called out, tossing the car into PARK.

They had been rear-ended.

"Mom!"

"Sorry, honey. Are you okay?"

"Yeah. Just surprised me is all."

"Okay, wait here, let me see what happened."

Nora unclenched her seat belt, not her teeth, as she made her way out of her prized car to assess the damage and to confront the dumb idiot who had crashed into her. What she saw was a battered old farm truck, two people up inside the high cabin. As she made her way toward the driver's side door, she stole a look at the back of her prized Mustang. The fool had taken out a brake light, left a small gash on the side bumper. She could see the bright red paint on the grille of the truck.

"Hey, look what you did," she said, pointing to the damage.

The man behind the wheel stepped out, closing the door behind him.

"What I did? You just pulled out, didn't even look to see if there was traffic."

"Traffic? In Linden Corners? Not exactly two concepts that go together."

"Nora?"

"Excuse me?"

"You're Nora, aren't you? Gerta's daughter."

Nora blinked away the snow that was falling in her face, clearing her eyes. Who was this farmer and why did he know who she was? She looked over at the other passenger in the truck, saw a young girl with a scrunched-up nose peering over the high dashboard, and that's when she knew who he was, knew who the girl was, and what they were doing here just a short distance from Gerta Connors's house.

"Brian Duncan," she said, placing her hands on her hips for effect.

"You recognize me?"

"No. But one and one in this case still equals four. I'm guessing that's Janey Sullivan in the truck. My mom talks about the two of you all the time."

"Small world, huh? She talks of you often, too, especially lately," he said. "We were just heading to your mother's house to pick her up to take her to the annual village Halloween party over at the community center. We call it the Spooktacular."

Nora allowed a knowing smile to cross her lips despite herself; she'd guessed it right. Linden Corners would never let a holiday pass by without some kind of celebration; like its middle name was "annual." "How nice. But I don't get your costume," she said, assessing his faded jeans, scuffed boots, and red flannel shirt. "You some kind of farmer?"

"Ha ha, no, I haven't changed yet. Janey in there, she's a windmill."

Of course she was, Nora thought.

"I'm sorry about your car," Brian said, "but you did just pull out without warning. I tried to warn you, but . . . you know, crunch."

"Yeah, crunch," Nora said.

Silence hovered between them, snow beginning to coat their shoulders.

Brian broke the quiet before it became deafening. "What do you say we get the kids inside where it's warm, then we can figure out what to do . . . about this." He spread his hands before the damage to her car. The truck appeared fine, just old and apparently indestructible.

Nora had other ideas about what she wanted to do, high on the list was wringing this guy's neck. Her car! But she knew Brian was right, get the kids out of the cold, deal with things then. Mother mode before lawyer, she told herself. She could hear her mother's words ring inside her mind, telling her that Brian is very practical and wise, and he had an easy, calming nature to his six-foot frame. No wonder Gerta liked to be around him, he had soothed her during a difficult transition period. Now it was Nora facing one, but she didn't need his bit of calm. She had no need for the services of Brian Duncan.

She gave him one last look. Even after an accident he had an affable way about him, from the gee-whiz smile to the thick brown hair where snowflakes were making him gray. Then she couldn't resist taking one last look at the damage to her car, wondering if it could be repaired. She wondered if the same applied to her.

"What's that they say?" Brian was asking.

Nora realized Brian was still talking to her. "I'm sorry, I must have zoned out. What did you say?"

"They say most car accidents occur when you're almost home."

Words failed Nora. What he'd said, she knew it was just another of those homespun adages courtesy of the quaint village of Linden Corners, yet the words rang deep inside her. She craned her neck to look over at her childhood home, so close she could almost touch it.

Yup, almost home. And it was no accident she was here.